contribution is gratefully received. If you would like
to help support the Foundation or require further
information, please contact:

THE ULVERSCROFT FOUNDATION
The Green, Bradgate Road, Anstey
Leicester LE7 7FU, England
Tel: (0116) 236 4325

website: www.ulverscroft-foundation.org.uk

0060395095

A SONGBIRD IN WARTIME

Shaftesbury, 1936. Mansfield House Hotel has been a refuge for Emily ever since she was orphaned at the age of 16. Not only did they give her employment as a chambermaid, but it's also where she met her fiancé Tom.

When theatre agent Roland stays at the hotel and hears Emily singing, he hatches a plan to get Emily away from Tom and make her a star.

Six years later, Emily has made a name for herself as 'The Bristol Songbird'. Her love for Tom is still as strong as ever, but she's not heard from him since that fateful night so long ago . . . And with the world enveloped in a war, it seems unlikely the two will ever meet again.

Will Emily and Tom find their way back to one another? Or will the war – and Roland – keep them apart?

KAREN DICKSON

A SONGBIRD IN WARTIME

Complete and Unabridged

MAGNA
Leicester

First published in Great Britain in 2021 by
Simon & Schuster UK Ltd
London

First Ulverscroft Edition
published 2022
by arrangement with
Simon & Schuster UK Ltd
London

A catalogue record for this book is available
from the British Library.

ISBN 978-0-7505-4943-1

Published by
Ulverscroft Limited
Anstey, Leicestershire

Printed and bound in Great Britain by
TJ Books Ltd., Padstow, Cornwall

This book is printed on acid-free paper

For Mum and Dad

Prologue
1920

A warm breeze ruffled the meadow grass as Eli Baker made his way up the hill to his cottage, Ralf the sheep-dog close at heel. Grazing sheep raised their heads to watch them pass.

He heard the singing before he reached the summit, the sound bringing a smile to his face and lifting his weary shoulders. At the top of the hill, he paused. Laying one hand on Ralf's head to prevent him from barking, he rested against the three-bar gate, gazing fondly on the woman and child in the cottage garden.

Mary hadn't noticed him. She was sitting on the doorstep, shelling peas, her chestnut-brown hair tumbling down her shoulders, a bowl resting on her lap. Four-year-old Emily sat beside her mother. Both were singing. It was a lullaby Mary had sung to Emily ever since she was a babe in arms.

Though it was a song he had heard many times, the sheer purity of their harmonized voices sent goosebumps up Eli's arms and stirred something deep in his soul.

'Lay down your head, sweet little child,
Mama and Papa are here by your side . . . '
She had a beautiful voice, had his Mary, but even at such a tender age, Emily's voice was deeper and richer, and Eli shuddered as the flawless purity of her voice stirred something deep within his soul . . .

1

PART ONE

PART ONE

1

1923

'I'm sorry, Eli,' Annie Scrivens said softly. 'She's gone.'

Eli Baker let out a low moan and dragged his rough hands through his thick, dark brown hair. He leaned forward in his chair, elbows resting on his knees, doubled over by the weight of his grief. 'The baby?' he suddenly thought to ask, his voice rough with unshed tears. Annie shook her head sadly.

With a grace that belied her bulk, Annie gently laid the stillborn little boy in his mother's arms and covered them with the sheet. Eli let out a loud sob. Annie looked across at him slumped on the spindle-back chair, weeping unashamedly, and sighed. He was only thirty-two, God love him, but he seemed to have aged twenty years overnight. His rugged, handsome features were haggard, and there were dark purple shadows under his brown eyes.

Annie had seen more than her fair share of misery and heartache in her twenty years as a midwife, but that didn't stop her heart breaking for Eli and the poor motherless girl downstairs.

She laid a large, capable hand on Eli's broad shoulder. His forearms were taut, muscled from long hours of manual labour. He had worked hard to make a good life for Mary and his little girl. She shook her head sadly at the cruelty of fate.

'I'll bring you a cup of tea and then I'll be off.' She paused. 'I'll call in to Alford and Sons on the way.' Eli

5

winced at the mention of the funeral directors. Annie gave his arm a comforting squeeze and left him alone with his poor dead wife and infant son.

At the sound of Eli's wretched sobbing, seven-year-old Emily Rose Baker looked up at the ceiling, blinking back tears of her own. She had been waiting for so long, listening for the telltale wail that would accompany the arrival of her new brother or sister, but instead, her mother's ever-weakening screams had ended in a deathly silence that was broken only by the sound of her father's sobs. Even at her tender age, she was aware something terrible had happened. Dread settled in the pit of her tummy like a stone.

She heard footsteps on the stairs and clenched her teeth, wrapping her thin arms around her skinny frame. She was a slight girl, thin and bony, with a thick mane of chestnut-brown hair that hung down her back in two untidy plaits. She sat in Eli's old arm-chair, close to the kitchen range, resting her bare feet on the dog, Ralf, who lay slumped morosely on the rug. For all intents and purposes, the aged mongrel was Eli's dog, but since puppyhood his canine heart had belonged solely to Eli's wife Mary. He had been whimpering for the past five minutes, as if notified by some sixth sense that his beloved mistress was no more.

'There you are, pet,' Annie Scrivens said, her bulk filling the doorway between the kitchen and the seldom-used parlour. Ralf raised his head an inch off his paws, sniffed the air and uttered a long-drawn-out sigh, before resting his head again.

Annie regarded the little girl with pity. It wasn't as if she even had brothers and sisters with whom to share the burden of her grief. Poor Mary had wanted a houseful of children, but Emily was the only one that had lived beyond a few months, not to mention the ones she hadn't carried to term. And now the poor woman was gone too. Annie clicked her tongue. Life just wasn't fair.

'Why don't you go outside and play a while?' she suggested to Emily, attempting to inject a cheerful note into her voice. Emily raised her tearful gaze to the window. From her low vantage point, she could just make out the fluffy white clouds skimming the crest of the rolling Dorset hills as they scudded across a cornflower-blue sky. The door was open a crack and she could hear the sigh of the wind through the budding trees and the bleating of Ned Sawyer's sheep across the track.

She turned her gaze to follow Annie as the midwife busied herself with making the tea.

'Can I go up and see Mama and the new baby?' she asked in a small voice. Annie's back stiffened, the heaped spoon of tea leaves hovering above the brown teapot. She cleared her throat.

'Not at the moment, pet,' she replied without turning around. 'Go outside. The fresh air will do you good. And take the dog with you.'

For a moment Emily thought about arguing, but at the sound of her father's continued weeping, she thought better of it. In mutinous silence, she slid off the chair and, calling to Ralf, slipped outside, the dog plodding dutifully behind her.

Emily sat down on the stone bench beneath the kitchen window and Ralf settled himself underneath. On either side of the cracked flagstone path, the lawn was awash with daisies and buttercups. Bees swarmed the yellow toadflax sprouting from the cracks in the lichen-covered wall and sparrows darted in and out of the ivy that clung to the side of the old stone cottage. Skylarks and swallows performed an aerial ballet over Emily's head and she could hear the bleating of the ewes and their lambs on the hillside that sloped down to the Sawyer farm nestled in the valley below.

Her chest felt tight and it hurt to breathe. A tear rolled down her cheek as she let out a sob. Ralf emerged from beneath the bench to lick her hand and she wrapped her arms around his shaggy neck, burying her face in his warm fur. She heard Annie Scriven's voice drifting from the window above her, saying goodbye to her father. Five minutes later, Annie emerged from the house in her hat and coat, handbag over her arm. 'Oh, pet,' she sighed at the sight of the sobbing child half-draped over the dog. Ralf whined softly. Nudging him gently aside, Annie wedged herself onto the bench beside Emily and put her arm around the shuddering child.

'My mama's dead, isn't she?' Emily sobbed. Annie's shoulders slumped.

'Yes, pet, I'm afraid she is.' She held the little girl while she sobbed into Annie's ample breast, stroking her head and whispering useless platitudes.

'You've got to be a brave girl for your father now, pet,' she said once Emily's sobs had abated.

'I want my mama,' Emily hiccoughed. Annie squeezed her tight.

'She's in Heaven with your baby brothers and sister,' she said.

'But I want her here.'

'I know you do, pet,' Annie said sorrowfully. 'I know you do.'

8

Eli ran a calloused palm over his chin, the day-old stubble rasping against his rough skin. Unable to bear the sight of his wife and child still and silent beneath the sheet, he turned his stricken gaze towards the window. Wispy clouds drifted across the sky.

'It's a beautiful day, Mary,' he said. 'You can see clear across the vale to Melbury Hill.' A sob caught in the back of his throat. 'Do you remember, Mary? It was at the church picnic up on Melbury Hill where you agreed to be my wife.' His lips twitched at the memory. 'The vicar was scandalized. We'd only been courting for eight weeks.' Now his eyes rested on the shrouded form of the woman he had loved since he was seventeen years old. He tried to say more but his voice failed him and he buried his face in his hands. What was he to do with Emily now? How could he care for a child when he worked every hour God sent? He and Mary had both been workhouse orphans, so there were no doting grandmothers or aunties to share the responsibility of raising the motherless girl.

He heard the front gate bang and crossed to the window in time to see Annie scurrying down the muddy track. Leaning over the sill, he looked down on Emily's bowed head. She had one thin arm slung around Ralf's neck and was picking frantically at a loose thread on her pinafore with the fingers of her other hand. With a weary sigh he made his way down the stairs and out into the warm spring sunshine.

Ralf greeted him in a subdued fashion before flopping wearily at his feet. The flash of hope he saw in Emily's eyes as she looked up cut him to the quick. He sat down heavily and pulled her against him, breathing in her comforting scent. She smelled of sunshine and fresh bread.

'I expect Annie Scrivens told you your mama's gone to be with the Lord?' he began, his voice gruff with suppressed emotion. He blinked. 'It's just us now, pet. You and me.' He kissed the top of her head. 'We'll be all right, won't we?'

Beside him, Emily stirred and nodded. Her face was pale and blotchy, and it broke Eli's already shattered heart that there was nothing he could do to spare his daughter this heartache.

★ ★ ★

Edwin Alford, the undertaker, and two of his five sons arrived just before noon. Emily and Eli stood and watched solemnly from the doorway while they carefully loaded Mary and her infant son into their horse-drawn wagon.

Annie Scrivens had spread the word and the first callers began to arrive soon after the undertaker left, bringing with them covered dishes of food along with their words of condolence. Ned Sawyer's housekeeper, Molly, arrived to oversee the making of endless cups of tea, and Emily was kept busy at the sink washing cups and saucers for the seemingly never-ending stream of visitors.

The sun was setting by the time Molly wrapped up her apron and set off on the short journey down the hill to the farmhouse to make a start on Ned's supper.

Without the hum of conversation and the rattle of crockery, the cottage seemed unnaturally quiet. It was now that Eli felt Mary's loss most keenly. She would have been preparing the evening meal, lifting

10

the rafters with the sound of her singing. She'd had a beautiful voice, had his Mary, and, young as she was, it was abundantly clear that Emily had inherited her mother's talent. Only last week the vicar had promised Emily a place in the church choir as soon as she turned ten. Nothing had given Eli more pleasure of an evening than sitting in his favourite armchair listening to his wife and daughter singing together.

Unable to be in the house, father and daughter huddled together on the stone bench as the sinking sun set the sky aflame and twilight crept across the hills.

2

Warm sunlight streamed in through the open doorway. Eli stared morosely at the bowl of lumpy porridge he'd cooked for himself and Emily. He had no appetite for the grey stodge and neither, it seemed, did Emily. He watched her as she pushed her porridge around listlessly. Poor mite, Eli thought with a sigh. She'd been up crying for her mother most of the night. No wonder she looked so washed out this morning.

He ran his hand through his thick, wavy hair and stifled a yawn. He'd barely slept himself. At midnight he'd given up on the bed, which was too cold and empty without Mary's presence, and moved to his armchair in the kitchen. With Ralf sprawled across his feet, he'd sat staring out of the darkened window until dawn.

He pushed his bowl aside and picked up his mug. His employer Ned Sawyer had, somewhat begrudgingly, granted him the rest of the week off to grieve. Eli had debated sending Emily to school but decided against it. Without work to take his mind off his grief, the empty day stretched endlessly before him and he'd be glad of her company.

He drained his mug and glanced at his pocket watch. It had been a gift from Mary on their first Christmas as man and wife. The hands stood at a quarter to eight. The vicar was calling at ten to discuss funeral arrangements. It wasn't a visit he was looking forward to. Eli's heart contracted painfully at the thought of laying his beloved Mary in the cold dank earth of St James's churchyard.

He scraped back his chair, rousing Ralf, who was dozing in a shaft of warm sunlight, and carried his bowl and mug to the sink.

'Can you manage at least a spoonful or two?' he said to Emily, nodding at her bowl. Shaking her head, Emily pushed her bowl away from her. The lump in her throat made swallowing difficult. She missed her mama so much. She pressed the heels of her palms against her eyes as they filled with fresh tears.

'Leave it then, pet,' said Eli gruffly. He turned his back to her, hiding tears of his own. 'Why don't you go collect the eggs?' he suggested, a noticeable tremor in his voice.

Wordlessly, Emily pushed back her chair and slipped outside. With Ralf trotting close at her heel, she rounded the side of the cottage. The chicken coop stood between a hedge of blackberry and hawthorn bushes and a disused shed in which the half-feral farm cats had made their home. Emily unlatched the door to the wooden henhouse and half a dozen chickens spilled out of the hatch, clucking and pecking at each other in their impatience to be free. Leaving the chickens to scratch contentedly in the grass and holding her breath against the sharp tang of chicken manure, she groped through the dank straw, finding six smooth brown eggs. She was about to return to the cottage when the sound of approaching voices caught her attention. She recognized the speakers immediately. It was the Tucker sisters, Edith and May, and they were talking about her.

Emily pressed herself against the cottage wall, breathing in the scent of the honeysuckle that clung

13

to its stone walls. It mingled with the smell of damp earth and the ripe odour of cow dung wafting from the field next door.

'What will happen to the poor mite, do you think?' Edith, the older of the two sisters, said as she paused outside Barrow Hill cottage to remove a stone from her shoe. She was a large woman, big-boned and weathered, her iron-grey hair hidden beneath a woollen shawl. 'Eli works long hours. He can't manage the child on his own,' she added, gripping her sister's arm to retain her balance while she slipped her shoe back on.

'He's a good-looking man,' May said as they set off again. Five years younger than Edith, she was slimmer, her complexion smoother and paler. Her greying blonde hair hung down her spine in a thick plait. 'And he's still young. He's bound to marry again, and quickly.'

'Of that I have no doubt,' Edith remarked. 'But will the new wife want the burden of another woman's child?' She shook her head sorrowfully. 'No,' she continued, answering her own question. 'It'll be the workhouse for the poor motherless soul.'

Emily stared after them, her mouth falling open in shock, but May's reply was lost on the breeze as the two sisters descended the track into the copse heading for their cottage further along the lane. A steel band tightened around Emily's chest. Would her father really send her away? Her heart beat rapidly and she blinked back the sting of tears. Sensing her distress, Ralf nudged her hand. She stroked his head absently, her vision blurred with tears. She missed Mama so much. How would she bear it if she was sent away from her father too?

14

'Emily? What's taking you so long?' Her father's voice startled her. Suddenly her churning emotions were too much to bear. Bursting into noisy tears, she let the egg basket fall to the ground as she ran to the shed and flung herself onto the dirty floor. A large ginger tom cat eyed her warily from the cobweb-shrouded rafters as several others slunk quickly into the shadows.

'Emily?' Her father filled the doorway, blocking the light. Ralf barked and licked Emily's wet face. The next moment, she was in her father's arms as he lifted her off the floor, brushing stray bits of straw and dirt from her pinafore. 'Oh, my precious child,' he murmured, cradling her tightly against him, feeling helpless in the face of her grief.

'Are you going to send me away?' Emily asked Eli tearfully as he carried her into the cottage.

'What?' His dark brows knit together in confusion. 'Send you away?' He set her on a chair and crouched down in front of her. 'Whatever gave you that notion?'

'I heard Miss Edith telling Miss May that your new wife won't want me.'

'New wife?' Eli barked, blanching at the thought. 'What new wife?' He raked his hand through his hair. 'And your poor mother not even cold . . . ' He cursed under his breath. The Tucker sisters were nothing but gossipmongers and troublemakers. Having been left comfortably off by their widower father, they had nothing better to do than meddle in other people's business.

'Take no notice of anything those two say,' he told Emily. 'I'm not inclined to find myself another wife and, even if I was,' he assured her, 'no woman would ever come between you and me, all right?' He handed

15

her his handkerchief. 'Now, wipe your eyes and wash your face. We've got the vicar coming in an hour.'

★ ★ ★

The Reverend Simeon Smedhurst was a pleasant-faced man in his mid-thirties, prematurely balding with thin sandy hair swept strategically across his pink scalp and the beginnings of a paunch. He perched on an armchair in the seldom-used parlour, a cup and saucer balanced precariously on his knee. The curtains were drawn as a sign of their mourning, plunging the room into a permanent state of twilight.

Emily sat solemnly on the sofa, wedged between her father's solid presence and the curved wooden armrest. Listening to the vicar talk about her mother in his soft, melodious voice had brought a lump to her throat and she kept her gaze fixed on her hands folded primly in her lap, her teeth clenched together in an effort not to cry.

'Do you have any family who are able to help you?' the vicar asked, taking a sip of tea.

Eli shook his head. 'I'm an orphan, as was my wife. But we'll manage. Emily is a sensible girl and capable. We'll muddle along well enough, I imagine.'

'Well, if you find it's too much for you,' the vicar said, his cup rattling against his saucer as he set it down, 'there's a woman over in Bimport who boards children.'

Emily stiffened. She could feel the vicar's scrutiny and didn't dare meet his eyes.

'Thank you,' Eli replied with a cool edge to his voice. He reached for Emily's hand. 'But that won't be necessary.'

Emily hadn't realized she'd been holding her breath

until that moment. She exhaled in a rush, her thin shoulders sagging in relief. She had trusted Eli to keep his word, but it was relief to hear him confirm it to the vicar. She wouldn't be sent away.

'Very well,' the vicar replied. He sounded unconvinced. Ned Sawyer's reputation as a hard task-master was well known and Eli's working hours were long. 'If you change your mind . . . '

'I won't.' Eli gave the vicar a tight smile. Reverend Smedhurst simply nodded and got to his feet.

'Very well,' he said, setting his cup and saucer on the parlour table. 'I will see you at eleven o'clock on Friday.' The two men shook hands and Eli walked him out.

Emily washed up the crockery, watching from the window as her father stood talking to the vicar at the gate. Daffodils growing against the wall nodded in the breeze and a kestrel hovered overhead. The sun had yet to burn off the mist that clung to the surrounding hills, shrouding them from view.

The cottage was quiet, too quiet, without her mother. Despite the sad loss of her babies, her mother's disposition had been a happy one. For as far back as Emily could remember, there had seldom been a day when the cottage didn't resound with Mary's singing or laughter. Softly, Emily began to sing. The melody came hesitantly at first, missing her mother's direction, but soon her voice seemed to take on a power of its own. She closed her eyes as her voice took flight, lifting her above the sadness, above the grief as she soared on the wings of the song.

Standing in the doorway, tears streaming down his face, Eli thought his heart might burst as he watched his daughter, singing her heart out.

17

* * *

The funeral service was well attended and mercifully brief. The sun was shining as Mary and her infant son were laid to rest in St James's tranquil churchyard beside her other lost babies. The mourners made their way back to Eli's cottage where, once again, the capable Molly dispensed endless cups of tea and plates of sandwiches and cakes she and Emily had spent the previous afternoon making.

Ned Sawyer was there, big and brawny, with a shock of black hair, and a sombre nature. A year older than Eli, the two men had been friends since Eli had come to work for Ned's father at the tender age of twelve. He stood now, in the corner of the dim, stuffy, over-crowded parlour, chewing contemplatively on a slice of Molly's Victoria sponge. He hated funerals and he'd been to his fair share of them, the first being his father's back when he was just a teenager. His father was followed barely a year later by his younger brother, Tommy, who succumbed to his injuries after being attacked by a neighbour's prize bull. His mother had lived to see Ned married, but not long enough to see him a widower at twenty-two, losing his wife Lizzie in childbirth when she was barely twenty years old.

He took a swig of milky tea, the dainty china tea-cup incongruous in his shovel-like hand. The sea of mourners parted slightly, affording him a glimpse of little Emily Baker, stacking dirty plates onto a tin tray he recognized as being from his own kitchen. Her face was pale and drawn, her black dress two sizes too big for her bony frame, and he felt a flicker of sympathy for the child before glancing away. His gaze came to rest on a small side table where Eli and Mary's

18

wedding photograph took pride of place and he felt a tightening in his stomach. Whether it was anger, regret or incredulity that a poor workhouse girl would choose a simple farmhand over himself, he couldn't say. He knew only that he had loved Mary Hamilton from the moment he first saw her.

With her waist-length brown hair, smiling eyes and upturned mouth, Ned had thought she was the most beautiful girl he had ever seen. His mother hadn't relished the idea of an ex-workhouse girl for a daughter-in-law and he had spent hours trying to persuade her otherwise. But in the end, his mother's opinion had proved irrelevant for Mary had chosen Eli.

He saw his friend approaching and swallowed down the last of his tea, wiping his mouth with the back of his hand.

'Thank you for coming, Ned.' Eli held out his hand. 'I appreciate it.'

'It's the least I could do,' Ned said, taking Eli's hand. 'Mary was a good woman, God rest her soul.'

'The best.' Eli scanned the room, pursing his lips at the sight of the Tucker sisters huddled in a corner, heads together, no doubt indulging in their favourite pastime of gossiping. He spotted the vicar talking to Annie Scrivens. So many friends and neighbours had turned out to pay their last respects.

'She's had a good turn-out.'

'Your Mary was well respected in the town,' Ned said with a nod. 'And a good friend to many. She'll be very much missed.'

'I'll be back at work first thing tomorrow,' Eli said, raising his voice to be sure Edith and May would hear him above the buzz of conversation. 'Emily is quite capable of looking after herself.' He caught the eye of the younger Tucker sister. May looked away quickly, but not before Eli had seen the embarrassed flush colour her cheeks. He allowed himself a smile of grim satisfaction.

Only half-listening to Ned, who had launched into a lengthy monologue about one of his prize-winning ewes, Eli's gaze sought out his daughter. He spotted her on the sofa and caught her eye. Emily smiled, and some of the anxiety shifted from his shoulders. They were going to be all right.

3

1930

The kitchen was filled with the aroma of baking bread. Putting the last of the cutlery in the drawer, Emily hung up the tea towel and refilled Ralf's water bowl. Her father reckoned the old dog to be about fourteen now. Grey-muzzled and suffering from arthritis, he seldom accompanied his master around the farm anymore, preferring to spend his days napping in the sun.

He licked Emily's hand and settled himself in the open doorway, resting his nose on his paws with a weary sigh. Singing softly to herself, Emily took up the broom and swept the floor. She loved the easiness of a Saturday morning. They breakfasted early as usual when Eli returned from the milking at six, but once breakfast was done and he had gone back to work, Emily could take her time with the seemingly endless household chores. During the week, she had to rush to get her chores finished to be at school by nine, and then, when she returned at half past three, there was the garden to see to, the evening meal to prepare. Not that she begrudged a single moment she spent caring for Eli and the cottage. She doted on her father and devoted her time to doing whatever she could to keep his life running smoothly.

The parlour clock chimed the hour and Emily opened the oven door, sliding the well-risen loaf onto a wire rack and setting it beside the open window to cool. Red and white gingham curtains framed a vista of rolling green hills, dotted with sheep, and a cloudless blue sky.

Ralf raised his head, sniffing the air, and got stiffly to his feet, his tail wagging in welcome.

'Who is it, Ralf?' Emily asked, going to stand in the doorway just as Molly reached the top of the hill. Leaning against the three-bar gate to catch her breath, she gave Emily a cheerful wave. Emily waved back. At twenty-four, Ned's housekeeper was a decade older than Emily, yet the two girls had become good friends over the past seven years. It had been Molly who taught Emily all she needed to learn about keeping house.

'Get me a glass of water, please, Emily,' Molly pleaded, pushing open the gate and stepping into the lane. 'That hill never gets any easier.' She fondled Ralf who had ambled over to greet her and collapsed on the bench, fanning her flushed cheeks with her hand. 'Thanks,' she said when Emily returned with a glass of water and sat down beside her. She gulped it down in one go. 'Ah, that was good.' She turned to Emily and grinned. 'I've got some exciting news. Sid has proposed, at last.' She beamed joyously. 'We're getting married.'

Not pretty in the conventional sense, with her auburn hair, pale freckled skin and too-wide mouth, it had been Molly's eyes — dark green and fringed with long, curling lashes — that had caught the attention of the sixteen-year-old Sidney Manners when Molly was just fifteen and they had been courting ever since.

'I'm so pleased for you,' Emily said with a smile, though her joy at Molly's news was tempered by the knowledge that her friend would be moving away.

Sid farmed a small tract of land on the other side of Compton Abbas, over an hour's walk from Shaftesbury.

'Have you set a date?'

'The first Saturday in August,' Molly told her. 'The banns are being read tomorrow.'

'That's quick. It's less than a month away!'

'We've been courting for nine years, Emily,' Molly said, rolling her eyes. 'I think I've waited long enough.'

'Mr Sawyer will miss you. He'll have to find himself a new housekeeper.'

'Yes, I wanted to talk to you about that.' Molly tucked a loose strand of hair behind her ear. 'I'd like to recommend you for the job.'

'Me?' Emily said, somewhat taken aback. 'I wasn't really intending to go into service.'

'There's not much else about,' Molly reminded her. Emily sighed. It was true. The daily headlines were a grim catalogue of job losses and business closures as the depression continued to tighten its grip on the country. Only yesterday, the owner of the glove manufacturer's had sent a message to say he could no longer offer Emily an apprenticeship when she left school at the end of the month.

'Mr Sawyer's a good employer. He pays a fair wage and you'll get every Sunday off.'

'Do you think he would agree?' Emily asked.

'I can't see why not. He knows your character, and he and your father are good friends.'

'I'll talk it over with Father when he comes home for his dinner,' Emily promised. The prospect of working for Ned Sawyer wasn't an unattractive one. She had known him all her life, after all.

'My last day is the thirty-first of July,' Molly said,

getting to her feet. 'If your father agrees, you could spend a few days before then learning how Mr Sawyer likes things done. He's not pedantic by any means, but there are one or two things he does like to be done a certain way.'

'I'll let you know my decision today,' Emily said as she walked with Molly the short distance along the lane. They paused at the gate, the valley spread out below them in a patchwork of green and gold fields. Her gaze caught the flash of sunlight on metal as a solitary motor car wended its way down the hill from Melbury.

'I'd appreciate that.' Molly pushed the gate and it swung open, startling a flock of five sheep huddled against the hedge. They shuffled out of Molly's way, bleating loudly as she started down the hill.

★ ★ ★

Emily was still pondering Molly's offer when Eli returned home for his dinner.

'It's been a hot one today,' he said, sitting down heavily on the stool beside the door and scratching Ralf behind the ears. 'I saw Molly heading up this way,' he said, removing his heavy boots. 'Came to tell you her good news, did she?'

'Yes,' Emily replied, handing Eli a bowl of warm water and a towel. 'And to offer me her job.'

Eli raised an eyebrow. 'I see. And how do you feel about working for Ned?'

Emily shrugged. 'It's as good a job as any.' She returned to her meal preparation, slathering butter onto thick slices of the freshly baked bread. 'And there's not much available in town.' She set the bread on the table along with a bowl of home-grown tomatoes and a lettuce.

'That's a fact,' Eli said, pulling up a chair and helping himself to a tomato. 'Well, Ned's a fair man. Work hard and he'll treat you well.'

'I'll have Sundays off so I'll still be able to sing in the choir,' Emily said, wiping her hands on her apron as she sat down at the table.

'The congregation will be pleased.' Eli grinned. 'Losing their best soloist would come as a huge disappointment.'

'Oh, Father,' Emily chided him, blushing at the compliment. Emily had joined the church choir four years before at the age of ten. Six months later the vicar had, none too tactfully, Emily remembered ruefully, elevated her to lead soloist over her eleven-year-old schoolmate, Lucy Hunt. Lucy's mother, a widow in her early forties, hadn't taken her daughter's demotion lightly, and the two of them had taken to attending services at the church on top of the hill. In the school playground, Lucy's resentment and jealousy had manifested in spiteful bullying that had blighted Emily's otherwise happy schooldays right up until the previous year when Lucy left school to go into service. To Emily's relief, their paths hadn't crossed since.

'Don't be coy, Emily,' Eli chided her mildly now. 'You have your mother's beautiful singing voice.' He smiled, the skin around his dark eyes crinkling with mirth. 'Unlike your old man. I couldn't carry a tune to save my life.'

Emily returned his smile. 'Reverend Smedhurst said if I had singing lessons, I could probably become a professional singer. Imagine that,' she said, folding tomato and lettuce in a slice of bread. 'Earning a living just for singing.'

'Ah, Emily, love.' Eli's expression clouded. 'Ambition of that sort is not for the likes of us. Smedhurst should know better than to fill your young head with such nonsense. The only places around here you'd earn money singing is in the pubs, and that's not the career I want for my daughter.' He smiled at Emily's crestfallen expression. 'Cheer up, you've got your choir and you earn a pretty penny singing at weddings and the odd funeral. And with that, I'm afraid, you will have to be content.'

4

1932

Emily stood in the farmhouse doorway, gazing out across the Blackmore Vale. A refreshing breeze blew across the valley, bringing with it the sweet-scented promise of much-needed rain after a lengthy spell of hot, dry weather.

It was the second week of August and Emily had been working for Ned Sawyer for two years. It had taken her a while to learn her way around Ned's vast farmhouse, and familiarize herself with the way he liked things done, but although a man of few words and given to bouts of melancholy, he had proved a patient and fair employer and she had soon settled into her new routine.

She saw him now, coming out the barn, shirt sleeves rolled up to the elbows, followed by Eli and several dogs. They had lost Ralf the previous winter at a grand old age. He had gone to sleep in front of the range one cold January night and never woken up. Eli had buried him under the apple tree in the back garden.

The two men and dogs approached the house. Chickens scattered, ruffling their feathers and squawking their indignation.

'We'll be off in a minute, Emily,' Ned called, untying the bandana from around his neck and wiping his forehead. 'Have you made a list?'

'It's on the table, Mr Sawyer,' Emily replied,

emptying the kettle into the washing-up bowl. The day Ned fulfilled on his promise to have indoor plumbing and electricity installed in this rambling seventeenth-century farmhouse would be a joyous day indeed, she mused, reaching for the dishcloth.

Oblivious to the dusty footprints his boots were leaving on the slate floor, Ned crossed to the table and picked up the list of items Emily needed him to pick up at the weekly market. The dogs milled about in the doorway, alternately panting and whining as streaks of lightning split the sky.

'Looks like we're in for a soaking,' Eli said, glancing out of the door at the rumble of distant thunder.

'Ah well. We'll have to dry off in the Knowles Arms over a pint then, won't we?' Ned grinned, shrugging on his jacket. He folded Emily's shopping list and put it in his pocket, along with his pipe and tobacco pouch.

'We'll see you later, Emily,' Eli said, giving his daughter an affectionate smile.

'Enjoy yourselves,' Emily replied with a smile of her own. Market day was an opportunity for her father and Ned to catch up on the local news and gossip over a few pints in one or two of the town's many public houses. She dried her hands on a tea towel and followed them to the door to see them off. Clouds billowed overhead, dark and foreboding. The dogs padded about the yard, hackles raised. Even the birds had fallen silent in anticipation of the coming storm. A solitary magpie preened himself on a telegraph wire.

'One for sorrow,' Ned remarked grimly, pulling on his cap.

'Good morning, Mr Magpie,' Eli said, doffing his cap. 'How is your wife this morning?'

Satisfied that the prospect of bad luck had been averted by the performing of the ancient ritual, Eli and Ned set off across the yard.

'Your Emily certainly favours Mary, doesn't she?' Emily heard Ned say as they walked away. She smiled. She liked it when people thought she looked like her mother. It made her feel closer to her, somehow.

'She's the spit of Mary at that age,' Eli agreed as they rounded the corner of the barn, the dogs trotting in their wake. Emily returned to her dishes, knowing that the dogs would follow the men as far as the lane before coming back to sleep the hours away until Eli and Ned returned in time for the afternoon milking.

The first drops of rain hit the window, sliding down the glass. The invigorating smell of rain on a thirsty land wafted in through the open doorway. Lightning lit up the sky and thunder crashed overhead. The dogs growled and paced restlessly around the kitchen, getting under Emily's feet until she finally lost patience and chased them out into the yard. The rain was coming down heavily now and they slunk off to find refuge in one of the barns.

Emily busied herself peeling and slicing vegetables for the mutton casserole she was planning for the evening meal. Eli and Emily had got into the habit of dining with Ned on market day. Seated around the large scrubbed-pine kitchen table, Ned and Eli would regale Emily with amusing anecdotes from their day before retiring to the parlour with its spectacular view of the rolling hills. After the dishes were done and the kitchen tidied, Emily would join them for a singsong. Often Ned would accompany her on his piano and, standing in the somewhat shabby parlour, silhouetted against a brilliant sunset, Emily would fantasize that she was a famous singer like her idols Gracie Fields and Lee Morse, the purity and beauty of her voice often reducing the two men to tears.

There would be no sunset tonight, she reflected, as rain lashed the window. A strong wind rattled the windows in their frames and howled under the eaves. It whistled down the chimney, sending a flurry of soot wafting across the floor. She fetched a broom, glancing out of the window.

The old Saxon hilltop town was shrouded in low cloud and pockets of swirling mist drifted across the valley. On the hillside the sheep were huddled close together, facing away from the driving rain. Lightning flashed and for a split second the landscape glowed silver. Huge puddles had formed in the yard, which was fast becoming a quagmire.

Emily shut the door, and wedged an old rag underneath it to prevent the muddy water seeping into the kitchen. The black clouds were so thick it was as if day had suddenly given way to night and she lit the lamp, thankful for the thick stone walls that had withstood centuries of tempestuous weather.

She put the casserole in the oven to cook then went upstairs.

Ned's bedroom was at the front of the house. It was a good-sized room, with heavy dark-wood furniture and brown striped wallpaper, overlooking the yard and farm buildings, with the sloping fields beyond. Eli's tied cottage, at the top of the hill, was almost completely obscured by swirling mist. The thunder and lightning were drifting towards the east now but the torrential rain continued, beating an incessant tattoo on the tiled roof and spilling over the guttering.

Emily made the bed and was straightening the quilt

when the dogs began to bark. Even over the hammering rain and the cacophony of barking dogs, she could hear the sound of an approaching vehicle. Puzzled, she crossed to the window and looked down into the yard in time to see a shiny black car pull up in front of the house. She saw Ned get out of the passenger side. He looked up at the house, his face ashen, and Emily felt a twinge of alarm. He silenced the dogs with a curt word, and leaned down to speak to whoever was driving.

Clutched by a sudden dread, Emily turned away from the window and hurried downstairs. She reached the kitchen just as Ned came in. He shooed the dogs away, and shut the door. Emily was dimly aware of the car driving away as Ned stood in the middle of the kitchen looking at her, water pooling at his feet. He took off his hat, wiping rainwater from his eyes. Something about his expression caused Emily's throat to close. She wanted to speak but no words would come.

'There's been an accident,' he said hoarsely. 'I'm sorry, Emily. Your father is dead.'

Emily stared at him in shock.

'No!' she said, her voice a strangled whisper. 'No.' She shook her head, unable to comprehend what Ned was saying. Her father couldn't be dead.

'I'm sorry,' Ned repeated, reaching for her hand. She snatched it away, as if burned. She was shaking, she realized, but the tears had yet to come. Blindly, she stumbled backwards, groping for support. Her hand found the back of a chair and she fell into it as her legs gave way.

'What happened?' she croaked.

Clearing his throat, Ned pulled out the chair opposite and sat down heavily. He cradled his face in his

31

hands and let out a low moan, then inhaled deeply and raised his head to look at her.

'We'd just reached the crossroads,' he said gruffly. Unable to bear Emily's stricken expression, he focused on the array of red and blue rosettes tacked to the blackened chimney breast, the legacy of generations of prize-winning ewes. The aroma of the lamb casserole filled the kitchen, turning his stomach.

'Angus Mullens was coming down Great Lane in his truck. Water was streaming down the road, like a river it was . . . ' He faltered and shook his head, as if trying to clear his mind of the horror he had so recently witnessed. 'Angus lost control . . . and . . . oh, God! It was awful. Eli was crushed against the wall.' He met Emily's gaze, his expression bleak. 'The doctor came but' — his broad shoulders slumped — 'it was too late.'

Emily let out a low wail and doubled over. Ned got to his feet, the chair legs scraping loudly on the slate floor.

'I had a bad feeling as soon as I saw that cursed magpie this morning,' he said, pacing in front of the hearth. He let out a shuddering sigh. 'The doctor said he'd call in at the vicarage.'

Emily lifted her head. Her pale cheeks were wet with tears as she stared at him with incomprehension.

'There'll be the funeral to plan,' said Ned, his tone gentle.

'Yes, of course,' Emily mumbled, ferreting in her skirt pocket for a handkerchief. She mopped her red-rimmed eyes and blew her nose. Ned glanced away, unable to stand her grief.

Emily thought back to her mother's funeral and how difficult it had been for her seven-year-old self.

32

Now, at just sixteen, she had lost both her parents and it would fall to her to arrange her father's funeral.

Eli hadn't been a religious man but he'd attended church every week, if only to listen to Emily sing — her throat ached at the realization that she would never again stand in the choir stalls and see the pride in her father's smiling eyes. A sob caught in the back of her throat as a fresh wave of grief tightened its vice-like grip across her chest.

Outside the dogs started barking and Emily caught a glimpse of a dark shape flash past the kitchen window.

'That'll be Smedhurst,' Ned said, going to the door.

'I'll make some tea,' Emily said dully, forcing herself to her feet. Ned opened the door and ushered the Reverend into the warm kitchen.

'My condolences for your loss, Emily,' Reverend Smedhurst said with a benign smile. 'I understand death was quick and Eli didn't suffer. That must give you a measure of comfort?'

'Thank you.' Emily looked away, blinking back tears as she turned her back on the vicar to fill the tea kettle and set it on the stove top to boil.

★ ★ ★

'Eli was a man of simple needs,' Simeon Smedhurst said a few minutes later. Emily handed him his cup of tea, but he waved away the plate of homemade biscuits. She offered the plate to Ned, who helped himself to a handful and set them on the parlour table. She sat down in a chair looking out over the rainswept valley, her cup of tea untouched on the tray in front of her.

'He wouldn't appreciate anything too elaborate for

his funeral,' the reverend continued. He was a man fond of his food, and his girth had expanded considerably over the years. Even the thick folds of his cassock couldn't hide his rotund belly. Though only in his mid-forties, he had lost his hair completely and his bald scalp gleamed in the lamplight. 'You will need to liaise with the undertakers, Emily. I presume you will be using Alfords?' Emily looked to Ned for guidance. He was hunched morosely in his armchair, chewing on a biscuit. He swallowed hastily and nodded.

'I'll speak to Edwin Alford, Emily,' he assured her with a half-smile. 'I'll cover all the costs. We'll have the wake here, of course. I'll see if Molly will come over in the morning to give you a hand.'

'Shall we say next Wednesday, then?' Simeon suggested. He looked at Emily. 'Two o'clock?'

She nodded dumbly, still unable to completely comprehend that she would never see her father again.

5

In the quiet of her own kitchen, Emily wound the clock and set it back on the dresser. Picking a speck of lint from her black dress, she settled herself in Eli's comfortable old chair and closed her eyes, inhaling the warm, familiar scent that still clung to the faded fabric. Out of habit she had put his slippers in front of the range to warm, forgetting for a few short, blissful moments that her father would never again come trudging up the hill, bone-tired and sweating, but with his good humour undiminished. She fished her handkerchief from her sleeve and blew her nose.

There had been a steady stream of visitors to the cottage all week as friends and neighbours came to pay their respects. Emily had found some solace in the mundane task of brewing endless pots of tea while Ned made clumsy small talk and munched his way through half a packet of Jaffa cakes.

And that afternoon, with glorious sunlight streaming in through the stained-glass windows, the pews in St James's church had overflowed with mourners. Many others had lined the narrow street as Eli made his final journey, and it had gone some way to easing Emily's grief to see how loved and respected her father had been by his fellow townspeople.

As Ned had promised, he had opened his home for the wake, swelling the centuries-old farmhouse with dozens of mourners. Molly had come over in the morning to help Emily prepare the sandwiches. She and Sid had been married for two years now and were the proud parents of a ginger-haired little boy named Samuel. They were expecting another baby in the New Year, Molly had confided to Emily in the kitchen as they sliced the tongue and ham for the sandwiches.

By the time the last mourner had left and the last cup had been washed and put away, Emily's temples had been throbbing with the beginnings of a head-ache. It had been an emotionally draining day and she had been glad to escape to the sanctuary of her cottage where the only sound was the rhythmic tick of the clock and the singing of the birds. She stared out of the kitchen window. The sky was turning salmon pink, the hilltops set aflame by the sun's dying rays. She sighed heavily, contemplating life without her father.

* * *

The knock at the door startled her. She frowned. It was gone nine o'clock; too late for callers. She stayed where she was, her eyes on the door.

'Emily? It's me, Ned.'

Surprised, she unlatched the door. Ned stood on the doorstep, silhouetted against a sky the colour of ripe damsons. In the west, the last vestiges of daylight broke through the clouds in vivid streaks of orange and yellow.

'May I come in?'

'Of course.' Emily stood aside to let him pass. He stood in the middle of the kitchen, his blue eyes trou-bled, and ran a hand through his thick hair. Strands of grey had begun to appear amongst the black and the creases around his eyes were more pronounced, but he was still an attractive man in a rugged, weathered sort

36

of way.

'Would you like a cup of tea?' Emily offered uncertainly. It felt strange being with Ned in the cottage without her father, and she was unsure as to the purpose of his visit. Surely whatever he wished to discuss could have waited until tomorrow?

'No, thank you,' Ned declined hoarsely. He cleared his throat. 'Please, won't you sit down?'

Perplexed, Emily lowered herself into the nearest chair, thinking her employer appeared nervous, and her stomach tightened. Surely he wasn't planning to let her go? She needed this job. The cottage was her home.

Ned paced the room, his obvious agitation only serving to further Emily's own anxiety.

'Is everything all right, Mr Sawyer?' she blurted out, unable to bear the heavy silence a moment longer.

Ned paused in his pacing to stare out of the darkened window. Emily could see his reflection staring back at him. The lamp sputtered, shadows dancing up the whitewashed walls.

'Eli was my best friend,' Ned said at length, turning towards Emily. He splayed his hands. 'I owe it to him to do my best by his daughter.'

Emily's shoulders sagged with relief. She wasn't about to lose her job after all. All too quickly, though, her relief gave way to shocked dismay as Ned dropped clumsily to one knee in front of her.

'Emily, I have admired you for some time,' he said, his voice gruff. 'And I would be honoured if you would consent to be my wife.'

'Marry you? But you're so old!' Emily blurted out before she could stop herself.

Ned's expression clouded. 'I'm only forty-two,' he

said with brusque indignation as he got awkwardly to his feet. He ran a hand through his thick hair. 'I'm still man enough to please a wife, and father an heir.'

Emily flushed. 'But I don't love you,' she said. 'I'm sorry.'

Ned shrugged. 'What has that got to do with anything? I'm offering you a home, security.'

Emily wiped her clammy palms on her skirt. She didn't want to hurt Ned's feelings, but marriage? Did he honestly believe she would consider being tied to a man twenty-six years her senior?

Taking Emily's silence as a sign she was coming around to the idea, Ned took her hand in his. They were the hands of a hard-working man, rough and calloused.

'As mistress of Barrow Hill Farm, you'd want for nothing. Even now, with the world economy going to pot around us, we'll be all right. I've enough put by to ride out the depression.' He smiled. 'I can make you happy, Mary —' Ned checked himself quickly. 'Emily,' he amended with a sheepish smile.

'I'm not my mother, Mr Sawyer,' Emily said with a flash of pity for the man as she slowly withdrew her hand. 'I'm sorry, but I cannot marry you.'

Ned's eyes flashed angrily and humiliation coloured his cheeks. He flexed his fingers, his nostrils flaring as he sought to compose himself.

'I see,' he said coolly. 'Very well.' He crossed to the door and paused, one hand resting on the door handle. 'The thing is, Isaac Goddard spoke to me at the wake today. He's been laid off and is desperate for work. They're being evicted from their cottage at the end of the month.' Ned pulled a face. 'I'm sorry, Emily. I had assumed you would accept my offer of marriage.'

He shrugged his broad shoulders. 'I've offered him Eli's job. You'll need to vacate this cottage by the end of the month.'

'That's two weeks away,' Emily said, panic catching at the back of her throat. 'Where will I go?'

Again, Ned shrugged. 'My offer of marriage still stands.'

Emily stared at him, mute with misery, her mind whirling as she contemplated the choices before her. A loveless marriage to a man old enough to be her father, or homelessness.

'Right, I see you've made your choice,' Ned said gruffly, correctly taking Emily's silence as a final refusal. 'Under the circumstances, I think it will be awkward for you to continue in my employ. You should look for another job. I shall pay you until the end of the week, of course, but I think it best you don't come in tomorrow.'

'You're letting me go?' Emily whispered hoarsely.

'I'm sorry. It's for the best. I'll give you a good reference.'

With that, he yanked open the door and stepped out into the night, leaving Emily staring at the door as it banged shut behind him.

6

Emily lay on her back in the grey, pre-dawn light, staring up at the ceiling. She had slept badly, as she had all of the past ten nights, waking before the cock crowed to the now all-too-familiar sick feeling in the pit of her stomach.

In just four days' time she had to leave her home to make way for Isaac Goddard and his family. With the depression tightening its grip on the town and surrounding villages, jobs were scarce. Over the last week she had applied at every shop and office in the High Street, and visited every farm within a five-mile radius in her quest for employment, but the answer was always the same: employers were cutting back, laying people off, tightening their belts, and her cheerful optimism had long since given way to despondency.

She threw back the covers and got up, wincing as the blister on the back of her heel brushed against the bedclothes. She flung open the curtains. A thin mist clung to the hills and there was already a hint of autumn in the cool morning air. She dressed quickly. The local newspaper was due out today. Emily knew they were usually delivered to the newsagents around a quarter to six, and she intended to be waiting outside when they arrived.

Despite the early hour, by the time Emily had ridden Eli's old bicycle into town, a lengthy queue had formed outside W. H. Smith & Son. Through the window, she could see the manager jangling his keys as he checked his pocket watch. Watchful pairs of eyes scanned the deserted street, ears attuned for the sound of an approaching engine. The smell of bacon frying wafted from a nearby café and Emily's mouth watered. She had foregone breakfast in her endeavour to be one of the first in the queue. Her stomach rumbled loudly and the woman in front of her laughed. She was a large woman, with big, work-worn hands, and she looked as if she were about to say something when a cry went up, rippling down the line as the grey delivery van rounded the corner, the words The Shaftesbury Gazette blazoned along its side in dark green letters.

The manager unlocked the doors and stepped out onto the shady street, snapping his braces with his thumbs and nodding greetings to his early-morning customers. The van drew up alongside the kerb and the driver, a grey-haired man with wire-framed glasses, got out and unlocked the back doors. It seemed to take an interminably long time for the two men to unload the bundles of newspapers, but finally the doors were slammed shut and the driver was getting back in his van and driving away.

Emily paid for her copy and hurried outside, fingers fumbling in her haste to find the right page. The Situations Vacant section was disappointingly thin and she scanned it quickly. A local chimney sweep was looking for an assistant; the accountants on the corner were in need of a ledger clerk. There were a few adverts for domestic assistants, and an elderly woman in Bell Street was advertizing for a paid companion. Emily was about to head that way when she saw three of the women who had been in the queue ahead of her already making their way there. She sighed and turned her attention to the cleaning jobs. Most had been placed by affluent families needing domestic help, but the one that caught her eye was for a chambermaid at the prestigious Mansfield House Hotel on the outskirts of town. The position included board and lodging.

Emily rolled the newspaper and stuffed it into the basket on the front of her bicycle. Straightening her hat, she freewheeled down the street, peddling past the grammar school and out into the open countryside.

Mansfield House Hotel was situated just two miles out of town on the Salisbury road. The elegant, late-Victorian building was situated at the end of a long, curving driveway lined with purple and blue-flowering rhododendrons. Emily had only ever caught glimpses of the hotel's many ivy-clad turrets and its imposing clock tower from the road in passing, so it was an impressive sight when she traversed the final bend and the drive opened up into a gravel parking area in front of the grand building. Gazing up at the myriad windows sparkling in the sunlight, Emily was dismounting when a rabbit suddenly shot out of the bushes. It was heading straight for her, followed by a small, wire-haired terrier in hot pursuit. At the last minute, the rabbit swerved. It veered to the left, disappearing between the gnarled roots of an ancient oak tree. The dog was not so nimble. He barrelled into the back of Emily's legs, sending her sprawling to the ground. The dog yelped in surprise as he rolled over several times before shaking himself and scurrying over to poke amongst the tree roots in search of his elusive quarry.

'Muffin! Muffin, come here you rascal!'

At the sound of the voice coming from behind the

rhododendrons, Emily got hastily to her feet. Slightly winded and dusty, she was relieved to find she was otherwise unhurt.

'I'm so sorry, miss. Are you all right?' The owner of the voice had emerged from the bushes. He was tall and tanned, with a shock of dark, curling hair. His brown trousers were grass-stained, and his shirt sleeves were rolled up to the elbow, displaying a pair of taught forearms.

'Thank you, yes. It's just my pride that's hurt,' Emily replied, with an embarrassed laugh, brushing dust from her skirt.

'Muffin's a good dog usually,' the man said, picking up Emily's bicycle and checking it for damage. 'It's just she's got a one-track mind when it comes to rabbits.'

'Well, I think that one got away,' Emily said, nodding to where Muffin was scrabbling frantically at the foot of the mighty oak.

'I'm Tom Harding, by the way. I'm a gardener here.'

'I'm pleased to meet you,' she replied, smiling at the rugged, handsome young man. 'Emily Baker. I'm here to apply for the chambermaid position.'

'Oh, you as well, hmm?' Tom said, lifting an eyebrow. Emily's heart sank.

'Are there many others?'

'At least four that I've seen. Two ladies arrived before the breakfast staff had even arrived for work.'

'But how did they know?' Emily asked in dismay. 'It only appeared in the paper this morning . . . '

Tom shrugged. 'Inside information. You'll probably find they've got relatives working in the hotel who let them know the position was going to be advertised today.'

Emily's shoulders sagged. 'I really need this job,' she whispered.

'Hey, don't lose heart,' Tom said. 'You've as good a chance as any.' He handed Emily her bike.

'Thank you.' She started pushing it towards the entrance but Tom stopped her.

'That's strictly for guests,' he explained. 'Mr Reynolds will have your guts for garters if you go in that way.' He grinned. 'Come on, I'll show you the staff entrance.'

Blushing at her mistake, Emily followed Tom around the side of the rambling building and down a set of narrow stone steps. A door in the wall stood ajar and from within came the sound of distant voices. Emily's heart beat quickened with nerves. Tom gave the door a shove and it opened up to reveal a dimly lit passageway. Emily could just make out another flight of stone steps at the far end.

'The kitchen and staff quarters are up those stairs. Someone will direct you to Miss Thompson's office. I presume it's her you need to see?'

Emily nodded. 'Miss Thompson, head of housekeeping.'

'Well.' Tom flashed Emily a grin. 'I'd better get back to work. Good luck.'

'Thanks.' Emily took a deep breath. 'I'll need it.'

Her footsteps echoed on the flagstone floor as she made her way, somewhat apprehensively, along the passageway, passing several closed doors, which she assumed were used for storage. She paused at the foot of the steps and inhaled deeply in an effort to calm her nerves. The sound of muted conversation drifted downwards, punctuated by bursts of laughter and the clatter of dishes. Wiping her clammy palms on her skirt, Emily climbed the steps and pushed open the door to find herself in the hotel kitchen, which was a steam-filled hive of activity.

A plump woman wearing a striped dress covered by a vast white apron was stirring something on the stove.

'Are you here for the job, love?' she asked, peering at Emily through a cloud of condensation.

'Yes, ma'am. I'm to see a Miss Thompson?'

'Miss Thompson's sitting room is the first door on your left as you leave the kitchen.' The woman pointed her wooden spoon. 'You can't miss it. There's a few others before you.'

Thanking her, Emily made her way through the busy kitchen, dodging kitchen staff. Normally the aroma of bacon frying would have her salivating, but now it only served to aggravate the nausea brought on by nerves.

Four pairs of eyes watched her intently as she entered the small, tastefully furnished sitting room. She recognized one of the women from church and gave her a tentative smile. The woman, who Emily knew to be in her mid-thirties, a widow living with her ageing father, returned Emily's smile with a curt nod. Emily took the only vacant spot on the end of the two-seater settee, her hands resting on her knees. The women sat in silence listening to the soft tick of the carriage clock on the mantelpiece.

'Thank you, Miss Reed. I shall be in touch,' Emily heard a voice say as the door to her left opened and a girl not much older than herself was ushered out by a tall, angular woman who looked to be in her late thirties. She had short, dark, sculpted hair and was wearing a green, striped calf-length dress. 'Who is

45

next, please?' she asked, her eyes coming to rest on Emily.

'That's me, Miss Thompson.' The lady Emily knew from church got to her feet. 'Mrs Crabb.'

'Thank you for coming, Mrs Crabb.' Miss Thompson stood aside to allow the woman into her office. She cast Emily another quick glance before shutting the door firmly behind her.

Emily waited her turn with anxious desperation. She was so lost in the contemplation of what exactly she would do if her interview proved unsuccessful that when Miss Thompson called her name she actually jumped.

Swallowing in an attempt to lubricate her dry throat and wiping her clammy palms on her skirt, she followed the woman into her well-appointed office.

'Please, have a seat.' Miss Thompson indicated a pair of chairs facing the large, walnut-veneered desk. A pretty watercolour hung above the fireplace. Red velvet curtains framed a bay window, which overlooked a paved terrace where several well-dressed couples were breakfasting in the warm sunshine.

'You're Eli's girl, aren't you?' Miss Thompson said, fingering the string of green beads hanging around her neck as she regarded Emily across the desk.

'Yes, miss,' Emily replied with a jerk of her head.

'I knew your father years ago. He was a year or so ahead of me at school but he used to come round to the house and do odd jobs for my mother when my father was laid up after his accident. He was a good man. I was saddened to hear of his death.'

'Thank you.' Her father's loss was still new and raw and her throat ached as tears threatened. She blinked quickly to keep them at bay.

'This hotel is in the fortunate position of being able to employ three new chambermaids,' Miss Thompson said, folding her hands in her lap. 'Thankfully,' she continued, her gaze drifting to the window with its view of the terrace where an elderly woman in emerald green was being ushered to a table by a younger, dapper-looking gentleman, 'our guests appear to be unaffected by the current financial crisis.' She leaned back in her chair. 'So, Miss Baker, what is your experience in housekeeping?'

'Well,' Emily began, 'I kept house for my father since I was seven, and for the past two years, since the age of fourteen, I have also worked as housekeeper and cook for Ned Sawyer of Barrow Hill Farm. I have a letter of reference.' She reached into her pocket and pulled out the letter Ned had popped through her door the previous week.

'Your former employer speaks very highly of you,' Miss Thompson remarked after reading it. 'He states, quite adamantly, that the termination of your employment was entirely due to circumstance and no fault of your own?'

'That's true, miss,' Emily said. She was grateful that Ned hadn't let his personal feelings colour his opinion of her work, which she had always done to the best of her ability.

Miss Thompson asked her a few more questions, then got to her feet. Realizing the interview was over, Emily followed suit.

'Thank you for coming in, Miss Baker.' Miss Thompson folded Emily's letter of reference and handed it back to her. 'You shall hear whether your application has been successful in the next day or so.'

The letter informing Emily she had got the job arrived the following morning.

7

'Edward's taking me dancing at the Grosvenor again on Saturday afternoon,' Betty James told Emily, plumping the soft, white goose-down pillows.

Emily grinned, smoothing down the corners of the plum-coloured eiderdown. 'Lucky you. He's quite the catch.'

'Isn't he?' Betty simpered dreamily. 'And he's such a wonderful dancer.' Picking up one of the pillows, she clutched it to her chest and waltzed across the room, humming a few bars from Strauss's 'Blue Danube' waltz.

Emily laughed, then stopped, startled, as she realized it was the first time she had laughed out loud, properly, since her father's death. She couldn't help feeling guilty, as if she were being somehow disloyal to his memory. She still missed him so much and the hard work of her daily regime was a welcome distraction from her grief. Her friendship with Betty had helped enormously, too. In the three weeks since she had started working at Mansfield House, she and Betty had grown very close.

At seventeen, Betty was a year older than Emily. She was small and thin, with pale, freckled skin, hair so fair as to be almost colourless and grey-blue eyes fringed by incredibly pale lashes. Betty had been working at Mansfield House for two years and Miss Thompson had assigned her to show Emily the ropes. The two girls shared a room in one of the hotel's many attic turrets and had been delighted to find they had much in common. Despite being in each other's company most of the day, they found they still had plenty to talk about once lights were out, often earning themselves a stern telling-off the following morning from Mr Reynolds, the hotel manager, and habitual insomniac, should he happen to hear them during his nocturnal wanderings.

The object of Betty's affections, Edward Secombe, worked as a waiter. Tall and fair, with violet-blue eyes and the beginnings of a moustache, Edward had the sort of handsome good looks that caught women's attention, staff and guests alike. Emily herself had been quite attracted to him the first day she had met him, but it had quickly become clear that Edward had eyes only for Betty.

'You should come with us,' Betty suggested, replacing the pillow and running a hand over its soft white cover to smooth out any wrinkles. 'There are always loads of eligible young men looking for partners.'

'My afternoon off is Thursday this week,' Emily reminded her ruefully. The one fly in their otherwise happy ointment was the fact that their afternoons off seldom coincided.

'Oh, that's a shame.' Betty pouted. 'Maybe next time.'

A gust of wind shook the window frame. It was late September. Many of the trees in the hotel grounds had gained their autumn colours and the air had turned noticeably chilly over the past few days. Now the sky was the colour of dishwater and big drops of rain spattered the glass.

'Maybe,' Emily agreed. She scanned the room, running through her mental checklist to make doubly sure no task had been left undone. Any complaints from guests regarding the cleanliness of their room would bring Miss Thompson's ire down on them like a ton of bricks.

It was almost midday by the time they had worked their way through the rooms in their section of the hotel. Emily wiped her arm across her forehead. Her skin felt dirty and she was aware of her own body odour as she wheeled the laundry cart down the stone passageway to the laundry room. She would spend her afternoon in the steam-filled washroom laundering the mountain of dirty bed linen and towels.

Thankfully the rain had been short-lived and a fresh breeze was blowing across the kitchen garden by the time Emily lugged her heavy basket of wet washing across the damp lawn to the clothesline. Patches of blue sky had emerged from amongst the grey clouds.

She set the laundry basket on the grass and took out the first of the sheets, gripping the pegs in her teeth as she draped it across the line.

'Well, hello again,' came a vaguely familiar voice. Emily finished pegging the sheet on the line and turned to find herself face to face with Tom Harding, the gardener she had met on the day of her interview.

She smiled. 'Hello.'

'You got the job, then?'

'Obviously.' Emily reached down to pick up another sheet, feeling oddly flustered by his unexpected presence.

'How are you enjoying it here?' Tom asked, as she straightened up.

'I like it a lot,' Emily said through a mouthful of clothes pegs. She stretched the sheet over the line and pegged it on. 'Your little dog not with you today?'

'Oh, Muffin's not mine,' answered Tom, shoving

his hands in his trouser pockets. 'She belongs to Mr Andrews, the head gardener.' He shrugged his broad shoulders. 'She'll have her head down a rabbit hole somewhere, no doubt.'

'Well, it's been nice seeing you again,' Emily said. She picked up the empty basket, resting it against her slender hip.

'Yes,' Tom agreed, returning her smile. 'I'll see you around.'

The encounter with Tom, brief as it had been, left a warm feeling in Emily that remained for the rest of the afternoon.

* * *

Her days were busy and it wasn't until almost a week later that Emily's and Tom's paths crossed again. It was the last Wednesday of September and Emily's first full day off in the four weeks since she had started working at Mansfield House.

The weather was mild as she walked into town, kicking at the leaves that littered the pavements. She ran her few errands and was studying the bus time-table outside the town hall, intending to pay Molly a surprise visit, when she spotted Tom across the street. Noticing her almost simultaneously, he raised his hand in a wave. Her pulse quickened with excitement as, glancing up and down the quiet street, he dashed across the road towards her.

'Hello, Emily. If I'd known it was your day off too, I'd have suggested we walk into town together.' He nodded at the bus timetable. 'Are you off somewhere, or have you time for a cup of tea?'

'I was going to visit a friend,' Emily said, trying to

52

ignore the butterflies in her stomach, 'but she's not expecting me, so yes, I'd love a cup of tea.'

She was very aware of Tom's presence at her side as they walked up the street to the Grosvenor Hotel, where they were met by a smiling maître d'.

'Inside or out?' he asked, indicating the French windows leading to the sunny courtyard.

Tom looked at Emily.

'Oh, outside, I think, please?'

'Of course. Follow me.' The maître d' led them out into the warm courtyard. Several tables were occupied but one close to the round stone fountain had just become vacant. Coins glittered on the algae-furred fountain bottom as they caught the sun's rays.

The maître d' quickly cleared the table and took their order for a pot of tea and two toasted teacakes.

'Well,' Tom said, grinning at Emily across the small oval table. 'This is pleasant.'

'Yes,' Emily agreed. Feeling suddenly self-conscious, she averted her eyes, glancing up at the pigeons cooing on the window ledges.

'New hat?' Tom asked, indicating the hat box Emily had been carrying and had now set down beside her shopping basket.

'It's Betty's,' she replied. 'She asked me to pick it up from the milliner's. She needs it for the Harvest Festival. Edward's taking her.'

'Ah, yes.' Tom nodded. 'Edward's a good chap. Totally besotted with Betty.'

Emily smiled. 'She'll be pleased to hear that. She rarely speaks of anything else.' The waitress arrived with their order. 'Shall I pour?' Tom nodded. The tea-cakes were warm and dripping with melted butter. Despite having not long since eaten breakfast, Emily found herself salivating.

'So, Emily, are you a local girl?'

'I am.' Emily bit into her teacake. Butter dripped down her chin and she wiped it with her napkin. 'I was born on Barrow Hill Farm. Do you know it?'

'Ned Sawyer's place?'

'Yes. My father worked for him.' Her voice shook. 'He was killed in an accident six weeks ago.'

'I'm sorry to hear that,' Tom said, sounding genuine. 'Your mother?'

'She died when I was seven. It was always just me and Dad.' Tears threatened and she looked away, waiting for the moment to pass.

'I understand,' Tom said gently. 'My mother died when I was three.'

Emily gave him a sympathetic smile.

'I was raised by my auntie until she and my uncle emigrated to Canada,' he explained. 'I was about ten at the time. My aunt was desperate for me to go with them but my father refused his permission.' Tom paused. He spooned sugar into his cup, stirring thoughtfully. 'I was angry with him. First for abandoning me when I needed him most and, well, by the time my aunt and uncle emigrated, I felt closer to them than to my father but . . . ' He shrugged. 'Dad and I have gone some way towards rebuilding our relationship but it's not quite the same.' He broke off and gave Emily a rueful grin. 'I'm sorry, I shouldn't be laying all this on you. We hardly know each other.'

'It must have been difficult,' Emily sympathized, recalling her own unfounded fears that her father would send her away after her mother's death. 'Does he live locally?' she asked, and lifted the dainty china cup to her lips.

'Motcombe,' replied Tom, referring to the small village two miles down the hill north of Shaftesbury.

' Are you still in contact with your aunt and uncle?'

'Sadly, my auntie passed away five years ago but my uncle and I exchange Christmas cards and the odd letter. He's a wheat farmer and I think the depression has hit him quite hard.'

'It is terrible, the way people are losing their jobs and livelihoods. We are so fortunate, you and I.'

'We are indeed.' Tom drained his cup. A warm breeze ruffled the ivy clinging to the walls. 'If you're finished, do you fancy a stroll along Park Walk?'

Despite Emily's protest, Tom insisted on paying the bill and carrying the round, striped box that contained Betty's new hat.

Emily found Tom easy company and his conversation witty and entertaining as they strolled along the popular promenade, which offered arresting views over the parish of St James and the Blackmore Vale. At the far end of the street, beyond a cluster of tiny higgledy-piggledy cottages, the church steeple rose up from amidst the trees. Now that she worked on Sundays, Emily had reluctantly given up her place in the church choir, and though she missed it dreadfully, she was consoled by the fact that Reverend Smedhurst had promised her that she would be welcome back any time.

The wind was brisker now and Emily shivered, despite her warm coat. Above the sigh of the wind through the trees came the chime of the town hall clock striking midday.

'Come on,' said Tom, cupping Emily's elbow with his free hand. 'Let's get out of this wind. I'll buy you dinner.'

'Thank you. I've had a lovely day,' Emily said later that afternoon as they walked along Salisbury Street, passing the boys' grammar school where a lively game of rugby was in progress on the playing field.

They had lingered over their meal at the quaint seventeenth-century café at the top of the High Street, and it was well into the afternoon by the time they'd emerged into the autumn sunshine.

'Me too,' said Tom with a grin. 'Let's do it again soon. When are you next off?'

'I'm off next Wednesday afternoon?' Emily replied hopefully.

'I'm off on Tuesday.'

'Oh,' said Emily, struggling to hide her disappointment.

'Now the nights are drawing in, I tend to finish work by around half past six most evenings,' Tom said. 'Would you like to meet up for a walk or perhaps a trip to the pictures?'

Emily smiled. 'I'd like that. I'm usually finished about six.'

'Great. What about tomorrow evening?' suggested Tom as they walked up through the hotel grounds. 'Shall we say a quarter past seven? We could make the pictures in time for the eight o'clock showing and get fish and chips afterwards?'

'Yes, thank you. I should like that very much.'

'Until tomorrow night then.' Tom grinned, handing Emily the hat box.

Emily smiled back. 'Until tomorrow.'

8

'Come on, Emily,' Betty cajoled from the doorway of their shared attic bedroom, her warm breath billowing in front of her face. It was early November and the single-bar electric heater barely took the edge off the frigid air. 'We shall miss the bus and there's no way I'm walking all the way to town in these heels.' She stuck out a foot, turning her slender ankle this way and that to admire her patent leather footwear.

'I'm sorry, Betty,' Emily panted. Shivering in nothing but her underclothes, she hastily ran a flannel over her face and neck.

'What took you so long anyway?' Betty lit a cigarette, despite it being against the rules, and inhaled deeply.

'Hilda's in bed with a migraine,' Emily explained, taking her new red wool dress off its hanger and tugging it over her head. 'I had three extra rooms to clean.' She tilted the dressing table mirror towards her and studied her reflection with a critical eye as she smoothed the dress over her lithe form. 'You'd better open the window a crack,' she added, giving Betty a sideways glance as she put on her lipstick. 'You know Mr Reynolds will go mad if he smells cigarette smoke.' She ran a brush through her curls and turned to smile at Betty. 'There, I'm ready.'

'About time,' Betty said, extinguishing her cigarette in the cracked saucer that passed for an ashtray. 'You look very pretty by the way. No wonder Tom's smitten.'

Emily's cheeks turned a bright shade of pink and she laughed in an attempt to hide her embarrassment but, as she put on her hat and coat and followed Betty down the stairs, she had to admit she was pleased at how close she and Tom had become over the past six weeks. They met up after supper at least twice a week and had managed to enjoy two afternoons off together in the past fortnight. Though she hadn't known Tom very long, Emily felt as comfortable with him as if she had known him all her life. Knowing he was waiting for her downstairs sent a tingle of excitement racing down her spine.

She had been looking forward to today all week. It was rare that her afternoon off coincided with Betty's and, as Tom and Edward had managed to wangle the time off as well, Betty had suggested they go to the cinema in town, which was showing one of her favourite films, *Tarzan the Ape Man*.

Tom and Edward were waiting in the corridor outside the hotel kitchen. Although not close friends, they shared accommodation above the old stable block and knew each other well enough.

'You look nice,' Tom said admiringly to Emily as she and Betty hurried towards them.

'Thank you.' Emily smiled, taking his arm.

'We'd better get a move on,' Edward said, a hint of irritation in his tone. 'The bus will be here any minute.'

'Sorry,' Emily apologized. 'My fault. I was late finishing work.'

They walked quickly, the gravel crunching beneath their feet. The sky was overcast and a cold wind stung their cheeks. They reached the road just as the bus rounded the bend. They paid their fare and climbed aboard. Even though the bus was quite full, having already done a circuit of the outlying villages, they managed to find seats together on the upper deck.

They got off outside the town hall where a group of boy scouts were rattling tin mugs at passers-by. Beside them, a crude effigy of Guy Fawkes reclined awkwardly in a muddy wheelbarrow.

A cold wind blew up the street and it was starting to drizzle as the two couples made their way down the bustling High Street. It was warm in the cinema foyer, with its plush ruby-red carpets and embossed wallpaper, the air hazy with cigarette smoke and smelling of chocolate. Tom bought the tickets and the usherette showed them to their seats.

Betty offered round a bag of barley sugars as the lights dimmed. The heavy curtains were drawn back to reveal the big screen and they settled back in their seats to enjoy the film.

'Not sure I'd want to live in the jungle with a man brought up by apes,' Betty said as the lights came on for the interval. 'But Johnny Weissmuller is gorgeous, so I might be persuaded. Anyone fancy an ice cream?'

'I'll have one,' Emily replied, reaching for her handbag. A few rows ahead of her, a man stood up, running a hand through his thick hair as he looked around. Emily recognized him immediately. It was Ned Sawyer, her old employer. She was debating whether to go over and say hello, for her father's sake if not her own — after all, Ned had had no qualms about seeing her homeless — when she realized that he'd spotted her. It would be churlish to ignore him now, she decided. 'I've just spotted my old employer, Mr Sawyer,' she said to the others. 'I'm going over and to say hello.'

'What ice cream would you like?' Tom asked. 'Choc-ice?'

'Yes, please,' Emily said, smiling at him over her shoulder as she made her way along the row to the aisle.

'Hello, Emily.' To his credit, Ned had the grace to look ashamed. 'How are you? I hear you're working over at Mansfield House.'

'I'm well, thank you, Mr Sawyer,' Emily replied, coolly. 'And yes, I am.'

'Look,' he said awkwardly, in a low voice, 'I owe you an apology. My behaviour was . . . appalling.' He broke off when the attractive blonde woman sitting beside him laid her hand on his arm. She looked up with mild curiosity and smiled.

Ned cleared his throat. 'Emily, I'd like you to meet my fiancée, Harriet Porter. Emily's late father was my dearest friend.'

'It's nice to meet you, Emily,' said Harriet.

'Likewise,' said Emily. 'And congratulations on your engagement.'

'Thank you.' Harriet blushed. She was an attractive girl with blue eyes and even features that suited her short hair. 'It was a bit of a whirlwind romance, wasn't it, Ned?' she said, turning to him. Ned nodded, avoiding Emily's gaze.

'We only met four weeks ago at the Harvest lunch,' Harriet continued, holding out her left hand to allow the modest diamond to catch the light. 'But we knew straight away we were right for each other. We're getting married on Christmas Eve.'

'Well, I wish you all the best,' Emily said, with genuine warmth. She looked at Ned. 'Both of you.'

'They're getting married in December,' Emily told

60

Tom when she returned to her seat. 'They've only known each other a month.'

'When you know, you know,' Tom said, handing Emily her choc-ice.

'Thank you. That's what Mr Sawyer's fiancée said.' Emily unwrapped her ice cream and licked chocolate from her fingers. 'I think I'd want to court a while longer than that before I made a lifetime commitment.'

Tom opened his mouth to reply but was interrupted by Betty returning from the ladies' and the usherette's announcement that the film would be restarting in five minutes and would people please return to their seats.

★　★　★

It was dark by the time they returned to the hotel. Lights blazed through the incessant drizzle, pooling on the front steps. A well-dressed couple were getting out of one of several cars parked on the gravel forecourt and the doorman hurried towards them, umbrella at the ready. The wet leaves were slippery underfoot and Emily was grateful for Tom's arm as the four of them made their way around the side of the building to the staff entrance.

They entered the brightly lit corridor to find Mr Reynolds, the usually unflappable hotel manager, in a state of high anxiety. His well-oiled dark hair was in disarray and he wrung his hands in agitation.

'What's the matter, Mr Reynolds?' Emily asked in alarm, blinking rain water from her eyes and shedding her wet coat. For once Mr Reynolds seemed oblivious to the water puddling around their feet.

61

'Are you ill, sir?' Edward queried politely. 'Is there anything we can do?'

'Miss Simms has let us down,' Reynolds snapped.

Melody Simms was a professional singer employed by the hotel. Her Saturday evening performances always drew a good crowd.

'That's not like her,' Emily said with a frown. 'She's usually so reliable. Perhaps she's poorly?'

'Oh no, she's not ill,' Mr Reynolds snorted. 'When she failed to turn up for her rehearsal this afternoon, I sent one of the lads round to her house. She's only buggered off to London, hasn't she?'

'London?' Betty exclaimed.

'So George says. According to her mother, Miss Simms has been offered a job singing at some posh hotel in Knightsbridge. She left this morning on the eleven-fifteen train.'

'That's a bit off, isn't it?' Tom said with a frown. 'Not to let you know.'

'Oh, what am I to do?' Mr Reynolds wailed, rubbing his furrowed brow. 'I've got a room full of diners looking forward to an evening of "Melodies with Melody" and the best I can offer them is Fred thumping out a few tunes on the baby grand.' He sighed deeply, shaking his head in consternation. 'Mr Mansfield is not going to be happy.'

'Mr Reynolds, wait,' Betty called after him as he turned away. 'Emily can sing.'

'What?' Emily looked at her in startled surprise.

'You're a singer?' Mr Reynolds asked Emily, his brows raised questioningly. She blushed, hearing the hope in his voice.

'Well, no,' she replied, a red flush creeping up her cheeks. 'Not really.'

62

'She's got a lovely voice, Mr Reynolds,' Betty assured him. 'She sings all the time when we're working.' She turned to Emily. 'Don't you?'

'Well, yes,' Emily acquiesced, 'but I'm not in Miss Simms's league.'

'Nonsense,' Betty declared stoutly. 'Give her a try, Mr Reynolds. She's brilliant.'

'No, I don't think . . . I've never sung in public before, apart from in the church choir. I wouldn't know what to sing.'

'Sing whatever you like,' Mr Reynolds said, his relief palpable. He looked at his pocket watch. 'You've got an hour to prepare. See Miss Thompson about a frock, then join me and Fred in the library for a rehearsal. If I'm satisfied with your performance, you're on.'

'Betty, what were you thinking?' Emily snapped, rounding on her friend in dismay as Mr Reynolds hurried off. 'I'm not a professional singer. What if they think I'm awful?'

'They won't,' Betty replied firmly.

'I didn't know you sang,' Tom said.

'It's just something I do,' Emily said, trying to ignore the butterflies congregating in her stomach. She thought of all the evenings she had watched Melody from the sidelines, dreaming that one day it might be her up there under the lights . . . She felt very queasy all of a sudden.

'Come on, Tom.' Edward nudged him. 'I'm on duty in fifteen minutes — I'll sneak you and Betty into the dining room. There are plenty of dark recesses you can hide in where Reynolds won't notice you.'

'Thanks, Eddie.' Betty kissed him, leaving a smear of crimson lipstick on his cheek. 'I wouldn't miss your debut for anything,' she added, turning to grin at Emily.

Tom gave Emily's hand a gentle squeeze. 'I'm sure you'll be amazing. I'll see you afterwards,' he assured her before leaving to go after Edward.

'I'm really not sure about this,' Emily said uncertainly as they waited outside Miss Thompson's sitting room.

'You'll be fine,' Betty assured her, rapping softly on the door. 'You said yourself how much that Mr Sawyer used to enjoy your little soirees.'

'That was different—' Emily's protest was cut short by Miss Thompson's invitation to enter.

★ ★ ★

Emily swallowed nervously. Her mouth was so dry she doubted she would be able to sing a note. She wore a long dress of midnight blue velvet that Miss Thompson had lent her. Betty had curled her hair and done her make-up. Both Mr Reynolds and Fred had been amazed during the rather hurried rehearsal, but now, facing a real, live audience, she felt like an imposter, a fraud. Her father's words echoed in her mind — *ambition of that sort is not for the likes of us* — and she wondered if he would approve. The scepticism emanating from her audience was tangible. They had come here expecting to see Melody Simms and instead they had been presented with a slip of a girl they'd never heard of. She glanced across at Fred, the pianist. He was an older man, with a head of grey hair and weathered features. He gave her a surreptitious wink and nodded as if to say he was ready whenever she was.

Emily's anxious gaze swept the room. She knew

Tom and Betty were out there somewhere, beyond the reach of the subdued lamplight. Edward walked by with a tray of filled champagne flutes and flashed Emily an encouraging smile.

She looked at Fred again and took a deep breath. The first note came out as a nervous squeak. Someone tittered and she looked at Fred in panic. He smiled and nodded as he played the introduction again. Emily took a deep breath and closed her eyes. As the music washed over her, she was transported back to Ned's cosy parlour, singing for her father. In her mind's eye she could see Eli sitting in one of Ned's overstuffed armchairs, his eyes brimming with paternal pride, and her nerves dissipated as she pictured him smiling at her. She would sing for her father.

She had chosen one of her mother's favourite hymns to start with. She sang hesitantly at first, but her voice soon gained strength, soaring to the rafters. The final notes faded away to deathly silence, and her heart sank. They hated her.

The sudden crash of applause made her jump. To her surprise, she noticed some of the women were dabbing their eyes. She caught a glimpse of Tom in the shadows, clapping for all he was worth. She smiled bashfully, letting the applause wash over her.

For the next two hours she entertained the diners with popular songs like 'In a Shanty in Old Shanty Town', 'Too Many Tears', and 'We Just Couldn't Say Goodbye'.

After two encores, the applause seemed to go on for ever, stopping only when Mr Reynolds bounded onto the stage, beaming from ear to ear. He took Emily's hand and gave a low bow.

'Ladies and gentlemen, our very own Miss Emily

Baker,' he said proudly, sending the audience into another frenzy of appreciative clapping. People were on their feet. 'Accompanied by our resident pianist, Fred Cordery.' Fred rose and gave a bow, to more thunderous applause.

'You've certainly been hiding your light under a bushel, Miss Baker,' Mr Reynolds whispered into Emily's ear as he led her off the stage. 'You were brilliant. Miss Simms has never received a standing ovation in all her years of singing at the hotel.'

Tom, Betty and Miss Thompson were waiting for her in the foyer.

'You were wonderful!' Tom exclaimed, impulsively flinging his arms around Emily and hugging her. Swept away by the exhilaration of her performance, Emily entwined her fingers in his hair and lifted her face to his. Their eyes met for the briefest moment before Tom's lips found hers and Emily closed her eyes, giving herself up to the sweetness of their first kiss.

'Well, well!" Mr Reynolds said, clearing his throat noisily. Emily blushed furiously as she and Tom parted, but she couldn't keep from smiling. 'You're wasted as a chambermaid,' Mr Reynolds continued, looking slightly embarrassed by such an exuberant display of affection. 'Come to my office first thing Monday, and we'll discuss your future role as our resident singer.' He grinned. 'It seems Miss Simms scarpering off to London was rather fortuitous. Well done for recommending your friend, Miss James,' he said, turning to Betty.

Betty grinned. 'I always knew she was destined for something better than cleaning bedrooms.'

'You were fantastic, Emily,' Tom praised her again a while later. They were sitting in the staff kitchen with Betty, mugs of steaming hot cocoa cooling on the table in front of them. 'I'm ever so proud of you.'

'Thank you.' Emily felt herself blushing. Word of her performance had spread amongst the staff and she was basking in the heartfelt congratulations and admiration of her colleagues.

'I wonder what offer Mr Reynolds will make you on Monday,' Betty said, with only the slightest twinge of envy.

'I can't imagine,' Emily murmured. 'I'm still in a state of shock. They really liked me.'

'Oi, Emily.' Edward came into the kitchen, his face beaming as he set a pint glass on the table, half-filled with change.

'What's this?' Emily asked, looking up at him in surprise.

'Tips.' Edward grinned. 'The customers always leave tips at the bar but we've never had this much before. The chaps thought it only fair that you get your share.'

'Blimey, Emily,' Betty exclaimed, holding the glass up to the light. 'You're going to be rich.'

9
1936

Emily walked off the stage to tumultuous applause.

'You were amazing, as always,' Betty said, handing her a glass of water.

'Thank you.' Emily gulped it down. 'I'm parched.'

'I'm not surprised.' Betty smiled at her friend proudly. 'Three encores!'

In the three years Emily had been singing at the hotel, her popularity had grown immeasurably, with her reputation drawing audiences from the surrounding villages and towns. She had received glowing reviews in the local newspaper and the previous month had been billed as the star attraction in the town's Christmas variety show.

She had begun by performing only on Friday and Saturday evenings, whilst continuing with her chambermaid duties during the day, but as her popularity had grown, and the dinner reservations had come flooding in, Mr Reynolds had taken the decision to have her sing every evening, bar Sundays. Despite the worsening depression throughout the country, it was rare that the dining room wasn't full to capacity, and they were often forced to turn away potential bookings.

'Another excellent performance,' Fred the pianist declared, joining Emily and Betty at the bar. 'A pint, please, Reg,' he said to the barman, flexing his fingers. As usual, the tip jar was overflowing and Emily knew from experience that there would be at least four or five drinks put back for her behind the bar. She rarely touched alcohol and, in reply to Reg's questioning glance, ordered a lemonade.

'Cheers!' Fred raised his pint.

'Cheers.' Emily and Fred clinked glasses. She took a sip of her lemonade, scanning the dining room. The pleasant hum of conversation blended with the clatter of cutlery and the soft tinkle of chamber music drifting from the gramophone.

Betty withdrew a cigarette from her case and put it to her lips. She leaned towards Fred, who immediately struck a match and lit it for her. 'Thank you, Fred.' Betty turned back to Emily, exhaling a cloud of cigarette smoke. 'So, have you decided whether you'll carry on singing here once you and Tom are married?'

'Tom is happy for me to continue for the time being, at least until we start a family,' Emily replied, blushing. To her delight, Tom had proposed on Emily's eighteenth birthday and there had been many occasions during the past two years when they had almost got carried away and given in to their desire for each other. The wedding was planned for the first Saturday in May so they only had to exercise self-control for three and a bit months, she mused, her blush deepening as she realized that both Betty and Fred were looking at her with knowing smiles.

'Right,' said Fred, draining his pint. 'I'd better get back to my piano. Enjoy the rest of your evening, ladies. Give my regards to Tom.'

'Speaking of Tom,' Betty said, sliding her empty glass across the polished walnut bar towards Reg for a refill, 'where is he? It's not like him to miss a performance.'

'He's gone to visit his father,' replied Emily. She wondered anxiously how the visit was going. Tom and his father didn't have the easiest of relationships, but Tom was trying hard to make things better. His father, Ernest, was keen to make things up to Tom too, but he did have an unfortunate habit of saying the wrong thing and rubbing Tom up the wrong way.

Betty glanced at the clock above the bar and drained her drink. 'Miss Thompson wants to see me in ten minutes,' she said. She crushed her cigarette butt in the ashtray. 'The new girl's moving in tonight and she's asked me to take her under my wing.'

'Well, I suppose now that Maggie is leaving to be married, you've worked here the longest.'

'Six years I've been here.' Betty pulled a face. 'I started the week after my fourteenth birthday.'

'I was sixteen when I started, so I've been here nearly four,' Emily reminded her.

'So you have,' Betty acknowledged drily. 'But you're not cleaning the guests' bedrooms anymore, are you? And in just over three months' time you'll be marrying the man of your dreams.' She sighed. 'I wish Edward would let me set a date. I sometimes wonder if we'll ever get married.'

'Of course you will,' Emily assured her. 'Tom says Edward's saving as much as he can.'

'But I've got savings too,' Betty exclaimed in exasperation. 'We've got more than enough between us to set up home, but he's too proud to take my savings into account. Anyway, I'd better go. I don't want to keep Miss Thompson waiting. I'll see you upstairs later.'

'All right. I'll go up after I finish this.' Emily stifled a yawn. 'I'm exhausted.'

70

Several of the diners came up to chat to Emily once Betty left and it was some twenty minutes before she managed to get away. The sound of voices drifted down the stairs as she made her way up to the turret and she smiled as she heard Betty laying down the law in the slightly bossy tone of voice she was prone to use when speaking to a new recruit.

'Smoking is totally forbidden in our rooms,' Betty was saying as Emily rounded the corner, shivering in the draughty air. The small corridor was dimly lit and it was a moment before she recognized the girl to whom Betty was speaking. Her mouth fell open in shock.

'Ah, Emily,' Betty said cheerfully, half-turning to smile at her friend. 'This is Lucy Hunt. She's taking over from Maggie.'

Emily stared at Lucy in dismay. The two girls hadn't seen each other since Lucy left school seven years earlier to go into service but, judging by the other girl's icy stare, she had clearly not forgiven Emily for her humiliation at the hands of Reverend Smedhurst all those years before.

'Hello, Lucy,' Emily said in as friendly a tone as she could muster. 'It's nice to see you again.' Betty's brow rose in surprise.

'Oh, do you two know each other?'

'We sang together in the church choir,' Emily explained.

'Until you started sucking up to old Smedhurst and persuaded him to make you lead soloist,' Lucy snorted with a toss of her sculpted blonde hair. 'I was lead soloist at St James's for six months before Emily came along,' she told Betty, whose blue eyes were darting between the two girls in bewilderment.

'Reverend Smedhurst told me he was very sorry when you left,' Emily said in a placatory tone. 'He had rather hoped you might stay in the choir.'

'What?' Lucy's nostrils flared angrily. 'And play second fiddle to you? The daughter of a farmhand?' She gave a brittle laugh and turned to Betty. 'My father was a very wealthy man, you know? We're related to the Mansfields.'

'And yet, here you are,' Betty interrupted coolly. 'Working as a chambermaid in their hotel, along with me, the daughter of a cowman.'

Lucy flushed an ugly crimson. 'Well, I won't be for long,' she snarled, anger distorting her pretty features. 'Mrs Mansfield promised me it is only temporary, until something better comes along.'

Betty gave her a condescending smile. 'Of course it is. Come on, I'll show you to your room. You're sharing with Cathy and Maggie. It'll be a bit of a squeeze until Maggie moves out at the end of the week,' she added drily. 'But I'm sure you'll manage.'

With one final glare at Emily, Lucy flounced after Betty. Emily watched them go, her heart sinking. In the ensuing years, it seemed, Lucy had grown from a spoilt, pampered girl into a spiteful, embittered young woman, and she was clearly still nursing a grudge. Emily just hoped it wouldn't affect the generally happy atmosphere that prevailed amongst the hotel staff.

★ ★ ★

'Is Lucy really related to the Mansfields, do you think?' Emily asked Betty a short time later as they lay in their narrow single beds, the covers pulled up to their chins. The wind howled under the eaves. January had brought a prolonged spell of bitterly cold weather with fresh snow falling almost daily.

'Distantly, on her mother's side,' Betty replied, turning to face her friend. 'She's certainly got an axe to grind with you, though?'

'So, it would seem,' Emily agreed ruefully. 'It's so silly. We were just children.'

'And it wasn't your fault if that Reverend What's-His-Name preferred your voice to hers. She needs to get over herself, that one.'

'I wonder who her father was. Her mother was already a widow when I knew them.'

'Well,' Betty said, her eyes glittering with mischief. 'Miss Thompson told me this in the strictest confidence, and you know I'm not one for gossip, but apparently, Lucy's father was descended from one of the big brewing families in Blandford. They weren't rich, but they were comfortably well off. They had a nice house with staff and what have you but the old man squandered all his money on some dodgy investments. He died in a hunting accident when Lucy was only six, leaving her and her mother penniless. If it hadn't been for the charity of relatives, they would have been destitute.'

'Golly, poor Lucy,' Emily murmured, feeling a stab of pity for the girl. 'How does Miss Thompson know all this?'

'Lucy's mother wrote to Mrs Mansfield practically begging her to give Lucy a job. Apparently, she was sacked from her last job, without references.'

'Sacked?' Emily's eyes widened in shock. 'Gosh, whatever for?'

'She's argumentative and doesn't like being told

what to do. According to what Mrs Mansfield told Miss Thompson, Lucy's mum has always made a big thing about them being an important family, so Lucy's grown up thinking she's a cut above the rest of us.'

'Yet, as you said,' Emily gave a small laugh, 'she's no better than us now.'

'Exactly.' Betty gave Emily a wry grin. 'Well, we'd better get some sleep. I don't have the luxury of a lie-in in the mornings like you do.'

'I wonder how long she'll last here,' Emily mused as she leaned over to turn out the lamp, enveloping them both in darkness. 'Miss Thompson's not going to put up with that sort of behaviour for very long, whatever her connections.'

'Ha, no,' Betty agreed sleepily. 'I don't think we'll have the pleasure of Miss Hunt's company for very long at all. Goodnight.'

10

Emily sipped her cup of hot, sweet tea and rubbed condensation from the window. The view from the hotel kitchen was of a grey and drab landscape. February had brought the beginnings of a thaw and everywhere was dripping with melting snow.

She smiled at the sight of Tom struggling to push a wheelbarrow across the waterlogged lawn in his wellington boots, Muffin trotting at his heels. He looked up and, catching sight of her at the window, grinned and waved.

Emily waved back.

She wrapped her cold fingers around her mug and glanced at the clock above the range. Around her the kitchen was a hive of activity as the luncheon preparation got underway. An array of tantalizing aromas hung in the steam-filled air as pan lids banged and oven doors slammed. Emily often felt slightly uncomfortable surrounded by the hustle and bustle that kept the hotel running so smoothly. She worried that her hard-working colleagues might look down on her in her role as 'entertainer'. But so far, apart from Lucy Hunt, no one ever seemed to begrudge her good fortune. And, for all the appearance of leading an easy, glamorous life, she did work hard. She spent her afternoons rehearsing with Fred, and she performed until late in the evening. If guests requested it, she often performed during luncheon or afternoon tea. Her biggest fear at the moment was catching a cold and being unable to work. As soon as she felt a tickle coming on, she gargled with honey and lemon, a remedy Betty had sworn was guaranteed to work. So far, her friend had been right.

A draught of cold air wafted through the vast kitchen as the door was flung open and Lucy flounced into the kitchen, her expression sour. Catching sight of Emily, she shot her a venomous glare as she reached for the teapot. Emily sighed inwardly. Lucy had been working at Mansfield House Hotel for just over a month now and had continually rebuffed all Emily's attempts at friendship. It seemed their working together had only exacerbated Lucy's grudge from all those years ago.

'This tea's stewed,' Lucy complained loudly, her strident tone cutting across the good-natured banter. 'And it's cold.'

'Make a fresh pot then,' snapped Mrs Young, the cook, stepping round Lucy, carrying a plump rainbow trout in her hands. 'I heard you were in Miss Thompson's bad books again, yesterday?' she said, slapping the trout down on the scrubbed table and reaching for her cleaver. 'You need to buck your ideas up, my girl, or she'll send you packing. Mr Reynolds expects this place to run like clockwork. We can't afford any shirkers.'

'What about *her?*' Lucy said, with a nod in Emily's direction. Emily felt herself blush as several of the girls looked up from their tasks.

'Emily earns her keep and more,' Mrs Young said firmly, waggling her finger at Lucy. 'She keeps the guests coming back time and again.'

Emily's blush deepened, this time from pleasure at the unexpected compliment.

'Well, I shall be writing to my Aunt Victoria,' Lucy pouted as she filled the kettle. 'I'm sure she didn't

76

mean for me to spend my days skivvying.'

Mrs Young raised an eyebrow. 'I'm sure Mrs Mansfield has more pressing concerns than the running of this hotel,' she said acerbically. 'Now, have your cup of tea and get back to work. I don't need you hanging around my kitchen making a nuisance of yourself.'

Studiously avoiding Lucy's contemptuous glare, Emily swallowed the remains of her tea and rinsed her cup under the tap. She glanced at the kitchen clock. She had a few minutes to spare before she was due to meet Fred in the billiard room to practise for the evening performance. Mr Reynolds had suggested some new songs and Emily, eager to have perfected them by the evening, had insisted on a longer rehearsal time than usual.

Leaving the warmth of the kitchen, she snatched her coat off the hook by the back door and stepped out into the grounds. The damp air settled on her hair and her face, filling her nostrils with the smell of wet earth and mouldering vegetation. She could hear Muffin snuffling about in the undergrowth and knew Tom couldn't be far away. She found him over by the compost heap, dumping a wheelbarrow load of garden rubbish. Muffin emerged from beneath a rhododendron bush and danced around Emily's feet, tail wagging frantically as Emily reached down to pat her wiry head.

'Hello, beautiful.' Tom let go of his wheelbarrow and wiped his hands on his trousers. His damp hair curled attractively around his shirt collar. Emily straightened up and he leaned over to kiss her. 'What are you doing out here?' He glanced up at the bleak sky. A solitary crow cawed in the bough of a nearby tree.

'I had a few minutes to spare so I thought I'd pop out and say hello.'

'Well, I'm glad you did. I missed you.' He rubbed his hands together and grinned. 'Dad sent a message up with the milkman. He's invited us over for tea on Sunday afternoon. What do you say? Will you come?'

'Of course.' Emily had visited Tom's father several times. Though there was often some underlying tension between Tom and his father, Emily thought Ernest a sweet, gentle soul and she had grown very fond of him. 'I'd like that very much.'

'Great.'

Neither of them noticed Lucy at the second-floor window, watching.

* * *

Lucy scowled as she stared down at the two figures deep in conversation on the hotel lawn. What was it about Emily Baker that held everyone in such a thrall? She could carry a tune — so what? So could she. Lucy had the voice of an angel, her mother had always said. That stupid vicar had made a huge mistake choosing Emily over her.

She'd had it hard growing up. Her early years had been pampered ones, doted on by an over-indulgent mother and equally forbearing father. The death of her father when she was six had come as a devastating blow. Not only had Lucy lost a beloved father, but she and her mother had suddenly found themselves homeless and at the mercy of whichever relative could be persuaded to offer them charity.

But despite their distressing circumstances, her mother hadn't allowed their problems to disguise that they deserved a higher station in life. It was seldom that Lucy did not get her own way, and being replaced by Reverend Smedhurst as his favourite soloist had cut deep. Over time the wound had festered, and she kept picking at it, like a scab she couldn't leave alone.

Now she gazed down at Emily with simmering resentment. Not only did everyone at the hotel, the manager included, treat Emily like she was something special, she'd also managed to bag herself the best-looking bloke around. Not that Lucy would ever settle for a gardener, of course. But she couldn't deny that it might be fun to get to know Tom a little bit better . . .

'What are you doing loitering in the corridor, Lucy?' Betty said crossly, coming out onto the landing with a pillow clutched to her chest. 'Do I have to do everything by myself?'

'I was on a break.'

'Pretty long break.' Betty clucked her tongue in annoyance. 'You've been ages.'

'All right, all right.' Lucy gave an exasperated sigh. 'I'm coming.'

11

'Another slice of cake, love?' Tom's father leaned forward in his armchair and indicated the Victoria sponge on the small baize-topped card table.

'Thank you.' Emily helped herself to a slice and settled back in her chair in his small but cosy parlour. A fire roared in the grate and from outside, where Tom was chopping wood out the back, came the rhythmic thud of an axe.

'It's delicious,' remarked Emily, while secretly thinking it was a little dry.

'Mrs Mullet next door baked it specially,' Ernest told her. 'She's always had a soft spot for my Tom. When his aunt emigrated to Canada and Tom came back to live with me, he could be a bit . . . difficult. She used to keep an eye on him for me.' He smiled at Emily over the rim of his teacup.

At fifty-five, Ernest was short in stature, with greying hair that was thinning on top, a ruddy complexion and a mouth that seemed to always be smiling. Apart from the dark brown eyes, Emily couldn't see much of Tom in Ernest at all and surmised that he must take after his late mother. An old sepia wedding photograph stood in pride of place on the mantelpiece but the bride's features were too indistinct for Emily to clearly detect any resemblance.

'Tom always speaks very fondly of Mrs Mullet,' Emily told him. 'And she and Mr Mullet are invited to our wedding.'

'She'll enjoy that.' Ernest nodded. 'She likes an

80

excuse to dress up, does Mrs Mullet.' Balancing his cup and saucer on his knee, he picked up his pipe and tobacco pouch that lay on the chair arm. 'Have you and Tom found anywhere to live, yet?'

'We're going to look at a cottage in Salisbury Street on Thursday morning. The rent's quite high but Tom's adamant we can afford it, especially as I'm going to be carrying on with my singing for the time being.'

'You could always move in with me,' Ernest suggested. Emily hesitated. Tom's feelings towards his father were . . . mixed. He loved him, but she didn't think he'd feel comfortable living under Ernest's roof. The rift between them was still too wide.

'That's very kind of you, Mr Harding,' she replied with a smile. 'But it's a distance to travel to work and back every day. It would cost too much in bus fare.'

Ernest nodded. 'Well, the offer's always there if you change your mind.'

The back door opened, and Tom blew into the cottage on a gust of cold wind. He came into the front parlour, his cheeks rosy from the biting cold, and arms full of freshly chopped wood which he dropped into the wicker basket beside the stone fireplace.

'The temperature's falling again,' he said, tugging off his thick gloves and shrugging out of his coat. 'I shouldn't be surprised if we get more snow tonight.'

'You two had better be off soon, then,' Ernest said, glancing out of the window with a worried frown. 'You don't want to be stranded down here if the buses stop running.'

'The next bus isn't due for another fifteen minutes,' Tom said, eyeing the clock. 'I've got time for a quick cup of tea.'

Lucy slammed the front door as she stormed out of the large, red-.brick manor house, her expression thunderous. What had started out as a pleasant luncheon with her late father's brother and his family had descended into a bitter disagreement that had left Lucy fuming with indignation. She walked quickly towards the bus stop, head bent against the brisk wind, her eyes smarting with tears of self-.pity, her Uncle David's parting comment echoing around her head.

'I refuse to fund your mother's extravagant lifestyle any longer, Lucy,' he'd said, placing his folded napkin beside his dessert plate and pushing back his chair. 'You're earning a fair wage. The two of you must learn to live within your means. Unfortunately, you seem to have inherited Amelia's misplaced sense of entitlement. You're turning into a thoroughly unpleasant young woman. Your father would be ashamed of you, God rest his soul,' he'd finished, before repairing to his study for a much-needed glass of cognac.

Shunning her aunt's rather reluctant invitation to join the others in the parlour, Lucy had remained at the table, crying and rudely ignoring the maid attempting to clear up around her.

She hurried up the road, conscious of the fact that, should she miss the quarter to four bus, she'd be forced to endure another two hours of her aunt and uncle's begrudging com.pany or risk freezing to death on the street. Looking up, she was surprised to see Tom loitering at the bus stop. Her spirits lifted immediately.

'Hello. It's Tom, isn't it?' she said, as she crossed the

road. 'We haven't been introduced. I'm Lucy Hunt.'

'Ah, yes.' Tom smiled, slightly taken aback. 'Emily's mentioned you.'

'I hope she hasn't maligned me too much,' Lucy said with a sly smile.

'Emily seldom has anything unkind to say about anyone,' Tom replied, coolly. Emily had told him a little about Lucy's behaviour towards her and, like his fiancée, he found it bizarre that a childhood incident could breed such a spirit of animosity.

'Where is your dear fiancée anyway?' Lucy asked airily, glancing up and down the deserted street. Night was falling and the cottage windows glowed orange in the growing darkness. From within the Methodist chapel behind them came the deep melodious strains of an organ. The tune was an old favourite Lucy recognized from her days as a churchgoer.

'She's just popped in to see a neighbour,' Tom replied, adding with palpable relief, 'Ah, here she comes now.' Seeing the joy on Tom's face, Lucy's ill humour returned. Her black mood was further deepened as she compared her own drab brown coat, a thrift shop purchase, to the tailored plum-coloured one Emily was wearing. Envy gnawed at her insides. If her mother wouldn't insist on Lucy handing over a large portion of her wages each month, and if her uncle wasn't so hard-hearted, she, too, might be able to afford fashionable clothes instead of being forced into wearing someone's casts-offs.

Walking down Mrs Mullet's garden path, Emily had been startled to see Tom talking to Lucy. In the moment before they both spotted her, she had paused by the gate, one gloved hand resting on the latch, a small frown between her eyes, watching as Lucy tilted

83

her face towards Tom. She was actually quite pretty when she wasn't wearing her usual scowl of displeasure, Emily reflected. Her own frown changed to a smile at the expression of relief on Tom's face when he caught sight of her walking through the gate.

'Hello, Lucy. What brings you down here?' Emily asked, tucking her arm into Tom's as the bus trundled into view, headlamps sweeping the verges.

'I was visiting my uncle, David Hunt MP,' she said smugly.

'Oh yes? He's your uncle, is he?' Tom remarked, as the bus pulled up in front of them with a hiss of brakes. 'My dad plays dominoes with him in the Royal Oak on Friday nights. He's a nice bloke.' He stood back to allow Emily and Lucy to climb aboard, following them down the aisle of the almost empty bus.

Despite the many empty seats, Lucy chose to sit directly across the aisle from Emily and Tom and tried to engage Tom in conversation.

'With my connections, I really shouldn't be working as a chambermaid, you know?' she said as the bus laboured up the hill. 'My aunt, Mrs Mansfield, promised my mother I would be offered a more elevated position, like receptionist.' She smiled sweetly, leaning forward to look around Tom and meet Emily's gaze. 'Perhaps I'll take your job, Emily. I'm of a mind to insist Mr Reynolds gives me an audition.'

'Emily's shoes would be hard ones to fill,' said Tom mildly before Emily could react.

'Oh, I'm not worried about filling your shoes, Emily,' Lucy said, with her customary hard tone.

Emily and Tom exchanged amused glances and Lucy flung herself back in her seat, pouting. She'd show them. She'd go and see Mr Reynolds as soon as she got back to the hotel. She'd wipe that smile of Emily Baker's face if it was the last thing she did.

★ ★ ★

'Can you believe her?' Tom said to Emily in a low voice a while later. 'She's totally deluded at the sense of her own importance.'

They were snuggled together on the sofa in the staff sitting room, watching the slowly dying embers in the fireplace. The hands on the carriage clock stood at a quarter to ten and they were alone, most of the staff having taken themselves off to bed in readiness for their early starts in the morning. 'And to harbour a grudge for all these years over such a trivial incident that took place when you were children, and one over which you had no control, is ridiculous.'

'It probably doesn't seem trivial to Lucy,' Emily said, stifling a yawn. 'I think her mother is to blame. I remember that she caused a big to-do about it, threatening to leave the church if Reverend Smedhurst didn't reinstate Lucy as soloist.'

'He obviously didn't give in.'

'No. He told me a long while afterwards that he had been sorry to see Lucy go but he'd stood by his decision, so they left. She was a right cow to me in the school playground after that.'

'It was a bit of bad luck her turning up here,' Tom said. Emily agreed.

'I can't help feeling sorry for her, though. From what Betty's gathered through working with Lucy, and she used the term "working" very loosely — apparently Lucy's as lazy as they come — her mother seems to have instilled it into her that because of who her father was, they should be treated as if they're better than the rest of us. What she doesn't seem to grasp is that, no matter what your connections, if you don't have two ha'pennies to rub together, you have to work.'

'Miss Thompson will take her down a peg or two,' Tom said confidently. 'Either that or she'll send her packing.'

'Betty thinks Miss Thompson's hands are tied, because of Lucy's connection to the Mansfields.'

'I doubt Miss Thompson will allow that sort of thing to influence her decisions. I know Mr Reynolds won't and if housekeeping standards start to slide, it's him Miss Thompson will have to answer to.'

'Maybe,' said Emily doubtfully. 'Anyway, that's enough about Lucy. I'm going to call in at the printers in the morning and order our wedding invitations. Do you think Mr Andrews might give you half an hour off to come with me?'

'It won't do any harm to ask,' Tom said. 'I suppose we'd better go up before Mr Reynolds does his rounds.' Reluctantly, Emily eased herself away from him. Hand in hand, they crept through the silent kitchen. Tom slid back the heavy bolts on the back door. Newly fallen snow glistened in the pale moonlight. An owl hooted and far away a dog was barking. 'I'll see you tomorrow, then.' Cupping her face in his hands, he kissed her long and hard. It was a kiss that left them flushed and breathless. 'God, I can't wait until we're married,' Tom rasped.

'Neither can I,' replied Emily. A floorboard creaked overhead. 'Go on,' she whispered. 'Off you go, before we both get a telling-off.' She bundled Tom out into the night and bolted the heavy door behind him. Pouring herself a glass of water as a ready excuse should she meet Mr Reynolds on her way up to bed, she crept upstairs.

should she meet Mr Reynolds on her way up to bed,
she crept upstairs.

12

The following morning as Emily made her way down
the staircase to meet Tom, she almost collided with
Lucy, who came flying towards her in floods of tears.

'Whatever's the matter?' she called after her.

'Leave me alone,' Lucy sobbed, wrenching open
the door to her bedroom and disappearing inside,
slamming it loudly behind her.

I wonder what that was about, Emily mused, continuing down the spiral staircase. Either Lucy had
suffered a bereavement, or she'd received a long-over-
due telling-off from Miss Thompson. She hoped it
was the latter.

Tom was waiting for her in the kitchen and, as they
set off down the snow-covered driveway, all thoughts
of Lucy vanished from her head.

★ ★ ★

'Have you heard what happened with Lucy this morning?'

Betty was waiting for Emily as she came in the door.
Flushed from the cold, she'd barely had time to stamp
the snow from her boots before Betty was ushering
her into the steam-filled kitchen. One of the kitchen
maids was setting out platters of roast beef sandwiches
on the table. As Emily took off her coat and hat, it
didn't take her long to realize that Lucy appeared to
be the main topic of conversation amongst the staff
gathering for their midday meal.

'I know you're dying to tell me, Betty,' she said, helping herself to a sandwich. 'So, what happened? She did seem very upset earlier. She almost knocked me down the stairs.'

'She somehow managed to persuade Mr Reynolds to let her sing for him,' Betty said, eyes glittering with excitement.

'Apparently, she tried to convince him she's a better singer than you, Emily,' Joe, one of the bell boys, said with a grin. 'As if.'

'That's right,' continued Betty. 'She clearly thought if she could prove to Mr Reynolds that she was the better singer, you'd be replaced.'

Emily's stomach contracted nervously. She loved her job and she didn't want to give it up — at least not yet, and certainly not in this way. 'And?' she asked, forcing herself to remain calm. 'From what I saw, it didn't look as though it went well.'

Betty grinned. Reaching for the pot of mustard, she leaned forward animatedly. 'She was awful, wasn't she, Joe?'

'Really bad,' Joe agreed. 'Claire and Una were listening outside his office. They said she sounded dreadful.'

'Really?' Emily frowned. 'But she has a lovely voice, as I recall.'

'Not anymore, clearly,' Betty smirked.

'As I understand it,' said Mrs Young, setting the big brown ceramic teapot on a trivet in the middle of the table, 'a person's voice can change as they mature. Poor girl,' she added with sympathy. 'She took Mr Reynolds's rejection to heart, I hear.'

'She spent the morning closeted in her room,' Betty said, clearly annoyed. 'I had to do all the work

89

by myself. Not that I don't anyway. She's about as much use as a wooden frying pan, the lazy so-and-so. Thankfully, we're a bit quiet this week.'

Kitty, the young scullery maid, came scurrying into the kitchen. 'Shush! She's coming.'

Conversation ceased instantly as Lucy appeared in the doorway, looking wan and tearful. Her red-rimmed eyes scanned the room.

'Talking about me, were you?' she said coldly. 'Mr Reynolds is a pig-headed bumpkin who wouldn't recognize talent if it bit him on the nose.' Someone tittered.

'Don't you dare speak about Mr Reynolds like that,' snapped Mrs Young, all traces of sympathy vanishing in the face of Lucy's contempt. 'You're lucky to have a job as it is. Now, sit down and eat your dinner, and keep a civil tongue in your head.'

Lucy pulled out a chair and glared across the table at Emily. 'And you can stop smirking, as well!'

Emily's mouth fell open in surprise. 'I wasn't.'

'Oh, you're so smug, aren't you? With your cushy job and your fiancé —'

'LUCY!' Mrs Young bellowed across the kitchen, cutting Lucy off mid-rant. 'Shut up or get out of my kitchen!'

Lucy scowled but fell silent. Ignoring the sly, mocking glances directed at her from around the table, she seethed with resentment. Sensing Lucy's eyes on her, Emily met her gaze, the expression of sheer malevolence on the other girl's face turning her stomach inside out. Emily swallowed and turned away. She tried to concentrate on what Betty was saying, but she couldn't shake the terrible feeling that Lucy Hunt was going to be trouble.

'What's Tom doing with her?' Betty hissed indignantly, grabbing Emily's arm. It was the following Friday afternoon and Emily had just finished rehearsing for the evening performance. She and Betty were sitting in the hotel's orangery, sipping mugs of warm cocoa while enjoying the view of the hotel grounds and the snow-covered hills beyond.

★   ★   ★

'What?' Emily followed Betty's scandalized gaze, frowning at the sight of Tom crossing the frosty yard with Lucy. Her face was turned towards him, and she appeared to be smiling. To Emily's relief, Tom's expression was one of polite disinterest.

'He's carrying her basket,' Betty snorted in disgust.

'As any gentleman would if he saw a lady carrying something heavy,' Emily said firmly, turning back to her friend as Tom and Lucy disappeared from view. 'I trust Tom implicitly.'

'Oh, I know you do. And so you should. Tom adores you. But I don't trust her, Emily. She's got it in for you and I wouldn't put it past her to use Tom to hurt you.'

'Tom's no fool, Betty.'

'No, you're right. I'm being silly.' Betty set her empty mug on the table. 'So, when do you pick up the wedding invitations?' she said, excitedly. 'I can't wait to see them.'

13

'Good evening, ladies and gentlemen.' Emily smiled at the sea of expectant diners. It was the third Saturday in March, the day before Mothering Sunday, and the dining room was full to capacity. 'In honour of all the lovely mums here tonight,' Emily said, 'I shall start with a Fred Astaire number, "Cheek to Cheek". I hope you enjoy it.' She nodded at Fred and, as she counted through the introduction, awaiting her cue to begin singing, her gaze sought out Tom. Standing in his customary spot in the shadows, he nodded and gave her an encouraging smile. Emily smiled back and started to sing.

Even the waiters, weaving between the tables, trays aloft, who heard Emily every day, paused to listen as she worked through her repertoire, eliciting both smiles and tears from her audience.

As always, when she took her final bow after several encores, it was Tom who led the thunderous applause.

'You were fantastic, as usual,' he said, meeting her at the bar a short time later. 'And you look amazing.' He leaned in to kiss her cheek.

'Thank you. And thank you for the dress. I love it.' Emily had walked up and down outside May's dress shop for several days admiring the red velvet, floor-length evening gown on display in the window. It was sleeveless, with a low-cut V-shaped back, and very expensive. When she'd mentioned to Betty that she couldn't justify the expense what with her upcoming wedding, her friend had gone straight to Tom, who had purchased it for her. A few alterations had been needed, which May had completed in record time in order to have it ready for the Mothering Sunday weekend.

'Miss Baker,' a male voice said behind her. 'May I buy you a drink?'

Emily turned to find herself face to face with a tall, thin man of around thirty, his well-oiled hair gleaming under the lights. She recognized him as one of the guests, having seen him checking in earlier that day. 'Er, yes, thank you. A lemonade, please.'

'Another doting fan,' Tom whispered in Emily's ear as the man turned away to order the drinks. 'I'll leave you to it. I promised I'd meet Edward and few of the chaps for a game of cards.'

'Don't let Mr Reynolds catch you gambling,' warned Emily, lowering her voice.

'He won't,' Tom assured her with grin. 'He never comes over to the stables.' He kissed her warmly. 'I'll see you later.'

★ ★ ★

'Here you go, Miss Baker. One lemonade.'

Emily accepted the glass. 'Thank you, Mr . . . .?'

'Thurston. Roland Thurston,' he replied, slipping a card from the breast pocket of his dinner jacket and handing it to Emily.

R J Thurston
THEATRICAL AGENT

'Nice to meet you, Mr Thurston,' Emily said as they shook hands. She forced herself to appear outwardly calm, but her heart was racing with excitement.

'Is there somewhere we can talk?' Roland asked, glancing around the busy dining room. 'Somewhere a bit quieter?'

'The staff sitting room,' suggested Emily. 'It should be empty at this time.' She led the way, Roland following with the drinks, and hoped he couldn't see how much she was shaking.

'In here.' She pushed open the door to the cosy room. A cheerful fire crackled in the grate and someone had left an open tin of toffees on the table. Emily drew the floral-patterned curtains and invited Roland to sit. He did so, perching his lanky frame awkwardly on the narrow sofa. Emily took the armchair closest to the fire.

'Cigarette?'

Emily shook her head. 'No, thank you. I don't.'

'Very wise.' Roland removed a cigarette and snapped his silver case shut. 'Ruins the voice.' He struck a match and lit up. Emily took a nervous sip of her lemonade. 'You must be wondering what I have to say, Miss Baker,' Roland said, exhaling a cloud of smoke. His pint sat on the table, ignored.

'I am curious,' Emily said with a nervous laugh. She was half-wondering if this was some sort of joke, an elaborate prank engineered by Lucy, or just a ploy by Mr Thurston to get to spend some time alone with her. It wouldn't be the first time a hotel guest had attempted to seduce her, and she was comforted by the knowledge that Miss Thompson was within shouting distance.

'I own a small theatrical agency in Bristol,' Roland said. 'I'm on my way back home after spending a few days in Poole. I read your review in the *Gazette* and was interested to see if you lived up to your reputation. And, boy, don't you just.' His thin lips curled into a smile. 'Miss Baker, in my six years as a talent scout, I have never heard a voice quite as exquisite as yours.'

'Oh, goodness,' Emily said, blushing at the compliment. 'Thank you.'

'With your looks, style and poise, Miss Baker, I can elevate you to stardom.'

It took Emily a minute or two to find her voice. 'That all sounds rather exciting, Mr Thurston. And a bit overwhelming. Are you . . . offering to represent me?' She put her hand to her chest. Her heart was pounding. Since her earliest childhood she had harboured a secret ambition to become like her idols, Gracie Fields and Lee Morse. Never in her wildest dreams had she imagined it might come true.

'I am, Miss Baker, I am. I can sign you up right now, if you're agreeable. I shall fetch a contract from my room.' He grinned. 'I am going to make you a star. Once you move to Bristol, the city will be your oyster. You'll have bookings almost every night of the week.'

'Move to Bristol?' Emily frowned.

'Well, yes.' Roland pulled a face. 'You're never going to amount to much here, are you? You need to be performing in the best theatres and music halls. Who knows, I might even get you a recording contract.'

'But my fiancé . . . I'm getting married in six weeks. Tom won't want to move to Bristol. He wouldn't be happy in a city.'

'Surely he could be persuaded to make the sacrifice? This is your career, after all,' Roland said in a slightly irritated tone, stubbing out his cigarette butt as he contemplated waving goodbye to the sizable agency fee he could command for having Emily on his books. She was a phenomenal singer and he had no doubt she would be in huge demand. The silence stretched out between them.

'I'm sorry, Mr Thurston,' Emily said, her words tinged with regret. She handed him back his card as she got to her feet. 'It's kind of you to think of me, but I must say no.'

'You're not even going to discuss my offer with your fiancé?' Roland asked, perplexed. Unfurling his long legs, he stood up. 'I could make you rich and famous beyond your wildest dreams.'

'I shan't tell Tom because I know he will insist I accept your offer. That's the kind of selfless man he is, and I will not pursue my dreams at the expense of his happiness.'

'But . . . But Miss Baker, please reconsider.'

Emily smiled. 'When I was a little girl, I dreamed of being a professional singer. My dad told me that sort of life wasn't for the likes of me. And it's true. I love what I do here at the hotel, and I'll carry on for the time being, until Tom and I have children.'

'So, you're throwing away the chance of a very lucrative career for marriage and a houseful of babies?'

'Yes, I am,' Emily said firmly. She inhaled, fuelling her resolve. 'I shall soon be marrying a wonderful man.' Her smile appeared a little wistful, Roland noted, giving him a measure of hope that perhaps all was not lost. 'I'm grateful for your offer and I'm pleased you think I have talent, but I'm afraid the answer is no.'

'Very well,' Roland said. 'I shall be at the hotel a few more days.' He dropped his card on the table. 'I'm in room twenty-two, if you change your mind,' he said as he stalked from the room.

Emily leaned against the doorframe as her heart-rate slowly returned to normal. For a few gloriously blissful moments, she had been seriously tempted by Roland's offer. She knew Tom would never stand in her way, and she loved him all the more for it, but her future was here, with him. Her unfulfilled dreams of stardom were easily eclipsed by her love for Tom, and her excitement over their approaching wedding and their future life together.

As she had told Roland, Emily didn't mention anything to Tom when she saw him the following morning. He was having enough troubles of his own recently, so why burden him with something that was never going to happen?

Tom's troubles had to do with, of all people, Lucy Hunt. It seemed that every time he turned around, she was there. She was always bumping into him, or needing to speak to him on some pretext or other. At first, he had put it down to coincidence, but after he had 'bumped into' Lucy for the fourth day in a row, he was astute enough to realize that she must be engineering the meetings.

He had told Emily straight away, of course, aware that other members of staff might see him and Lucy talking and get the wrong end of the stick. Her initial response had been to laugh it off, but Lucy's persistence was becoming something of a problem and they were both at a loss as to how to deal with it. He'd even told Lucy straight out that he wasn't interested, but she'd simply given him that strange sly smile of hers and muttered something about what the eye didn't see, the heart couldn't grieve over.

'She's got it bad, mate,' Edward said with a grin, when he confided in him later that night as they prepared for bed in their chilly dormitory. 'And she's not exactly subtle, is she? She follows you around like a lovesick puppy. The lads think it's hilarious.'

'It's not funny,' Tom grumbled morosely. 'I'm marrying Emily in six weeks' time. Apart from being downright rude, I don't know how I can get through to her.'

'How's Emily dealing with it?' Edward asked. 'Betty says she doesn't seem too bothered.'

'She laughed it off at first but even she's finding it a bit wearing now.' Tom threw his shirt over the end of the bed and climbed under the covers. 'I mean, does Lucy seriously expect me to jilt Emily for her?'

Edward chuckled. 'Probably. She's as thick-skinned as a rhino, that one.'

'She's flipping annoying, I'll say that.'

'You're going to have to be brutal, mate,' Edward said, slipping into bed and blowing out the candle, enveloping them in thick darkness. 'Goodnight.'

'Night, Ed.' Tom lay on his back, hands behind his head, listening to the snores reverberating up and down the dorm as the lads drifted off to sleep. He heard a rat scurrying along the rafters above his head, and the far-off screech of a barn owl. He sighed, hoping that Lucy would get the hint and leave him alone. In a short few weeks he would marry the woman he loved more than life, and he wasn't going to let a selfish, spoilt little minx like Lucy Hunt spoil what was going to be the most exciting time of his life.

14

Lucy smiled at her reflection in the full-length mirror. The peacock-blue frock matched her eyes perfectly and came down to her calves, showing off her figure to its full advantage. She did a little twirl, fingering the string of glass beads that swung from her slender neck. She looked a million dollars, as their American guests would say, and there was no way Tom would be able to resist her charms. She was going to knock him dead. Now, she just had to find a pair of shoes to match. The old biddy who occupied room twenty-nine certainly had plenty to choose from.

Careful not to crease her dress, she knelt in front of the wardrobe and pulled out the first of the cardboard boxes stacked neatly in the bottom. Nestled in pale cream tissue paper was a pair of black dance shoes. Totally unsuitable. She tried the next one.

Helping herself to the guests' belongings was an illicit pleasure she had only recently discovered. It had started about two weeks before, when one of the girls realized she'd left a bottle of Windolene on the sill in one of the bedrooms and Lucy had been sent up to retrieve it.

Though she had complied begrudgingly, once inside the silent, empty bedroom, and faced with such an array of expensive perfume bottles, velvet-lined jewellery boxes and the rich mink fur coat draped over the back of a chair, the temptation to indulge her extravagant tastes was overwhelming. And as she spent a pleasant fifteen minutes spraying her wrists with perfume and trying on jewellery dripping with diamonds, the thought came to her that the guests were seldom in their rooms during the day. She'd opened the wardrobe doors, a shiver of excitement running down her spine as she imagined the feel of the silk gowns against her skin, or burying her face in the rich furs.

She saw nothing wrong with what she was doing. She never took anything from the rooms, except the lingering scent of perfume — until now.

Lucy opened the third shoebox to find a pair of delicate peacock-blue silk slippers nestled in a bed of diaphanous blue tissue paper. They matched the dress perfectly. She slipped them on and pirouetted around the room, craning her neck to admire her reflection from every angle. Laughing quietly to herself so as not to draw attention should anyone happen to be passing in the corridor, she sank onto the bed and gazed around the opulently furnished room. Room twenty-nine, with its rich ruby-red brocade and polished walnut furnishings and large four-poster bed — which was a total waste for an old dear like Mrs Beaumont-Clarke, in Lucy's opinion — was one of the hotel's most luxurious.

Safe in the knowledge that its occupant wouldn't be returning until late in the evening, Lucy strolled over to the window, which afforded her the perfect view of the kitchen gardens — and Tom.

She sighed. Had fate treated her fairly, she would be the one with the furs, the diamonds, the beautiful frocks and gowns. She had always planned to marry well in order to live the life of luxury she had dreamed of ever since her father's passing had plunged her and her mother into poverty. But she would happily relinquish that dream for Tom.

It was ridiculous, of course. What had started as a bit of fun on Lucy's part had backfired. Somehow, she realized, she had fallen in love with Tom, and his indifference was driving her insane.

She pressed her palms to the windowsill and rested her forehead on the cool glass to gain a better view of him. He was leaning on his hoe and ran an arm across his forehead, wiping the sweat from his brow. Against the crumbling wall of the kitchen garden, daffodils nodded in the brisk March wind. In the orchard beyond, which provided the hotel pantry with a vast stock of jams and preserves, the trees were in bud, with clouds of pink and white blossom interspersed amongst the newly sprouted green.

Lucy glanced at the small travel clock Mrs Beaumont-Clarke kept beside her bed. It was a quarter to three on a Monday afternoon. At three o'clock Tom would head for the gardener's shed to brew up for himself, Mr Andrews and the other gardeners. If she timed it right, she could get to the shed just after he did. She was confident that once Tom saw her in Mrs Beaumont-Clarke's finery, he would be unable to resist her charms.

Finding a silk shawl draped across a chair that was a similar hue to Mrs Beaumont-Clarke's frock, Lucy draped it around her slender shoulders and, after listening at the door to make sure the corridor was deserted, she slowly opened the door and peered out. There was no one about.

She slipped down the stairs and out of the back door, gasping as the cold air took her by surprise. She shivered. Mrs Beaumont-Clarke's thin shawl and frock offered little protection against the bitter wind.

The gravel bit through the soles of the thin silk slippers as she hurried towards the hedge-lined path that would take her to the shed. She should remain undetected, unless someone happened to be looking out of an upstairs window.

She stood shivering behind a bank of yew trees, feeling the damp seeping through her slippers while she waited for Tom to down tools and make his way over to the shed. Muffin the terrier appeared as if from nowhere and trotted after him, nose to the ground. Lucy watched as Tom and the dog disappeared inside, and then followed. Outside the door, she hesitated. When Muffin started to bark, Lucy took a deep breath, lifted the latch and stepped inside.

'Lucy!' Tom stared at her in surprise, almost dropping the lit match he had used to light the stove.

Muffin danced around her ankles and Lucy pushed the dog away with her knee, trying to prevent the dog's claws snagging the delicate material of her dress. Tom narrowed his eyes suspiciously.

'What are you doing in here?' he demanded, flicking the spent match into a metal bucket.

'I came to see you,' Lucy said with what she hoped was a seductive smile. The shed was small, filthy and crammed with gardening implements. Cobwebs hung from the corners, the tiny window was covered in grime and it smelled of compost and damp. Not the ideal place for a romantic assignation, Lucy mused wryly, but it was the only place she could think of where she could get Tom alone, if only for a short time. She wouldn't need long to convince him she was worth ten of Emily.

'Mr Andrews and the lads will be here shortly,' Tom said, setting the kettle on the stove. 'I'd get going if

I were you.' He looked pointedly at her outfit. 'You wouldn't want to soil your dress — or your reputation.'

'Teatime is half past three,' Lucy said firmly. 'We've got half an hour.'

Tom's brows shot upwards. 'Half an hour for what?'

'To get to know each other a little better,' Lucy said, inching closer. She had sprayed a generous amount of perfume on her wrists before she left Mrs Beaumont-Clarke's room, and the cloying scent stung the back of Tom's throat. He coughed, his shoulders sagging in resignation. He would have to take Edward's advice and be blunt. He had to make it clear to Lucy, once and for all, that he just wasn't attracted to her in any way.

'Look, Lucy, I apologize if I've misled you in some way and given you the impression that I'm interested in you romantically. I assure you, I'm not. I love Emily.' He held out his hands in a gesture of supplication. 'We're getting married in six weeks. I'd never dream of looking at another woman.'

'Oh, come on, Tom,' Lucy said, her smile faltering slightly as she moved closer, thrusting her hips out suggestively. She put out a tentative hand and let her fingers trail lightly down his forearm, taking his shudder of revulsion for desire. 'See?' She battered her eyelashes and giggled. 'There's no point resisting. You know I always get what I want.' She tilted her face upwards, closing her eyes in expectation.

'Not this time.' Tom pushed her away and she half-stumbled, her eyes popping open in shock. 'This has got to stop, Lucy,' Tom said, sternly. His fists were clenched at his side as he fought to control his anger. 'Emily and I are sick of you following me around.

You're a laughing stock, do you know that?' He stopped abruptly at the sight of Lucy's stricken expression and realized that she was about to cry. 'Look,' he continued in a gentler tone, 'I'm sorry. That was cruel.'

Lucy's cheeks burned. Blinking back tears of humiliation, she turned and ran for the door, scattering flowerpots and seed trays in her haste. She was so desperate to get away, she failed to notice her shawl slipping from her shoulders. It fell silently to the floor, landing in a silken heap behind an upturned plant pot.

She ran across the lawn, sobbing tears of self-pity, and stumbled into a bramble bush. The thorns snagged at Mrs Beaumont-Clarke's dress. With a sob of frustration, Lucy yanked herself free, ripping her sleeve badly in the process, and continued running.

'Lucy?'

Wiping her tearstained face with the back of her hand, she glanced over to where Rosie Smith, a timid laundrymaid barely fifteen years old, was staring at her in confusion. 'Whatever's happened?'

'It was Tom,' Lucy blurted out before she could stop herself.

'Tom?' Rosie stared at her in dismay. 'Tom the gardener?'

Lucy nodded and, giving into a fresh wave of tears, ran off towards the back of the hotel.

'Rosie, stop wool-gathering.' Miss Thompson appeared in the laundry doorway. A cloud of steam billowed around her as she glowered at the young girl. 'And look, you silly chump, you've draped the edge of that sheet on the wet grass. You'll have to wash it again now.' Still frowning, Rosie stuffed the offending sheet back in the wicker basket. It would take her ages to rewash the sheet and put it through the mangle. She'd probably end up missing her tea. Fuming over the unfairness of her lot, she carried the basket back to the laundry room.

Half an hour later Rosie was summoned to Mr Reynold's office by a very worried-looking Miss Thompson.

★ ★ ★

The lads arrived as Tom was spooning sugar in a row of tin mugs. Joking and laughing, they rubbed their cold hands together in an effort to get the blood flowing.

'Here you go, lads. This'll warm you up.' While Tom handed out the mugs of steaming hot tea, Jim retrieved the biscuit tin from underneath a pile of hessian sacks and passed it around. Perched on upside-down crates, they munched on Bourbon biscuits, fed crumbs to Muffin and sipped their tea, voicing their surprise that Mr Andrews, usually the first on the scene when tea and biscuits were on offer, had yet to make an appearance.

It was nearly four o'clock by the time he finally pushed open the shed door and looked around at his 'boys'. There were five of them, including Tom, varying in age from seventeen to twenty-five. Having lost his own young son in a drowning accident twelve years before, Mr Andrews was inordinately fond of them all.

'We saved you a Bourbon, Mr Andrews,' one of the boys said with a grin.

'Thanks, lad.' Mr Andrews nodded, turning his troubled gaze on Tom. 'Tom,' he said with a sigh.

105

'Mr Reynolds wants to see you in his office. Now.'

Tom looked up in surprise. 'Did he say why, sir?'

'Mr Reynolds will explain,' Mr Andrews said, shuffling his feet uncomfortably.

Feeling only slightly apprehensive, Tom left his workmates to clear up after their tea break and made his way to Mr Reynolds's office. From the corridor he could hear Emily rehearsing in the dining room, and he smiled. He still felt bad about upsetting Lucy the way he had but, hopefully, she had got the message and would leave him alone in future.

He arrived at the manager's office and knocked on the door. Opening it when he heard Mr Reynolds's curt 'Enter', he was surprised to find Miss Thompson, head of housekeeping, sitting in one of the two chairs facing Mr Reynolds's vast, tidy desk.

'Ah, Tom, come in and have a seat,' Mr Reynolds said, indicating the chair next to Miss Thompson.

'Mr Reynolds, Miss Thompson, good afternoon.' Tom sat down, nodding at each of his superiors in turn.

'Good afternoon, Tom,' Miss Thompson replied, stiffly. She looked at him with what appeared to be disappointment and Tom's feeling of disquiet increased.

'Is something the matter, sir?' he asked, his dark eyes clouding with concern as he wracked his brain to recall to mind some dereliction of duty.

'Tom, I'm afraid a rather serious allegation has been made against you,' Mr Reynolds said solemnly as he leaned back in his leather chair and regarded Tom with a serious air.

'What sort of allegation, sir?' Tom asked, puzzled.

'Lucy Hunt said you lured her to a shed and attempted to molest her.'

'What?' Tom exclaimed, almost falling out of his chair in shock. 'I did no such thing!' He turned to Miss Thompson. 'She told you this?'

'We have to take this sort of accusation seriously, Tom,' she replied, her tone neutral.

'Mr Reynolds,' he said, turning back to the manager. 'You know me. You know I would never behave so deplorably.'

'We have a witness who saw Lucy running away from the gardeners' shed in a state of severe distress around a quarter past three this afternoon,' Mr Reynolds said, removing his spectacles. He cleaned the lenses with his handkerchief and returned them to his face. 'Mr Andrews has told us that you went to the shed to put the kettle on at three o'clock. Miss Hunt claims you'd arranged for her to meet you there, knowing the others wouldn't arrive until half past.'

'Oh, come on, sir,' Tom exclaimed. 'That's a lie. She just turned up. It was her who tried to seduce me!'

Mr Reynolds lifted an eyebrow. 'Her clothing had been ripped.'

'What?' Tom blurted out incredulously.

'As I said,' Mr Reynolds continued. 'We have a witness.' Though how reliable, he wasn't quite sure. Rosie had appeared utterly terrified when he'd spoken to her earlier. The entire time he'd been questioning her, she had kept glancing at the weeping Lucy.

'She says she saw you open the shed door and invite Miss Hunt inside.'

'No, that's ridiculous,' Tom cried. 'Why would someone lie like that? It's not true. I was making the tea and Lucy just walked right in. Why would I invite a young lady round in order to seduce her knowing full well that my mates, and not to mention my boss, were due to arrive in half an hour? It makes no sense!'

'You leapt on her like an animal,' Miss Thompson said, icily. 'You tore her dress.'

'I didn't!' Tom declared hotly. 'I didn't lay a finger on her. Well,' he amended, 'only to push her away when she tried to kiss me.'

'It was you who tried to kiss her,' Miss Thompson responded acidly. She didn't like the girl, but she wasn't about to stand by after some man had tried to take advantage of her.

'Miss Thompson, I swear I did not.'

'What about Miss Hunt's shawl?' Mr Reynolds demanded.

Tom turned back to him. 'Pardon?'

'Miss Hunt claims you grabbed at her shawl when she fled your advances. She had no choice but to leave it behind.' He regarded Tom coldly. '

'Look!' Tom inhaled deeply, in an attempt to control his emotions. He couldn't believe Lucy would make up such outlandish claims against him. 'It's true that Lucy stormed out of the shed in tears,' he said as calmly as he could, 'but only because I was unkind to her. I made it quite clear I wasn't interested in her romantically. Everyone knows I'm marrying Emily in a few weeks' time. When Lucy left me, her clothing was intact. If she did tear her dress, it had nothing to do with me.'

They were interrupted by a knock. The door opened and Mr Andrews poked his head into the room. Studiously avoiding Tom's gaze, he nodded at Mr Reynolds. 'One of the lads found it, sir. Hidden behind a plant pot.'

'I see.' Mr Reynolds nodded gravely. 'Thank you, Mr Andrews. Miss Thompson, if you'd be so kind?'

Miss Thompson rose and took the shawl from Mr Andrews, laying it carefully on the corner of the desk. Tom stared at it in dismay as the door clicked shut.

'Lucy must have dropped it as she left the shed,' Tom said, running his hand through his hair. 'That's the only explanation.'

'The police will have to be informed, Tom,' Mr Reynolds interrupted him, grim-faced. 'In the meantime, you're confined to your dormitory. Under no circumstances must you attempt to speak with Miss Hunt.'

'But, sir!' Tom protested.

'That is all. You're dismissed.'

Tom got to his feet in a daze. In the corridor outside Mr Reynolds's office, he leaned against the wall, the noise from the kitchen sounding far-off as his ears buzzed. He felt like he was falling down a deep hole. He shook his head and rubbed his temples. How could this be happening to him?

Emily walked out of the dining room, clutching her songbooks to her chest.

'Tom!' She grinned in delight at encountering her fiancé so unexpectedly, but her smile faded as she took in his look of despair. 'Tom, what's the matter?'

Tom shook his head. To Emily's horror, he looked close to tears. Dumping her books on the nearest table, she went to put her arms around him but he shrugged her away.

'Tom, what is it?' she asked again, beginning to panic. 'Please tell me.' At that moment Mr Reynolds's door swung open, emitting Miss Thompson. She scowled at Tom.

'Don't let Mr Reynolds catch you still here,' she said sternly, flashing Emily a look of pity as she passed her.

'Tom,' Emily hissed in exasperation. 'Will you just—'

'Lucy went to Mr Reynolds and accused me of attacking her,' Tom said in a low voice.

'What?' Emily stared at him, appalled. 'But that's ridiculous! Surely no one believes her?'

'She's managed to persuade someone to corroborate her story,' Tom said hoarsely. 'I'm to stay in my room until the police arrive.'

'The police?' Emily's stomach clenched in fear.

'It'll be my word against hers,' he muttered morosely.

'Oh, Tom. Come here.' Emily held him close for a few seconds before he pulled away.

'I'd better go. I'll see you when I can.' He started to walk away, then paused. Turning back to Emily, he said, 'You believe me, don't you? You know I'd never . . . .?'

'Of course,' Emily assured him, attempting a smile. 'It will be sorted out, Tom. No one will believe it of you, I promise.'

'I hope you're right,' he replied wearily.

With a queer heaviness in the pit of her stomach, Emily watched him walk away.

15

Rumours spread around the hotel like wildfire. A police constable had arrived as the evening meal preparation was underway and spent an hour interviewing everyone involved, including Miss Thompson and Mr Andrews. The frock, shawl and shoes belonging to the unsuspecting Mrs Beaumont-Clarke had been taken away as evidence. Tom had not yet been arrested but was confined to quarters for the foreseeable future and Emily was sick with worry as she took her place in front of the microphone that evening.

As Fred played the opening bars to 'Moon Over Miami', she took a deep breath and tried to focus on the job at hand. She spotted Roland lounging at a table set for one close to the stage, smoking a cigar. He smiled and raised his glass in salute. Emily looked away. She didn't see him get to his feet and leave the room.

The atmosphere in the dining room appeared dark and malevolent. Thinking about what Lucy had done made the bile rise in her throat and, for a moment, she thought she might throw up right there on stage. Instead, hearing her cue on the piano, she emptied her mind of everything except the music and began to sing.

★ ★ ★

Roland crushed his spent cigar underfoot as he tripped down the front steps, the splash of the water fountain loud in the quiet stillness. It was cold and he wished he'd taken the time to go back for his coat as he followed the moon-dappled path in the direction of the old stable block.

Roland Thurston prided himself on having a good business brain. There was no place for sentimentality when it came to making money and Roland liked making money — lots of it. And, if the occasion called for it, he was even prepared to play a little dirty. He was a great believer in the old adage that the ends justified the means. And one such occasion had just arisen. Along with the other guests, he'd listened to the hotel gossip with avid interest and he'd been quick to realize how he could turn Tom's misfortune to his advantage. Hence why he now found himself in the old stable yard. He peered in through one of the downstairs windows where a group of lads of various ages were playing what appeared to be a serious game of cards. Roland couldn't hear their conversation but he was in no doubt that most of it, if not all, would revolve around their mate Tom.

He glanced upstairs to where a single window glowed with orange lamplight. The full moon was bright and he easily negotiated the flight of stairs, and knocked on the loft door. He heard the creak of a bed, and then silence. Just when Roland was about to give up and leave, he heard a movement. The door swung open.

'Oh,' Tom said, clearly puzzled. 'I thought you were the . . . Never mind.' He frowned. 'You were talking to Emily last night. Who are you?'

'My name's Roland Thurston,' Roland said, his fingers moving instinctively to his breast pocket before he thought better of it. 'I'm a theatre agent. May I come in?'

'A theatre agent?' Tom repeated, moving aside to let Roland in. 'Emily didn't mention it.'

'No, she said she wouldn't. Tom — may I call you Tom?' Tom nodded and sank down on his narrow bed. In the lamplight he looked haggard and pale, but Roland felt little pity for the man. If Roland had a fiancée like Emily, there was no way he'd jeopardize their relationship by carrying on with another girl. 'From what I hear, you're in a spot of bother?'

Tom rubbed his hands across his face. The police interrogation had been brutal. The constable had spoken to him like he was a common criminal. Clearly, like Mr Reynolds and Miss Thompson, and even, to his dismay, Mr Andrews, Constable Moreton seemed determined to believe Lucy's version of events over Tom's. He was seriously worried. Constable Moreton had told him there was a good chance he could be arrested, and even go to prison. He was so desperate to see Emily it was a physical ache in his chest.

'The way I see it, Tom,' Roland said, leaning against the wall, 'you're likely looking at a few years inside. At the very least, you'll lose your job.'

'But I'm innocent,' Tom insisted, running his hand through his hair.

'That's as may be,' Roland said. The lamp flickered in a sudden draught, sending shadows dancing across the floor. 'But there will always be folk who'll believe in the old saying that there's never any smoke without fire. The mud will stick for years, and what about Emily, hey? With her talent she should be on the stage. I can offer her a glittering career, Tom. I can make her rich.'

'What do you mean?' Tom asked.

'I offered to take Emily on as a client but she refused.' Roland pushed himself off the wall and came to stand beside Tom. 'Because of you.'

Tom frowned. 'She never said.'

'No, because she's loyal to you. But I could see the excitement in her eyes, Tom. The hunger. She wants it. She really does.'

'Then she must do it,' Tom said indignantly, his own problems momentarily forgotten. 'I'm not the sort of chap who'd stand in the way of his wife's career.'

'The trouble is, this thing with this Lucy girl isn't going away any time soon, is it? When Emily becomes well-known — and she will be, of that I have no doubt — what do you think the newspapers will make of the fact that her husband has a criminal record?'

'It won't come to that,' Tom said, earnestly. 'They'll have to believe me eventually, because I'm telling the truth.'

'Oh, don't be naïve, Tom. Have you any idea how many innocent people end up in prison every year? And you know how the newspaper reporters work. They'll get hold of this girl, get her side of the story splashed all across the front page. Emily's career will be over before it gets off the ground.' He laid a hand on Tom's shoulder. 'Forgive me, I'm going to be blunt. In all likelihood you're going down for this, Tom, and you don't want to take Emily with you.'

Tom regarded Roland with a frown. 'I'd never do anything to hurt Emily.'

Roland smiled. 'You already have, mate. How long will it be before she starts to believe the rumours, hey?'

'No, she wouldn't. Emily loves me. She trusts me.'

'Look, mate, do the right thing.'

'And what do you suggest that is?' asked Tom coldly.

Roland shrugged his shoulders. 'You could leave.'

'What?'

'Just go, now. While it's dark. By the time the coppers come back tomorrow you'd be long gone.'

'I couldn't leave without saying goodbye to Emily,' Tom said, incredulous that Roland could even think that he would.

'You can't. She's performing and you're confined to your room. You don't want to get yourself into more hot water, Tom. *I'll* talk to Emily. She'll understand. Once things have died down a bit, say in a few months perhaps, you can come back.'

'But we're getting married.'

'Not if you're in prison, you're not.' Roland squeezed Tom's shoulder in what he hoped was a big-brotherly manner. 'Listen to me, mate. You know it makes sense. Get right away from here. Give me an address where I can contact you, and I'll let you know once the dust has settled.'

Tom sank onto the bed and cradled his head in his hands. Images of himself being handcuffed and bundled into a police van swirled around in his head. He pictured Emily, her face drawn, her eyes filled with . . . what? Disappointment? Disgust? And he groaned. 'Greenstones, Motcombe,' he told Roland hoarsely. 'My dad's address.'

'Great.' Roland slapped Tom on the back. 'You're doing the right thing, Tom. You're a decent chap. I'd hate to see you go to prison for something you didn't do.'

Tom grabbed Roland's arm. 'And you'll explain everything to Emily?'

'Of course, I promise.'

'Tell her I love her. And that I'm sorry, and I'll

come back for her.'

Roland nodded. 'Course I will, mate.'

After Roland left, Tom sat on his bed, his face buried in his hands. Was he doing the right thing? He wasn't sure, but how could he clear his name stuck in a prison cell? And what of Emily? Could he really expect her to wait for him while he served time in prison? Surely it was better for both of them if he stayed away until the dust had settled, as Roland put it. All he could do was hope that she would understand why he had to go. He didn't even have any paper with which to write her a letter. He would just have to trust Roland to pass his message on.

With an ache in his heart like no other he'd ever experienced before, he got to his feet and started to pack.

16

'Emily, Emily, wake up.' Emily opened her eyes the next morning to find Betty leaning over her, her expression grim.

'What time is it?' Emily groaned. She had barely slept all night, worrying about Tom. She'd lain awake until well into the early hours, and even then, she'd only managed a fitful doze.

'A quarter to eight,' Betty said impatiently. 'Emily, something's happened.'

'Oh, no!' Emily sat up in alarm. 'What now?' She blinked. Her eyes felt scratchy from lack of sleep.

'Tom's gone,' Betty said, gently, her eyes filling with tears. 'I'm so sorry, Emily.'

Emily stared at her, uncomprehending. 'Gone? What do you mean, gone?' she said hoarsely. 'Gone where?'

Betty shrugged. She sat down on the edge of Emily's bed and put her arm around her friend's shoulder. 'He left sometime last night. It was before lights out. He wasn't in his bed when Edward went up but he just assumed he'd snuck out to see you. He'd never snitch on a mate, of course, but when he still hadn't returned by this morning . . . the other lads noticed and of course Mr Andrews had a duty to inform Mr Reynolds.' Betty's eyes clouded. 'Oh, Emily, he's phoning the police.'

'Tom wouldn't just leave,' Emily said, starting to shake. 'He wouldn't go without saying goodbye.'

'They're saying downstairs that it proves his guilt.

Lucy's walking round like the cat who got the cream.'

'They know Tom,' Emily declared angrily. 'And everyone knows what sort of person Lucy is. How could they believe her over him? It's ludicrous!' She put her hands over her face and burst into tears.

'I know,' Betty agreed, giving Emily a hug. 'It's unfair. But not everyone believes her, Emily. Mrs Young certainly doesn't, neither does Edward, and most of the girls, but, unfortunately, a lot of them are starting to wonder. If he is innocent, why do a runner?'

Emily raised her tear-stained face to her friend. 'You don't believe that, Betty, surely?' she asked, bleakly.

'Certainly not!' exclaimed Betty indignantly. 'And I'm sure that if it wasn't for Lucy's very tenuous connection to Mrs Mansfield, they wouldn't have given her outlandish accusations the time of day.'

'Yes, but as it is, everyone's regarding her as a victim while my poor Tom . . . ' She couldn't go on. More tears came, soaking the front of Betty's blouse as she sobbed in her friend's arms.

* * *

Tom's father opened the door with a weary smile. 'Hello, Emily, love. I thought you'd be by soon enough. Come on in, girl. The kettle's just boiled.'

Emily followed Ernest into his sunny kitchen, the last vestiges of hope that she would find Tom at his father's house quashed as she sat down on the sagging armchair closest to the stove.

'Like I told that miserable bugger Constable Moreton,' Ernest said, taking the kettle off the hob, 'Tom was here.' He filled the teapot with boiling water.

'Turned up late last night, but he was gone before first light this morning.'

'Did he say where he was going?' Emily asked. She was numb with shock and felt cold, despite the cheerful blaze and the slanting rays of sunlight streaming in through the window.

'He didn't,' Ernest said, pouring the tea and handing Emily a mug. She accepted it gratefully, cradling it in her cold hands. 'He's always been a bit impetuous, my Tom. I just hope he doesn't do anything rash.' He pulled out a straight-back chair and sat down stiffly, his expression sad. 'It's a bad situation, Emily,' he said with a sad shake of his head. 'What possessed the girl, do you think? Why would she tell such lies about my boy?'

'I don't know,' Emily said miserably. 'She's always been jealous of me, ever since we were children, but I never would have believed she'd stoop this low. To ruin Tom's life just to get back at me. It's unforgivable.'

Ernest nodded. 'It is that, love. It is that.'

★ ★ ★

On the bus back up the hill, Emily kept her eyes fixed on the window but she could feel the curious gazes she was attracting from her fellow passengers. Motcombe was a small village and the arrival of a police constable at Ernest Harding's door would have set tongues wagging. Her arrival soon after would have made it obvious that it had something to do with Tom.

'Everything all right, love?' a middle-aged woman in a black coat and headscarf asked, leaning across the aisle to attract Emily's attention as the bus wended its way along the narrow tree-lined road.

'Yes, thank you,' replied Emily with a tight smile. The woman drew back, clearly disappointed.

'Only we noticed Mr Harding had a constable call this morning,' said her slightly younger companion. 'Everything all right with young Tom?'

'Yes, thank you,' Emily said again with forced politeness. The two women exchanged glances and put their heads together, clearly finding Emily's response unsatisfactory. Emily was pleased when they both got off outside the town hall.

She got off the bus opposite the hotel and walked slowly up the long driveway, her heart growing heavier with every step. She couldn't believe that Tom had actually gone. Grief lay like a rock in her chest. At times she could hardly draw breath.

She found Betty in the kitchen. She was sitting alone, a mug of tea in her hands, seemingly oblivious to the hectic luncheon preparation going on around her. She looked up, caught sight of Emily and her eyes lit up with hope, but Emily shook her head as she joined Betty at the table.

'He wasn't there,' she murmured softly, acutely aware that the noise level had receded somewhat with her arrival. Betty placed her warm hand over Emily's cold one.

'Oh, Emily, I'm sorry.'

Emily shook her head, her eyes filling with tears.

'Here, love,' Mrs Young said, placing a mug of beef tea in front of Emily. 'Get that down you.'

'Thank you,' Emily whispered.

'It'll be all right, love,' Mrs Young said, giving Emily's arm a gentle pat. 'The truth will come out in the end. It always does.'

Emily nodded, unconvinced. With Tom God knows where, what difference would it make?

The afternoon passed slowly. She rehearsed with Fred but her heart wasn't in it. Even so, Roland Thurston, who was listening from the adjoining library, couldn't fault her performance. His instinct had been correct: Emily was a true professional.

17

'Why don't you come into town with me this morning, Emily?' Betty suggested as she took her place at the breakfast table. Emily shook her head.

'No thanks.' Picking up her mug of tea, she ignored her bowl of cooling porridge. It was Thursday and Tom had been gone for two full days. Any hope she'd harboured that he might come back was slowly fading.

'Maybe I should speak to Rosie,' Emily said, her voice low as she swivelled around to glare at the girl slumped in her chair at the far end of the long refectory table. 'She must be mistaken in what she saw.'

Betty followed her gaze, her eyes narrowing. 'Or she's lying. She certainly doesn't look happy.'

'You know Tom would never do what Lucy's accused him of.'

'Of course he wouldn't,' Betty agreed, ladling a dollop of honey on her porridge. She glanced over at Rosie. The girl certainly did look out of sorts. And no wonder, for no one seemed to be talking to her. 'Why are you up so early, anyway?' she asked.

Emily shrugged. 'I didn't want to be on my own. I think too much.'

Betty looked at her sorrowfully. 'Oh, Emily, I'm so sorry this has happened to you. I swear I could swing for that Lucy.'

Emily managed a wan smile. 'You're a good friend, Betty.'

At that moment, Betty spotted Rosie leaving the

table, her expression stricken. She wiped her mouth on her napkin and pushed back her chair. 'I'll be back in a minute.'

Surprised, Emily watched as her friend disappeared in the direction of the pantry. As she turned back to the table, her engagement ring caught the light. She gasped as a sharp stab of pain shot through her. Listening to the light-hearted banter around her, she just wanted to scream. For a brief moment she contemplated taking her mug and throwing it against the wall. The idea brought a sad smile to her cold lips as she imagined everyone's shock should she behave so out of character. Instead, she lifted it to her lips and forced herself to take a sip.

Out of the corner of her eye, she saw Betty emerge from the pantry, march over to Mrs Young and whisper something into her ear. Instantly, Mrs Young was on her feet and bustling after Betty towards the pantry. As if sensing some drama was about to unfold, conversation abated until Mrs Young's angry voice could be heard emanating from the pantry, interspersed by loud sobbing. Moments later, the cook came storming out of the pantry dragging Rosie by the arm. The girl was red-faced and crying bitterly.

'You're going to tell Mr Reynolds exactly what you just told me, my girl,' Emily heard Mrs Young say as she propelled Rosie out of the kitchen. The heavy doors swung shut behind them, leaving everyone staring after them in stunned silence.

'She lied,' Betty said, returning to the table. 'That bitch Lucy told her what to say.'

As the table erupted in noise, Emily stared at Betty in stupefaction. 'She *did* lie?' she said, trembling with anger. 'But why?'

'Apparently Rosie happened to be bringing in the washing when she saw Lucy in the garden all upset. Then later, Lucy came to find her and told her she'd better corroborate her story and swear she'd seen Tom invite Lucy into the shed or she'd tell Miss Thompson she'd seen Rosie stealing.'

'What an evil cow.' Emily frowned. 'But is it enough to exonerate Tom?'

The kitchen door opened, drawing dozens of expectant glances.

'What's up with you lot?' Lucy asked, scanning the room with her usual supercilious glare as she helped herself to a mug of tea. She caught sight of Emily and stifled a grin.

'Ah, Emily. Such a shame the wedding's off,' she said, not quite able to hide how much she was relishing Emily's heartache. She hadn't exactly planned to get Tom into trouble but she'd been so upset when she'd run into Rosie that the lie had just slipped out, and then, when Mr Reynolds had seen her in the torn dress, she'd felt compelled to continue the deceit. Though she couldn't deny it was somewhat satisfying to see Emily and Tom get their comeuppance.

'I think you'd better shut up, Lucy,' Betty said coldly. 'Before I throw this mug of tea over your head.'

Lucy's laughter was cut off by the return of Mrs Young, her angry gaze sweeping the room.

'You,' she said, pointing at Lucy. 'Mr Reynolds wants to see you in his office. Right now.'

'I've just poured a cup of tea, Mrs Young,' replied Lucy petulantly.

'I SAID NOW!' Mrs Young's bellow made everyone jump. Lucy flushed crimson. Meekly, she got to her feet and fled the room.

124

Emily and Betty exchanged glances. Mrs Young took a deep breath and returned to her seat. 'Come on, you lot,' she said. 'Eat up. We don't want to get behind with our work now, do we?'

★ ★ ★

Emily's afternoon rehearsals were interrupted by a message from Mr Reynolds asking all staff to meet him in the kitchen. She had been on tenterhooks all day, waiting to see what would happen. By the time Emily arrived, most of the other staff were already there and the air was thick with speculation.

She found Betty leaning against the sink.

'What's going on?' she whispered, but before Betty could reply, Mr Reynolds entered, followed by Miss Thompson. The room fell silent.

'Good afternoon, staff,' Mr Reynolds said, clearing his throat. His gaze swept the kitchen, coming to rest on Emily. His cheeks coloured slightly and he looked away, seemingly flustered. 'I've called you all here this afternoon to inform you that Lucy Hunt and Rosie Smith have been dismissed.' There was a collective gasp and Emily gripped Betty's arm. 'Lucy admitted to me earlier today that her allegations against Mr Harding were a complete fabrication,' Mr Reynolds continued, looking rather sheepish. 'Constable Moreton has been informed and, of course, the investigation has been dropped.' He coughed. 'Right, well,' he said, flapping his hands. 'That will be all. You may return to your duties.'

'She admitted she made it all up,' Emily said, a wave of relief washing over her as the others began to disperse. 'Tom has been vindicated and it's thanks to you. What did you say to Rosie in the pantry to make her confess?'

'I didn't have to press too hard,' Betty admitted. 'The guilt was making her ill.'

'I hope Miss Thompson gave her a reference, though she doesn't deserve it.'

'No, she does not,' declared Betty stoutly. 'Nor your sympathy, either. Are you going to go and see Tom's dad? He might have heard from Tom by now and you can let him know it's safe for him to come back.'

Emily glanced at the clock on the wall and grimaced. 'Damn! I've missed the bus. I'll have to wait an hour for the next one.'

'Why don't you ask Mr Andrews to run you down in the van?' suggested Betty.

'It's worth asking, I suppose,' agreed Emily. 'He is very fond of Tom.'

The head gardener was only too happy to oblige and, twenty minutes later, after a somewhat hair-raising journey along narrow winding roads, he was pulling up outside Ernest's cottage. Clutching her hat, Emily ran up the front path and hammered on the door.

'Oh, Mr Harding,' she blurted out when it opened. 'Lucy confessed to making up the whole thing.' Ernest smiled at her sadly and Emily faltered. 'Do you understand, sir? She made the whole thing up. Tom's safe.'

'Come on in, love.' Ernest stood aside to let Emily into the small front parlour. He shut the door behind her and shuffled over to the sideboard. 'This came the morning.' A brown envelope was propped against the carriage clock. He picked it up. 'It was sent from aboard RMS *Duchess of Atholl*.' Ernest's voice trembled. 'Tom sailed for Canada from Liverpool this morning.'

126

'What?' Emily's heart plummeted. She stared at Ernest in shock. 'He can't have. No!' she wailed, as she sank into the nearest chair. 'Why would he do that?' She looked at Ernest, her eyes pleading for him to say it was all a cruel joke. 'Why?'

'I don't know, love. Perhaps he thought he had no choice.' Ernest sat down opposite her. 'He wasn't to know that girl would recant her story.'

'Do you think he'll come back?' Emily asked, as the tears ran down her cheeks.

'I reckon once he arrives, he'll head for my late sister's place. I'll write to my brother-in-law and tell him what's happened. I'm sure Tom will be home within a few weeks,' Ernest said, his warm fingers closing over hers.

★   ★   ★

'He's gone,' she said in reply to Mr Andrews's questioning glance. With his large frame hunched over the steering wheel, he stared out of the misted-up windscreen and nodded. He cleared his throat and gunned the engine. Her tears spent for now, Emily kept her gaze fixed on the road ahead, as Mr Andrews drove them both home in grim silence.

18

Emily woke early the following morning with a sore throat and aching, red-rimmed eyes. She had cried herself to sleep, only to wake barely a few hours later. Lying in the dark, listening to Betty's gentle breathing, she had forced herself to think long and hard about her future. She had to cling to the hope that Tom would return. She still couldn't comprehend that he would leave without a word. He hadn't even left a note, but surely, as soon as he reached port in Canada, he would send word and she would be able to let him know all was well and he could return home. In the meantime, she didn't know if she could bear to continue working in the hotel without Tom, and she was sure that, once Tom did come back, he wouldn't feel comfortable working for Mr Reynolds either. The fact that even Mr Andrews had been inclined to believe Lucy's lies must have cut him to the quick.

By the time the sky had begun to lighten an idea began to form in her head. She just hoped she would have the courage to follow it through.

'You look awful,' Betty told her, sitting up in bed and regarding her friend sorrowfully. 'Shall I bring you a cup of tea?'

'No, thank you, Betty,' Emily replied, throwing back the covers. 'I need to talk to you. It's important.' Barefoot, she crossed the narrow space between the beds. 'Move over.' Betty made room for Emily to climb in beside her.

'You know, Emily,' Betty said, putting her arm around her friend as Emily rested her head on Betty's shoulder, 'I'm inclined to agree with Mr Harding. As soon as Tom reaches his uncle's place and realizes that he's no longer in trouble, he'll come back.' She gave Emily a squeeze. 'I'm sure of it.'

'I'm hoping that's what will happen,' Emily said, raising her head to look Betty in the eye. 'But that's not what I want to talk to you about. I'm leaving the hotel.'

Betty drew back in shock. 'What?'

'If Mr Thurston's offer still stands, I'm going to accept.'

'You're going to Bristol with him? Are you mad? You don't know the man.'

'I've heard enough hotel gossip to know he has a good reputation as an agent.'

'But — how will Tom know where you are?'

'The hotel can forward my mail to Mr Thurston's address in Bristol and I will write to Ernest too.' She paused, looking thoughtful. 'I realize Tom may not be able to book his passage home immediately, so if what Mr Thurston promised me is true, I'm hoping to earn enough to give us a fresh start somewhere.'

'I shall miss you,' Betty wailed.

Emily smiled sadly. 'I'll miss you, too, Betty. But I can't stay here. Not after the way Tom was treated.'

Betty sighed. 'When will you leave?'

'Mr Thurston is due to check out today so . . . ' She shrugged. 'That's if he's still interested, of course.'

'Oh, he'll be interested all right,' Betty replied drily. 'You can count on that. But Mr Reynolds won't be happy.'

'I know,' Emily said, unabashed. 'I feel bad letting

the guests down, but as for him . . . ' She shrugged. 'Anyway, if I don't go today, I'll miss my chance.'

* * *

'I'm catching the eleven-fifteen train,' Roland said, checking his pocket watch with a sigh of irritation. 'Please see that my luggage is delivered to the station in plenty of time.'

'Of course, sir,' the pretty receptionist assured him with a smile. 'Would you like to settle your bill now, sir?'

Roland was reaching into his pocket for his wallet when he spotted Emily crossing the foyer towards him. Instantly, his irritation vanished as he turned to greet her with a smile.

'My dear Miss Baker,' he said. 'I had hoped to run into you before I left. May I say that your performance last night was even more hauntingly beautiful than usual?'

'Thank you, Mr Thurston. I wonder, may I have a word?'

'Certainly. Why don't we go into the library? Would you send in a pot of tea, please, miss,' he said to the receptionist. 'Add it to my bill and I shall settle up shortly.'

'Certainly, Mr Thurston. I'll have one of the waiters bring it through directly.'

Resting his hand lightly on her back, Roland ushered Emily into the warm library. He could barely contain his excitement. Since that Lucy girl had come clean about what had really transpired between herself and Tom, he'd given Emily up as a lost cause, which had gone a long way to fuelling his irritation.

The library was a pleasant room, with floor-to-ceiling shelves crammed with books. Nests of easy chairs were placed at intervals around small tables, and Gershwin played on a gramophone behind a large potted fern.

Roland indicated a chair and Emily sat down. Her heart was racing and her palms were clammy. She gazed through the French windows over the dew-drenched lawns. Once the sun burned off the fine mist that hung in the air it would be a pleasant spring day.

'So, Miss Baker,' said Roland, lighting a cigarette and leaning back in his seat. 'How can I help you?'

'Mr Thurston,' Emily began nervously, 'I was wondering whether your offer might still be open?'

Resisting the urge to leap to his feet in jubilation, Roland simply took a long drag of his cigarette and smiled. 'Am I correct in assuming that you have changed your mind, Miss Baker?'

Emily blushed. 'Yes. My circumstances have changed. Tom has gone away . . . ' Her voice wobbled and she took a deep breath to steady it. 'Mr Thurston, my wedding may well have been . . . postponed.'

'Oh, I'm sorry to hear that,' Roland said with what he hoped was a sympathetic tone.

'Thank you. I find myself in need of a change of scenery, and so, if your offer still stands, I would like to accept.'

Edward arrived with the tea tray. Giving Emily a sad smile, he set it on the table between them. She thanked him and busied herself setting out cups and pouring the tea.

'My train leaves at eleven fifteen,' Roland said. 'Could you be ready to leave by then?'

'Yes,' Emily said firmly. 'I will need somewhere to

live. I have savings.'

'I know of several boarding houses with excellent reputations,' Roland assured her, dropping a sugar lump into his cup and stirring.

'I must tell Fred before I speak to Mr Reynolds,' Emily said, her heart sinking at the thought of having to let down a man who, over the years, had become a dear friend.

'Of course,' Roland said. 'I've booked a taxi for twenty past ten. Shall we meet in the foyer at a quarter past?'

'Yes, thank you.' Emily set down her teacup. 'That will give me plenty of time to do everything I need to.' She stood up. 'Thank you, Mr Thurston. I shan't let you down.'

'I know you won't.' Roland grinned, getting to his feet. 'And it's Roland, please.'

Emily smiled. 'Thank you, Roland.'

★ ★ ★

Emily wiped her eyes and knocked on Mr Reynolds's door. It had been hard saying goodbye to Fred. He had taken her news stoically, as was his way, but beneath his gruff exterior, she could see that he was hurt by her leaving.

She sniffed, and on Mr Reynolds's invitation, pushed open the door.

'Ah, Emily,' Mr Reynolds said, looking decidedly flustered at the sight of her. 'Come in, do.' He smiled at her. 'I expect you've heard about Miss Hunt? That the clothes she was wearing during Tom's so-called attack actually belonged to a guest? Mrs Beaumont-Clarke's not pressing charges, thankfully.' He indicated one of the chairs. 'Please, my dear, have a seat.'

'Thank you, that won't be necessary.' Emily stood in front of his desk and took a deep breath. 'Mr Reynolds, I am leaving the hotel. Today.'

'Leaving?' Mr Reynolds stammered with a frown. 'Whatever for?'

'Mr Thurston has offered to represent me. I'm going to Bristol.'

'But, you have responsibilities. Our guests will be expecting you to sing this evening.' Mr Reynolds flapped his hands in consternation. 'Is this to do with that regrettable business with your fiancé?' he blustered. 'I thought the matter was resolved.'

'I'm sorry to be letting the guests down, but you should have believed Tom in the first place,' Emily said, with a flash of anger. 'I knew the truth would come out eventually, it always does. But it's too late. He's gone, Mr Reynolds. Tom has gone to Canada, believing he's a wanted criminal.' Her eyes filled with tears.

'Emily,' Mr Reynolds said, his face crumpling in anguish. 'I'm sorry. I didn't realize.'

'I'm sorry too,' Emily said sadly. 'Goodbye, Mr Reynolds.'

She shut the door quietly behind her.

Saying goodbye to Mrs Young and Miss Thompson was harder for she was fond of the two women, and she was close to tears again by the time she came to meet Roland in the hotel foyer.

'Goodbye, Emily,' Edward said, giving her a hug. 'I'm going to miss you.'

'I shall miss you too.' Emily pressed her face into his neck. 'If you hear anything from Tom . . . ' she whispered.

'You'll be the first to know.'

Betty clung to her, crying unashamedly. 'Promise you'll keep in touch?'

'I promise.' She pressed a piece of paper into Betty's hand. 'This is Mr Thurston's address. You can write to me there.'

'We really must go,' Roland chided her. 'The taxi is waiting.'

Her trunk had already gone ahead to the station with Roland's, and she gave Betty one last, lingering hug and headed outside. A brisk wind was blowing but it was pleasantly mild with fluffy white clouds scudding across a sapphire-blue sky.

Roland opened the door to the taxi and she settled herself inside. He climbed in beside her. Blowing her nose, she leaned out of the window, waving.

'Don't forget me when you're rich and famous,' Betty yelled after her, making Emily smile as the taxi drove around the fountain and set off down the drive.

★ ★ ★

The train pulled into Bristol's Temple Meads Station at a quarter to one that Thursday afternoon. To Emily's relief, after a few attempts to engage her in conversation, Roland had seemed content to hide behind his newspaper, leaving her free to gaze out of the window at the changing landscape and try to make sense of how much her life had changed in barely a week.

'I expect you want to freshen up?' Roland said as they stepped down onto the bustling platform. He had to shout above the cacophony of blowing whistles, the screech of metal against metal and the cooing of the hundreds of pigeons roosting on the iron girders above their heads. 'The cloakroom's over there.' He pointed through the cloud of dispersing steam. 'I'll sort out the luggage and meet you over by the newsagent's stand.'

Grateful to have a few moments to herself, Emily threaded her way through the crowd to the cloakroom where she washed her hands and splashed her cheeks with cold water. Wiping her face on the towel provided, she caught sight of the sad-eyed, pale-faced girl staring back at her. She missed Tom so much it felt like an iron vice squeezing the very breath from her lungs. Blinking back the tears that threatened, she pulled on her gloves and straightened her hat. Taking a deep breath to steady herself, she went in search of Roland.

★ ★ ★

'I've arranged for your luggage to be sent on to the Pines Guest House,' he told her. 'Mrs Wilson always has vacancies.' With his hand resting lightly on her spine, he guided her out into the bright March sunshine. 'And now I shall treat you to a late luncheon. There's a lovely little place not far from here. We can go over your contract while we eat.'

'Is the guest house expensive?' Emily asked anxiously. She had her savings, but she would need to use them sparingly until she had an income.

'It's on me,' Roland said, waving his hand expansively as he steered her down a wide, crowded street lined with shops, cafes and restaurants. 'You can pay me back once you're earning. This is the place.'

They were standing beneath a striped red and white awning. Elaborate gold writing on the window spelled out the name 'Gabriella's'. 'Best pie and mash in the city,' Roland said, pushing open the door and standing aside to let Emily enter. Her senses were instantly assailed by the savoury meaty aroma. Most of the red-and-white-checked tables were occupied, she noticed. It was obviously a popular place. The door at the back swung open and a large blonde-haired woman of about fifty came bustling out, bearing two plates of steaming food.

'Roland,' she said, beaming at him from across the restaurant. 'How lovely to see you again. Sit yourself down. I'll be over in a jiffy.'

'That's Hilda Wright,' Roland said to Emily as he pulled out a chair for her. 'She gave me my very first job.'

'You used to work here?' Emily asked with genuine interest as Roland took his place opposite her.

He nodded. 'I was fourteen. I'd lost my mum and my older sister to the Spanish flu the year before. We'd already lost Dad at Passchendaele so it was only me and my younger sister, June. We were squatting in the basement of a derelict, rat-infested tenement block. We had no heating, no food, but we didn't dare apply for parish relief. I was terrified they'd take June away.' Roland paused to clear his throat. Emily gave him a sympathetic smile.

'June and I used to scavenge for scraps outside the cafes and restaurants,' he went on. 'One day, I got too bold and attempted to steal a loaf of bread out of Hilda's kitchen. Her husband caught me red-handed and was about to box my ears when Hilda turned up. She took pity on me and gave me a job washing up. It was hard work and long hours, but it kept June out of the workhouse. She's married now with a couple of

136

kiddies. Lives over in Clevedon.'

Hilda came bustling over, her round face red and perspiring. 'Right,' she said, 'pie and mash twice, is it?'

'Definitely.' Roland grinned up at her. 'Hilda, this is Miss Emily Baker, my latest star in the making.'

'Pleased to meet you, Miss Baker,' Hilda said with a friendly smile. 'Two pie and mash coming up,' she said, heading back to the kitchen.

'How did you go from being a washer-upper in this place to a theatrical agent?' Emily asked while they waited for their food to arrive.

'My parents were both involved in the theatre. That was how they met. One day an old friend of theirs came into the restaurant and recognized me. He gave me a job as stagehand. I realized I was good at spotting who had talent and who didn't. I opened my own agency when I was twenty-two and I've never looked back.'

'I knew he was too clever to waste his life waiting tables and washing up,' Hilda said, placing two steaming plates in front of them. Having had barely any appetite over the past few days, Emily realized she was suddenly hungry. 'Enjoy,' Hilda said, shuffling off as the bell over the door jangled, heralding the arrival of more customers.

'It smells lovely,' Emily said, picking up her knife and fork.

'I assure you it tastes as good as it smells. I'm not sure what's in it . . . ' He grinned. 'I always thought it best not to enquire, but it is jolly delicious.'

Emily had to agree and surprised herself by clearing her plate. She washed it down with a mug of Hilda's strong, sweet tea.

'That's better,' Roland said approvingly, as Hilda collected their plates. 'You've got a bit of colour in your cheeks.'

Emily looked down at her hands. For a few blissful moments she had managed to forget about Tom, but now the pain and grief came crashing down on her like a ton of bricks. Sensing her change of mood, Roland called for the bill.

'Let's get you settled at Mrs Wilson's,' he said, once he'd paid. 'I'll flag down a taxi.'

138

19

Roland rang the bell at a quarter to eleven o'clock on Monday morning. Emily had been watching for him from the dining room window and she was already buttoning up her coat and putting on her hat.

She had written to Molly and Betty and had then spent the weekend exploring the surrounding streets, wishing Tom was at her side. Despite his aversion to big-city life, she was sure he couldn't help but be awed by the sights and smells of the historic city. She couldn't wait to enjoy them with him.

Now a new week beckoned, bringing with it a new chapter in her life and she was determined to make the most of the chance she had been given. Pushing aside her anxiety over Tom, she opened the door with a cheery smile.

'Good morning, Roland.'

'Morning, Emily. Your carriage awaits.' Roland indicated the black Ford parked alongside the kerb. 'May I?' She took his proffered arm and trotted down the steps beside him. 'I'm as good as my word,' he said, opening the car door for her to climb in. 'I've been busy all weekend and I have got you a booking for every day this week at the Barley Mow.'

'What's the Barley Mow?' Emily asked, slightly apprehensively. She had never performed anywhere other than the Mansfield House Hotel and she couldn't help feeling nervous. The last thing she wanted to do was let Roland down.

'It's a music hall on Castle Street,' he said. 'Very

popular for its variety shows. You're quite a way down the bill,' Roland said with an apologetic sideways glance, 'but you won't stay down for long. I'm sure you'll be top of the bill in no time, with your name in lights.'

Emily laughed. 'I'm just happy to have the chance to sing again,' she said, as Roland tuned the key in the ignition and pulled into the flow of morning traffic.

★ ★ ★

Roland parked the car in nearby Tower Hill and they walked briskly up Castle Street, dodging the throngs of morning shoppers. It was cold, the sun yet to break through the mist that had drifted over from the Severn estuary, and Emily was glad of her warm coat.

'This is it.' Roland came to a halt halfway along the street. 'The Barley Mow music hall.'

A handsome medieval jettied building, the Barley Mow was tucked between a dealer in musical instruments and a wireless shop.

'There you are,' Roland said, pointing to a poster board propped up in the doorway. 'Your name on the bill.'

'Emily Rose?' She looked at him questioningly.

'I noticed your second name on your contract. I think Emily Rose has a nicer ring to it than Emily Baker, don't you think?'

Hesitantly, Emily acquiesced. She wasn't quite sure how she felt about losing her surname, but her misgivings did nothing to dampen the thrill of seeing her name in bold print, sandwiched between a Nellie Simpson and Pedro the Amazing Magician. 'Oh, I do hope I won't disappoint.'

140

'I can assure you, you won't,' Roland said, taking her firmly by the arm and leading her into a dimly lit, somewhat stuffy foyer that smelled of stale tobacco smoke and damp. There was a lot of dark blue velvet and the distempered walls were emblazoned with framed advertizing posters and photographs of now famous artists who had started their careers at the Barley Mow.

'We're shut, love,' a brassy-haired woman in a flowing pink dressing gown and holding a cigarette between her long fingers emerged from the gloom. 'Oh, Roland, it's you.' She smiled, showing a row of uneven teeth. 'And who's this? Another of your protégés?' She held out her hand. 'Lulu Tremain. Burlesque dancer.'

'Pleased to meet you, Lulu.' Emily shook the proffered hand. 'Emily Baker.'

'Ah, yes, Roland's been singing your praises all weekend.'

'And with good reason,' Roland said amiably. 'She's damn good.'

'It's not often you back a wrong 'un, Roland,' Lulu admitted, exhaling a cloud of smoke towards the discoloured ceiling. 'George is downstairs,' she added, nodding towards a door marked 'Stage'.

'Thanks, Lulu.' Roland nodded. 'Get us a cup of tea, will you? I'm parched.'

'What am I, the tea girl now?' came Lulu's good-natured retort as she flounced off into what Emily would later discover was the theatre kitchen.

'George Atkins is the stage manager,' Roland explained as they descended the thickly carpeted stairs. 'He's the one you need to impress.' He pushed open a door and Emily found herself in the wings of the stage. A ladder ran up to the gantry from which large spotlights beamed down on a dark-haired girl singing a popular music hall ditty. Apart from the stage, the rest of the auditorium was in darkness. All Emily could see were the first few rows, lit up by the lights. Several of the red velvet seats were occupied. One man, wearing a black velvet dinner jacket and an expression of abject boredom, shuffled a deck of playing cards. Carefully stepping around discarded props, a coil of rope and an elaborate pully system seemingly designed to allow people to fly through the air, Emily followed Roland across the stage and down the steps. A well-built man in shirt sleeves, with thick, wavy black hair, leapt to his feet. 'All right, Nellie,' he called to the dark-haired girl. 'That was great. Take a break.' Nellie stopped singing and reached down to retrieve the glass of water at her feet.

'Roland, good morning,' the man said, coming towards them.

'George.' The two men shook hands.

'So, this is your new girl?' His dark eyes looked Emily up and down.

'Emily, this is George Atkins. George, Emily Rose.'

'Pleasure to meet you, Emily. It seems you've really impressed young Roland here. So, let's see what you've got. Have you brought your music with you?' George said. 'Well, hand it over to Max,' he continued when Emily confirmed that she had. 'And let's hear you.'

Nerves made her clumsy and she fumbled her music, letting some sheets fall to the ground. Flustered, she crouched down to gather them up.

'Don't be nervous.' Nellie, the dark-haired girl appeared at her side. 'Max is a brilliant accompanist and none of us bite.' She glanced over at the man with the deck of playing cards. 'Except perhaps Pedro, but he's weird anyway.' She smiled. Nellie's friendly manner went some way to putting Emily at her ease. She finally got her music sheets in order and gave them to Max.

'Take your time,' he told her kindly. He was an older man, with dark hair greying at the temples and creases around his pale blue eyes. 'Take a deep breath and give me the nod when you're ready.'

She had chosen to start off with a Shirley Temple number, 'On The Good Ship Lollipop', followed by Fred Astaire's 'Cheek to Cheek', which Roland had suggested, it being one of the first songs he'd heard her sing. Standing on stage, staring out into the inky blackness, seemed surreal. She looked down at her fellow performers draped over the front row. Some were chatting quietly; a few stared up at her expectantly. Inhaling a deep, shaky breath, she glanced over at Max and gave a nod.

From the moment she began to sing, all conversation ceased, her audience captivated by her voice. George raised an eyebrow and glanced at Roland, who flashed him a smug grin and shrugged as if to say, 'Told you so.'

Emily finished her first song to a burst of applause. Blushing, she barely had time to draw breath before Max launched into the opening bars of her second number. By the time she'd worked through her entire repertoire for the upcoming performance, she felt as though she were walking on air. She floated off the stage to tumultuous applause and shouts of congratulations from the other performers. To her surprise, Roland flung his arms around her.

'You were fantastic!' He was beaming. 'Didn't I tell

you so, George?' he said with unbridled enthusiasm as he released Emily from his embrace.

'You've got a fantastic voice, Emily,' said Nellie without a hint of jealousy. 'This is Leah. She's a singer too.'

Emily smiled at the willowy, auburn-haired woman with slanting green eyes. 'Hello, Leah.'

'Nice to meet you, Emily,' Leah said with genuine warmth. 'You've got a wonderful voice. Have you had formal training?'

'No, nothing. My only teacher was the choirmaster at church.'

'That's amazing,' said Leah admiringly. 'It took me months to learn how to project my voice enough to fill an auditorium this size. Nellie too.'

'That's where Leah and I met,' Nellie said. 'We both attended Madam Marie's singing school. Look, Pedro's rehearsing now. Do you want to get a cup of tea? We won't be needed for at least another hour or so.'

'I'd love one,' Emily said, massaging her throat. 'I'm as dry as the desert.'

Huddled in the small kitchen over mugs of weak, milky tea, Emily learned that Nellie was twenty-two years old and had lived in Bristol all her life. Leah was twenty-four and had moved to Bristol from Burnham-on-Sea five years earlier.

'My parents weren't very happy,' she told Emily, getting up to fetch the biscuit tin. 'I think Dad thought I was headed for a life of debauchery.' She placed the tin in the middle of the table. 'He has a very dim view of people who earn their living on the stage. He's a fisherman,' she added, as if this explained the reasoning behind his opinion.

144

'What did you do?' Emily asked, taking a biscuit and dunking it in her tea.

'I helped Mum in the smokery.' Leah pulled a face. 'And sang in the local pub on Saturday nights. Then my boyfriend decided he wanted to get engaged. I was nineteen years old and I suddenly saw what my life would be like if I stayed put — marriage, babies, a husband away at sea for days on end — and it filled me with dread. I broke up with the boyfriend, packed my bags and headed for the bright lights of Bristol. I enrolled in Madam Marie's singing school, got myself an agent and here I am. It's been hard going but I wouldn't have changed a thing, apart from the fact my dad still won't speak to me.'

'I was lucky,' Nellie said. 'My mother was a professional singer before she married so both my parents were very supportive. I was always performing as a child and I attended singing school from the age of twelve.'

'Do you still live at home?'

Nellie shook her head. 'Coming in at all hours of the night, I felt it unfair to my parents so I moved out last year. I board with Leah and Lulu in College Street.' Emily looked blank and Nellie added, 'It's about a twenty-minute walk from here. What about you?'

'I was singing in a hotel in Dorset where Roland happened to be saying,' Emily said, keeping her story short. 'He offered to take me on as a client.'

'When's the wedding,' asked Leah, eyeing the ring on Emily's left hand.

'I . . . we . . . ' Emily faltered. 'I'm not sure,' she ended lamely, self-consciously folding her hands on her lap. 'Tom, my fiancé, is working away at the moment.'

'Oh, what does he do?' Leah asked.

'He's a gardener.'

Sensing that the new girl was loath to divulge any more information, Nellie swiftly changed the subject. 'Where are you staying?' she asked, helping herself to another biscuit.

'The Pines Guest House in West Street but I'm going to need somewhere more permanent very soon.'

'You could move in with us,' said Lulu, coming into the kitchen and catching the drift of the conversation. 'We've got a vacancy.'

'I was about to suggest that,' Nellie said, smiling at Emily over her mug. 'Poor Ethel. She was a burlesque dancer like Lulu, but her mum passed away recently so she's had to go home and keep house for her dad and brothers.'

'Such a waste of talent,' Lulu added glumly.

'So, anyway, her room's free. I don't think Miss Anne's advertized it yet, has she?' She glanced at Leah and Lulu for confirmation. Both girls shook their heads.

'I think she was going to put a card in the window this week. Miss Anne's our landlady,' Leah added for Emily's benefit. 'She's a lovely old dear. Mothers us all to death.'

'Why don't you walk back with us this afternoon?' Nellie suggested. 'You can meet her and have a look at the room. If you like it you could move in tomorrow.'

Emily smiled gratefully. 'That would be wonderful.' She'd been dreading having to traipse around the city in search of lodgings. 'Thank you.'

* * *

146

They finished their tea and returned to the auditorium for more rehearsals. Promptly at midday, George called a halt for dinner. Someone had been out to a nearby bakery and bought meat pies which they ate sat along the edge of the stage or lounging on the plush velvet seats. As she picked crumbs from her skirt, Emily tried to imagine what it would be like later with the auditorium full and her stomach flipped with nervous excitement. She only wished that Tom could be there, hiding in the wings, silently cheering her on.

20

Sixty-one College Street was halfway down a row of elegant red-brick houses. Nellie mounted the three steps to the shiny black door and slid her key in the lock. The door opened into a small entrance hall illuminated by dusty sunlight spilling out from the parlour. On Emily's right was a staircase, its runner moth-eaten and frayed at the edges. A tantalizing aroma drifted from the back of the house.

'Hello, Miss Anne,' Lulu called out as the four girls took off their coats and hung them on the coat stand. Emily heard the clatter of saucepan lids and a short, plump woman with curly greying dark brown hair appeared, wiping her hands on her apron.

'Hello, girls. Your supper's all ready for you. You'll be wanting to get back to the theatre by six.' She stopped short when she noticed Emily. 'Oh, you've brought a friend home. Hello, love, I'm Anne Philips, but call me Miss Anne — all the girls do.'

'Emily Baker. I'm pleased to meet you, Miss Anne,' Emily said with a smile.

'Emily's interested in Ethel's room,' Nellie said, removing her hat and fluffing up her hair.

'Well, you're welcome to go up and have a look, love,' Miss Anne told her. 'Nellie, do you want to show her up? Supper will be ready as soon as you come down.'

'Come on, this way.' Nellie led Emily up the narrow stairs. 'This is where Miss Anne and Barbara sleep,' Nellie said as they reached the first landing.

148

'Barbara's also a singer, but she's appearing over at the Hippodrome at the moment.'

'The Hippodrome?' Emily repeated, her eyes wide. Nellie gave her a rueful grin.

'Yes, we're all so jealous. The bathroom's that door there. Hot water's a premium which, as you can imagine in a household of six women, is an absolute nightmare. You'll have to time your ablutions accordingly.' Hand on the intricately carved bannister, she led the way up to the next floor. 'Leah and Lulu have the two attic rooms,' she said, indicating a further flight of stairs. 'I'm in there, and this,' she said, flinging the door open with a flourish, 'is you.'

Emily stood in the doorway, taking in the room. It was simply furnished. A single bed covered by a lemon candlewick bedspread was pushed against one wall. Against another stood a tall dark-wood wardrobe, and beside it, a six-drawer chest, the interiors of which smelled strongly of mothballs. The wallpaper was coming away at the edges and there was a damp patch on the ceiling, but the carpet and bedding were clean and smelled fresh. Floral-pattered curtains hung at the window overlooking the street.

'It's a lovely room,' Emily said, turning to Nellie. 'I'd like to take it.'

'Excellent.' Nellie tucked her arm through Emily's. 'Let's go tell Miss Anne.'

'Emily's going to move in,' announced Nellie as they entered the kitchen where Leah and Lulu were seated at the table.

'Oh, that's good news,' Miss Anne said, handing round bowls of delicious-smelling vegetable soup. 'Have you got much in the way of belongings?'

'Only my clothes and a few books,' Emily replied,

149

helping herself to a hunk of bread.

'I can ask the lad next door to fetch them over for you, if you like?' Miss Anne said, joining them at the table. 'When would you like to move in?'

'Would tomorrow be too soon?' Emily asked.

'That's fine with me, love.' Miss Anne beamed. 'Right, girls, it's almost half past four. You'd better eat up if you want a wash and what have you before you go back to the theatre.'

'You can use the bathroom if you want to freshen up,' Leah told Emily, mopping up the last of her soup with a crust of bread.

'Good luck to you all,' Miss Anne said as she got up to start clearing the table. 'I'll have the cocoa waiting for when you get back tonight.'

Emily was in the bathroom when Miss Anne shouted up the stairs to tell her that a Mr Thurston was waiting in the parlour for her. Nervous that something had gone wrong and Roland had come to tell her that she wouldn't be performing after all, Emily bounded downstairs, her heart racing.

'Roland?' she said breathlessly, her anxiety waning in the light of his cheerful grin.

'I thought you might prefer to arrive at your first performance in style so I've come to drive you.' He glanced around the tidy parlour, taking in the comfortable three-piece suite and crocheted antimacassars, the framed sepia photographs jostling for space on the mantelpiece, the cheap watercolours on the walls. 'How do you like the place?'

'Very much,' Emily replied. 'I'm moving in tomorrow.'

'Great. I'll have your things delivered in the morning.'

'Miss Anne said her neighbour wouldn't mind fetching my trunk.'

'Nonsense,' Roland said with a wave of his hand. 'I'm quite happy to oblige. Now, I took the liberty of going by Mrs Wilson's and picking up one of your frocks. It's in the car. Shall we?' He started for the door.

'Do you mind if we give the girls a lift?'

'What?' Roland said, slightly irritated as he had hoped to spend a few minutes alone with Emily, getting to know her better. 'Oh, very well. As long as they hurry.'

Emily ran up the stairs to shout to the girls that if they could be ready in five minutes, Roland would drive them to the Barley Mow.

It was a further ten minutes before they set off. Roland sat staring straight ahead, his face tight with annoyance.

'Our agent doesn't drive us to shows,' Leah complained once Roland had dropped them off and gone to find somewhere to park the car. 'We only hear from him when he's got a booking.'

'He's just being extra kind because it's my first time performing in a proper theatre,' Emily replied, as she hurried after Leah, her gown draped over her arm.

The dressing rooms were situated in the bowels of the theatre where the cool air smelled of greasepaint and powder. Nellie was already in a state of undress by the time Leah and Emily appeared at the right dressing room door.

'I almost ended up in Pedro's dressing room by mistake,' Lulu laughed, sticking her head around the doorframe on her way to join the other dancers for a last-minute run-through of their routine. A plume of

151

vibrant pink ostrich feathers sprouted from her hair. 'Why they decided to swap us all round at the last minute, I don't know.' She smiled. 'Break a leg, girls.'

The dressing room was a tangled mess of discarded clothing and shoes. Nellie sat down at the mirror and, clearing a space amongst the many bottles and jars, leaned forward to apply her make-up. The dress she would wear for the performance hung on a rack, along with Leah's silvery-sequined number. Leah was top of the bill, so she had plenty of time to relax. She was reclining in an easy chair flicking through a magazine, her auburn hair in curlers.

Emily, third from bottom after Pedro the Amazing Magician, didn't have the luxury of time. She hung her dress beside Nellie's and took a seat in front of the mirror. Her heart was racing and her hands were shaking so much she was terrified she'd poke herself in the eye with her mascara wand. From upstairs came the sound of music. The audience were starting to arrive.

* * *

'You're on in ten, Emily,' George Atkins, the stage manager, called, banging on the door. Emily took another sip of water. She'd been to the toilet twice in the last twenty minutes. Her nerves were so bad it felt as though a million butterflies were fluttering in her stomach. She wiped her clammy palms on a towel and checked her reflection in the mirror for the hundredth time.

She was wearing the ruby-red velvet dress Tom had bought her. Of course, Roland would have chosen that dress for her to make her debut in. It was what she had been wearing the first time he saw her. Just

152

feeling the soft velvet against her skin brought tears to her eyes. She missed Tom so much. By sheer strength of will, she pulled herself together. She couldn't let Roland down.

Forcing thoughts of Tom from her mind, she took a deep breath and, with both Leah and Nellie's good wishes ringing in her ears, she set off up the brightly lit passageway to the stage.

Standing in the wings while Pedro took his bows, she couldn't stop trembling. Her throat was dry and her mind had gone blank. She was struggling to remember the first line of her first song. Panic washed over her in a hot flood and she glanced about her anxiously, fighting the urge to turn tail and run. Suddenly, Roland was at her side.

'Breathe,' he commanded, taking her sweaty hands in his. 'Breathe deep, in and out, in and out.'

Emily did as he said, breathing deeply, and she felt the panic slowly begin to subside. By the time the applause for Pedro had faded away, she felt calmer and more in control.

'Are you all right?' Roland asked, his eyes full of concern. Emily nodded and he gave her a smile. 'That's my girl. Now, go knock 'em dead.'

Taking another deep breath, she walked out onto the stage to enthusiastic applause. She stood in the spotlight, heart thumping. As she stared out into the darkness, she imagined Tom was there, standing in the shadows, as always and that she was singing for him. Turning to Max, she gave him an almost imperceptible nod. He struck the first note, and Emily began to sing.

Her performance brought the house down. The applause thundered on for a good five minutes as

Emily took bow after bow. To her surprise, a few long-stemmed roses came flying out of the darkness, landing on the stage near her feet. *Oh, Tom,* she thought sadly, stooping to gather them up. *What would you think if you could see me now?* Clutching the roses to her chest, she gave one final bow and hurried into the wings where Roland was waiting with open arms.

'Emily, you were fantastic!' Roland laughed, swinging her off her feet. 'Absolutely brilliant. You are going to go far, my girl,' he said. 'I can see it now, your name up in lights in every theatre from Land's End to John O'Groats. I'm taking you out after the show. This calls for a celebration.'

She watched the rest of the show from the wings, applauding each act with enthusiasm. Both Leah and Nellie's performances were top-notch and Emily couldn't have been prouder of her new-found friends. Holding hands with Leah and Nellie, she took her place on stage as the ensemble took their final bows to whistles and thunderous applause. *This is what I was born to do,* she thought as the curtain finally came down. And she couldn't wait to do it all over again the following night.

21

Emily quickly settled in at the house in College Street. Though having Nellie, Leah and Lulu as constant companions went some way to easing her worry over Tom, some mornings it was an effort to get out of bed and face the day. The only time she felt truly alive was when she was on stage.

She had written to Betty, Molly and Tom's father, giving them her new address. Tom had been gone for over a week now. He was bound to have written. Every morning she waited impatiently for the postman but it was another two days before she received any letters, three arriving simultaneously on the Saturday morning.

To her dismay, there was nothing from Tom, but, laying the letters from her two friends aside, she tore eagerly at the envelope from Ernest. Sitting at the foot of the stairs, she scanned his spidery scrawl. Ernest wrote that he had received a telegram from Tom the previous day informing him only that he had docked safely in Montreal. Relieved that Tom had landed safely, Emily determined to be positive. A letter would come tomorrow, she was sure of it.

Ernest went on to ask after her health and exclaim in wonderment at her blossoming career. Emily folded the letter and replaced it in its envelope. Much as she was enjoying her new life as a performer, she would give it up in an instant when Tom came home.

Molly's and Betty's letters were upbeat and full of envious admiration. Molly's was filled with news of her children and Betty's was full of the exciting news that she and Edward had finally set a date for their wedding. They were to be married on the last Saturday in August. Thinking of her own wedding, which should have been in just a few weeks' time, Emily tried to feel happy for her friend. Betty continued that she'd heard Rosie was working at the local glove factory but nothing had been heard of Lucy. Mr Reynolds had hired a new singer, 'But she's nowhere near as talented as you.'

'Mrs Young, Miss Thompson and the girls all send their fondest love, as do Edward and I,' Betty concluded, signing her name with a flourish and a string of kisses.

★ ★ ★

Emily's run at the Barley Mow finished at the end of April, the day before what would have been her wedding day. With no word from Tom in almost six weeks, Emily was growing increasingly anxious that something had happened to him. He would have written, even if it was just to say goodbye. Tom would never leave her in the lurch. She'd never believe he would be that cruel.

Despite Emily's growing disquiet, Roland had been busy and she was booked to sing at venues all across the city. Leah left Bristol in the first week of May for Southampton. She was topping the bill on one of their transatlantic cruise liners and would be away for several weeks. Lulu and her troupe of dancers were spending the summer season in the nearby seaside resort of Weston-super-Mare. Without the two girls, the house felt quiet, though both Emily and Nellie were so busy with their singing engagements that they were seldom home.

As the summer wore on with still no word from Tom, Emily's sense of foreboding increased. Either something awful had happened to him or — and this she could scarcely contemplate — he had moved on without her. Another long week passed, and on a balmy summer's day in early July, tears streaming down her cheeks, she finally took off her engagement ring. Sliding it onto a thin silver chain that had once belonged to her mother, she fastened it around her neck, and tucked it under her blouse where it lay close to her heart.

A few days later both Emily and Nellie had a rare evening off together. Miss Anne had gone to bingo so the girls were alone. Sitting on Nellie's bed, painting their toenails, mugs of cocoa cooling on the bedside cabinet, Nellie was regaling Emily with tales of life in the theatre before the conversation drifted onto the topic of love and romance.

Given their profession, neither girl was without her fair share of admirers. Emily had so many bouquets of flowers delivered to her dressing room it was beginning to resemble a florist's.

Nellie had dated a few of the young men who hung around the stage doors but, as she told Emily now, none of them had taken her fancy for very long.

'What about you?' she asked, screwing the lid back on her bottle of cherry-red nail varnish. 'I know you like to keep your private life private but, well, you've been very quiet lately and I notice you're no longer wearing your ring?'

Emily smiled sadly. 'I haven't heard a word from him in over three months,' she said, her lip trembling as her eyes filled with tears. 'Oh, Nellie, I think he's forgotten all about me.'

Resting her head on Nellie's shoulder, she poured out the whole sorry tale.

'That Lucy sounds like a right cow,' Nellie fumed, feeling angry and indignant on Emily's behalf. 'I sincerely hope she gets her comeuppance. And you say Tom's dad hasn't heard from him either, except for that one telegram?'

'No,' Emily sighed. 'Not a word from either Tom or his uncle.'

'Perhaps he never intended to go to his uncle's,' said Nellie thoughtfully. 'And if he is still under the assumption that he's a wanted man, he's afraid to give his father an address, in case the police go after him. Is he close to his father?'

'Their relationship is strained, but surely Tom would trust his own father not to reveal his whereabouts to the police,' Emily cried in frustration. 'I just hope nothing's happened to him,' she said, blowing her nose, though the alternative was equally as painful. 'If he would only write to Ernest, at least I'd know he was all right, even if he doesn't want to come home.'

'Oh, Emily,' Nellie said gently.

'I miss him so much.'

'Here,' Nellie said, leaning over to reach for the bottle of sherry she kept under the bed. 'I keep this for moments just like this,' she said, pulling out the cork and taking a swig before offering the bottle to Emily.

Emily took a sip. Syrupy and overly sweet, it slipped down her throat. 'I've got some chocolate in my bedside drawer, too,' Nellie said. 'A gift from

a besotted admirer. We may as well indulge. Chocolate won't cure your heartache, but it will go a long
way to making you feel better.'

22

'Whoa, there, boy, whoa!' Samuel Jones pulled on the reins and the heavy wagon rolled to a halt in the middle of the wide dirt road. The long prairie grass undulated in the warm wind and buzzards circled in the vast empty sky. 'This here's the place, boy?' Samuel took off his wide-brimmed hat and ran a gloved hand through his white-blonde hair.

Perched on the wagon seat, squinting against the low afternoon sun, Tom read the name burned into the wooden sign. 'MARCHWOOD'. Suspended from a roughly hewn wooden arch by two metal chains, it creaked as it swung slowly in the breeze.

'I believe so, sir,' Tom said, grabbing his knapsack as he jumped to the ground. 'Thanks for the ride.'

'My pleasure,' Samuel said, settling his hat back on his head and slapping the reins. 'I was glad of the company.' The horse moved off, the wagon creaking along behind it. Tom shouldered his knapsack and looked down the rutted track. He could see the red-tiled roof of his uncle's farmhouse shimmering in the late spring sunshine. He licked his dry lips and started down the track. The only sound was that of the wind singing through the long grass. His stomach twisted anxiously as he approached the house, wondering if his uncle would recognize him. He had changed a lot in the thirteen years since his uncle and late aunt immigrated to Canada.

He felt a pang of loss for his aunt. From the age of three until the year he turned ten, his father's sister,

Aunt Polly, had been a mother to him. As a young boy, he had suffered keenly from the loss of his mother and then, within days of the funeral, he had been taken away from everything that was familiar, abandoned by a father too wrapped up in his own grief to realize how much his son needed him.

Then, seven years on, his world had again been ripped asunder when his aunt and uncle had emigrated and Ernest had refused his permission for Tom to go with them. Tom had been devastated and, although both he and Ernest had worked hard to put the past behind them, there was still a distance there that they couldn't seem to bridge.

Tom's thoughts turned now to the night he'd left Shaftesbury, and he experienced a guilty twist in his gut. Sleep often eluded him as he relived the moment he'd turned up at his father's cottage after fleeing the hotel.

Terrified by Roland's warning and half afraid that the police would arrive to arrest him at any moment, he'd panicked. Throwing a few things into a bag, he'd slipped undetected from the hotel and made his way cross-country in the pitch darkness, down to Motcombe, pounding frantically on his father's door until Ernest's startled face appeared at the window.

'Tom! Lad, what is it?' His father had ushered him inside, his face creased with concern. 'What's happened? Is it Emily?'

Tom shook his head. He was breathing so hard he could barely speak but eventually he'd managed to blurt out what had happened at the hotel. As the words spilled from his lips, he'd watched Ernest's expression change from disbelief to shock.

'Why would the girl make up something like that?'

Ernest shook his head in bewilderment.

'You don't believe me capable of such a thing, surely?' Tom had roared.

'Of course not. All I'm saying is perhaps you did something that she might have misconstrued . . . '

Tom had just stared at him in disbelief. That his own father could believe him capable of such behaviour both stunned and angered him. He couldn't sleep that night. The idea began to manifest in his tired, troubled mind that, if his father could believe Lucy's lies, perhaps Emily might too. Feeling sick to his stomach, he'd slipped out of bed and dressed quickly.

He had boarded a train heading north. From Manchester he'd hitched a lift to Liverpool in the back of a delivery truck, thinking he could find work on the docks. RMS *The Duchess of Atholl* was anchored in the harbour and, signing on as a steward, he'd worked his passage to Canada, his fear lessening with every nautical mile.

He'd been in the country for three months now, moving steadily west in his efforts to reach his uncle's farm. He'd travelled by train, ox-cart and on foot, working where he could to supplement his meagre savings.

His thoughts inevitably turned to Emily. He missed her so much it hurt. There hadn't been a second since he left England that he hadn't thought about her. Did she still work at the hotel, or had she taken up Roland Thurston's offer? As soon as he was settled at an address, he would write to Emily and let her know how she could reach him. He knew he should probably leave her be. With a criminal record, he would be nothing but a millstone around Emily's neck. But he couldn't let go of the hope that, someday, his name would be cleared and he could go home. Emily would wait for him, wouldn't she?

He was nearing the house now and he paused, sensing something was not right. Sunlight glinted off the windows. The barn door banged in the wind but otherwise the place was silent. A battered truck was parked in the yard close to the house. An empty washing line was strung between the barn and a small lean-to attached to the side of the two-storey farmhouse. Then the realization hit him. There were no cattle in the pens and the fields had been left fallow. Tom frowned as he walked slowly up the front steps to the wrap-around porch. Two wooden rocking chairs sat on either side of the screen door. He peered through the dusty window to the empty room beyond. Clearly the farm had been abandoned, but why? What had happened to his uncle?

He turned at the sound of an approaching vehicle. A car, black paintwork streaked with dust, was bumping along the track towards the farmhouse, a thin cloud of swirling yellow dust following in its wake. Tom descended the steps as the vehicle came to a halt in front of the house. The man who got out of the passenger seat was tall and thin with a handlebar moustache.

'Good afternoon,' he said, regarding Tom with surprise. 'Albert King.' He thrust out a hand.

'Tom Harding,' Tom said, shaking Albert's hand. 'I was hoping to see my uncle. This is his farm.'

'Ah.' Albert pursed his lips. 'You obviously haven't heard. I'm sorry to tell you that Mr March passed away some weeks back. I'm the solicitor handling his estate.'

'Uncle Joe has died?' Tom absorbed the news solemnly.

'I'm afraid so. He had been ill for some time.' Albert frowned. 'You didn't know?'

'No,' Tom said regretfully. He inhaled deeply and held out his hand. 'Well, thanks, Mr King. I guess I'll be on my way. Please pass on my condolences to my uncle's family.'

'I can give you their address,' Albert offered, giving Tom's hand a firm shake.

Tom shook his head. His cousins had been born after his aunt and uncle had immigrated. They were strangers to each other. 'No, that won't be necessary, thank you.'

'All right then. I can give you a lift back to town if you're happy to wait five minutes?'

'Thanks.' Tom nodded. He waited in the front passenger seat while Albert did a quick check around the house. At the end of the driveway, Albert left the engine idling while he unlocked the mailbox and skimmed the pile of mail that had accumulated since his last visit. Bills mostly, and another letter postmarked England. He slipped them into his jacket pocket and got back in the car.

'Right,' he said, pulling out into the empty road. 'Where can I drop you?'

'The bus station would be great,' Tom said, staring straight ahead at the long ribbon of tarmac shimmering in the haze of the afternoon sun. He wondered if his father had been informed of his brother-in-law's passing.

'So, you got any idea where you're headed?' Albert asked.

'Not yet,' Tom replied. Albert nodded.

164

'Well, it's a pretty big country,' he said, then commenced to regale Tom with the wonders Canada had to offer, as the car ate up the miles and the town appeared in the hazy distance.

Two days later, Tom found himself in Manitoba province, working as part of a crew on a large wheat farm some twenty miles east of Winnipeg. He wrote to Emily at once, care of the Mansfield House Hotel, and spent the next couple of weeks eagerly awaiting her reply.

Though the hours were long, he relished the hard work. His crew were good company and he enjoyed the friendly banter of the bunkhouse in the evenings but, as the weeks passed with no letter from Emily, he had to face the painful realization that she must have moved on without him. His old life began to seem like a dream, and one day, as he stood looking out over the undulating prairie, he realized he had stopped thinking of England as home. Even if he wanted to, he couldn't go back now. He'd burned his bridges, with his father and with Emily.

But, try as he might to push Emily out of his head, she haunted his dreams and filled his every waking thought. He withdrew into himself and the other men soon learned not to ask questions and respected his privacy. He wouldn't allow himself to get close to anyone. In an effort to exorcize the ghosts of his past he threw himself into his work, the more physical and exhausting the labour the better.

He lay on his narrow bunk at night, listening to the call of a nearby barn owl. It was late summer and the harvest would be coming to an end. It would soon be time for him to move on. He folded his arms behind his head, staring up at the dark ceiling, his mind filled with thoughts of Emily, and wondered what she was doing now.

23

Summer drifted into autumn and there was still no word from Tom. Emily's heartache was tempered only slightly by the news that Roland had secured her a fortnight's booking at Bristol's Hippodrome Theatre.

'Wow! This place is amazing,' she breathed in excitement as she walked out onto the stage one Monday morning in late September.

'I told you it was something else, didn't I?' Roland grinned at her as she took in the sheer beauty of the auditorium's architecture and design. Referencing the city's long history with the sea, the baroque decorations featured a nautical theme. There were two rows of three boxes each on either side of the grand circle, surrounded by Doric columns painted salmon pink and cream.

'And look at the ceiling,' exclaimed Emily. 'It's incredible.' Set in the roof above the stalls was an ornate dome decorated with water nymphs swimming in the sea.

'There's some mechanical device that allows the dome to open for ventilation,' Roland explained, coming to stand beside her. 'So, are you impressed?'

'It's so huge,' Emily said by way of reply.

'It has the capacity to seat nearly two thousand people.'

'So many?' Emily said breathlessly, the thought of performing in front of such a large audience at once both exhilarating and terrifying. 'Though I shan't probably have that huge an audience,' she said, modestly.

'Perhaps not the first few nights,' Roland agreed, 'but certainly by the second week you'll be packing them in. Your star is on the rise, Emily Rose.'

'Hello, Mr Thurston?' a voice said. 'Mildred Pearce.' A tall, boyish-looking woman perhaps a few years older than Emily emerged from the shadows. She wore a pair of men's trousers and a baggy dark green hand-knitted jumper. 'I'm one of the stage hands. Do excuse me.' She grinned, indicating the splashes of paint on her jumper. 'We're working on the scenery for our next production.' She turned to Emily. 'Welcome to the Hippodrome, Miss Rose. What do you think of our theatre?'

'I think it's amazing,' Emily said enthusiastically. 'I feel privileged to be able to perform here.'

'Right, come on. I'll show you to your dressing room. I'm afraid it's not half as glamourous below stage as it is on top.'

Emily smiled. After spending nigh on six months in various theatres, she was well accustomed to the cramped quarters that passed for dressing rooms.

'Mind how you go,' Mildred said, leading the way down the staircase and along a corridor. Snippets of conversation and bursts of laughter wafted from doorways as they passed, and the air smelled of cigarette smoke and hair oil.

'The cast are preparing for this afternoon's dress rehearsal,' Mildred said, stopping to pick up a silk stocking that had inadvertently found its way into the corridor. 'Someone will be looking for that later,' she muttered, stuffing it into her trouser pocket. 'This is where you'll be next week.' Mildred rapped loudly on one of the doors and pushed it open. The half-dozen young women in various stages of undress sitting at a long table in front of mirrors studded with bright lights turned to peer at the intruders through a haze of cigarette smoke.

'Oh, it's you, Mildred,' drawled one young lady with a pout.

'Sorry, ladies. I'm just showing Miss Rose around.'

'Hello.' Emily gave a shy wave.

'Hello, Miss Rose,' chorused the girls absently.

'We'll leave them to it,' Mildred said as she and Emily joined Roland in the corridor. 'Well, do you think you'll find your way around all right?' Mildred asked as she led them back upstairs to the foyer.

'She'll be fine,' Roland said. 'Won't you, Emily?'

'I'm sure I shall, Mildred. Thank you for your help.'

'You're welcome, Miss Rose, and remember, if you need anything just give me a shout.' She stuck out her hand. 'I look forward to seeing you next week.'

★ ★ ★

Emily waited nervously backstage. Her heart was thumping so loudly she was sure the audience would be able to hear it over the crash of the orchestra. 'You'll be absolutely brilliant,' Roland assured her, giving her a quick kiss on the cheek and looking very debonair in his black dinner jacket. 'And you look absolutely stunning,' he added, admiringly. Emily blushed beneath her make-up. She was wearing a new gown. It was emerald green and hugged her slender figure, the hem just brushing the tip of her sequined emerald shoes.

Beyond the curtains, the orchestra reached a crescendo, signalling that it was almost time for her

169

entrance. Emily clutched Tom's ring, hung around her neck on a chain, and took a few deep breaths to steady her nerves. Her tension was heightened by the knowledge that some of the people she cared about most in the world were seated in the audience. Nellie would be there, with Betty and Edward; Lulu and her new beau, Colin; Miss Anne; as well as Ernest who had travelled up by train that afternoon. Unfortunately, Molly, now with three children under five, couldn't come but she had sent Emily a card congratulating her on her success. Leah too had been unable to attend. Back from her transatlantic cruising, she was herself performing in a different venue. She'd promised to come the following night with Barbara, who, having returned from her north of England tour only that morning, had wanted an early night.

The orchestra fell silent to an explosive round of applause.

'Knock 'em dead, kid,' Roland hissed, as Emily walked onto the stage. Closing her eyes, she concentrated on her breathing while she waited for the applause to end and the curtain to rise.

'Ladies and gentlemen,' a voice boomed from above. 'Miss Emily Rose!' The heavy velvet curtains lifted to another round of thunderous applause, punctuated by whistles and catcalls. Emily gazed out over the darkened auditorium and smiled. With a little curtsey, she waited for her cue from the orchestra, and began to sing.

* * *

'You were absolutely amazing, girl,' Ernest said, tears of pride welling up in his eyes when Emily and Roland walked into the Pig 'n' Whistle half an hour after the performance. Emily hugged him warmly. He had aged in the six months since Tom had been gone, she noted sadly. There were more grey streaks in his hair and lines around his eyes that hadn't been there before.

'I wish our Tom could have been here.'

'You've still not heard anything?' Emily asked, with little hope. She knew full well that, had Ernest heard anything, he would have told her straight away.

'No, lass, not a word. I've written to my brother-in-law again, just in case.'

They were interrupted by Betty, who flung her arms around Emily and gave her a hug. 'You were brilliant, Emily. I'm so proud of you, my dear friend.'

'Thank you, Betty. Thank you, Edward.' She leaned forward to accept Edward's rather awkward peck on the cheek. 'I'm so pleased you both could come.' Emily hadn't seen her two friends since their wedding day back in August.

'I wouldn't have missed it for the world,' declared Betty. 'Edward, get Emily a drink, will you? Emily, what are you having?'

'I'll get the drinks,' Roland interjected quickly. 'Whatever everyone wants and damn the expense. This is a celebration, after all.'

The pub was packed and Emily was grateful that Roland had had the foresight to have booked the snug in advance. A warm fire crackled in the grate, giving off the pleasant aroma of burning pine cones.

'We're all so very proud of you, dear,' Miss Anne said, leaning forward to pat Emily's knee, pink from the warmth of the fire. 'Aren't we, Nellie?'

'We certainly are,' Nellie replied, without a hint of envy. Lulu and Colin offered their congratulations.

'Thank you.' Emily grinned. 'When do you start rehearsals, Lulu?'

'End of the week,' replied Lulu, with obvious relief. She had been out of work since returning from Weston-super-Mare but had recently secured a role in a pantomime at the Prince's Theatre. 'We open on the twenty-eighth of November and run for six weeks.'

'We'll definitely want tickets,' Nellie said, as Roland returned with the drinks. '*Aladdin* is one of my favourites.'

★ ★ ★

'Good morning,' Emily sang, coming downstairs two days later to find Nellie, still in her dressing gown, sitting at the breakfast table reading the newspaper. The sky was dark and rain battered the windowpane.

'Where's Miss Anne?' she asked, pouring herself a cup of tea.

'Gone to the shops,' Nellie said. Briefly scanning the article about a march of two hundred strong, that had originated in Jarrow and was now continuing towards London, she flicked to the entertainment section. 'Oh, hey, look at this,' she said, with obvious excitement.

'Bristol Songbird, Emily Rose, delivered another outstanding performance last night at the Bristol Hippodrome.' Wow! Emily, he's given you a five-star review. Well done,' she said, glancing at Emily across the table. 'Arnie Muirs is one of the toughest art critics about. This is definitely one for the scrapbook. I'd better pick up another copy on my way to work. Miss Anne's going to want one. Bless her, she keeps every word written about us.'

Emily smiled. 'She's such a dear.' She took the paper from Nellie and scanned the article with warm pleasure. 'Roland will be pleased.'

'And so he should be,' Nellie said drily. 'He's going to make a fortune out of you.'

★ ★ ★

'Have you seen this?' Roland said, without preamble, waving the newspaper in front of Emily when he arrived to pick her up twenty minutes later.

'I have,' she replied. 'It's a very good review. I'm very grateful to Mr Muirs.'

'Good?' Roland exclaimed with incredulity. 'It's absolutely bloody brilliant.'

Emily's smile didn't quite reach her eyes and he knew she was thinking of Tom, again. Why couldn't she just forget him? he thought with a flash of irritation. Thank God, he'd intercepted his letter. Forwarded on to him by the hotel, it had arrived back in the summer, the Canadian postmark a certain giveaway as to whom it was from. In all fairness to himself, he had wrestled with his conscience for some time before ripping it up, unopened, into tiny shreds and burying them deep in the wastepaper basket.

Now, as he ruminated on Emily's glowing review, he felt confident that, in light of her growing success, his behaviour had been completely justified. Emily knowing that Tom had tried to get in touch would only complicate matters.

'Bristol Songbird,' he mused, as he turned the key in the ignition. 'I like it. I like it a lot.' He pulled away from the kerb. 'I think that should be your stage

173

name from now on,' he said with a grin. 'Emily Rose, the Bristol Songbird.'

PART TWO

24

1942

A cold wind howled down College Street as Emily stepped out of the front door. All over the city, buildings were burning, clouds of black acrid smoke hanging like a pall in the clear January sky.

As an important harbour and shipyard, as well as being home to the Bristol Aeroplane Company, who supplied aircraft for the RAF, Bristol was a prime target for the Luftwaffe. Over the past fourteen months, Bristolians had suffered a pounding by German bombers. Between November 1940 and April 1941, over twelve thousand civilians had been killed and over a thousand more seriously injured in raids that had left much of the city centre in ruins. Much of Castle Street had been destroyed, including the Barley Mow Theatre and the Pig 'n' Whistle pub. Poor Willis the barman, who had been sheltering in the cellar below, had died of suffocation when the building collapsed. Hilda Wright's pie and mash restaurant, Gabriella's, a favourite of Emily and Roland's, had been bombed the previous January, along with the railway station. Thankfully, Hilda had been safely tucked away in her Anderson shelter and soon afterwards, she had evacuated to her brother's farm down in Devon.

The New Year had brought a fresh wave of terror. Almost every night, Emily's performance at the Palace Theatre was interrupted by the wail of the air raid siren. Huddled beneath the stage, Emily and her colleagues listened to the shriek and whine of the bombs raining down on the city.

She clutched her coat tighter around her as she hurried down the street, her gas mask slung over her shoulders. She didn't have to walk far to see the devastation caused by the months of raids. A group of children were playing amongst the rubble of a bombed-out church. A street along, a middle-aged woman in a headscarf and threadbare coat stood crying outside the blackened ruins of a house. She was being comforted by a younger woman with a solemn-faced toddler on her hip. Two slightly older children sat on the kerb, wrapped in blankets and sharing a slice of bread. The street was teeming with firemen and ARP wardens. Some of them recognized Emily and called a greeting as she passed, while the soles of her shoes crunched on broken glass and shattered masonry. Scattered across the road were reminders of the people who had lived here: a child's shoe; a framed wedding photograph, the glass cracked; a library book, its singed pages flapping in the wind. An old man sat amongst the rubble, crying unashamedly, one arm slung around a mongrel dog that was trying to lick his master's tears. A policeman stood over him, holding a mug of tea. Emily looked away, unable to bear the man's grief.

The WVS van was parked further down the street and Emily smiled as she caught sight of Nellie's dark head bent over the knee of a small boy of about five. She glanced up as Emily approached.

'Glad you could make it,' she said, raising an eyebrow.

'I'm sorry,' Emily said sheepishly. 'I forgot to set my alarm. Why didn't you wake me?'

'There you are,' Nellie said to the little boy, smearing

178

antiseptic ointment on his grazed knee. 'You'll be as right as rain in a day or so.' The child tilted his tear-stained face and grinned. He was missing his two front teeth. 'And stay off the bomb sites,' she called after him as he ran off to join his friends.

'Miss Anne knocked on your door just before she left for the shops. She told me you'd mumbled something about getting up in five minutes.'

'Oh golly, I must have dozed off again,' Emily said, blushing guiltily. She yawned. 'I was at the recording studio until really late last night. The air raid warning sounded, so Roland and I had to shelter in the studio basement. I only got home after the all-clear sounded. I hope I didn't wake you?'

'I slept like a log once I got back in my own bed,' Nellie said, turning to the huge tea urn in the back of the green van. 'Which is just as well, or I'd have been worried sick about you, out in that fire storm.' She unwrapped a pack of bacon. 'How did it go at the recording studio?'

'Good,' Emily said, reaching for the frying pan. 'Roland's pleased with the result. Sam does write lovely songs.'

Emily had met American songwriter Sam Arnold while touring the south of England during the spring of 1937. He had gate-crashed an after-show party given for her at the Pavilion Theatre in Bournemouth and introduced himself. He was a thirty-nine-year-old divorcee from Wisconsin and had been living in England for the past three months. He'd heard Emily sing, he said, and he wanted to write songs for her. Roland checked him out, liked what he found, and Sam had moved to Bristol the following month.

In August 1937, Emily had travelled to London

179

with Roland to perform her first radio broadcast. Six months later, on Valentine's Day 1938, she had released her first record, *On The Way Home*, which had enjoyed moderate success.

In 1940, she had recorded her first hit, 'Laying the Ghost'. Although Sam had written it as a way to exorcize the ghost of his ex-wife, for Emily the lyrics perfectly expressed her heartache over Tom.

It had been six years now since he had sailed to Canada, yet her heart refused to relinquish the faint hope that one day he might get in touch. A year after Tom had left, Ernest had received a letter from his late sister's son Bradley, informing him of his brother-in-law's death in January of 1936, two months before Tom had travelled to Canada. Ernest's letters had been enclosed.

Knowing Tom as she did, she knew it was inevitable he would have enlisted, and she worried constantly about his safety. She could only pray that he had put Ernest down as next of kin so that, should the worst happen, they would at least be informed.

The policeman she had seen comforting the old man and his dog appeared at the van's serving hatch. 'Can you get us a refill, love?' he said, handing over an empty mug. 'With plenty of sugar. It's for the old boy over there. Poor bloke.' Emily filled the mug from the urn. 'He only popped out to take the dog for a walk. Came home to find his house obliterated, and his wife 'as been killed.' He shook his head sadly. 'Fifty-three years they'd have been married this year,' he said. 'Thanks, love.' He took the mug of tea and carried it back to where the old man sat, his face buried in the matted fur of his dog.

'Tears your heart out, doesn't it?' Nellie said,

grabbing a loaf of bread and starting to slice it. 'Six houses gone in this street alone.' She sighed. 'The manager of Dempsey's Department Store dropped off a load of blankets this morning. Mrs Higham's taken them over to the emergency shelter in Frog Lane.'

'It makes you wonder just how much more we can take, doesn't it?' Emily said, staring out at the city skyline. Smoke billowed over the rooftops and she could make out the orange glow of the fires that still burned in the distance.

'We don't have a choice,' Nellie said, smearing the slices of bread with jam and piling them on a plate. 'Here you are, hand those round. Most of the firemen and ARP wardens have been working throughout the night. They must be ravenous.'

'I sometimes feel like I should be doing something more,' Emily said, stepping carefully down from the van with the tray bearing mugs of sweet tea and the plate of bread and jam. She opened her mouth to say something more but spotted two ARP wardens coming towards her, their faces black with soot, their eyes tired.

'Morning, boys, get that down you,' Emily said, as the men helped themselves to a mug of tea and a slice of bread. 'Bad night?'

'Houses hit all over the city,' one of them said, with his mouth full. 'Hundreds homeless, God knows how many killed and injured.'

'I'm getting on home after I've had this,' said the other. 'Just praying my house is still standing. A few hits looked pretty close.'

The two men wandered off, leaving Emily standing in the middle of the rubble-strewn street staring after

181

them.

She felt unable to explain to Nellie the restlessness in her soul. They had joined the Women's Voluntary Service soon after war was declared, both girls adamant that they wanted to do their bit. They had worked tirelessly and had seen suffering and horror the likes of which they wished never to experience again. Yet, just lately, Emily couldn't shake the feeling that she should be doing more. But what?

A fireman, his face streaked with white dust, accepted a mug of tea gratefully. 'Thanks, love,' he croaked. He pointed to where two women in WVS uniforms were talking to an elderly couple. The older woman held a baby in her arms. A wailing toddler clung to her skirt. 'They could all do with something to eat and drink. They've been out here since first light. The poor kiddies are practically blue with cold. Your colleagues are trying to persuade them to go to a shelter.'

'Thank you. I'll take this over right away.' Emily's brow furrowed. 'Oh, the poor woman. She looks distraught.'

'Her daughter and three older grandkids are still inside,' the fireman said sombrely. Emily followed his gaze. The house outside which they stood was an empty shell. Only the back wall and the staircase remained intact. 'The old couple and the two little ones spent the night in their Anderson shelter. Apparently the other kids suffer from claustrophobia so Mum stays with them in the house. They were sleeping under the kitchen table,' he added grimly.

Wearily, Emily picked her way across the street towards the little group. Firemen and civilian volunteers were searching through the wreckage in the vain hope of finding someone still alive. One of the volunteers, spotting Emily and her much-needed mugs of tea, gave her a cheerless wave.

'Oh, Emily, thank you,' said Carole, the older of Emily's two colleagues, leaving the group to come over to her. 'We've got a sad situation here. Three kiddies and their mum buried under all that lot. Dad's away fighting.' She sighed. 'We're trying to get the grandparents to go to the shelter before the kids freeze to death, but they're refusing to go.'

'Perhaps they'll have a cup of tea, at least,' said Emily, hopefully. 'The children must be hungry. Here.' She handed the other woman her tray. 'Take this and see if they'll have something. The volunteers must be in need of a break, as well? I'll run back to the van and see if I can scrounge a few blankets. We usually keep a few for emergencies.'

'Are you all right, Emily?' Nellie asked, when Emily returned to the van, blinking back tears of frustration.

'Oh, it's horrible, Nellie,' she replied, tearfully. 'A young mum and three of her children most probably dead, two little ones without a mum. It's too awful to think about.' She took a deep breath and scanned the inside of the van. 'Have we got any spare blankets? The little mites are freezing.'

'There are some in the cupboard under the tea urn,' Nellie said over her shoulder, as she served two civilians who'd spent the last few hours dragging survivors from under the rubble of their bombed-out homes. 'Here you go, love — two mugs of tea and a bacon butty.' She turned back to Emily, wiping her greasy hands on a tea towel. 'Did you find them?'

'Yes, thanks.' Emily stood up. 'I'll just take these over to those poor people. Hopefully they'll be persuaded to go to the shelter soon.' She hugged the blankets to her chest. 'Poor things. I feel so sorry for them.'

'It's so tragic,' Nellie agreed, coming to stand next to her friend. 'But when you come back, I want to talk to you about something. It's something I've been thinking about for a while, and what you said just now, about doing more? Well, I've had an idea.'

'What?' asked Emily, intrigued.

'Go deliver your blankets first,' Nellie urged her. 'Then we'll talk.'

★ ★ ★

'I've been thinking about joining ENSA,' Nellie said. They were sitting on the top step of the van, their gloved fingers wrapped around mugs of hot tea. It was perishingly cold. Carole and her colleague had finally, with the gentle coaxing of a kindly policeman, persuaded the old couple to take their grandchildren to the shelter. They had no sooner gone than a shout went up from one of the volunteers. An ARP warden had gone running with his first aid kit, but it had been four bodies that were carried out a short while later. Emily and Nellie had watched in grim silence as the covered stretchers were loaded into the waiting ambulance.

'ENSA?' repeated Emily. 'You're thinking of performing for the troops?'

'Yes. There was an article in *Woman* magazine this week. I think it would be a great thing to do. We'd be helping the war effort by entertaining our brave boys and we might even get to travel abroad.'

'It does sound exciting,' Emily admitted. 'I'll have to speak to Roland. I've got bookings for the next six weeks, at least.'

'We'll have to go to their headquarters in London to join up. Just think, Emily,' Nellie said, eyes gleaming. 'All those men.'

Emily laughed and nudged her friend's arm with her elbow. 'You're man-mad, Nellie Bedford. What happened to that Brian you were seeing? I thought you were keen on him?'

Nellie pulled a face. 'Too much of a mummy's boy,' she said with a dismissive wave of her hand.

'Well, what about Jerry? He seemed nice.'

'Oh, we still exchange letters, but he's stationed abroad now so it's unlikely I'll ever see him again.' She shivered. 'Just think, when we're with ENSA, we might be posted somewhere sunny and tropical.'

'Oh, I hope so,' said Emily, draining her mug and glancing up at the gulls wheeling overhead. 'I could do with some warmer weather. They're forecasting snow for this afternoon.'

★ ★ ★

The first flakes began to fall late that afternoon as Emily was leaving for the theatre. As always, Roland was waiting on the pavement to walk her to the bus stop. Roland had upgraded his car since Emily's career had taken off, but, with the rationing of petrol and the worrying rumours that soon petrol for private use would be banned altogether, his Ford Prefect spent more time locked away in the garage than on the road.

'The bombing was bad again last night,' Roland said. A mild heart condition had precluded him from enlisting so he was doing his bit as an auxiliary ambulance driver. 'I just heard that one of my colleagues was killed when part of a house collapsed on him,' he added, running his hand across his face.

'It's simply awful,' Emily agreed. In an attempt to banish the harrowing scenes she'd witnessed earlier in the day, she tucked her arm in his and said, 'There's something I want to discuss with you, but first, I've got some happier news to share. I had a letter from Betty waiting for me when I got home this afternoon. She gave birth to a little girl on New Year's Day, weighing eight pounds and ten ounces. She's called Olivia, after Betty's mum.'

The previous summer, Emily had travelled down to Dorset to spend a weekend with Betty and her two little boys, Eddie and Harry, aged four and two. Betty had been five months pregnant and fretting over Edward who had recently been posted to North Africa.

'Poor Edward,' Roland commiserated. 'Goodness knows when he'll get to meet his new daughter.'

'I know. It's such a shame. Betty's going to take the children to a photographer so at least he'll have a picture of them all.'

'So, what did you want to discuss?' Roland asked as they boarded the bus.

'Nellie wants to join ENSA,' Emily told him, as the bus wended its way through the devastated city. 'And I'm thinking of doing the same.'

'You can't!' Roland said, aghast. 'You've got a string of engagements. You can't let your fans down. Not at a time like this.'

'I wouldn't dream of letting them down,' Emily replied, slightly annoyed that Roland would jump to such a conclusion. 'I would honour all of my bookings, of course, but it's just that any future bookings will be done through ENSA. I think it would boost morale for the troops, both here and abroad.'

'There are thousands of performers in ENSA,' Roland told her, raising his eyebrows sceptically. 'It's not as glamorous as it's made out to be, you know. I've heard that some of the billets leave a lot to be desired.'

'Roland, people are sleeping on the floor in church halls! I'm not bothered about sleeping arrangements. I just want to do something to bring a little bit of pleasure to all those millions of men and boys so far from home.' As always, Tom was never far from her mind and she wondered if that was what had prompted her enthusiasm for Nellie's suggestion. If she could bring joy to servicemen and women far from home, it might go some way to rubbing salve on her aching heart, and if, maybe, there was a chance she might run into Tom . . .

25

'Well, I don't know,' said Roland, still unconvinced some twenty-odd minutes later as they got off the bus in Talbot Road. 'I'm not sure I'd like you being surrounded by thousands of men,' he teased. 'You might fall in love with one of them.'

'I doubt there's any chance of that,' Emily replied with a rueful smile as they approached the sweeping steps of the Jubilee Theatre. The theatre's brickwork was plastered with posters displaying the words 'EMILY ROSE, THE BRISTOL SONGBIRD' across an artist's impression of Emily in a silver, sequinned gown, one hand holding a microphone.

'And why's that?' Roland asked, holding open the door to the thickly carpeted foyer.

'I'm not sure I could ever feel about anyone else the way I feel about Tom,' Emily replied, removing her gloves and stuffing them in her coat pocket.

'It's been six years, Emily,' sighed Roland with more than a hint of irritation. 'You're too old to believe in fairy tales.'

'God knows I'm the last person to believe in fairy-tale endings,' Emily retorted, 'especially with the state the world is in right now. I know I'm probably being silly. I am being silly,' she amended. 'But I had such a strong feeling Tom and I were meant to be.' She paused, one hand resting on the stage door. 'You know?'

'You still love him,' said Roland quietly. He slid his left hand into his jacket pocket, his fingers closing over the small, velvet box he had been carrying around for the past three months, just waiting for the right moment.

'I don't think I'll ever stop,' Emily said, turning the door handle. A cold draught blew up the corridor and she shivered. Laughter and voices drifted from the dressing rooms, light spilling from doorways. She took a few steps and glanced back over her shoulder. 'Aren't you coming?' she asked, puzzled. Roland always sat with her in her dressing room, reading snippets from newspaper reviews and making her laugh with his silly jokes.

'No,' Roland said, a peculiar expression on his face. 'No, actually, I won't. I'll see you after the show.' He gave her a thin smile. 'Break a leg, sweetheart.' He blew her a kiss and was gone, leaving Emily staring at the door as it swung shut behind him.

★ ★ ★

Roland strode down the street, pulling up his collar as he went. It was snowing harder now, big white flakes settling on the frozen ground. Shoulders hunched against the cold, he turned the street corner and headed for the nearest pub.

He pushed open the door and was immediately enveloped in the welcoming fug of cigarette smoke, burning coal fire and stale beer.

As it was a weekday afternoon, the pub was relatively quiet. The handful of men seated at the bar twisted around when Roland blew in on a gust of swirling snow and icy air. They gave him a cordial nod, and returned to their conversation. Two young men in uniform occupied a table near the window.

'What can I get you?' the smiling, dark-haired barmaid asked him as he approached the bar.

'A whisky, please.' The barmaid raised her eyebrows but didn't comment as she reached for the bottle and poured a generous measure into a glass. Roland gulped it down in one, coughing and spluttering as the liquid scorched his throat. 'Another one, please,' he croaked.

Thin-lipped, the barmaid obliged. 'I'm not going to have any trouble from you, am I, love?' she asked, sternly.

'No, ma'am,' Roland said. He handed over his money and carried his drink to a small table in the corner. He slung his coat over the back of the spindle chair and sat down, staring morosely into the flames dancing in the grate and cursing himself for his foolishness in allowing himself to believe that he and Emily had a future together.

'For Heaven's sake,' he muttered under his breath. They were like a courting couple in almost every respect. They went out to the cinema together, dancing, dinner when Emily's busy schedule allowed. Several newspaper reporters had speculated over the possibility of a romance between them and no wonder. He had believed it himself. Fool that he was, he had even bought the ring.

He swallowed his drink down in one, and got up to get another.

★ ★ ★

The air raid siren sounded just as the curtain was coming down on Emily's performance. Pandemonium erupted in the auditorium as the audience surged for the exits. Losing precious minutes, Emily ran back to her dressing room to grab her coat. Her evening gown would offer little protection against the bitter January night.

'Emily!' She heard Roland's slurred shout above the frantic shrieks as she was swept along with the crowd spilling out into the snowy night. The snow was inches deep underfoot, soaking Emily's satin slippers instantly.

'Roland!' she shouted, scanning the dispersing crowd in the pale moonlight. In the distance, search-lights swept the night sky and from far away came the distinct drone of approaching aircraft.

'Emily!' Roland grabbed her arm. Shivering wildly, her toes turning numb, Emily stared at him in shock, taking in the bloodshot eyes, the askew tie and his general dishevelled appearance.

'Have you been drinking?' she asked with surprise. He gave a harsh laugh. The smell of spirits on his breath was all the confirmation she needed. 'Roland?' She frowned. 'Are you all right?'

'Sir, ma'am, for your own safety, you must get under shelter, now,' an ARP warden shouted.

'I'm not afraid of you, Hitler,' Roland bellowed, raising his fist to the sky.

'Ma'am,' the ARP warden said with a weary sigh. 'Get your husband under cover.'

'Ha, ha, I'm not her husband,' Roland slurred, almost falling as he stumbled on the kerb.

'Come on, Roland.' Confusion furrowing her brow, Emily managed to get Roland to the railway bridge where dozens of people were sheltering beneath its solid brickwork, most of them theatre goers unable to get home. They huddled together for warmth.

Emily found a space for herself and Roland. Roland seemed to have mislaid his coat and was shivering uncontrollably in his thin jacket. Emily wrapped her arms around him in an effort to share her body heat. Her frozen feet throbbed painfully. Somewhere in the darkness, a woman was quietly sobbing.

Emily started to sing the song that Vera Lynn had made so popular, 'There'll Always Be an England'. Softly at first, the words barely audible, her voice gained strength and people began to join in. Hesitantly, then their voices growing louder until the archway reverberated with song. Emily worked her way through her repertoire of well-loved songs until they were drowned out by the drone of aircraft overhead and the bombs and incendiaries raining down over the city. Several times they fell close enough to dislodge some of the bridge's brickwork, eliciting shrieks of terror from those sheltering beneath it as they were covered in showers of dust and falling debris.

She felt as though her chest was in a vice, her fear was so acute. She could hear the wail of sirens as ambulances and fire engines raced through burning streets. The acrid smell of smoke singed her senses as she huddled against Roland. Listening to his drunken snores, she almost envied him his oblivion.

After four hours of almost constant bombardment, the bombs finally fell silent. They sat in stunned silence, listening to the dwindling drone of departing aircraft. Roland was awake now, his head lolling against Emily's shoulder as they waited for the all-clear. Emily had lost all feeling in her hands and feet and tried to console herself with the knowledge that with the all-clear would come the WVS vans with hot tea and blankets. She thought of Nellie, Miss

Anne, Lulu, Leah and Barbara, and prayed that they were safe. There would be no way of knowing which streets had been hit until daylight revealed the night's destruction.

'I'm sorry, Emily,' Roland mumbled, groaning as he adjusted his position. His joints were stiff with cold, and his head pounded painfully. He vowed then and there that he would never drink spirits again.

'I've never seen you drunk before,' Emily said, her voice low. 'Is everything all right? Roland?' she said, when she received no response. Roland let out a long, shuddering sigh.

'I've got a confession to make,' he said, his voice barely audible in the near-darkness. The fires raging in the surrounding streets provided just enough light to make out the faint outline of those closest to her.

Despite her discomfort, Emily smiled. 'What did you do?' she whispered, wondering what drunken antics he'd got up to the previous evening.

'It's about Tom,' he said softly.

'Tom?' Emily exclaimed in surprise.

'Shush!' someone hissed irritably. Now that the danger had mostly passed, a few people were trying to doze. Emily lowered her voice.

'What are you talking about?' she asked with a puzzled frown.

'It's my fault he left,' Roland blurted out. Emily stared at him in disbelief. In the faint glow of the flames, she could see the shame written across his face.

'What are you talking about?' she asked in bewilderment.

'I persuaded him to go,' Roland muttered miserably. 'I knew you had a wonderful career ahead of you and he would only hold you back. I told him you'd be better off without him. That the accusations against him, whether true or not, would blight any career you might have.' Roland's shoulders slumped. His reasoning sounded lame even to his own ears. How could Emily ever forgive him?

'I don't believe you,' Emily whispered, staring at him with incomprehension.

'And that's not the worst of it,' Roland said, unable to meet her eyes. 'There was a letter.' He cleared his throat. 'The hotel forwarded it on to me.'

'A letter?' Emily said hoarsely. 'From Tom? When? Where is it?' she demanded in confusion, her heart quickening.

'I . . . I threw it away.'

'What? Why? What did he say?' Emily asked, fleetingly wondering if Roland had destroyed her letter out of some misguided desire to protect her.

'I didn't open it,' he replied bleakly. 'Things were going so well for us, I . . . I didn't want to complicate things. I'm so sorry.'

'How dare you?' Emily spat bitterly. 'How dare you? I thought you were my friend.'

'I am your friend,' Roland insisted.

'A friend wouldn't deliberately destroy my one chance of happiness!'

'I'm sorry, Emily,' he said again. 'I swear, there's not a day gone by that I haven't regretted my actions. Emily, wait!' he cried, as she got stiffly to her feet. Her toes were so numb, she almost stumbled, and her cramped leg muscles screamed in agony. She regained her balance and turned to look at him.

'I shall never forgive you,' she said coldly.

'Emily, please.' Roland struggled to his feet, grabbing her wrist. 'I'm sorry.'

'Leave me alone.' She brushed his hand away and turned, making her way clumsily between the huddled groups of bemused onlookers.

'Emily, wait!' Roland shouted, going after her. 'Don't be stupid. They haven't sounded the all-clear yet. Emily!'

Choking back tears of rage, she ran down deserted streets where fires raged, lighting up the sky for miles around. She could hear Roland shouting after her but she ignored him. The snowy streets were littered with smouldering debris and broken glass. A water pipe had burst, sending gallons of water gushing across the road. Sirens echoed across the ravaged city.

★ ★ ★

The all-clear sounded just as she staggered up College Street over an hour later. Exhausted, soaked through and frozen to the bone, she let herself in the front door just as Nellie was coming in the back, having spent the duration of the raid in the Anderson shelter in the yard.

'Oh my God! Emily!' Nellie gasped, taking in the bleak expression, the filthy, ruined dress, the satin slippers that were now little more than rags. 'What's happened?'

'Roland!' Emily choked as she stood shivering in the hallway.

'Oh my God!' Nellie's hand flew to her mouth. 'Is he . . . dead?'

Emily stared at her with incomprehension. 'What? No, no, he . . . he . . . ' Unable to continue, she burst into tears.

'Oh, come here.' Nellie gathered Emily into her arms. 'Good grief, girl, you're frozen. Come on, let's get you upstairs and into the bath.'

The landing light flicked on and Miss Anne appeared at the top of the stairs in her dressing gown. 'Is everything all right?' she called down anxiously.

'I'm not sure,' Nellie replied, helping Emily up the stairs. 'Emily's had some sort of shock and she's frozen stiff. I'm going to run her a bath.'

'There might not be much hot water,' Miss Anne warned. 'I'll boil a couple of kettles and then I'll make us some cocoa. It was a bad one tonight,' she added, worriedly. 'Are the girls in the shelter?'

'Yes,' Nellie replied as they passed on the stairs. 'Lulu's on duty tonight but Leah and Barbara were asleep by the time the all-clear went.'

In the steam-filled bathroom a short while later, Emily rolled up her ruined gown and tossed it in the corner. The soles of her feet were scratched and bleeding and throbbed painfully as they began to thaw. She lowered her aching body gingerly into the hot lavender-scented water — Miss Anne had insisted she use some of her soothing bath salts — her face red and swollen from crying. Nellie perched on the lid of the toilet.

'What's happened? Is Roland hurt?'

Emily shook her head and scowled. Her skin was turning pink in the hot water and her fingers and toes tingled painfully, but, according to Miss Anne, that was a good sign. It meant she didn't have frostbite.

The door opened and Miss Anne entered with three mugs of steaming cocoa. She handed one each to Nellie and Emily and leaned against the sink, cradling her own mug in her hands.

'Roland told me that he's the reason Tom left,' Emily said bitterly. 'He persuaded him to go because he thought that with Tom out of the way, there'd be nothing to stop me having a career. He ruined my life and I'll never forgive him,' she said through gritted teeth. 'Never.'

At that moment the doorbell rang. Miss Anne frowned. 'Who on earth can it be at this time?'

'It'll be Roland,' Emily spat angrily. 'Tell him to go away.'

'I'll tell him you need a bit of time,' Miss Anne said. 'You've had a shock and you're understandably angry. I'll tell him to call back in a day or two, shall I?'

'No,' Emily snapped. 'I don't want to see him again. I'll fulfil my obligations over the next six weeks but then I want nothing more to do with him. I want out of my contract.'

'You don't mean that, Emily!' Miss Anne said in dismay.

'Yes, I do,' insisted Emily, as the doorbell chimed again.

'I'd better go and answer it,' Nellie said, 'before he wakes the neighbours.'

'I doubt they're asleep anyway,' Miss Anne said sorrowfully, taking a sip of her cocoa. 'Mavis got a telegram this evening. Her eldest boy's ship was torpedoed and poor Graham was killed. He only turned nineteen in November, poor love.'

'That's so sad,' Emily said, forgetting her own misery for a moment to think of the smiling young lad next door. He'd been a boy of thirteen when Emily had first moved into the house. Usually out playing football with his mates or off on his bike, he'd always been willing to run errands for the girls in number sixty-one. He'd started courting in the months before he joined the navy; a pretty young thing called Jenny, Emily recalled. She pulled a face, imagining the poor girl's devastation on leaning of her boyfriend's death.

'If this damn war has taught me anything, Emily love,' Miss Anne said as they heard the front door close, followed by the sound of footsteps ascending the stairs, 'it's that life's too short to bear grudges. Roland did a terrible thing and you've every right to be angry, but try and find it in your heart to forgive him.'

'I shan't get over it,' Emily said as Nellie came back into the bathroom. Emily gave her a questioning look.

'He's full of remorse,' Nellie said. 'The poor chap was practically in tears. It's all right,' she added as Emily shot her a dirty look. 'I sent him away. Told him to wait a few days until you feel like talking to him.'

'Nellie!' Emily cried. 'I don't want to talk to him. Not now, not ever. You don't understand. Tom and I were getting married. If it wasn't for Roland's interference, Tom would have been there when Lucy recanted her story and we'd have been married a few weeks later.'

'What's done is done,' Miss Anne said, handing Emily a clean towel. 'Now come on, you two need to get to bed. You'll have to be up in a couple of hours.' She ushered Nellie from the room and left Emily to fume alone.

★ ★ ★

A large bouquet of flowers was delivered the following day. Leah, bounding down the stairs to answer the doorbell, could barely see the delivery man for the size of the arrangement.

'Emily,' she called. 'They're for you.'

'Who're they from?' Emily asked, emerging from the kitchen to stand in the passageway.

'I don't know. The envelope's sealed.' Leah handed them over. 'See you all later. Stay safe, ladies.'

The front door banged shut as Emily slit open the envelope. She read the card with a snort of disgust, marched into the kitchen and dumped the bouquet in the dustbin.

'That's what I think of Roland's apology,' she said tartly in reply to Miss Anne's raised eyebrows. 'If you see him,' she said over her shoulder to Nellie, seated by the kitchen fire shining her shoes, 'tell him not to bother sending any more flowers. He'll just be wasting his money.'

★   ★   ★

For the next five days, Roland called at the house on College Street every afternoon as Emily was about to leave for the theatre. Studiously ignoring his pleas, Emily carried on as if he wasn't there. When he turned up at the WVS station, she got one of the ARP wardens to send him packing. On the day she finally opened the front door and he wasn't there, she tried to rejoice that he had finally given up, but for some reason she couldn't fathom, it felt a hollow victory.

26

The small Morris van splashed down the waterlogged track. Squashed in the front seat between Nellie and the driver, a Welsh singer named Dave, Emily surveyed the drab landscape through a curtain of rain. The horizon was an indistinguishable blur in the distance.

In the back of the van, where the doors were tied together with rope to allow for ventilation, were the two other members of the small touring company: Bill, a comedian in his early forties; and Nik, a twenty-six-year-old tap dancer and second-generation Greek immigrant. They were resting against the kitbags on either side of a small piano.

They had been on the road for over two hours, travelling from Northamptonshire to an army base on the moors in Derbyshire, the weather growing progressively worse with every mile.

Emily had lost count of the number of military bases she had performed at over the past ten weeks since joining the Entertainments National Service Association — ENSA — in early February. She had been released from her bookings in Bristol a month early after the theatre in which she was due to appear took a direct hit. Three days after completing her run at the Jubilee Theatre, Emily and the girls had travelled up to London to the ENSA headquarters at Drury Lane. Lulu was currently part of a dance troupe touring the military camps along the east coast while Leah and Barbara were based somewhere in the southwest.

Miss Anne had happened to bump into Roland whilst queueing outside the butcher's shop and reported that he looked a shadow of his former self. Apparently, he had asked after Emily, and had given Miss Anne a sad smile when she'd told him Emily was touring the north with a company of ENSA entertainers. The landlady had ended her letter by passing on Roland's fondest regards, which had left Emily feeling unsettled for the rest of the day.

The truth was — and she hated to admit it, even to herself — she missed Roland's company. He had been more than her agent; he had been one of her dearest friends, and she felt bereft without him. But his actions had destroyed her chance of happiness with Tom, and for that she would never forgive him.

'The turning shouldn't be too far now,' Nellie said, peering through the windscreen at the road ahead. They were flanked on either side by steep, rocky hills, dotted with grazing sheep. 'See, we're here.' She ran a crimson fingernail along the Ordinance Survey map, tracing the route. 'So, according to this, we need to take the next left.'

'There, that's it,' Emily said, pointing to a signpost. Dave braked sharply and made the turn. They jolted along uncomfortably as Dave steered the van up the slippery track. The wooden barracks were visible through the sagging barbed-wire fence, a variety of military vehicles parked in the foreground. A company of soldiers in khaki-green combat trousers and T-shirts jogged past, many of them letting out loud wolf-whistles as they caught sight of Emily and Nellie through the van windows.

They waved back, smiling. Dave wound down the window.

'Excuse me. We're from ENSA.'

'Park over by the officer's mess,' the sergeant major shouted. 'They're expecting you.'

Dave thanked him and wound up the window. He turned off track, the van bouncing and rocking across the rough grass to park as close to the officer's mess as possible. A face appeared at the window and, seconds later, the door opened, a young soldier — Emily wouldn't put him any older than eighteen — running down the wooden steps and unfurling an umbrella.

'Good afternoon, ma'am, ma'am, sir,' he said, opening the door and saluting the occupants. 'Private Harry Ryall. I'm to escort you to your accommodation. Would you care to follow me?'

'There's two more of us in the back,' Dave said, leaning forward to peer around the two girls, 'and a piano.'

'Someone will be over to collect the piano, sir,' young Ryall replied. Nellie got out of the van and Emily followed. They huddled under Private Ryall's umbrella while he ushered them up the steps into the mess, leaving Dave, Bill and Nik to follow.

The officers' mess was warm and dry, and nests of shabby armchairs and small card tables were set about the room. Against one wall was a shelf crammed with battered paperback novels and out-of-date periodicals. A window looked into an office where two girls in military uniform were clicking away at typewriters.

'Can I offer you any refreshments?' Private Harry asked as the three men trooped through the door, shaking rainwater from their clothes.

'Tea would be lovely, ta,' said Dave, rubbing his hands together.

The others all agreed and Harry disappeared off

through another door.

'I hope we're not sleeping in tents again,' Nik grumbled as the rain drummed on the tin roof.

'Me too,' agreed Dave, flopping down on one of the chairs. He was in his early thirties, with dark hair and a beard. He'd been invalided out of the army the previous year after an accident had left his right leg noticeably shorter than the left. He wore a specially adapted shoe now and his limp was barely noticeable. 'I shall be glad to get home at the end of the week,' he added, stifling a yawn.

'So will I,' said Nellie, taking one of the other chairs. 'I can't wait to sleep in my own bed and have a proper bath.'

'Oh, don't, Nellie,' Emily groaned. 'I long for a nice, long soak with some of Miss Anne's bath salts.'

'Luxury.' Nellie smiled and glanced over at Nik. 'What about you, Nikolaos? Will you be glad to get home?'

'I will be happy to eat my mother's cooking again,' Nik replied with a grin as the door opened and Harry came in with the tea.

★ ★ ★

Some twenty minutes later, Emily and Nellie were standing in the middle of what could only be described as a shed. A cold draught blew in through the cracks in the walls and the single pane of glass rattled noisily in its frame. And the roof leaked, as evidenced by the inch of rainwater in the bucket standing in the centre of the room.

There were two camp beds, one against either wall. Each held a pillow, two army-issue blankets piled up at the end, and two metal buckets, one for washing and one to use as a toilet.

'Oh well,' Emily said philosophically. 'We've slept in worse.'

'Thank God it's only two nights,' Nellie agreed, sitting down on the camp bed. 'I don't think my back could cope with much more.'

'Is it really hurting?' Emily asked with sympathy.

'It's bearable. I'll take some more aspirin before we go onstage.'

'Take some now,' Emily advised, taking her dress out of her kitbag and hanging it on the back of the door to get rid of the creases. She laid her hat on the bed and took off her jacket, flexing her shoulders. 'It's certainly not all glamour and glitz, is it?' she laughed.

'Ha, no!' Nellie gave a wry smile. 'And then there's Lulu staying in three-star hotels every night. Where did we go wrong?'

'Never mind. As you say, it's only two nights.'

'Well, I shall insist on a hotel room on our next tour,' Nellie said, leaning back on her hands. Then, 'Do you think Nik fancies me?'

'Of course he does,' Emily said. She dipped her flannel in the water bucket and wiped her face and neck, wincing as the cold water touched her skin.

'Why hasn't he said anything, then?' Nellie pouted.

'Because he's obviously worried about hurting Dave's feelings.'

'Dave and I were over weeks ago,' Nellie protested. Emily raised a quizzical eyebrow.

'I don't think Dave's properly over you yet, Nellie. I've seen the way he watches you. He's still besotted.'

'I made it quite clear at the time I wasn't looking for anything long-term or serious. We had a bit of fun and it's over.'

'People can't just turn off their feelings on a whim,' Emily said. Her tone was slightly sharper than she'd intended. She loved Nellie like a sister, but she didn't always approve of her somewhat callous approach to romance. 'One day, you're going to fall really hard for someone, and I only hope they don't break your heart.'

'I may well break my heart over Nik,' Nellie said with a pout. 'We've only got two nights before we go back home. After that I may never see him again.'

'I'm sure you'll cope,' Emily said drily, rummaging in her bag for her make-up. 'We won't be back in Bristol a day and you'll have forgotten all about him.'

She propped her mirror on the windowsill, and began to apply her make-up. 'At least we've got a proper stage tonight,' she said, squeezing foundation onto her fingers and rubbing it onto her face. 'One of the requisitioned buildings is the old community hall. That nice private said the amateur dramatic society used to perform there.'

'That's a relief,' Nellie said, grimacing as she massaged the base of her spine. She'd hurt her back during a fall when a makeshift stage had partially collapsed three nights earlier. 'Now, do you want to start with the duets tonight, or finish with them?'

27

'Will you marry me, Miss Rose?' The soldier with the boyish face and red hair smiled cheekily as he stowed Emily's kitbag into the back of the van.

'I'm not the marrying kind, sweetheart,' Emily said, straightening the jacket of her ENSA uniform as she came down the steps.

'May I write to you then?' he persisted, his green eyes gazing at her with adoration.

'Of course you may.' Emily gave him the address of the ENSA headquarters in London. 'They'll forward any letters on to me,' she assured him.

'Come on, Nellie,' Dave called impatiently, shooting a sour glare over to where Nellie was signing photographs surrounded by a group of love-struck squaddies. They had a three-hour drive ahead of them, and they were already leaving later than planned.

The two shows at the camp had gone down a storm. Emily and Nellie had been called back for encore after encore the night before. It had been gone midnight before either girl got off the stage.

To Nellie's unbridled delight, Nik had finally plucked up the courage on their final evening on tour to declare his feelings for her and the two had slunk off into the night. Emily had been woken by the sound of Nellie sneaking back into the hut just before dawn, declaring in a loud stage whisper that she had finally fallen in love, before slipping under the rough blankets and falling soundly asleep. She'd overslept, which had delayed their departure, though

Dave's annoyance was, Emily was certain, fuelled by jealousy rather than his desire to be on the road.

'Miss Rose, Miss Rose!' A surge of soldiers enveloped her, waving black-and-white photographs of herself. Aware that Dave was drumming his fingers on the roof of the van in growing irritation, she scribbled her name as fast as she could. She was pleased to see that Nik, Dave and Bill were signing a few too.

They'd had their photographs taken at a studio in Bristol before leaving for the tour. At first, Emily had been amazed that strangers would want a picture of her, but as the tour progressed, she became aware of how important she and others like her were to the morale of the servicemen and women. Life in the camps could be boring and monotonous and any entertainment was welcome. She had soon discovered that photographs of the performers could become a comfort to the young men who treasured them, especially for those who had no wives or sweethearts waiting for them back home.

So, no matter how time-consuming, she never begrudged the time she spent signing autographs, or engaging in conversation with a homesick serviceman.

★ ★ ★

Ten minutes later they were finally on their way. The sky was clear and it was a perfect April day. But for the barrage balloons drifting over Birmingham in the distance, it was almost possible to forget that a war was raging. Fluffy white clouds chased each other across the sky, casting swiftly moving shadows on the hillsides. Driving down lanes flanked by drystone walls, flocks of bleating sheep and frolicking lambs dotting the landscape, it was the perfect late-spring morning.

They spoke little on the journey. The past few weeks of early-morning starts and late-night finishes had taken their toll. Combined with hours on the road and the trauma of learning of the deaths of young men and boys who had been singing along to well-loved hits such as 'The White Cliffs of Dover' only the night before, they were all feeling fatigued.

It was almost late morning by the time the barrage balloons hovering over Bristol's forever altered sky-line came into view. From the plumes of rising smoke, it was clear that the city had taken another pounding during the night and Emily sent up a quick prayer for Miss Anne's safety. Emily worried constantly over her landlady, especially given her aversion to using the Anderson shelter, and it was with huge relief as they turned the corner to find that College Street remained unscathed.

'Goodbye, girls,' Dave said, pulling up alongside the kerb. 'It's been a pleasure working with you.'

'You too, Dave,' Emily said. 'Stay safe.'

Nik had untied the back doors and was unloading the kitbags. Emily said goodbye to him and Bill and, leaving Nellie and Nik to say their fond goodbyes, she shouldered her bag. She was about to climb the front steps when the door flew open and Miss Anne stood on the threshold, her face ashen.

'Oh, Emily,' she said, her voice quivering with shock. 'It's Roland. He's in hospital.' Tears filled her eyes. 'They don't think he'll make it.'

★ ★ ★

Dave dropped her outside the Bristol Royal Infirmary and she ran up the front steps. There were people everywhere; the walking wounded with makeshift bandages, bloodied and white-faced with shock as nurses tried to assess those in most urgent need of attention. Somewhere a child was screaming. Several women sat about on chairs, solemn-faced babies and toddlers clutched to their chest. One teenage girl, in obvious pain, sat slumped on the floor, cradling her right arm.

'Excuse me,' Emily said, pushing her way through the crowds to the information desk. 'I'm looking for someone.'

'So are a lot of people, love.' The nurse, a woman in her late forties, didn't even look up from the notes in her hand. 'It's chaos in here today. Take a seat and someone will get to you as soon as they can.'

'It's urgent,' Emily said, her voice breaking. 'Please, I think he may be dying.'

The woman looked up. Her tired eyes flickered with recognition. 'Aren't you the Bristol Songbird?'

Emily nodded. 'Please, if you can just tell me where he is?'

'It's not visiting hour yet,' the nurse said, looking pointedly at the clock above the door. But then she sighed. 'I don't suppose it matters. Who is it you're looking for?'

'Roland Thurston.'

'When was he brought in?'

'This morning,' Emily replied. From Miss Anne's hurried explanation, she'd learned that Roland had been driving his ambulance to the hospital when the street had been hit by an incendiary bomb. His patient, an elderly woman, had been killed instantly,

209

as had his co-driver. Roland himself had suffered terrible burns to a large part of his body.

'These are today's intake,' the nurse said, scanning her list. Emily was aware that the crowd of anxious, desperate people behind her was growing by the second. They pressed against her, crushing her against the desk.

'Here we are,' the nurse said finally, and Emily let out a sigh of relief. 'He's in Orchid ward, love. Out those doors, down the corridor, then up the stairs and take the first left.'

'Thank you so much.' Emily pushed her way through the doors and raced down a corridor lined with patients on stretchers awaiting beds.

She flew up the stairs and finally arrived at the ward. Pausing for a moment to catch her breath, she pushed open the door. Immediately she was hit by the sickly-sweet stench of charred flesh. Most of the beds in the ward had the curtains drawn. 'May I help you?' A nurse seated at a small desk rose to her feet. 'I'm the ward sister, Nurse Swann.'

'I'm here to see Mr Thurston,' Emily stammered nervously, her heart hammering.

'It's not visiting time yet,' Nurse Swann replied sternly. 'But as you're here, I suppose I can make an exception. I must warn you,' she added as she led Emily between the rows of beds, her rubber-soled shoes squeaking rhythmically on the shiny linoleum, 'he's a very poorly man. He's suffered burns to fifty per cent of his body and he's unconscious, so he won't know you're here.'

She paused halfway down the ward and took hold of a curtain. 'Are you ready?' Barely able to speak, her mouth was so dry, Emily nodded and Nurse Swann drew it back.

For a moment all Emily could do was stare in horror at the mummified figure on the bed. Roland's arms, legs and torso were thickly swathed in white bandages. A bandage covered the right side of his head but, to her immense relief, his actual face appeared unharmed.

'He's luckier than most in here,' murmured Nurse Swann softly as Emily approached the bed. 'Some of these poor boys . . . well, even their own mothers wouldn't know them.'

'Hello, Roland,' Emily said, laying her hand tentatively on his bare shoulder. 'Can he hear me?' she asked the sister.

'Whether or not he can hear you, I think it does patients the world of good to have someone chat to them. Many of these poor lads are far from home and don't have visitors. My nurses try to spend as much time with them as time allows but, as you can imagine,' Nurse Swann said, 'they're all extremely busy. Perhaps you might like to read to him.' She nodded at a rather dog-eared copy of Robinson Crusoe. 'Sometimes it's easier than making small talk with someone who is unable to respond.'

'Thank you. Yes, I will.' Emily drew the single wooden chair closer to the bed and picked up the book.

'I'll bring you a cup of tea,' Nurse Swann said, slipping through the curtain. Emily listened to the squeak of her shoes mingling with the grunts and moans emanating from beyond the blue curtain.

'Oh, Roland,' Emily whispered, her eyes filling with tears. 'I'm so sorry.' She watched his face, willing him to make some sign that he knew she was there, but he remained motionless. Only the gentle rise and fall of his chest and his ragged breathing gave any sign that he was alive at all.

She opened the book and tried to read but the words blurred as her tears fell, splashing on the page.

'Here's your cup of tea, dear.' Nurse Swann pushed the curtain aside. 'Oh, now, come on, dear. Dry those eyes. Your Mr Thurston doesn't want you to be all sad and melancholy. It'll take some time, but he will be all right.' She set the tea on the bedside cabinet and gave Emily's shoulder an awkward pat. 'The heat scorched his throat and lungs, which is why his breathing sounds so laboured, but the doctor is satisfied there's no lasting damage. There'll be some scar tissue on his body of course but, thanks to the quick action of the ARP boys on duty who doused the flames, his burns aren't as serious as they might have been.' She gave Emily an encouraging smile. 'Keep your chin up, dear.'

'Thank you.' Emily managed a weak smile. She wiped her eyes and blew her nose. She was grateful he hadn't been killed. She would have felt awful if she'd been robbed of the opportunity to make amends. She was still angry with him for what he'd done to Tom, and perhaps she always would be, but like Miss Anne had said, if war taught a person anything at all, it was that life is too short to hold grudges.

28

Roland regained consciousness five days later. When Emily arrived at the hospital in the afternoon, his curtains were drawn back and he was sitting propped up against his pillows. Unable to turn his head much, he blinked in surprise at the sight of Emily standing at the foot of his bed, her face wreathed in smiles.

'Emily!'

'I hardly dared believe it when they said you were awake,' she said, taking off her hat and sitting down. 'How are you feeling?'

'You were here before .....' Roland croaked, frowning. 'I thought I was dreaming.'

'I've visited every day this week,' Emily assured him.

'You were reading ..... something .....' He was interrupted by a fit of coughing that left him gasping for breath. Emily held a glass of water to his lips and he took a tentative sip. 'Thank you,' he said once he'd regained his breath.

'It was *Robinson Crusoe.*' Emily smiled at him fondly. She reached out to take his hand, realized her mistake and patted his shoulder instead.

Roland's face clouded. 'Why did you come?'

'Oh, Roland,' Emily sighed. 'You were – are – one of my dearest friends. I know I was angry, and I still am, but I can't blame you alone. Tom should never have run away in the first place, whatever you said to persuade him, and it breaks my heart to say it, but if he really loved me, he would have written again.

213

He should have realized I didn't receive his letter and written to his father instead.'

'I'm so ashamed, Emily,' Roland wheezed.

Emily held up her hand. 'It's all right. You don't have to say anything. Save your strength for getting better.'

Roland shook his head. 'No, please, let me speak ..... I was so blinded by the thought of our success that I didn't even stop to consider your happiness.' He coughed again. 'Once we became friends, I knew I could never tell you what really happened between Tom and me. He asked me to tell you he loved you and that he would come back for you. I'm sorry I kept that from you too.'

Emily absorbed Roland's words in silence as a nurse wheeled a metal trolley down the ward. The patient in the bed next to Roland's was sobbing quietly.

'Poor Jim.' Roland's gaze flickered sideways. 'They took his bandages off this morning. He's only twenty-one.'

'Poor man,' Emily murmured. She pulled the chair nearer the bed and sighed. 'So why tell me now, after all this time?'

Roland cleared his throat. 'I don't want to keep anything from you anymore. Why did I feel the urge to confess in the first place? To be honest, I don't really know. I think the drink had something to do with it but .....' He sighed heavily. 'Emily, you must know I'm in love with you. I know you don't feel the same, and that's all right. I've finally accepted that you'll never feel the same way about me. I wanted to clear my conscience I suppose.'

'And do you feel better for it?' Emily asked, a slight bitter edge to her words.

214

'No,' Roland admitted, shame faced. 'The truth is, I hate myself for hurting the one person in the world that I care most deeply about and, believe me, if I could go back and undo what I did, I would, without a moment's hesitation.' He coughed again, a harsh hacking sound that brought the nurse hurrying over to make sure he was all right.

'Not too long, miss,' she said to Emily. 'We don't want to tire him out.'

'I won't stay much longer,' Emily said. 'But I will be back tomorrow,' she assured Roland as she got up to leave a few minutes later.

'If I knew how to find Tom, I would,' he said, his eyes pleading.

'If he wanted me to know where he was,' Emily said sadly. 'There's no excuse. He could have written to his father.' She gave Roland a wry smile. 'It's time I accepted the fact that God, fate, the universe, whatever, had different plans for Tom and me.' She leaned over and kissed his forehead. 'Get some rest now. I'll be back tomorrow.'

★ ★ ★

Emily visited Roland every day, staying no longer than an hour as he tired quickly. It would be some weeks before his bandages could come off, but he seemed in good spirits.

The raids over Bristol appeared to have stopped for the time being, and as spring turned to summer, the city breathed a collective sigh of relief in the hope that, just possibly, they were over the worst.

After six weeks in hospital, Roland's bandages were removed. He had suffered severe scarring to his arms, legs and back, but his doctor was confident that they would fade significantly over time. He was also left with a bald patch of scar tissue on the right side of his head and was partially deaf after losing an ear.

The doctor's main concern was the state of Roland's lungs, and he suggested he convalesce on the coast in the hope that the fresh sea air would aid his full recovery. So, at the end of May, Roland left Bristol for the Dorset seaside town of Lyme Regis.

Throughout the summer, Emily and Nellie toured the hospitals in Bristol and Bath, performing for wounded servicemen. On occasion, they were joined by Dave, which involved engaging the services of a couple of hospital porters to carry his small piano up and down the many stairs.

Emily still found it rather surreal to hear her songs playing on the wireless. The BBC Overseas Service was broadcasting her voice across the globe and she couldn't help wondering if Tom was listening or, indeed, if he ever thought of her.

One warm day in August, Betty and the children came up on the train. Emily met them at Temple Meads Station.

'Gosh, you've had such a dreadful time of it,' Betty said. With one arm wrapped around her wriggling baby daughter, she flung the other around Emily and hugged her. 'I knew it was bad but I couldn't grasp the scale of the devastation until I saw it with my own eyes.'

'It's been hard,' Emily said, smiling down at the two little boys. 'Hello, Eddie. Hello, Harry. Are you going to give your Auntie Emily a hug?'

The boys, aged five and three respectively, nodded shyly. Emily crouched down and held out her arms.

Glancing at their mother, who nodded, they moved into Emily's embrace. 'My, how you've both grown since last summer,' she said, kissing their rosy cheeks. 'And as for you, Miss Olivia Grace .....' She stood up, and held out her arms to the little girl squirming in Betty's arms. 'Aren't you just gorgeous.'

'She's almost seven months now,' Betty said, handing over her daughter gratefully. 'She's an angel but she does get heavy.'

'Have you heard from Roland?' Betty asked as they made their way out into the summer sunshine.

'He's doing well,' Emily said, jiggling Olivia on her hip. 'He sends his regards.'

Holding her sons by the hand, Betty looked around at the bomb-damaged street. 'Oh, Emily,' she sighed. 'It's awful, isn't it? Yeovil was bombed again two weeks ago. A thousand homes were hit.' She shook her head.

'We saw a dog fight,' Eddie told Emily, his face glowing with excitement. 'The planes flew right over our house.'

'One crashed in the field behind our house,' Harry added, animatedly. 'There was lots of smoke.'

Emily met Betty's gaze over Olivia's head.

'The pilot and crew survived,' Betty said. 'They were taken to a POW camp somewhere. It was the talk of the town for a while.'

'Horrific thing for the boys to witness, though,' Emily said, her voice low. 'Have you heard from Edward lately?'

'His letters are weeks out of date by the time I receive them,' replied Betty brightly, though her smile trembled slightly. 'The last one was dated July. He sounds cheerful enough, though I'm sure that's for our benefit. It can't be much fun over there, what with the heat and the flies.'

Emily took them to a small café down a narrow side street, which had, miraculously, survived the bomb blast that had destroyed much of the surrounding area.

'How's Nellie?' Betty asked once they were seated and the waitress had brought the tea and glasses of milk for the boys. 'Is she still seeing that Greek fellow?'

'Nik? Yes. He's a lovely chap.' Emily blew on the surface of her tea to cool it. 'And Nellie seems smitten.'

'Good for her. Eddie, stop blowing bubbles. It's rude. And what about you? Isn't it time you found someone?'

'I'm far too busy,' Emily said with a smile as Olivia beamed at her across the table.

'All those army camps and air bases?' Betty raised an eyebrow. 'Come on, Emily, you spend most of your life surrounded by hundreds of eligible men.'

'Whom I shall never see again, once they get shipped out,' Emily reminded her with a wry grin.

'Well, we've got Americans stationed over near Sturminster Newton now. They're very popular at the dances, what with most of the local lads away fighting. And with the kids,' she added as Eddie piped up:

'They gave us chocolate, Mum, didn't they?'

'They did, indeed,' Betty said drily. 'We were visiting Edward's sister when they arrived. Such a noise, and all these huge green lorries taking up all the road. Everyone came out and lined the streets, cheering and waving and the soldiers were waving back and blowing kisses, and throwing chocolate bars and chewing gum to the children. It was like a carnival.'

'It was fun, wasn't it, Mum?' Eddie said, his little pink tongue licking the milk from his upper lip. 'I wish we could go to Aunt Chrissy's and see the 'Yanks' again.'

'I want to see the "Yanks" again too,' Harry said.

'Drink your milk,' Betty told them both. Olivia had fallen asleep in her arms, and Betty adjusted her position to relieve the pressure on her arm. She gave Emily a mischievous grin. 'I heard some gossip about our old enemy Lucy Hunt the other week,' she said.

'Lucy?' Emily said, her dislike of the girl making her scowl. 'Is she back in Shaftesbury?'

'No,' Betty replied, leaning forward and lowering her voice slightly. 'I bumped into Miss Thompson. Oh, did I mention in my letters that the Mansfield Hotel has been requisitioned as a convalescent home for wounded soldiers?'

Emily nodded. 'Yes, you did.'

'I thought I had. Anyway.' Betty took a sip of her tea and set the cup in its saucer. 'As I said, I bumped into Miss Thompson. She's an ARP warden now in Yeovil but she was in Shaftesbury visiting her mother. Her brother-in-law is in military intelligence based in London. Their work's all very hush-hush, but apparently, he let slip to Miss Thompson's sister that the chap he's working with is married to none other than our Lucy Hunt.'

'Oh,' said Emily bitterly. 'Good for her.'

'Well, not exactly.' Betty grinned. She glanced at the two boys who were growing restless and kicking each other under the table. 'Boys, you may go and sit in the window seat and read your comics.' Eddie and Harry slid off their chairs and scampered over to the window seat, which was bathed in mid-morning sunlight. 'Now,' Betty continued once she was sure her sons were doing as they were told, 'according to Miss Thompson's sister, Lucy's husband keeps her stuck down in Devon while he's living the high life in London.'

'There is a war on,' Emily said. 'He can hardly pop home to the country every weekend, especially if he's with the intelligence service.'

'Well, yes, that's true but ...' Betty lowered her voice even further. 'He keeps a mistress. He's out every evening wining and dining her, by all accounts. Doesn't care who knows.'

'Do you think Lucy knows?' Emily asked, aghast. Much as she despised Lucy, she was appalled that a husband could treat his wife so callously.

'Miss Thompson believes she does.'

'Poor Lucy,' Emily said, but with little sympathy, as she refreshed their cups.

'If you ask me,' Betty said, with a wicked grin, 'it serves her bloody well right.'

★ ★ ★

Emily saw Betty and the three children off on the four-fifteen train. Feeling slightly deflated by her friend's absence, she decided to take a stroll along the harbourside. The port was a hive of activity and heavily guarded, the surrounding buildings fortified with coils of barbed wire and sandbags. Despite the heavy security and evidence of bomb damage, the harbourside was bustling with couples, mostly servicemen and their sweethearts making the most of their precious time together.

Emily bought herself a bag of chips and went to

220

stand as close to the harbour edge as the strict security precautions allowed, the aroma of chip fat, salt and vinegar mingling with the briny sea air. The late afternoon sun danced on the water and gulls wheeled noisily overhead.

Betty's news about Lucy had unsettled her, opening up old wounds. But, much as her anger against Lucy was never far from the surface, it was nothing compared to the pain she felt at Tom's abandonment. The fact that he had never tried to contact her in six years was an agony she could never assuage. And her heart ached for poor Ernest. He was in his early sixties now and not in good health. She couldn't understand how the Tom she had known and loved could be so unfeeling as to not get in touch. She shook her head. It made no sense.

★　★　★

By the time Emily got home, it was getting on for six o'clock. She let herself in to find Nellie and Miss Anne in the kitchen.

'This came in the second post,' Nellie said, handing Emily an official-looking sheet of paper. 'ENSA are sending us on tour. Our first performance is on Saturday in Portsmouth.'

'We're to travel down on Thursday,' Emily read out loud, 'to make allowances for any delays on the lines. We're touring all around the south-east.'

'Promise me you'll be careful,' Miss Anne implored them, anxiously, wringing her hands. 'Portsmouth's a prime target for Hitler's bombs.'

'We will,' Emily promised, unable to contain her own excitement. She wondered what her father, a man who'd barely set foot outside of Dorset, would have made of her traipsing up and down the country. The thought of his amazement made her smile. 'I'd better write to Roland and let him know,' she said, heading for the stairs. 'I'll write to Ernest, Molly and Betty too. And then' – she grinned at Nellie – 'we'd better crack on with our packing.'

29

1943

Tom sipped his pint and looked out across the cold English Channel. The smell of diesel oil hung on the salty breeze that ruffled the sun-dappled grey-green waves, and the crying of the gulls mingled with the steady throb of engines.

Being back on English soil had brought painful memories of the past flooding back and the temptation to try to get in touch with Emily had been almost overpowering. He cast his mind back to the newspaper headline that had caught his eye just before he boarded his ship in Canada:

BRISTOL SONGBIRD PERFORMS FOR US TROOPS AT BROADLAND
Emily Rose tours South-East for second time to entertain Allied troops

Reeling with the knowledge that she would be travelling around the south-east at the same time as him had caused him to wonder if the fates might, at last, be working in his favour. If he could just see her and explain . . . but he pushed the thought aside angrily. In all the photographs he had seen of Emily, she looked happy. And he still had the threat of a criminal record hanging over him. No matter how much it hurt to admit it, she was better off with Roland.

It didn't stop him constantly searching the crowds

wherever he went in the hope of catching a glimpse of her face, he thought ruefully, inhaling a lungful of briny air. He flexed his shoulders. His skin was tanned and he had the weathered complexion of someone who spent much of his time working out of doors. He had spent his first three years in Canada as an itinerant farm labourer, finding work wherever he could. When Canada declared war on Germany in September 1939, a week after Britain, he'd joined the Royal Canadian Air Force. During his time working on various farms, he'd grown quite fluent in the French language, and so, when a request came down the line for a competent French speaker to apply for a special mission overseas, his squadron leader had put Tom's name forward.

A week earlier, on a bitterly cold early spring day, with no idea yet as to what this mysterious mission entailed, Tom and his team of five had set sail for Liverpool, where they had immediately boarded a train for Southampton. And so here he was, sitting on a bench outside the Nelson Arms pub awaiting transport for the next leg of his journey. He'd hoped the mellowing effect of the ale would go some way to assuaging his guilt for not contacting his father. He loved him, but time had done little to allay his deep-seated bitter. ness at his father's unspoken but obvious condemnation six years earlier, and now Tom's stubborn pride would not allow him to attempt a reconciliation.

A trio of young women in ENSA uniform hurried across the street towards him and his heart quickened, Emily, as always, never far from his thoughts. They smiled at him as they bundled past into the pub. Tom swallowed a mouthful of beer, and wiped froth from his upper lip with the back of his hand. He had hoped the pain of her loss might have eased as the years went by, but, if anything, the passage of time had only intensified his longing for her.

He allowed himself a bitter smile, squinting against the light bouncing off the water. Thurston had certainly been proved right in his predictions. Emily had hit the big time. Her songs were frequently played on Canadian radio. The first time he'd seen her photograph in the newspaper, he'd been blown away by how glamorous she looked. So many times over the years he'd thought of writing to her again but the sight of her standing arm in arm with Roland, her smiling face tilted towards his, had confirmed his suspicion that she had moved on. They inhabited different worlds now. It was too late, for both of them.

From his breast pocket, he withdrew a crumpled photograph. One of Emily's publicity shots, it showed her in full ENSA uniform, posing in front of a plain background. He had found it fluttering under a bench at the station by the docks, presumably left behind in error by some fortunate young lad lucky enough to be heading home on leave. It wasn't signed so Tom hoped whoever had lost it wouldn't be too disappointed. After all, he could always write to ENSA HQ for a replacement.

'Hey, Tom.' He looked up as his friend and co-pilot Rich Drummond emerged from the pub carrying two foam-crested pints of beer. 'You okay?' Rich frowned, noting his friend's bleak expression. 'You thinking about that girl again?' he asked, sloshing beer as he sat down beside him.

The youngest son of a wheat farmer from McLennan in Alberta Province, twenty-four years old, Rich was five years younger than Tom. They had met during their basic training, hit it off immediately and had been friends ever since. Tom knew instinctively that if ever he were to come under enemy fire, there was no one he'd want at his side more than Rich Drummond.

'I'm all right,' Tom said, arranging his features into the semblance of a smile.

'I came to tell you the lads are getting up a game of darts. Do you fancy it?'

'Sure,' Tom said, getting up. Anything to put thoughts of Emily out of his head, he mused silently, shoving her picture deep into his breast pocket. 'Come on,' he said to Rich with a grin. 'Let's go show those guys a thing or two.'

* * *

Two hours later Tom, Rich and their crew were in the back of a truck being driven through the New Forest. They sat in relative silence for the forty-minute journey down leafy lanes and across open heathland to the village of Beaulieu. There, the truck turned into the gravel driveway of a large Victorian country house. Several Jeeps and a smart car were parked in front of the old stone building. The front door opened and a young soldier came hurrying down the broad steps.

'Good evening, gentlemen,' he said, nodding at the young driver. 'Major Chadwick is waiting for you in his study.'

Massaging his cramped calf muscles, Tom and the others followed the young solider into the hallway. Despite having been requisitioned by the military for some time, the entrance hall still retained much of its charm. Framed portraits hung on the duck-egg blue walls and a majestic chandelier hung from the ceiling.

A wide staircase swept up to a galleried landing, along which two uniformed soldiers walked with purpose, disappearing out of view around a wide stone column.

'This way please, gentlemen.' The soldier led Tom and his men to a nearby door and rapped on it loudly.

'Come,' said a voice. 'Ah, Captain Harding, good evening,' the major said, getting up and moving around his wide, teak-veneered desk as Tom stepped into the tastefully furnished study. 'Welcome.'

Major James Chadwick was a large man, clean-shaven with thinning dark hair and blue eyes. He shook Tom's hand and welcomed the others. His manner was brisk and businesslike as he invited them to sit down and ordered tea to be brought.

'Now, gentlemen,' he said, once they had dispensed with the small talk and the tea had been poured. 'You may wonder what this special mission entails.'

'Yes, sir,' Tom replied, leaning forward.

'I've been informed that all five of you are fluent speakers of French?' The men nodded and the major continued. 'This mission involves you passing your-selves off as French citizens in enemy-occupied towns and discovering as much as you can of their plans.'

'Will there be any sabotage involved, sir?' asked Rich.

Major Chadwick shook his head. 'Your role is to gather intelligence, which will be passed on to mem-bers of the Resistance. They'll take care of the rest.'

Rich leaned back in his chair and folded his arms across his chest, looking disgruntled.

The major went on to explain the finer details of the mission before inviting them for dinner in the officer's mess.

It was late in the evening by the time a solider led

Tom and Rich up the grand staircase and along the galleried landing lined with paintings of long-dead aristocrats to their room. He flung open a door at the furthest end of the landing and stood aside to allow the two men to enter.

The room was tastefully furnished in light green and cream, though the army's occupation had taken its toll on the delicate fixtures and fittings. Tom dumped his kitbag on the stained pale green carpet and looked around in appreciation. Compared to barracks and the cramped ship's cabin, this was luxury indeed.

'The lads are all very jealous about you getting this room,' the young soldier, Jackson, informed them with a grin. 'Emily Rose and Nellie Bedford were billeted in here when they visited Beaulieu just last week.'

'You all right, Tom?' Rich asked with as Jackson left the room, closing the door quietly behind him. 'You've gone all funny-looking.'

Tom managed to grunt something unintelligible as his brain tried to comprehend that Emily had been in this very room only a week before. He hadn't told Rich much about his past and, respecting his privacy, Rich had never pressed him. He'd certainly be surprised to learn that the old girlfriend Tom still carried a torch for was none other than the so-called Bristol Songbird, Emily Rose.

'It's all that brandy you drank at dinner,' Rich went on, oblivious to his friend's inner turmoil. 'You never could hold your drink.' He stripped off his uniform and climbed under the covers.

Tom followed suit and Rich blew out the light. Tom lay on his back in the all-consuming darkness, staring up at the ceiling. Emily had slept in this very room, perhaps in this very bed. He sniffed the pillow, inhaling the clean smell of soap powder, and chided himself for his foolishness. It would be several weeks before he would be smuggled over to France and Emily's tour was due to continue for some weeks yet. Perhaps he might cross paths with her after all. With that thought going around his head, he finally fell asleep and dreamed of Emily in her red dress singing in the dining room of the Mansfield House Hotel.

30

Emily shivered as the lorry bounced along the rough track. In the distance, she could just make out Dover Castle in the thin early morning mist.

It was early May, eight weeks since Emily, Nellie, Nik and Dave had embarked on their second tour of the south-east. Along with new recruit Samuel, a jazz musician from New York, they had toured field hospitals and army camps over several counties. They had sung to the sound of distant shelling and artillery fire.

The lorry rumbled up a steep track lined with derelict barns and empty animal pens. As the road levelled out, Emily could see fields of olive-green canvas tents and military vehicles, tanks, Jeeps, lorries and trucks, most of them draped in camouflage nets.

As the lorry lurched across the rough terrain, soldiers streamed towards them, waving and laughing. By now Emily and Nellie had grown used to the adoration of their legions of fans and waved through the dust-smeared windscreen, smiling.

The young soldier, Jack, who had been assigned as their driver, brought the lorry to a halt and the excited troops surged forward, many of them waving photographs of the two women.

'Hello, boys,' Nellie sang, alighting from the cab with a smile. Emily clambered out behind her, smoothing down the skirt of her olive-green ENSA uniform.

The three other soldiers, who travelled as their escort, jumped out of the tarpaulin-covered lorry bed, rifles in hand. They were followed by Dave, Nik and

230

Samuel, who looked very dapper in his snappy black suit.

'We need some muscles to get the equipment out, chaps,' one of the young soldiers yelled into the crowd. At once, about twelve eager volunteers stepped forward.

While the willing soldiers unloaded the equipment, the performers were kept busy signing autographs. Samuel unfastened his saxophone case and blew a few notes, to the delight of the crowd.

'Good morning, ladies and gentlemen.' The crowd parted slightly at the approach of a young, fair-haired officer. He smiled warmly and held out his hand. 'Welcome to camp. I'm Second Lieutenant Higham. It's a pleasure to meet you, Miss Bedford, Miss Rose.' He smiled as he shook Emily's hand. 'If you'd like to follow me, I'll show you to your quarters. My men will bring your kitbags.'

Dew sparkled on tussocks of grass sprouting on uneven ground churned up by heavy vehicles and a thousand footprints. The troupe followed Second Lieutenant Higham past the mess tent and a huge field hospital, military ambulances parked haphazardly outside, to where two large tents had been set up close to a makeshift stage.

'I'll leave you to get settled,' Second Lieutenant Higham said with a quick salute. Thanking him, Emily and Nellie ducked beneath the canvas flap and surveyed their surroundings.

'Well, as accommodation goes, we've experienced worse,' Emily said. They had slept in rat-infested barns, bombed-out churches, derelict farmhouses, leaky tents and, for five memorable nights, in a stately home, so the small tent with its twin camp beds was more than adequate.

'As long as it's waterproof, I'll be happy,' Nellie said, perching on the edge of a camp bed and rubbing the small of her back. She'd suffered recurring backache ever since her fall the previous year, but it had been exacerbated by her pregnancy. She was almost three months gone now but, so far, only Emily and Nik were aware of her condition. She had tearfully confided in Emily six weeks earlier when a camp doctor had confirmed her worst fears, and it had taken her another two weeks to pluck up the courage to tell Nik. To her relief, Nik had been ecstatic at the news and proposed to Nellie there and then. He was adamant that they should marry as soon as their tour ended. His mother, he told Nellie after reading her latest letter, was over the moon at the prospect of becoming a grandmother. Nellie wasn't quite so sure how her own parents would react on discovering that their only daughter had got herself in the family way, but she wasn't planning on telling them until after the wedding, hoping that Nik making an honest woman of her would go some way to softening the blow.

Three eager-faced young privates arrived with their luggage, and Nellie and Emily spent the next few hours chatting to the troops before their evening performance.

They were invited to eat supper in the officer's mess and Emily was inordinately pleased to find herself seated beside Second Lieutenant Higham. Some of the officers holding court around the table came over as pompous and opinionated, but Second Lieutenant Higham proved to be good company: polite and full of amusing anecdotes about camp life.

'I have all your albums, Miss Rose,' he said, blushing in a boyish way that Emily found quite endearing.

'Please, call me Emily,' she said, as the camp cook brought in the main course of pork and vegetable stew.

'Then, please, you must call me Kit,' Second Lieutenant Higham said.

'Nice to meet you, Kit,' Emily said. To her dismay, her attention was then claimed by the ruddy-faced major seated on her other side, who proceeded to bore her with a long-winded account of his army career.

★　★　★

Their first performance went down a storm; both Emily and Nellie were called back for several encores and it was gone midnight by the time they returned to their tent.

'Oh, I'm exhausted,' Nellie groaned, collapsing onto her camp bed.

'That Second Lieutenant Kit Higham seems nice,' Emily mused, wiping away the greasepaint by lamplight.

'Emily Rose Baker!' Nellie exclaimed, sitting up, her eyebrows arched in surprise. 'Have you finally met a man you're actually interested in?'

Emily blushed. 'I just think he's nice, that's all. There's no need to read anything into it. We're only here for three days and then I'll likely never see him again.'

'Er, you can write, you know? Millions of love affairs are being conducted by post across the world right now.'

'He's a bit posh,' Emily said. 'He's not going to be interested in me.'

'He certainly seemed so at supper,' Nellie said. 'He

was hanging on to every word you said, until that pompous bullfrog of a major butted in. I didn't bother to say anything earlier, given your usual aversion to relationships, but he's definitely interested.'

Emily smiled as the tiny flicker of something she hadn't felt in a long time ignited in the pit of her stomach. Had she finally met someone who might help her to lay Tom's ghost to rest? She shook her head at her foolishness. She would be at the camp for only two more days; certainly not enough time to build a relationship and she wasn't one for a quick fling. She carefully hung up her uniform and changed into her pyjamas, slipping under the covers as Nellie extinguished the lamp.

'Goodnight.' Nellie's voice cut through the inky darkness.

'Goodnight, Nellie,' Emily murmured sleepily. 'Sleep well.'

* * *

'Good morning, Miss Rose,' Kit said with a grin, falling into step with Emily as she crossed the dew-soaked field to make use of the camp's rudimentary toilet facilities.

Emily smiled. 'Good morning, Second Lieutenant.'

'It's Kit, please,' he reminded her. 'I just wanted to say how much I enjoyed the show last night. The lads have been in a state of excitement ever since we heard that you were coming.'

'That's nice to hear,' she said as two nurses emerged from the wooden hut that housed the women's wash-room. They smiled warmly and wished Emily and Kit a good morning.

'I wondered,' Kit said, hesitantly. 'I've a couple of hours free this morning. Would you care to take a walk? There's a pretty stream just beyond that copse.' He pointed to a clump of trees at the far end of the field. Plumes of smoke rose in the distance and the morning breeze carried the sound of distant shelling. He cleared his throat, nervously. 'May I call for you in half an hour?'

'Thank you, yes. I'll be ready,' promised Emily, trying to quell the rising tide of excitement. It wouldn't do to get her hopes up. It was a walk, nothing more.

'Nonsense!' Nellie scoffed when she voiced the thought to her friend twenty minutes later. Nellie was sat on her camp bed towelling dry her long hair. 'He fancies you. For goodness' sake, Emily, we're at war. The normal rules of courtship don't apply. You have to grab whatever bit of happiness you can. No one knows how long we've got. Every day is a gift. Look at poor Bill. Dead of a heart attack at forty-two. You go for it, girl. You've been faithful to Tom for years. It's time you started living. Grasp this chance with both hands — that's what I say.'

Shaking her head in amusement, Emily did however take a little more care with her appearance than usual. Kit was waiting outside her tent when she emerged ten minutes later, straightening her beret. Her ensigns gleamed in the sunlight and her polished shoes shone.

'Shall we?' Kit said, extending his arm to point the way.

Carefully, they made their way over the rough ground. Emily caught her foot on a loose clod and Kit had to grab her arm to prevent her from stumbling.

'Thank you,' she said, her stomach flipping as she

met his gaze.

Kit cleared his throat, breaking the spell.

'Come on, it's not much further,' he said.

They slipped and slithered down a steep bank. Through the trees, Emily could see the reflection of sunlight on water.

'It's lovely here,' she said, as they emerged through the small copse to the water's edge. The stream tumbled musically over sun-bleached pebbles. Dragonflies skimmed the surface, iridescent in the sunshine. Spreading their jackets on the damp grass, they sat down, legs stretched out in front of them.

'It's a nice place,' Emily said as a kingfisher came to perch on an overhanging branch.

'I come here when I want to be alone,' Kit said. 'Commanding thousands of soldiers can be exhausting.'

'You're very young to be an officer, aren't you?' Emily asked curiously.

'I'm twenty-nine,' replied Kit, somewhat indignantly. 'But you're right. I was fast-tracked. My father pulled a few strings. I got quite a lot of stick from the lads at first but I think I've finally earned their respect. I'm not afraid to get my hands dirty and when we're posted to Italy, I'll be in the thick of it right alongside them. I've made some good mates.'

'I think friendships made during wartime are very strong,' Emily said. 'Nellie's as close as a sister to me.' She closed her eyes, tilting her face to the sun, contemplating the time in the not-too-distant future when she would have to continue on tour without her dear friend. She pushed the thought aside and shuddered.

'Are you all right?' Kit asked with concern.

'I think someone just walked over my grave,' Emily said.

The shadows dwindled as the sun climbed ever higher. For the time being the guns had fallen silent, and the birds began to sing in the branches above their heads.

Kit told her that he lived in Hampshire and would, one day, inherit the title of Viscount.

'Viscount?' Emily raised an eyebrow. 'I am impressed.'

'Oh, my family has titles aplenty,' Kit said with an unselfconscious grin. 'As well as a crumbling manor house outside Cheriton. Unfortunately, they have very little in the way of money.'

'Well, I'm just a simple farmhand's daughter from Dorset,' Emily said wryly.

'I think you're wonderful,' said Kit in earnest.

'Thank you,' Emily said, blushing.

Kit took a deep breath. 'May I write to you?'

'Of course,' Emily replied with a flood of pleasure that surprised her. 'If you write to me care of the ENSA headquarters in Drury Lane they'll forward it on to me.'

Kit's face fell. 'You must get fan mail by the sack load.'

'I do get a lot,' Emily said. 'But I will be very happy to hear from you.'

They sat in companionable silence for a while, listening to the birdsong and the babble of the brook. As she felt the sun's warmth on her face and listened to the gentle breeze whispering through the meadow grass, it was almost possible to imagine that the war was merely a horrible nightmare from which she had only recently awoken. But all too soon, the tranquillity was, once again, shattered by the sound of distant explosions.

'I'd better be getting back to camp,' Kit said, getting up reluctantly and offering Emily his hand.

'Thank you,' she said, as he hauled her to her feet. 'So must I. We're going round the hospital this afternoon, singing to the men who are too badly injured to make it to the shows.'

They walked slowly, both wishing to delay the moment of parting as long as possible.

'May I see you again later?' Kit asked as they neared the edge of the camp. 'After tonight's show?'

Emily smiled broadly. 'Yes, I'd like that.'

31

It was late by the time Emily met Kit around the back of the makeshift stage.

'Seven encores,' he said with a grin, his teeth very white in the moonlight. 'Impressive.'

'They were a very appreciative audience,' Emily croaked ruefully, massaging her aching throat.

'Insatiable,' Kit amended. 'Not that I blame them. Entertainment's been a bit thin on the ground out here. A man gets fed up playing cards every night and there's precious little else to do. I think I've read every book in the camp at least twice.'

Walking close together, but not touching, they made their way to the perimeter of the camp. Behind them, they could hear the sounds of men retiring to bed. A joke cracked, a guffaw of laughter, an exclamation of anger, a muffled curse as someone stumbled over a guy rope.

Kit took off his jacket and laid it on the damp ground for them to sit on. The night air was cool on Emily's face as she gazed up at the vast star-studded sky. There had been no bombing raids for some time and, for now, the anti-aircraft guns along the coast were silent.

Emily found Kit so easy to talk to and felt as though she'd known him for months, not barely forty-eight hours. He told her about his childhood. The eldest of two brothers, with parents who took a somewhat detached approach to childrearing, he and his brother William had been raised by a succession of nannies until they were old enough to be sent off to boarding school.

'I heard from Mother that Will's out in North Africa somewhere,' Kit said.

'Are you close?' Emily asked, thinking she detected a note of regret in his words.

'As children we were,' he said. 'But we drifted apart once I went off to school. I was seven years old and very homesick.' He smiled ruefully. 'I cried myself to sleep every night that first week, so I'm afraid I gained a reputation as a bit of a cissy.'

'That's very young to be away from one's mother,' Emily said, her heart aching for the lonely little boy he had been. 'I was that age when my mother died.'

'I'm so sorry to hear that,' Kit said, taking her hand. Emily swallowed and looked away. 'But, sadly,' he continued, 'it wasn't Mother or Father I missed. It was my nanny. Nanny Pat had been with us the longest and she was more of a mother to me and Will than our own. Of course, once Will joined me at school the following year, Nanny Pat was dismissed and I never saw her again.'

Emily told him about Betty and her children, Roland, and her friends back in Bristol. She didn't mention Tom. His was a memory she wasn't yet ready to share with this young, attractive man who made her pulse race and set her heart pounding. How was it possible she could feel so attracted to someone she barely knew? Yet she knew Kit felt the same. She could see it in his eyes when he looked at her.

In the pale glow of the moon, Kit took hold of Emily's hand, sending a shiver up her arm. With his other hand, he gently tilted her chin so she was gazing directly into his eyes. Then he kissed her. Softly at first, then harder, fuelled by an urgency as their time together was short.

Emily couldn't help but compare his kiss to Tom's. It was different, but nice, she thought as they pulled apart.

'You're so beautiful, Emily,' Kit gasped, his voice hoarse as he struggled to regain control over his desire. 'When this madness is over, I will come to Bristol and woo you properly with dinner and roses.'

Emily laughed. 'I shall look forward to that.'

With Emily's departure looming, they stayed up talking and kissing all night, watching as the sky lightened in the east.

'You'd better get back to your tent,' Kit said with obvious reluctance. 'I'd hate to be the cause of your reputation being tarnished.'

It was on the tip of Emily's tongue to say to heck with her reputation, but they were both distracted by the scream of the air raid siren from the nearby towns of Dover and Folkstone, followed by the almost imperceptible drone of approaching aircraft. At once, Kit was on his feet, scanning the dark sky.

'Get back to camp,' he hissed urgently. 'Get your friends and get under cover. All hell's going to break loose.' Kissing Emily hard on the mouth, he pushed her roughly towards the camp and began to run, screaming orders as the men erupted into action.

Soldiers were running in all directions, and Emily ran as fast as she could over the rough ground. She almost collided with Nellie emerging sleepily from the hut.

'What's happening?' Nellie grabbed Emily's arms.

'Planes,' Emily gasped, her chest burning as she fought to catch her breath. 'Get under cover. I'm going to wake the boys.'

'Nik!' Nellie screamed as Nik stumbled sleepily out of his tent, pulling on his shirt. Nellie ran to him, flinging her arms around his neck. Dave and Samuel emerged, still wearing their pyjamas. They surveyed the chaos in bewilderment.

'Get undercover,' Emily screamed as loud as she could, struggling to be heard over the roar of the aircraft and the clatter of the guns. The flak lit up the sky in a horrific tableau as enemy guns raked the campsite. Emily stood frozen to the spot as she watched soldiers, young men who had so recently been applauding her singing, mowed down.

'Emily, come on.' The touch of Dave's hand on her arm galvanized her into action, and she scrambled under the closest lorry, pressing her hands over her ears to block out the screams of agony, and praying that Kit would be all right.

The attack was brutal but short-lived. Emily pressed her face into the ground, listening to the sound of engines fading into the distance. The gunners fired a last round of shots as the medics busied themselves tending to the wounded and dying.

Emily crawled out from under the lorry and stared in horror as the emerging daylight highlighted the extent of the carnage and devastation. Tents had been shredded, flaps of canvas fluttering feebly in the faint breeze. Several vehicles had been badly damaged, but that was nothing compared to the casualties. Bodies were strewn across the ground. One young man, barely old enough to shave, lay just outside his tent. He looked so peaceful, as though he were sleeping. Emily looked away, fighting the urge to vomit. Her stomach was a knot of anxiety over Kit, and she glanced around frantically for a glimpse of him amongst the confusion.

'Give us a hand, will you?' asked a young stretcher-bearer. 'We're a bit overrun at the moment.'

'Of course,' Emily said, without hesitation. For the next two hours, she held the hands of the dying and staunched gaping wounds, oblivious to the blood and dirt. By the time the wounded had all been transferred into the field hospital, and the dead taken away for burial, she was exhausted. Her uniform was smeared with blood and mud. Her petticoat was in shreds where she had ripped a strip off to use as a tourniquet.

She sank wearily onto the grass outside the hospital tent, trying not to hear the cries of agony on the other side of the canvas wall. Nellie handed her a mug of water. She had blood on her face and shirt, but seemed not to notice as she sank down next to Emily, stifling a yawn.

'Have you seen Kit?' Emily asked, anxiously.

'No,' Nellie croaked. 'But that's a good thing. If he'd been injured or killed, we'd know by now.'

Emily nodded. She lifted her mug to her lips. Her hands were shaking so much she spilled some water down her jacket. She looked over towards Folkestone. A few small fires were visible but it seemed as though the camp had taken the brunt of the unexpected attack.

'Emily!'

'Kit!' Letting her mug fall to the ground, Emily scrambled to her feet.

'Oh God, Emily! I was so worried.' Kit pulled her into a rough embrace and she rested her head against his chest, and closed her eyes. Her relief was overwhelming.

'I was so frightened for you,' she whispered.

His eyes clouded. 'I lost some good men,' he said, bitterly. 'Bastards.' He glanced up at the clear blue sky, his expression grim.

'I'm sorry,' Emily said, filled with sorrow.

'I shall write to their wives or mothers,' he said with a sigh. 'I like to do that. The telegram is so blunt, I like to hope my letters offer a measure of comfort.'

'I'm sure they bring them a lot of comfort,' Emily said. 'You're a good man, Kit.'

'Duty calls,' he said, giving Emily a final squeeze as the chaplain approached, clutching a well-thumbed Bible. 'We'll be holding a short service within the hour.' Emily followed his gaze to where the new graves were being dug beyond the camp. Dave and Samuel were among the grave diggers, bare torsos gleaming with perspiration.

'What time are you leaving?' Kit paused to ask.

'As soon as Nik and the chaps have repaired the wheels on the lorry,' Emily said, her voice trembling as she realized that she might never see Kit again.

'It will be all right,' he said, as if reading her thoughts. 'I'll be here to see you off, I promise.'

★ ★ ★

It was mid-afternoon by the time they were ready to leave.

'I'll write often,' Kit promised in their last few moments together before he helped Emily up into the cab. A few of the soldiers crowding around the lorry whistled and cheered as they pulled away, but the overall mood was sombre.

Emily leaned out of the window, her gaze locked

244

on Kit's amidst a sea of soldiers. She waved and blew kisses until the lorry turned onto the road, and then slumped back in her seat.

'Are you all right?' Nellie asked gently, taking Emily's hand in hers.

Not trusting herself to speak, Emily simply nodded and fixed her tear-filled eyes on the road ahead.

'Emily! Hey, Emily, hey, wait up!' Clutching her hat in the stiff sea breeze, Emily whirled round at the sound of her name being shouted above the noise of the crowds thronging the quayside at Southampton docks. She scanned the faces of the many civilians and servicemen and women, and then she saw him, hobbling towards her on a pair of crutches.

'Edward!' Emily exclaimed, her pleasure at seeing him quickly changing to concern. 'Your leg?'

'It's nothing serious, thank God. Just bad enough to get me sent home for a week or two.'

'Betty will be thrilled,' Emily said. 'Is she expecting you?'

'No.' Edward grinned. 'I'm going to surprise her.' His smile broadened. 'And I'll get to see my baby girl at last. Except she isn't a baby anymore,' he added, with not a little regret. 'She's eighteen months old now.'

'I'll be heading home soon myself,' Emily said. 'I've been performing with ENSA.'

'I wish you'd made it out to North Africa,' Edward replied sardonically. 'The chaps we got sent were abysmal. Couldn't carry a tune if their lives depended on it.' He nodded at Emily's kitbag. 'When's your train?'

Emily shook her head. 'I'm not going back to Bristol yet. I've been granted a couple of days' leave. I've got a wedding to attend.'

'Oh?' Edward said.

'You remember Nellie? You met her at one of my

performances in Bristol.' Edward stared at her blankly. 'Well, anyway, she's getting married, hopefully within the next few days. She and her fiancé have gone to see about getting a licence and booking a date. In the meantime, though, I'm going to see Roland. Dave's got a performance tonight in Bridport so he's dropping me off in Lyme Regis on the way.'

'Ah, yes, Roland. Betty wrote and told me he'd been injured. How is he?'

'He's coming along nicely, thank you for asking,' Emily said with a smile. 'The sea air has done his lungs the world of good. He's hoping to be discharged before too long.'

'Tell him I send my regards, won't you?' Edward said, turning his head at the sound of the railway conductor's whistle. 'That's my train. Take care of yourself, Emily.'

'You too, Edward. Give my love to Betty and the children.'

She watched Edward swing his way through the crowds towards the waiting train and spotted Samuel making his way towards her. Picking up her kitbag, she waved.

'Dave's waiting with the van,' he said, taking Emily's kitbag and slinging it over his shoulder. 'I've booked you both into a boarding house for tomorrow night,' he told her, moving through the crowd with the grace of a panther as Emily hurried to keep up with him. 'The landlady's got a shed out the back where we can store our stuff until after the wedding. She's even offered to put on a bit of a do after, just for the five of us.'

'That's kind of her. Oh, there's Dave,' she said, spotting the Morris van idling alongside the kerb. 'Tell

Nellie I'll see her tomorrow.' Samuel stowed Emily's bag in the back of the van and she clambered in beside Dave. She gave Samuel a wave, and Dave pulled into the traffic. They had a two-hour drive ahead of them.

★ ★ ★

It was late afternoon by the time they drove into the quaint seaside town of Lyme Regis. The sea sparkled aquamarine in the sunshine and a brisk salty breeze tugged at Emily's hair when she got out of the van.

'The convalescent home is along there, according to the map,' Dave said, pointing through the open window. 'I'll meet you back here around one o'clock tomorrow afternoon?'

'Thanks, Dave. I'm really grateful,' Emily said. Dave had used his petrol ration to drive her here.

'It made no odds,' Dave said with a shrug. 'I was coming this way anyway.'

'Good luck for tonight,' Emily called after him as the van pulled away. Dave stuck his hand out of the window and waved. He'd been rather quiet on the journey and, watching the van disappear around the corner, Emily couldn't help wondering just how much he minded that Nellie was marrying Nik.

The seafront was bustling with day trippers, and fishing boats rocked the gentle swell in the harbour. Emily walked along the seafront. The sand shimmered in the sunlight, but the effect was marred by the coils of barbed wire and signs warning people to 'KEEP OFF'. The aroma of frying fish drifted from a nearby café and seagulls cried overhead.

The convalescent home was situated up a steep incline. It was an old Georgian manor house that had been requisitioned by the military at the start of the war. Set in immaculate grounds, the salmon-pink house commanded a spectacular view of the sea.

Emily climbed the steps and rang the bell.

'Good afternoon,' she said to the pretty young nurse who opened the door. 'I'm here to see Mr Roland Thurston. It's Emily Baker.'

'I know who you are, miss,' the nurse said, blushing. 'I've seen your picture in the papers.' She stood aside to allow Emily into the airy hallway. 'This way, Miss Rose.' She led Emily through a large drawing room, where three men in dressing gowns and slippers were involved in a game of cards. 'You sang at my brother's camp in February,' the nurse continued, leading Emily into a sunlit conservatory and out onto the lawn where a game of croquet was in progress watched by several patients in wheelchairs. 'Jerry didn't talk about anything else in his letter home except you. My little brother Martin was dead jealous. He's only fifteen, you see, and can't wait to join up. He'll be even more jealous when I tell him I've actually met you. He's got your picture pinned on his bedroom wall, I believe.'

'I shall sign an autograph for him,' Emily offered, spotting Roland sitting in the shade of a horse chestnut tree.

'Oh, would you, miss? Thank you. He'll be over the moon.'

'Emily,' Roland said, laying his book aside and getting to his feet as Emily approached. He held out his arms and they embraced. He kissed Emily's cheek. 'You're looking well. Please, have a seat.' He indicated the chair beside his and sat down. 'They'll be doing the tea rounds in a bit.'

'That will be nice. I am rather thirsty.' She laid her

hat on the grass by her feet. 'So, how are you?'

'I'm as right as rain,' Roland declared triumphantly. 'Most of the scarring is barely noticeable now and my lungs are almost up to ninety per cent capacity. My doctor reckons I'll be able to leave within the month.'

'That's brilliant news.' Emily beamed. 'You've been here what, twelve months?'

'Give or take a week or two. But enough about me,' Roland said with a cheeriness he didn't feel. 'Tell me about this second lieutenant of yours. Kit, isn't it?'

Emily blushed. 'Yes, Kit Higham.'

Roland wrinkled his nose. 'I gathered from your letters that you are rather smitten, but now I can see your face, I see that you're in love with him.'

'I believe I am,' Emily said with a sigh. 'I know how ridiculous it must sound. We've spent less than three days in each other's company, but I think about him all the time. When a day goes by that I don't receive a letter from him, I'm actually relieved because that means I have something to look forward to the next day.' She gave a little laugh. 'Does that make sense?'

'Completely,' Roland replied drily, raising an eyebrow. 'But what about Tom? I thought he was the love of your life.'

The brightness in Emily's eyes dimmed briefly. 'Tom and I were never meant to be, Roland. I've finally accepted that. With Kit, I can have the life I always dreamed of. He's such a kind, gentle man. I can't wait for you to meet him. You'll like him, I know you will.'

'I'm sure I will,' he said with a smile that didn't quite meet his eyes. He would never reveal to Emily how much it hurt that, having at last let go of Tom, she hadn't chosen him.

'Now, tell me,' he said, giving himself a mental shake. 'How are Nellie and the others?'

'Nellie is getting married, hopefully in the next day or so. She's five months gone now and starting to show, so time is of the essence. Miss Anne is well, bless her. She keeps us updated on what each of us is doing. Lulu was in Belgium last we heard, and Leah and Barbara are both somewhere in North Africa.'

'I'm proud of you, Emily,' Roland said as an orderly approached with the tea tray. 'It sounds like jolly hard work.'

'I'm proud to have done it. Thank you,' Emily said, taking the proffered cup of milky tea. Balancing the saucer on her lap, she said, 'Our boys need as much encouragement as we can give them. I've got a week's leave so I'll go home and see Miss Anne.' She grinned as she sipped her tea. 'I've forgotten what it's like to sleep in a proper bed.'

★　★　★

Emily and Roland sat on a bench on the seafront, eating fish and chips out of newspaper. Sunlight bounced off the water and gulls bobbed on the gentle swell. Laughter drifted from the nearby pub. She had slept badly; the sound of anti-aircraft guns further along the coast had kept her awake much of the night, her stomach in knots of anxiety. Portsmouth and Southampton were prime targets for the Luftwaffe, and she was worried for Nellie and Nik.

Trying to put anxious thoughts out of her mind, she had enjoyed a pleasant morning with Roland, strolling along the cliffs above the town.

'What time is Dave coming?' Roland asked now,

squinting against the glare of the diamond-patterned sea.

'One o'clock,' Emily replied, licking her fingers. 'What's the time now?'

'A quarter to.' Roland scrunched up his greasy newspaper and lobbed it in a nearby rubbish bin.

'Southampton Docks hit again,' shouted a voice, sending Emily's stomach churning. The newspaper seller shouted again, and, dropping the rest of her dinner on the bench where it was immediately snatched up by a flock of seagulls, Emily ran over to him, digging into her bag for her money.

'There you go, miss,' the vendor said, handing over the paper. Emily thanked him, absently, her eyes already scanning the leading article.

'. . . docks and surrounding areas,' she read aloud to Roland. 'Oh God, Roland, the boarding house was just around the corner.'

'They'd have gone to a shelter,' Roland tried to assure her. 'There's a telephone box outside the post office. Why don't you phone the boarding house just to set your mind at rest?'

'Yes, I will.' Emily hurried down the street to the telephone box and gave the operator the name of the boarding house.

'I'm sorry,' the operator said after several interminable minutes had passed, 'I have been unable to connect your call. Please try again later.'

Emily let out a wail of frustration. She felt sick with worry.

'The phone lines are probably down,' Roland said. 'Try not to panic.'

'I know something's happened,' Emily said, frantically. 'I can feel it. Oh, where's Dave? Oh, thank God,' she said with relief as the van turned the corner. Dave pulled up against the kerb in front of her and got out of the car, his face ashen.

'Oh, Emily,' he said bleakly, coming towards her.

'Nellie?' she whispered with dread, already knowing what he was going to say.

'Nik telephoned me half an hour ago,' he said, and Emily burst into tears and fell into his arms. 'It was a direct hit. It would have been quick.' His voice was thick with emotion. 'She wouldn't have known anything about it.'

'Didn't she have time to get to a shelter?' Emily sobbed, as Roland looked on helplessly.

'Nellie was in the Morrison shelter right where the bomb hit,' Dave said in a choked voice as they drew apart. He wiped his tears away roughly. 'Nik wasn't there. He'd bumped into an old friend earlier in the day and they'd arranged to meet for a drink. He was in the pub in the next street when the bomb hit.'

'Oh, poor Nik,' Emily groaned. 'And the poor baby.' She rubbed at her swollen eyes. 'It never even got a chance to live.'

Dave swallowed hard as more tears threatened. 'Come on,' he said gruffly. 'We'd better set off. Nik and Samuel are waiting for us.'

'Is Samuel all right?' Emily asked, anxiously.

'He'd gone to a jazz club and was sheltering in the basement. He's fine.'

'My condolences, mate.' Roland shook Dave's hand, and Dave nodded. Wordlessly, he got back in the van.

'Look after yourself, Emily,' Roland said, squeezing her tight.

Emily nodded. 'You too, Roland.'

She got in the van and stared ahead as Dave pulled away from the kerb. Neither of them spoke, both lost in their own grief. Roland watched from the pavement as the van turned the corner, catching a brief glimpse of Emily's tear-stained face before they rounded the bend and were gone.

★ ★ ★

Almost seven hundred miles away in northern France, Tom was huddled behind a bank of oil drums close to the railway station. He carefully adjusted his position in an effort to relieve the ache in his cramped muscles. They had been in position since early that morning and the tension was palpable.

The warm air was thick with the smell of diesel oil. Beside him, Rich glanced at his watch and held up two fingers. The train was due into the station in two minutes. Tom nodded. The mission had taken weeks in the planning. If everything went according to plan, a high-ranking member of the Gestapo would be taken out and the German hierarchy would be left reeling.

From far away came the distant shriek of a train whistle. Tom tensed. He gave Rich the thumbs-up, and Rich nodded. This was it.

Suddenly, there was an ear-splitting explosion and Tom found himself lifted high into the air. He landed heavily on the track, his nostrils filled with the stench of burning oil. He heard shouting but it sounded muffled, as if it was coming from far away. He forced his eyes open. Rivers of burning oil dripped from the platform onto the tracks like molten lava. Blood trickled into his right eye and he blinked frantically, trying to clear his vision. His throat closed in terror as a young German soldier appeared above him. The soldier, barely more than a boy, grinned and took out his revolver.

33

Nellie's funeral was held four days later. Her parents, an attractive-looking couple in their fifties, were clearly devastated by their daughter's death. They knew nothing of the unborn grandchild they had lost, and Nik confided in Emily that he had resolved not to tell them. Why add to their grief, he had said.

The service was mercifully short, and Nellie was laid to rest in the pretty graveyard. When the coffin was lowered into the ground, Nik was inconsolable in his grief, drawing raised eyebrows from some of Nellie's more conservative relations. Lulu and Leah had managed to make it home for the funeral, and Miss Anne was there, of course. Emily clung to her arm at the graveside while Roland and Leah did their best to support the grief-stricken Nik.

Afterwards, they retired to a nearby hotel for a modest buffet. Emily managed a few words with Mrs Bedford, whom she thought was very like her daughter, and, despite Nellie's fears to the contrary, she was certain would have been overjoyed at the prospect of being a grandmother, however soon after the wedding the baby would have arrived.

★ ★ ★

In the days that followed, Emily threw herself into her work with ENSA. She spent the rest of the summer touring hospitals and convalescent homes around the country. Her relationship with Kit was moving along

256

nicely. His unit had been sent out to the Mediterranean soon after Emily had left the camp but she wrote to him often, looking forward to getting home to find his replies waiting for her. She savoured every word, reading them again and again until the letters were imprinted on her memory. She had a photograph taken at a studio in town and sent it to Kit, wanting him to have something more personal than the standard ENSA portrait she handed out to fans. One evening, as she undressed for bed, she slowly unclasped the chain that held Tom's ring from about her neck and folded it away in her underwear drawer. She finally felt ready to say goodbye to the past.

She heard occasionally from Dave and Samuel who were touring the American bases along the south coast again, and once from Nik. Grieving for his beloved Nellie and unborn baby, he had returned to the naval unit from which he had been seconded when he joined ENSA.

In early August, Roland finally received a full bill of health from his doctor and returned to Bristol. He immediately set about arranging a recording session for Emily, and on one of her rare days off, they travelled up to London to record an album of all her well-loved songs.

'I wonder what my dad would think if he could see me now?' she mused to Roland when they entered the recording studio.

'He'd be proud as punch,' Roland said. Overcome with emotion, Emily could only nod as she gave Roland a grateful hug.

Throughout October and November, the papers were full of news of battles on the other side of the world and of the allied victory in Italy. She fretted constantly about Kit's safety. The only time she managed to forget about the war was when she was singing.

* * *

'I'm just nipping to the post office, Miss Anne,' Emily called one day in early December as she buttoned up her coat. She wound her scarf around her throat and picked up the brown-paper-wrapped parcel waiting on the bottom step of the stairs. It was Kit's Christmas box and she wanted to get it sent off in good time. 'Is there anything you need while I'm out?'

Her landlady appeared in the parlour doorway, duster in hand. 'Thank you, love, but I did a bit of shopping yesterday. Queued for almost an hour, I did, for a bit of sugar and what have you.' She smiled. 'Still, I shouldn't complain. There's a lot of folk who've got it a lot worse than us. They're starving in Greece, you know?'

'I know. It's terrible,' Emily agreed as she checked her appearance in the hall mirror and tucked a stray wisp of hair under her cap. 'How's Leah? Such tragic news about her brother.' In the middle of November, Leah's parents had received a telegram informing them that their son had been killed.

'She's coping,' Miss Anne said with a sigh. She had aged rapidly in the months since Nellie's death. Fond as she was of all 'her girls', Nellie had been like a daughter to her and she felt her loss keenly. 'Like we all have to do.'

Emily nodded. She missed Nellie in so many ways. She missed their lazy Sunday mornings, sitting at the kitchen table in their pyjamas and rehashing the pre-

258

vious evening's performance over tea and toast. She missed their pre-show chats, the giggles and laughter in the dressing room. Even the nights spent in a leaky tent in a waterlogged field, huddled together for warmth, held a more poignant place in her memory now.

'I'll be as quick as I can,' she said, opening the door and glancing up at the overcast sky. Snow was forecast for later that morning and it appeared they might be right. The wind was cold and she was glad of her warm scarf. Her cheeks and nose were tingling by the time she reached the post office and joined the lengthy queue. The Salvation Army band were playing Christmas carols on the street corner, and across the street, a sign in the butcher's shop advertized rabbit as an alternative for Christmas dinner since turkeys were in such short supply.

Emily smiled as fond memories of childhood Christmases filled her thoughts. When her mother was alive, they had often had rabbit for Christmas dinner rather than the more traditional bird. She could remember her father coming in from the cold, stamping his feet to rid his boots of the snow, a dead rabbit swinging from his gloved hands, and her mother would laugh as she took it from him. Emily would sit at the large kitchen table watching as her mother skinned and prepared the rabbit for roasting, and soon the cottage would be filled with the tantalizing aroma of roasting meat. No part of the rabbit would go to waste, and now, as she entered the post office, her cold fingers tingling with cold in her woollen gloves, she thought longingly of the velvety rabbit-skin mittens her mother used to make.

34

'I received a letter from Edward yesterday,' Betty said, handing Emily a mug of tea. It was Christmas Eve and they were sitting in Betty's cosy kitchen helping Eddie and Harry, now aged six and four respectively, to make paper chains out of strips of old newspaper to decorate the small Christmas tree in the parlour. Olivia, a sturdy toddler a week off her second birthday, was sitting by the hearth playing with the paper dolls Emily had cut out of an old magazine. 'He's stationed quite far from any fighting at the moment, so that's a relief.'

Hearing his father's name, Eddie looked up from his colouring. 'Is Daddy coming home?'

'No, darling,' Betty said sadly. 'But he will be thinking of us, and he'll have the lovely pictures you drew for him, so he'll know we're thinking of him too.'

'At least he got to see the children in the summer,' Emily said cheerfully.

'I'm grateful for that,' Betty said, getting to her feet to replenish the teapot. 'But, in a way, it made it worse.' She leaned against the dresser, arms folded across her chest, and bit her lip. 'I know it sounds ridiculous, and it is. I loved having him at home, it's just that I'd got used to doing without him, so when he went again after the fortnight, it made the wrench even harder to bear.' She returned the teapot to the table. 'Do you think I'm being silly?'

'Certainly not,' replied Emily, dabbing paste onto a strip of newspaper and fastening the link. 'I understand perfectly. There,' she said, smiling at the boys. 'I think we have enough to cover the whole tree. Shall we go and see?'

Yelping with excitement, the boys scampered into the other room, Olivia toddling after them.

'Poor Livy,' Betty said, as they followed the children into the parlour. 'She won't know her father if this war goes on much longer.'

'It's so hard — for everyone,' Emily agreed, with a pang at the thought of Kit spending another Christmas away from home. She rallied herself, smiling fondly at the sight of the children gathered around the tree, silhouetted by the light of the fire. For the next half-hour they dressed the tree and placed the presents Emily had brought with her underneath it. They were only second-hand toys she'd picked up at a thrift shop, wrapped in newspaper and tied up with pretty coloured wool, but she knew the children would be thrilled.

'I think it's time for cocoa and a bedtime story, and then bed, or Father Christmas won't come,' Betty said, smiling fondly.

'Can Auntie Emily read us a story?' asked Harry.

'I'd love to,' Emily said, taking Olivia on her lap while Eddie and Harry dashed up to their bedroom, fighting over who got to choose the book.

'If you're very good and stop squabbling, I'll read two stories,' Emily shouted up the stairs after them. 'You can choose one each.'

★ ★ ★

Once the children were tucked up in bed, stockings hanging on the bedposts, Emily and Betty curled up

261

on the sofa with a mug of cocoa.

'Doesn't this remind you of our evenings in the staff sitting room at Mansfield House?' Betty said with a grin.

'We had some good times, didn't we?' Emily smiled, reminiscing. 'The four of us.'

'How are things progressing with you and Kit?' Betty asked, quick to steer the conversation onto safer ground.

'Good.' Emily stretched her stockinged feet out towards the fire. 'I honestly believe we have a future together,' she said, staring into the flickering flames. 'I'm really happy. Obviously I'm terrified every minute of the day that something might happen to him, but I am happy. I finally feel like I have something to look forward to once this blasted war is over.'

'I'm so pleased for you, sweetheart,' Betty said, putting an arm around Emily's shoulders. 'God knows you deserve some happiness.'

They sat in silence for a while, listening to the pop and crackle of the flames.

'Will you be seeing Ernest while you're here?' Betty asked, getting up to throw another log on the fire.

Emily nodded. 'I've arranged to see him on Boxing Day morning on my way to the station.' She pulled a face. 'I haven't told him about Kit. I'm not sure if I should. What do you think?'

'Perhaps you should wait a while,' Betty advised. 'See how things work out.'

'I agree, although I'm sure he'd understand. After all, neither of us have heard from Tom in years. We have to face it: he's not coming back, is he?'

Betty gave a shrug. 'I've always thought it odd that he's never written. You two were so close. I'd have bet all I had that you were meant to be.'

'That's what I believed too,' said Emily. 'It doesn't make any sense. The Tom I knew would never behave so cruelly.'

'Unless,' Betty began, with a pained expression.

'Something happened to him?' Emily finished bleakly. 'I've wondered that often. Sometimes I think it's the only rational explanation, but I'd have known, deep inside, I'm sure I would.'

'Poor Ernest. The not knowing must be tearing the poor man apart,' Betty said. 'Right, bedtime, I think. The children will be up with the sparrows.'

'Thank you for this, Betty,' Emily said as they climbed the stairs to the bedroom at the front of the small cottage. 'It would have been a pretty lonely Christmas otherwise.'

'You're always welcome,' Betty said, patting her arm fondly. 'You know that.'

35

The children were up early. In her dressing gown, rubbing sleep from her eyes, Emily perched on the arm of the sofa watching as they unwrapped their modest presents, squealing with delight at every new surprise. The boys loved the comics and board game Emily had bought them, and the wooden toy cars Roland had made during his recuperation. He had also made a cradle from an old cigar box for Olivia to go with the second-hand doll Emily had bought.

Leaving the children to play with their new toys, Emily helped Betty prepare the vegetables for the midday meal. After putting the chicken in the oven to roast, they set off for church.

It was a bright, crisp day. Snowdrifts glinted in the sunlight and a robin redbreast sang joyfully on top of a snow-capped pillar box. A dog had left paw prints in the snow along Layton Lane, and the boys followed them, laughing in glee, convinced that they had been left by Father's Christmas's reindeer.

The churchyard was a wonderland of white as they made their way down the snowy path to where the Reverend Smedhurst was waiting to welcome his parishioners to the morning service.

'Emily,' he exclaimed, his pleasure at seeing his one-time choirgirl evident in his joyous expression. 'How lovely to see you.' He held her gloved hands in his cold ones. 'Mrs Smedhurst and I have been following your career with interest.'

'I didn't know you had married,' Emily said with

genuine delight. 'Is Mrs Smedhurst here?'

'I'm afraid she has a bad cold and so has stayed at home today. She will be sorry not to have met you. She is a great fan.'

Aware that the children were growing restless, and that a small crowd had gathered behind her, Emily excused herself and went into the church where the flower ladies had worked wonders with sprigs of holly and ivy. A Christmas tree adorned with paper chains and paper angels made by the Sunday school class stood beside the altar. Candles burned on every available ledge.

After the service, many of the congregation who remembered Emily as a young girl wanted to congratulate her on her success.

'Your mum would be ever so proud of you, love,' a plump, middle-aged woman told her, beaming. 'She had a lovely voice herself, as I'm sure you remember?'

'I do,' Emily replied with a friendly smile. 'She was always singing around the house.'

She spotted Ned Sawyer making his way towards her, and her friendly smile broadened.

'Merry Christmas, Emily,' Ned said. 'You've come a long way since you used to sing in my parlour on a Friday evening. You remember Harriet?'

'Nice to see you again, Mrs Sawyer,' Emily said, smiling at Ned's wife who was gathering up her four children. Two boys and two girls, they appeared to range in age from about three to eight.

'Likewise,' Harriet smiled. 'Merry Christmas. Children, this is Daddy's old friend Miss Rose whom I was telling you about the other day. We were dancing to one of her records, remember?' The four children stared up at Emily in open-mouthed awe and she laughed.

'I'm sure you don't need me to tell you, Emily,' Ned said, 'but your mum and dad would have been so proud of you. A workhouse lad like your dad, well, he'd never have dreamt a daughter of his could achieve so much.'

'Thank you, Ned,' Emily said, swallowing the lump in her throat. 'That means a lot.'

'Can we go home yet, Mummy?' Eddie whined petulantly. 'I'm hungry.' Betty shot Emily a mortified glance as she hissed at him to be quiet. But, seeing one of the ill-spirited Tucker sisters heading her way, Emily was glad of the excuse to make her farewells and join Betty and the children for the walk home.

'How does it feel to be so famous?' Betty asked Emily curiously, as they took off their coats in the tiny lean-to hallway, the mouth-watering aroma of roasting meat wafting from the kitchen.

'A bit surreal,' replied Emily truthfully, following Betty into the kitchen while the children disappeared into the parlour to play with their toys. 'Would they be so interested in me if I was still just plain old Emily Baker, hotel chambermaid?' She grinned, tying her apron strings.

'Enjoy it,' Betty told her with a shrug as she lit the hob. 'You deserve it. You've done as much for this war effort as anyone, and you deserve all the credit you get.'

Christmas dinner was a jolly, pleasant affair and, afterwards, Emily and Betty sent the boys out to play in the snow while they washed the dishes.

★ ★ ★

266

Boxing Day dawned bright and sunny. The snow was beginning to thaw and the trees and window ledges dripped with water as Emily got off the bus outside the Methodist church opposite Ernest's cottage.

Tucking her hands in her pockets, she crossed the deserted street and let herself in the garden gate. Ernest had the door open before she was even half-way up the path.

'Emily, it's lovely to see you.' They embraced on the doorsteps.

'Hello, Ernest. Merry Christmas.'

'Merry Christmas, Emily love. Come on in.'

'Thank you. Did you have a good day yesterday?' Emily asked, as she hung up her wraps and followed Ernest into the cosy parlour.

'It was very pleasant. I was invited next door to the Mullets' again.' Ernest rubbed his hands together. 'Now, the tea's just brewing. Will you have a cup?'

'Tea would be lovely, thank you.' Emily sat down close to the fire and held her cold hands towards its cheery glow.

'How are Betty and the children?' Ernest called from the kitchen over the clatter of crockery.

'Very well, thank you. Olivia's such a poppet. She'll be two next week.'

'It doesn't seem possible, does it?' Ernest said, coming into the room with the tea tray, which he placed on the parlour table.

'I saved up my dried fruit ration so Mrs Mullet could make a half-decent Christmas cake,' Ernest explained, handing Emily a slice of fruit cake on a plate. 'I told her you were coming this morning, so she sent me home with a couple of slices. It isn't at all bad, is it?'

Emily took a bite. 'It's delicious,' she agreed. 'How have you been, Ernest?'

'Oh, I can't complain, love,' he replied cheerfully. 'I had a bit of a chest infection last week, but Mrs Mullet picked up some concoction from the chemist which seems to have sorted it out, and I keep myself occupied with my garden and my chickens. Which reminds me, I've got half a dozen eggs for you to take with you.'

His cheery tone was tinged with sadness and Emily's heart went out to him. Though only in his early sixties, he had aged a lot in the years since Tom had been gone. Thinking of Tom, and how much she had loved him, her thoughts turned to Kit. Hopefully her Christmas box had arrived in good time but even so, what sort of a Christmas would he have had, on a battlefield so far from home?

'What's the matter?' Ernest asked in concern, getting up to refill her teacup.

'I was just thinking how this will have been a miserable Christmas for so many people,' she replied, woefully.

'We just have to make the best of it,' Ernest said, leaning over to stoke the fire. 'And hope for better things.'

She stayed an hour with Ernest before it was time to leave to catch her train.

The journey back to Bristol was without incident. Roland was waiting on the platform as the train pulled into Temple Mead Station.

'I've missed you,' he said, giving her an affectionate peck on the cheek and picking up her suitcase. 'How was your trip?'

'Very good, thank you,' Emily said, cradling the

bowl of eggs as they walked through the cavernous terminal. 'Betty sends her regards.' They stepped out into the cold, crisp sunshine. 'Did you have a nice time at your sister's?'

'I did, thank you. They are all in frightfully good health,' Roland said. 'June put on a decent spread despite the rationing and I managed to bear the company of my rambunctious nephews.'

'They must have loved having their uncle to play with,' Emily said with a grin.

Roland grinned back. 'I think they found the fact that I'd been blown up quite exciting. The younger lads did, anyway. Alexander's a teenager now and a bit more reticent. He's counting the days until he can join up.' His grin turned into a grimace. 'As you can imagine, June is praying the war will be over long before he's old enough.'

'Oh gosh, let's hope so,' Emily agreed wholeheartedly. 'There is an air of optimism around now, isn't there? The tide appears to be turning in our favour.'

36

Miss Anne was at the stove boiling eggs when Emily came downstairs the following morning.

'Morning, love.'

'Good morning, Miss Anne,' Emily said, going up behind her landlady and giving her a hug.

'It was kind of your Mr Harding to spare us these eggs,' she said, lifting the eggs from the water and setting them in the waiting cups. 'Please tell him I'm grateful when you next write. And speaking of letters,' she added, indicating the envelope propped against the salt cellar. 'That's just come.'

'It's from Kit,' Emily said, unable to keep the delight from her voice as she ripped open the envelope and scanned the now familiar handwriting. 'He's coming to Bristol,' she cried, her eyes shining. 'He's got two weeks' leave and he wants to see me. Oh, I'm so excited!'

'I'll look forward to meeting your young man.' Miss Anne fixed a slice of bread onto the toasting fork and thrust it into the flames. 'When does he arrive?'

'The eighth of January on the eleven-fifteen train.' Emily glanced at the calendar hanging on the back of the door. 'In ten days' time. Oh, Miss Anne, it will be wonderful. I can't wait.'

★ ★ ★

'I'm excited,' she told Roland an hour later as they walked by the quayside, buffeted by an icy wind.

'But I'm nervous too.'

'That's understandable,' Roland said, tucking Emily's gloved hand through the crook of his arm. 'You spent barely three days together seven months ago. You're bound to feel apprehensive.'

'And yet I believe we know all there is to know about each other through our letters,' Emily said. 'Anyway, enough about me. What about you? Is everything all right? You look as though you've something on your mind.'

Roland took a breath. 'I'm joining ENSA,' he said, stopping Emily in her tracks.

'Really? Roland, that's great.'

'I've got to go up to London to see them but' — he grinned bashfully — 'if you're in need of an at-best mediocre pianist, I'm your man.'

Emily gave his arm a playful punch. 'Don't be so self-deprecating,' she laughed. 'You've accompanied me before and you're very good. When do you go to London?'

'The eighth.'

'Oh, that's the day Kit arrives.'

'I shall look forward to meeting him on my return then. Look,' he said, nodding towards the misted windows of a tea shop across the street. 'I've lost all feeling in my toes. Do you fancy a hot drink? My treat.'

'That's an offer I can't refuse,' Emily replied with a smile.

★ ★ ★

Despite throwing herself into touring hospitals and camps across the southwest, the days in the run-up to Kit's arrival dragged, but at last the day came. She

271

waved Roland off on the 9.45 train to London and found a quiet corner in the station café where she lingered over a cup of tea. She bought a newspaper but found herself unable to concentrate and eventually gave up, preferring instead to watch the comings and goings of the commuters and pigeons roosting high up in cavernous ceiling, her stomach clenching with excitement.

By the time the 11.15 thundered into the station, hissing clouds of steam and twenty minutes late, she was a bundle of nerves. Leaving her newspaper folded on her seat, she gathered up her coat and hat and hurried onto the platform, standing on tiptoes to see over the throng of servicemen and civilians. Starting to fret that she might have missed him, she made her way up and down the platform, scanning faces as sweethearts embraced and children flung themselves into fathers' arms. People were starting to embark and soon the carriage doors closed. The whistle blew and the train rolled out of the station, leaving Emily staring after it in dismay. Again, she scanned the platform, a sick feeling in the pit of her stomach. He'd missed the train, common sense told her. Trains were unreliable these days and the likeliest explanation was that he'd missed his connection. He'd surely be on the next one.

Nursing yet another cup of tea, she sat down to wait. Two trains came and went, disgorging their passengers, but still Kit failed to arrive. Feeling dejected and sick with worry, Emily made her way home.

She found Miss Anne in the parlour.

'He wasn't on the train,' Emily said, in a trembling voice.

'Oh, Emily love,' Miss Anne said, getting to her

272

feet and holding out her arms. 'I'm sure there's an explanation. He's probably stuck somewhere. It'll be all right, you'll see. Now sit down,' she said, releasing Emily from her embrace. 'You're frozen to the bone. I'll put the kettle on.'

★ ★ ★

The days passed and still there was no word from Kit.

'I've written to Kit, but do you think I should write to his parents as well?' she fretted to Roland as they drove through the beautiful Cotswolds on their way to perform at an army barracks.

'Like Miss Anne said,' Roland said in what he hoped was a reassuring tone, 'he's likely been delayed.'

'It's been almost a week, Roland,' Emily cried. 'He'd have been in touch by now.' She glanced out of the window. They were driving through rolling farmland, and frosty fields glistened in the hazy sunshine. Her bottom lip trembled. 'I'm scared something's happened to him.'

Taking one hand off the steering wheel, Roland gripped her hand in his. 'We're at war,' he reminded her, giving her fingers a squeeze. 'Everything's up in the air. Communication could be out wherever he is, or maybe the trains aren't running.' He gave her an encouraging smile. 'It's too early to worry.'

Feeling only slightly mollified, and making a valiant effort to push her anxiety aside, Emily turned her mind to the task ahead. She gave Roland a sideways glance. He was looking very dapper in his uniform. It would be their first official performance together since he became a fully fledged member of ENSA. His piano was strapped in the boot, the doors tied open in order to accommodate it. Every time they rounded a corner or hit a bump in the road, it slid about precariously and Emily could only hope and pray it would make it to their destination in one piece.

It was late evening by the time Roland dropped her off outside her front door, and she was exhausted. 'I'll see you tomorrow,' she said, leaning over to kiss his cheek. 'I'm home,' she called, stepping into the hall and shutting the door behind her.

'I saved you some supper,' Miss Anne replied from the kitchen. 'A letter came for you this morning. It's on the mantelpiece.'

Not bothering to take off her coat, Emily hurried into the warm parlour, her heart racing. It had to be from Kit. But the handwriting on the envelope was unfamiliar and excitement gave way to trepidation as she ripped it open and withdrew the single sheet of army issue writing paper.

Dear Miss Rose,
I hope you don't mind me writing to you, but I felt it my duty to inform you of the sad news that Kit was killed on New Year's Day.

'Oh, no!' wailed Emily, slumping into the nearest armchair and allowing the letter to flutter to the carpet.

Miss Anne came hurrying into the room, her face creased in concern. 'What's happened?' she asked, her heart sinking as she took in the letter on the floor and Emily's obvious devastation.

Emily could hardly bring herself to say it. 'Kit's dead,' she choked.

'Oh, my dear,' Miss Anne sighed. 'I'm so sorry.'

274

She crouched beside the sobbing girl, stroking her hair and whispering useless platitudes.

Sometime later, Emily sat slumped at the kitchen table, her chilled hands wrapped around a mug of hot sweet tea. For the moment she was dry-eyed, her tears spent, her gaze focused on the floral-patterned tablecloth as Miss Anne read the letter.

'This chap Jim,' Miss Anne said now, glancing up from the sheet of notepaper. 'It seems he was a good friend of Kit's.' She took off her reading glasses and wiped the corner of her eye with her handkerchief. She cleared her throat and put her glasses back on. 'He writes that they were out on patrol together when they came under fire. Kit was shot by a sniper while trying to rescue one of his men.' Emily raised her head to meet Miss Anne's sympathetic eyes. 'Jim says Kit's heroic act saved the other man's life. He found your address amongst Kit's personal effects as he was preparing for them to be sent to his parents and thought you deserved to know what happened to him.'

'That was thoughtful of him,' Emily whispered dully.

'He also says that Kit had your photograph in his pocket when he died. He was buried with it.'

'Three days,' Emily said bleakly. 'That's all we had. Three days. I don't even have a photograph of him.'

Miss Anne's chair scraped on the linoleum as she got up and rounded the table, putting her arms around Emily. 'I'm so, so sorry, my poor girl,' she said. 'I'll pop down to the telephone box first thing in the morning and call the hospital. You're in no state to entertain tomorrow.'

'I can't let them down,' Emily objected with a shake of her head. 'I need to keep busy. I'd be grateful if you'd telephone Roland though.' She took a deep, shuddering breath. 'I must write to Kit's parents and offer my condolences. They must be devastated.'

★ ★ ★

She opened the door to Roland just after nine o'clock the following day and gave him a tearful hug. They sat in the parlour where Miss Anne plied them with tea and mince pies left over from Christmas, which she had made using wholewheat flour and blackberry and apple preserve in place of mincemeat. Emily had no appetite, but Roland, who had missed his breakfast, polished off half a dozen.

'I'm sorry for your loss, Emily,' Roland said with genuine sympathy. It broke his heart to see her so pale and broken. He leaned forward in his chair. 'You need something to take your mind off your grief, a change of scenery.' He paused, unsure on how to proceed. 'I'm not sure if you're ready to hear this but, well, I was at ENSA HQ last week. I didn't say anything before in case nothing came of it, but the recruiting officer asked how I thought you'd feel about us touring the Far East.'

'The Far East?' repeated Emily apathetically.

'Yes,' Roland replied. 'The lads over there are having a rough time of it by all accounts and need some morale-boosting entertainment.'

Emily walked over to the window. The sky over Bristol was sombre, much like her mood.

'What do you think?' Roland asked gently. 'Might you be up for it?'

She closed her eyes, wrapping her grief around her like a heavy cloak. Perhaps a long tour abroad was the

276

distraction she needed. 'Yes,' she said, quietly. As she turned to face Roland, it crossed her mind to wonder what her father might have thought about the prospect of her flying halfway around the world. Despite her heavy heart, the thought made her smile.

'It'll be dangerous,' Roland said, his tone turning serious. 'The Japs are pretty ruthless. If they got hold of you ... Well, you've read the newspaper reports about what happened to those poor nurses.'

'I'm not naïve,' Emily replied. 'And anyway, we're just as likely to be killed at home as we are abroad. Our boys deserve our support. How soon can we leave?'

'We're to go up to HQ on Saturday to sort out the details, but I think they're looking about the first week of March.'

'The Far East? Are you mad?' Miss Anne threw up her hands in disbelief when Emily revealed her and Roland's plans.

'It's important our boys out there don't feel they've been forgotten,' Emily said in an attempt to mollify her landlady.

'Even Mr Churchill is encouraging it,' Roland added.

'You know Moira up the road? Her son is out there somewhere,' Miss Anne retorted sharply. 'It's awful, by all accounts. It's stinking hot and there are all manner of nasty insects. You could catch malaria, or worse.' She gave Emily an anxious look. 'You could get yourself killed.' Her lower lip trembled and Emily went to her.

'I'll be careful, I promise.'

Miss Anne's shoulders sagged in resignation. 'I'm not happy,' she said, her hand shaking so much she spilled the tea.

'Look,' Roland said in an attempt at appeasement. 'Why don't you come up to London with us on Saturday? It'll be a nice day out.'

'You could do a bit of shopping,' Emily agreed. 'You've been saving up your clothing coupons. You could treat yourself to a new dress.'

'I might,' snorted Miss Anne, only slightly mollified. 'I'll think about it.'

Three days later, the morning post brought a brief note from Kit's parents. As cold and impersonal as she had imagined the viscount and his wife to be from Kit's description, it simply thanked her for her condolences as if she were nothing more than a mere acquaintance. She read it through twice, then screwed it up and threw it on the fire.

PART THREE

PART THREE

37

Burma, 1944

With one hand scratching the mosquito bite on her ankle, Emily clung to the side of the Jeep as it bounced along the rugged track at an alarming rate. Perspiration ran in rivulets down her spine and her damp uniform clung to her wet skin. Roland slouched in the front passenger seat, his feet up on the dashboard, his hat pulled low over his eyes. His left arm sported a bandage where a mosquito bite had turned septic.

The jungle was hot and humid, the birdsong and jabbering of monkeys punctuated by the sound of distant gunfire.

Emily lifted her ponytail away from her clammy neck in a vain attempt to cool her skin, but no breeze stirred the thick soupy air. It had been almost three weeks since they'd left the port of Chittagong in India; three weeks spent driving through enemy-occupied territory to reach British troops stationed in remote parts of the Burmese jungle.

Their driver and guide, a small Burmese man called Maung, had come highly recommended by the hotel manager who assured them that Maung knew the roads into Burma 'like the back of his hand' and was well versed in the martial arts, as well as being a competent marksman: a useful skill in a jungle teeming with enemy soldiers.

Since departing England two months earlier, on a wet and windy Saturday in March, Emily's hectic schedule had been the welcome distraction she needed. She'd lost count of the number of planes she had flown in, or the army bases she had sung at en route.

They had travelled throughout India, performing wherever they came upon an army base. Emily would always remember the wounded men, those who were too ill to attend her shows. She made sure to find the time to visit the wards, sitting by the men's bedsides and listening to them talk about their sweethearts or wives back home. She would sing for them, often with Roland accompanying her on his small, well-travelled piano that was growing more battle-scarred with every leg of the journey.

Roland, with his scars and stump of an ear, was a hit with the men and, like Emily, he enjoyed spending time at their sickbeds, playing cards, helping them to write a letter, or simply just talking.

The Jeep bounced over a deep hole, almost flinging Emily out of her seat, and she tightened her grip. Clenching her teeth, she used her cap to bat away the flies that swarmed around her face. During her travels, she had grown used to extremes of heat and the variety of creepy-crawlies and reptiles. Now, apparently, she would have to get used to the rain for, according to Maung, the month of May was the start of Burma's monsoon season.

'How are you coping in the back there?' Roland asked with a grunt.

'I'm all right,' Emily replied, stifling a yawn. 'How's your arm?'

'It's feeling much better.' He reached for the water canteen hanging around his neck and took a long swallow. 'Urgh! Warm,' he said with a grimace. Taking his cigarette case from his shirt pocket, he offered it

282

to Maung.

'Thank you,' the driver said with a nod.

'How much further?' Roland asked, lighting the cigarette and passing it over.

Cigarette clamped between his lips, Maung held up two fingers.

'Two hours?' Roland raised his eyebrows. Maung shrugged. In the backseat, Emily adjusted her position in an effort to get more comfortable, her tired eyes scanning the shadowy undergrowth for anything that might give cause for concern. Maung had assured her that as long as she could hear the birds and the monkeys, she was safe. At least she thought that was what he had meant. She glanced at him through eyes narrowed against the sun's glare, relieved that he appeared to be quite relaxed as he steered the little Jeep along the track, the little piano rocking wildly on the seat beside her.

★ ★ ★

Late in the afternoon, they drove through vibrant tea plantations shimmering in the sultry late afternoon heat. A little further on, Maung brought the Jeep to a halt at the side of the dusty road. Below them lay the port of Chittagong, nestled on the banks of the Karnaphuli River. A few buildings showed signs of bomb damage and there were several large naval ships anchored out in the bay. Several small boats and skiffs skimmed the river, silhouetted against the water that shone like gold in the reflected light of the sun.

'I shall be glad to have a bath again,' Emily said, massaging her stiff shoulders just as the air was shattered by the far-off thud of an explosion. Maung pressed harder on the accelerator and the Jeep sped down the winding road towards the city, putting a welcome distance between them and the plumes of black smoke rising above the treetops.

★ ★ ★

A two-storey building built at the end of the previous century, the Palm Court Hotel had seen better days. The stucco walls were studded with bullet holes and the paintwork was flaked and peeling. While Maung talked with two sturdy young lads about carrying the piano away for safekeeping, Emily and Roland made their way into the large vestibule. The mosaic floor was cracked and the sluggish ceiling fan creaked ineffectually in the steamy air.

The hotel had been requisitioned by the British army and was swarming with military personnel, all of whom conveyed their pleasure at seeing Emily back safe and sound.

'It's very brave of you to come all this way, dear,' said a whiskered colonel, pumping Emily's hand with enthusiasm. 'It's very much appreciated.'

'We just want our brave lads to know they're not forgotten, sir,' said Roland. 'I hope we'll see you at our concert tomorrow?'

'You can count on it,' the colonel said.

They were shown to their rooms by a young Indian boy whose name Emily didn't catch. In the privacy of her second-floor room, she stood her suitcase in the middle of the floor and crossed to the window. Throwing open the wooden shutters, she looked out over the hotel grounds. Verdant lawns were surrounded by a thick forest of indigenous trees and flowering bushes.

284

Sunbirds darted between the colourful blossoms of fragrantly scented frangipani and hibiscus flowers and a crane stalked regally across the lawn to the vibrating background thrum of cicadas.

There was a knock on the door and she turned as an elderly Indian man brought in a tin bath. He was followed by three younger men, each carrying large jugs of water.

'Oh, thank you so much,' Emily said, delighted by the prospect of washing away the sweat and dirt of the past three weeks. Once the men had left, she stripped off her damp uniform and stepped into the bath. The water was only lukewarm, and she had worn her bar of soap to a sliver, but after weeks of travelling, it felt like sheer luxury to lay her head against the edge of the bath and close her eyes, listening to the shriek of a parakeet outside her window.

★ ★ ★

The troops were camped high up on the dunes above the city. As Maung drove the Jeep between rows and rows of tents, soldiers emerged into the waning light to cheer and applaud Emily and Roland's return. Emily and Roland joined the men in their canteen, talking and joking with them over supper. Afterwards, Emily clambered onto the bonnet of the Jeep and sang for them. She sang the old favourites, as well as a couple of new songs her writer, Sam Arnold, had sent her and which Roland was very excited about. He couldn't wait to get back to London to start recording them.

The men joined in, cheering and singing along, and posing for photographs that Roland took with his trusty Box Brownie.

It was gone midnight by the time Emily retired to her room. Despite the slats in the shutters, her room was airless and humid. She flung the shutters open in a vain attempt to circulate the still air and changed into her pyjamas. She climbed between the mosquito netting and stretched out on top of the bedsheet, listening to the exotic nocturnal chorus of tree frogs, crickets and cicadas until she drifted off, waking several hours later to shards of brilliant sunshine.

38

Tom sat on the edge of his narrow camp bed and laced up his boots with practised speed. From outside the tent came the all too familiar throb of approaching aircraft and he knew from bitter experience that he had literally minutes to get airborne before the base was raked by enemy gunfire.

Amidst the shouting and barking of orders, he grabbed his helmet and sprinted towards his plane, his co-pilot Rich Drummond close on his heels. All around him, his squadron were scrambling into action. The anti-aircraft gunners were already at their posts, scouring the skies for enemy planes. Tom swung himself up into the cockpit and started the propeller. The plane chugged to life and he rolled onto the grass runway. The plane bounced over the uneven ground and took off, shuddering as it hit a pocket of warm air. Tom held her steady, drawing back on the throttle, the wheels just clearing the tops of the trees as he coaxed her higher.

It had taken him almost two months to recover from the injuries he'd sustained in France. And, if it hadn't been for Rich, he wouldn't have survived at all. His insides turned to water every time he recalled just how close he'd come to death that day. He'd heard the click of the German soldier's gun, the sun glinting on metal as he'd pointed it at Tom. He'd closed his eyes and thought of Emily . . .

The gun had fired. Tom had opened his eyes, and the soldier was gone. Rich stood in his place, grinning like an idiot. He'd hoisted Tom over his shoulder and he'd found himself staring into the sightless eyes of the German soldier before passing out. It was only afterwards that he'd learned how Rich had carried him through the ensuing gun battle, not slowing his pace until he'd got Tom to the nearest safe house. As soon as he'd recovered sufficiently to withstand what would prove to be an arduous and dangerous journey, he'd been smuggled back to England.

On his discharge from the Queen Alexandra hospital in Cosham, he'd rejoined his squadron at the Royal Canadian Air Force base in the Far East. Since arriving in Burma late the previous year, his job had consisted mainly of supply drops to the many isolated camps scattered throughout the jungle. He'd had to rely on his skill as an aviator many times, attempting extremely steep approaches and take-offs, and his natural ability to remain calm under severe stress had enabled him to outmanoeuvre enemy aircraft on more than one occasion by flying at death-defying low altitudes in order to escape Japanese fighter planes.

Now, he arced the plane around, squinting into the shaft of sunlight breaking through the bank of thick cloud.

'Dead ahead, Tom,' Rich said calmly. With a steady hand, Tom eased off on the throttle as the plane was rocked by turbulence, and suddenly the sky was full of enemy planes.

★ ★ ★

The dogfight lasted several hours and they were joined by several other units but, eventually, the Allies forced the Japanese to retreat.

Tom's unit had lost two planes and four crew members. Several other planes limped home, trailing smoke. There had been injuries on the ground, too, and a mechanic had been killed, mown down as he ran for cover.

As always after a battle, the mood among the men was sombre. While medics treated the wounded, Tom grabbed a fold-out chair and set it up just inside his tent, out of the rain. Rich joined him, a cigarette dangling from his sunburnt lips.

'There were a few close calls out there today,' he said, shuffling a deck of cards. He ran a large hand through his sandy hair and flicked ash onto the damp ground.

'We sent them packing, though,' Tom said, stretching his tired, cramped muscles. The rain was growing heavier, drumming on the canvas and forming rivulets in the mud, which meandered beneath the tent flaps and seeped under the ground sheet.

If the monsoons only got rid of the mosquitoes, Tom mused wryly, scratching absently at a bite on his neck, he could bear the seemingly endless rainfall with more equanimity, but the puddles of stagnant water appeared to provide the ideal breeding ground for the annoying insects. He could hear one now, humming around inside the tent. Several of his squadron had gone down with malaria in recent weeks and stocks of quinine were running low.

'Shame about Wilder,' Rich said of the mechanic who'd been killed. 'He'd only just become a dad.' He licked his fingers and laid a card on the bed, face up. 'A little girl — Ginny. He showed me her picture. Bonny little thing.'

Tom laid his own card beside Rich's. 'Another little kiddie who'll grow up not knowing her father,' he said, with a twinge of guilt as an image of his own father came to mind. He reached for his canteen and took a swallow of tepid water. He tried not to think of Ernest, if he could help it, but, at times like this, when his survival had hung so precariously in the balance, his head would flood with thoughts of the father he hadn't seen in eight years.

★ ★ ★

He was still thinking of his father that afternoon as he lay on his camp bed, listening to the beat of the rain on the tent roof. Time had not erased the memory of that night so long ago, when he'd turned up on his father's doorstep, desperate and frightened. He had never got round to writing to his father about his uncle's death. It was something that weighed heavily on his heart, but as more time had passed, the more the imagined gulf between him and home had widened. It was far too late to put things right.

Thinking of his father inevitably turned to thoughts of Emily. He had often wondered how life might have turned out if he hadn't heeded Roland's advice to flee. Would they be married now? Or would he still be languishing in prison for a crime he hadn't committed? He smiled bitterly. He used to listen out for her songs on the radio, look out for mentions of her in the press. But every time Tom caught a glimpse of her photograph in the newspaper, posing with troops or, even worse, with Roland, it was like a red-hot poker to his heart and so he'd long since tried to stop torturing himself with what might have been. Now, when the rest of his squadron whistled and swooned over grainy newspaper images of the Bristol Songbird, he walked away. When her songs played on the camp wireless, he found something else to occupy his time, well out of earshot.

Tom stifled a groan and rubbed his hand across his eyes. The rain hadn't brought any relief from the humidity and, even wearing just his shorts and socks, his skin was soaked in perspiration.

He'd had his share of female attention over the years. He was an attractive man and the years of war had given him a ruggedness that had enhanced his good looks. There had been a brief romance with a young army nurse. It had ended when she was posted abroad and, sadly, he'd later learned that she had been killed when the ship she was travelling on was torpedoed.

Tom rolled onto his side and lit a cigarette, filling his lungs with nicotine as he tried to blot out the painful memories.

'Hey, Tom, get out here quick!' Rich ducked his head through the flap. His hair was plastered to his skull, rain streaming down his face. 'Come on! Hurry up.'

Bemused, Tom swung his feet to the floor and reached for his hat. Pushing the tent flap open, he was confronted by a sheet of rain that reminded him of the time he'd stood behind a waterfall up in the mountains. Setting his hat on his head, he squelched through the mud to the edge of the camp where most of his squadron seemed to have gathered, their excited chatter rising above the thunderous roar of the deluge.

'Hey, glad you could make it,' Rich said, slapping Tom on the back with a grin.

It was on the tip of Tom's tongue to ask what was

going on when he spotted her being helped out of a battered old Jeep by a young airman. Another held an umbrella open above her head, though to what point, Tom couldn't tell; she was already soaked to the skin, the Jeep's flimsy tarpaulin cover seemingly unfit for purpose. Her uniform clung to her in all the right places, eliciting catcalls and whistles of appreciation from the crowding men.

'Hello, boys,' Emily called with a cheery wave. She'd caught the sun, Tom noticed as she briefly removed her cap to wipe the rainwater from her eyes. It suited her, he thought, annoyed with himself for noticing. She wore her long, chestnut-brown hair scraped back in a ponytail and, when she smiled, she appeared to Tom even lovelier than he remembered. He was plucking up the courage to push his way through the crowd towards her when Roland appeared, grinning as he slipped his arm around her waist.

'Hello, chaps,' he called with a wave. 'Great to see you all. Good grief, but you're stuck out in the arse-end of nowhere aren't you?'

There were guffaws among the assembled men. Tom glowered at Roland, his smouldering jealousy tempered by a measure of sympathy for the man. He'd clearly suffered some horrific injury. One side of his head was badly scarred, and his ear was nothing more than a misshapen lump.

Whatever else Roland said was lost in the laughter but by then Tom was already walking away.

★ ★ ★

'Let's get you out of the rain, Miss Rose,' the young airman holding the umbrella said, ushering Emily

292

and Roland across the boggy ground to where four men were hastily erecting a tent. 'I'm afraid we weren't expecting you,' he said apologetically, 'or we'd have tried to arrange more suitable accommodation.'

'Don't you worry about us,' Emily laughed. 'We've slept in much worse.'

'We didn't know we were coming here either,' Roland told the boy. 'We were on our way to Ramu Airfield but our guide' — he indicated Maung, who was waving his arms about in an attempt to convey to a couple of RCAF servicemen the urgency of getting the piano undercover as quickly and as safely as possible — 'spotted your camp from the ridge back there and we thought a surprise visit would be good for the morale. We heard about the fighting this morning. We're sorry about your comrade.'

'Thank you, sir. I'm Joel, by the way. Aviator Joel Robinson.'

'We're pleased to meet you, Aviator Robinson,' Roland said.

'I'm so happy you decided to stop by.' He grinned. He was a cheeky-faced chap with freckles and ginger hair that was just visible below his cap. 'Well, miss, sir, your tents are ready. I shan't keep you out in the rain any longer.' He handed Emily the umbrella.

They thanked him and the men who had so effortlessly put the tents up, and crawled inside. Emily was wet through, the Jeep's makeshift tarpaulin roof having offered little protection against the deluge. At least it was warm, she mused, stripping off her jacket. Thankfully, though her suitcase had leaked a bit around the edges, most of her stuff was dry and she quickly found another shirt, which she pulled on over her damp underwear.

It was the middle of May, two weeks since the start of the monsoon season. The incessant rains, mudslides and inevitable flooding had all conspired to make travelling around the area even more hazardous. Not to mention the possibility of stumbling upon Japanese soldiers out on patrol. There had been a rumour doing the rounds recently that a company of ENSA performers had been taken captive by the Japanese but a rumour was all it had turned out to be. It had made them all a little more anxious just the same.

'I hope the piano's all right,' Emily said, a short time later as she and Roland huddled beneath the umbrella and picked their way across the boggy ground towards the mess tent. 'It got quite wet today. I think today's the worst we've had. I hope we can get back across that creek tomorrow. It looked like it was rising quite rapidly.'

'Maung will manage. He seems able to navigate any manner of obstacles. I'm more worried about enemy fire. If we were closer this morning . . .' He let the rest of the sentence trail away. They'd watched the dogfights from an army base twelve miles away, their hearts in their throats as they willed the Allies to victory.

'I'm not naïve to the dangers, Roland,' Emily reminded him. 'I know we wouldn't stand a chance if we got caught by the Japanese, but it's a risk I'm willing to take for the sake of these boys.'

'I know. And I commend you for it. You're braver than me, most of the time.'

'I'm not brave at all.' Emily smiled. 'I'm frightened a lot of the time — more for the troops than for myself, though. When I'm standing on stage looking out at all those smiling, happy faces, it's so hard not

294

to wonder which of these boys will still be alive next week, or next month. It's horrible.'

Roland gave her arm a squeeze. 'And that's what makes you so special,' he said, softly. 'You make sure you give them a great time, and you don't only entertain them, you take the time to talk to them, and get to know them. That's important, Emily. Especially when they're so far from home. They like to know that someone cares.'

'I do care,' said Emily fervently. 'I care very much.'

'I know you do, sweetheart,' smiled Roland. 'We need to find out where we can perform tonight. Hopefully it's somewhere undercover. I don't fancy singing in the rain.'

'It wouldn't be the first time,' Emily quipped, shaking the rainwater from the umbrella as they reached the mess tent and ducked inside.

39

Emily and Roland performed in the mess tent for several hundred men with many more crowded outside in the pouring rain. It was raining so hard, the sound of it drumming on the canvas roof almost drowned out Emily's voice at one point. But she persevered, and the men went wild. Every song was met by a standing ovation, and by the time she was finished, her make-up was running and she was bathed in perspiration. Her throat ached, but she continued to smile at the waving, cheering men.

Suddenly, amongst the crowd she glimpsed a face from her past. The colour drained from her cheeks, and despite the oppressive heat, her skin erupted in goosebumps.

'Tom,' she mouthed over the roar of stamping feet and resounding cheers. She blinked and scanned the sea of faces, but he was gone. She stared at the spot where he had been just moments before. Had he been a figment of her imagination? She frowned. Had her fevered mind, fatigued by the stress of travelling in a war zone, conjured him up? No, he had definitely been real. When she brought Tom to mind, he was the young, fresh-faced twenty-three-year-old man she remembered. The Tom she had seen in the crowd was older, worldlier. Her heart skipped a beat and her stomach somersaulted, her eyes searching the crowd desperately.

'Are you all right, Emily?' Roland asked, his voice low enough to be heard above the cheering. 'You look as though you've seen a ghost.'

'I think I have,' she said simply. Roland frowned, following Emily's frantic gaze. 'I've just seen Tom.'

'Your Tom?'

Emily pulled a face. 'Well, he isn't my Tom, is he?' she said, her stomach plummeting with the awful realization that Tom could, conceivably, have a wife waiting for him back home. It had been eight years, after all. He was bound to have met someone else, as she had with Kit.

As she moved amongst the crowds, chatting to the men, asking after their families, their hometowns, her thoughts were on Tom. If it was indeed him, then he clearly didn't want to see her. She bit her lip in consternation and tried hard to concentrate on the photographs a pleasant-faced airman was showing her of his wife and son back home.

The rain had stopped by the time Emily and Roland groped their way between the rows of tents, slapping at exposed parts of flesh in a futile attempt to kill the mosquitoes that whined incessantly around their heads. The steamy air throbbed with the hum of cicadas and the dark night sky glittered with a million stars.

'Wow, it's so beautiful,' Emily said, stopping to look up at the star-studded canopy. 'The sky seems so huge here.'

'Emily.' She froze, recognizing his voice instantly.

'Tom,' said Roland with a cheeriness that sounded forced. 'What a surprise.'

'Roland,' said Tom curtly, emerging from the shadows, his face gleaming in the starlight. His gaze rested on Emily. She swallowed hard.

'Hello, Tom,' she croaked.

It was as if the years had fallen away. They stared at each other for what seemed like the longest time until the spell was broken by Roland's awkward cough.

'I'll get back to my tent, Emily. I'll see you in the morning.'

'Are you and Roland a couple?' Tom demanded bluntly, as soon as Roland was out of earshot. Emily shook her head.

'No. He's my pianist and chaperone, and a dear friend.'

'A dear friend, hmm?' drawled Tom with a smirk.

'I know he encouraged you to leave, Tom,' she said, involuntarily stepping closer to him, her heart hammering against her ribcage.

'And yet you call him a friend?' Tom sneered in disgust. 'After what he did to us? I don't suppose he told you that I asked him to apologize to you, to tell you I love you and that I'd come back for you one day when it was safe for me to do so?'

'No, he didn't,' Emily admitted. 'Not straight away. But you didn't have to leave! He didn't make you.'

'He said people would believe I was guilty, that I'd drag you down,' Tom said, his voice ragged with emotion. 'And you could have answered my letter!' he added, bitterly.

Emily looked down. 'Oh, Tom. Your letter was sent on to Roland after I left the hotel. He threw it away — I didn't know about it until years later, and by then I didn't know how to reach you.' Then her anguish turned to defiance. 'But you could have tried again! Or written to your father — Ernest hasn't heard from you once since you landed in Canada.'

'You still see my father?' Tom asked, surprised.

'As often as I can. He misses you, Tom.' As do I. The

298

words came unbidden into her head but remained unsaid. 'Why did you never write again?'

'I thought . . . ' Tom rubbed the bridge of his nose with his forefinger. 'I thought that if Dad could believe Lucy's lies, maybe you did too. I assumed that was why you never wrote back.'

'Oh, Tom,' Emily said quietly. 'Lucy recanted her accusations.'

'What?' Tom said, aghast, his eyes wide in shock. He frowned. 'Is that true?'

'Yes,' she said softly, her eyes sad. 'It was the day Ernest received the telegram saying you'd sailed for Canada. And, Tom, Ernest never believed Lucy for one second. He's desperate for you to come home.'

Emily took a deep breath as she struggled to control her emotions. Despite her lingering grief over Kit, seeing Tom had brought back all the heartache. She was still so much in love with him, she realized, and probably always would be.

'Captain.' The voice in the darkness startled them both.

'Brigadier General,' Tom said, saluting quickly as his superior was illuminated by the faint light emanating from the tents. 'Perhaps you'd be so kind as to escort Miss Rose to her tent,' the brigadier said pointedly.

'Yes, sir.' Tom nodded as the brigadier general bade them both goodnight. They made their way between the rows of canvas, excruciatingly close, yet worlds apart. They came to a halt outside her tent. From nearby came a burst of laughter as someone attempted to sing one of her songs. The air between them seemed to crackle with expectation. Emily shivered in anticipation.

From deep in the jungle came a loud explosion that lit up the sky. Emily jumped and the moment was lost.

'It's all right, lads,' Tom called out reassuringly as heads peered out of tent flaps. 'It's nowhere near us.' He turned back to Emily, a pained expression on his face. He gave her a wry smile. 'Goodnight, Emily,' he said softly, holding the flap of her tent open. 'Sweet dreams.'

Struggling to hide her disappointment. Emily crawled inside, groping through the darkness for her camp bed. Not bothering to undress, she curled up on top of her sleeping bag, her emotions in turmoil.

How could Tom have possibly believed his father to be ashamed of him for all these years? Ernest would be devastated. She groaned in frustration. So many wasted years. If only Tom hadn't acted so impulsively.

She lay awake in the all-consuming darkness, listening to the high-pitched whine of mosquitoes and the endless, vibrating hum of insects, punctuated by bursts of distant gunfire.

She heard the soft cough of a sentry on patrol as he passed by her tent, the soft sucking noise of heavy boots on boggy ground and she rolled onto her side, letting the tears fall.

★ ★ ★

Despite another heavy rainfall during the night, the following morning dawned sunny and steamy. Emily emerged into dazzling sunlight, drenched in perspiration and struggling to breathe in the high humidity. The surrounding jungle reverberated with the croak of tree frogs and exotic birdsong.

The camp was a hive of activity as morning chores

were completed and breakfast was served to thousands of troops. The men fought to share Emily's table, all wanting to talk and recount stories of their lives back home in Canada.

As she smiled and chatted to the troops, she cast her eye around the vast dining tent in search of Tom. After their conversation the night before, she was upset that he appeared to be avoiding her and she was terrified that she would leave the camp and never see him again.

She and Roland spent their final hours in the camp posing for photographs, visiting the sick and wounded and signing autographs while Maung and two airmen manhandled the little piano through the mud and onto the Jeep, covering it with the tarpaulin. The sky had darkened again, and a hot wind whipped the surrounding foliage. Even the birds and insects had fallen silent.

Troops swarmed their Jeep as they prepared to leave.

'Thank you so much for taking the time to visit us, Miss Rose, Mr Thurston,' said Brigadier General Lewis, shaking Emily and Roland by the hand. He was a tall man in his early forties with severely cropped dark hair and a weathered complexion. 'We appreciate it.'

'Thank you for your hospitality, sir,' Emily replied with a heavy heart. She was still hoping to see Tom again before she left, but much as she scanned the sea of smiling faces, he was nowhere to be seen.

Maung started the engine and the Jeep spluttered reluctantly to life. The camp erupted in cheers and whistles as they drove away. Emily twisted in her seat to wave, smiling bravely, despite the tears that threatened. The Jeep rounded a bend and she slumped back in her seat, closing her eyes.

They had barely gone a mile down the rough track when the first drops of rain began to fall. Within seconds, it had turned into a deluge of biblical proportions, the tarpaulin cover offering little protection from the driving rain. Steam rose up from the hot ground, and the road soon became a quagmire. Maung had his work cut out trying to control the vehicle as it slithered and slipped in the mud.

From somewhere terrifyingly close by, Emily heard the sound of gunfire.

★ ★ ★

Tom lay on his narrow camp bed, hands behind his head, thinking about Emily. It had been clear last night that all the old feelings between them were still there and, if they hadn't been interrupted, who knows how things might have turned out? But that morning, in the cold light of day, he'd managed to convince himself that he had no place in her world, and so he had deliberately absented himself until she left the camp, foolishly believing that if he avoided her, the ache in his heart might go away. Instead, it had only intensified. Now he was regretting his pig-headedness. There was so much he wished he'd said but it was too late.

'Captain Harding,' a young private said, poking his head through the tent flap and breaking Tom's reverie. 'Brigadier General Lewis wants a word, sir.'

Getting up, Tom grabbed his jacket and cap and hastened out into the pouring rain in the direction of the brigadier general's tent. Nodding at the sentry, he ducked inside.

The large, roomy tent had been laid out exactly like Brigadier General Lewis's study at his headquarters back in Montreal. He was sitting behind his large teak desk when Tom entered, studying a piece of paper with a worried frown upon his face.

'Brigadier General.' Tom saluted him. 'You wished to see me, sir?'

'Captain, I've received a worrying report that there are enemy patrols in the vicinity.'

Tom caught the man's meaning instantly. 'Emily!' he cried in alarm.

'Yes,' the brigadier general nodded solemnly. 'I fear that Miss Rose and Mr Thurston may be heading straight into an ambush. I've radioed ground support but the nearest patrol is over half an hour away. Go after them, Captain.'

'Yes, sir.' Barely taking the time to salute, Tom dashed from the tent, already calling for back-up as he raced towards the vehicle pool. Jumping into the nearest Jeep, he turned the key in the ignition, moving the vehicle forward even as men were piling in behind him.

'What's going down?' asked Rich, clambering into the passenger seat.

'Japs on patrol,' Tom said grimly, gunning the engine as the Jeep bounced across the churned-up ground. 'Right where Emily is headed.'

Rich blanched and swore. 'We'd better get a move on, then. They've had at least a twenty-minute head start.'

'I'm praying their Burmese driver doesn't drive as fast as me,' Tom said through gritted teeth as the Jeep slewed across the road. He fought for control, easing off on the accelerator slightly as he led the convoy down the slippery track.

Emily slid low in the back seat. Her heart was racing. Fear had squeezed the air from her lungs and she could hardly breathe. She had never been so frightened in her life. So far, Maung assured her, the Japanese were unaware of their presence.

'If they knew we were here, we'd be dead already,' he said matter-of-factly as Emily and Roland exchanged terrified glances. 'We just need to get to the river,' the young Burmese man said, tightening his grip on the steering wheel as they careered down a steep incline. Emily could just hear the roar of the river in the valley below over the tumult of the rain. 'We'll be safer on the other side. There are British and Allied soldiers there.'

Emily craned her neck, scanning the waving fronds of the dark, forbidding jungle. She knew stealth was one of the Japanese soldiers' greatest attributes. If there were soldiers nearby, by the time the three of them spotted them, it would be too late.

The Jeep continued its downward slide, the sound of rushing water thundering in Emily's ear. She could see the river now, a tumultuous, heaving mass of brown, foam-flecked water swallowing everything in its path. Maung rolled the Jeep to a halt as close to the bank as he dared and the three of them got out, transfixed by the sight of the raging maelstrom. Tree branches and other debris swirled in the seething cauldron. A dead ox floated by, swept along by the swift current.

'We'll never make it across,' Roland said in alarm.

Maung shrugged his thin shoulders. 'No choice,' he said, simply. He cocked his head as another round of gunfire echoed through the valley. 'They're close.'

Emily looked at the river, her throat dry.

'We either risk being washed away, or being caught by the Japanese,' she told Roland. 'At least this way we'll have a chance.'

Roland didn't answer. Instead, he walked to the water's edge, staring at the debris tumbling and swirling as it was dragged along by force of the water. He flicked his cigarette butt into the river where it spun frantically for a few seconds before being whipped downstream.

'It's difficult to tell how deep it is,' he said, looking up and down the bank. There were a lot of low-hanging trees, their branches dragging in the water.

'No choice,' Maung said again with an urgency that brooked no argument. They got back in the Jeep, their clothes clinging to them like a second skin, and Maung started the engine.

Slowly he rolled the Jeep forward. Emily held her breath as the water slammed into the front of the vehicle, but the wheels held firm. The car rocked as Maung eased it into the river. Water gushed over the bonnet, splashing Emily in the face as it swamped the back seat.

So far, the wheels were managing to find purchase on the riverbed. For a second, they became embedded in the silt, but Maung revved the engine loudly and the Jeep inched forward. From the dense jungle came a shout. Emily's heart froze and she fixed her gaze on the approaching bank; so tantalizingly close, yet their progress was excruciatingly slow.

Just as the front wheels made purchase on the opposite bank, the water level surged and the Jeep rose from the ground. Emily squealed, clinging to the front seat as the Jeep was swept downriver. Maung wrenched the steering wheel in vain. They were swept along helplessly. All attempts to grab hold of an overhanging branch proved fruitless. They were moving too fast. Something large and solid slammed into the Jeep, and the next moment, Emily found herself in the water. Choking on a mouthful of silt, she spun round and round in dizzying circles until she was dragged under by the current. Her cheeks grazed the riverbed and water thundered in her ears as she groped blindly for something to grab hold of. The pressure in her chest was intense as her lungs screamed for oxygen and her strength was beginning to fail. But just as it felt as though she might give up and drift into oblivion, her fingers closed over a tree root. Praying it would hold, she forced her head above the water, gasping for air. With supreme effort she managed to drag herself up the slippery bank. Blinking water out of her eyes, she scanned the riverbank for a sign of Roland and Maung, a sob rising in her throat as she realized she was completely alone.

She crawled further up the wet grass, wedging herself between two tree trunks, their bark wet with slime. She was filthy. Mud and twigs clung to her hair. Her uniform was caked in silt and her face and hands stung where she'd grazed herself on the riverbed. Knowing an infected wound was one of the most common killers in the jungle, she carefully inspected each abrasion. Satisfied that they appeared clean enough, she scanned the riverbank, pondering her dilemma. She was alone in a jungle teeming with enemy soldiers, without food or water.

Sporadic bursts of gunfire erupted further up the bank and she whimpered in terror as she pressed herself against the trees. Then she heard someone call her name. She shook her head in bewilderment, thinking she must be hallucinating for it sounded very much like Tom's voice.

'Emily!' She heard it again and relief surged through her veins.

'Tom.' Her hoarse croak was barely audible above the roar of the water and she forced herself to her feet. She tried again. 'Tom!' Her legs shook with the exertion of standing up and she had a throbbing pain above her left eye. In her panic, she hadn't realised she'd hit her head.

'Emily! Where are you?' Roland's voice this time.

'Miss Rose! Emily!' The jungle seemed to suddenly vibrate with people calling her name. There was more gunfire but further away this time.

'Here,' she tried to shout. 'I'm over here.'

'Emily! She's here!' Shouldering his rifle, Tom slithered down the bank. Without another word he pulled her into his arms. Emily clung to him, shivering despite the sticky heat of the day. 'It's okay,' he said softly as he stroked her hair. 'It's okay. I've got you. You're safe now. Medics!' he bellowed over his shoulder. 'Over here, hurry.'

The medics came sliding down the bank, followed by Roland, white-faced and wide-eyed with terror.

'God, Emily,' he said, pushing Tom aside and grabbing her in a clumsy embrace. 'I thought we'd lost you.'

'Let us do our job, sir,' one of the medics said firmly, nudging him aside.

'I'm okay,' Emily croaked with the semblance of a smile, as Roland reluctantly released her. She glanced about her uneasily. 'Are we safe here? The Japanese?'

'We've pushed them back for the time being,' Tom replied. 'But we haven't got long. Now they know we're here, they'll be back with reinforcements. We need to get you back to Chittagong as quick as possible.'

'You'll be okay, miss,' the first medic said. 'A lot of scratches and abrasions but they're superficial. You've taken a nasty bump to the head, but that'll heal in a day or so. Get plenty of rest.'

'Thank you,' Emily said hoarsely.

The medic grinned. 'You might want to rest that voice of yours for a day or two, as well.'

'She's going to have plenty of R and R,' Roland said firmly. 'I shall insist on it.'

'We need to get you away from here,' Tom said, his dark eyes serious. 'I'm afraid it'll be a while before your Jeep's drivable, if at all.'

'Maung?' Emily asked, anxiously.

'He's fine,' Roland assured her. 'Oh, good grief,' he said in astonishment. 'Look at that.' Everyone turned in time to see the little piano bobbing along down the river.

'Our piano,' Emily wailed. 'Oh, what a shame. It's travelled so far with us, too.'

'We'll find another one,' Roland said. 'What matters is that we're all safe.'

'Hear, hear,' agreed an airman with sandy hair. He gave Emily a wink. 'I think Captain Harding is waiting to drive you back to your billet, Miss Rose,' he said.

'It's a long drive,' Tom said, avoiding his mate's curious, teasing gaze. 'And we want to be back at base before nightfall.'

40

'It's very kind of you to drive us back,' Emily said, massaging her throat. It felt as though it had been scoured with sandpaper.

'Think nothing of it,' replied Tom, more sharply than he'd intended. He was still reeling with the knowledge of how close to death Emily had come.

Rain drummed on the canvas roll-top as the Jeep splashed along the rutted track. It had taken Tom's men less than thirty minutes to construct a makeshift bridge across the flooded river and now they were a mere sixty miles from the border, but given the arduous terrain, it would be several hours before they reached Chittagong.

'You will write to your father, won't you?' Emily said quietly, needing to fill the heavy silence that had fallen between them.

'Yes,' replied Tom brusquely. Acutely aware of Emily's presence beside him, he kept his gaze fixed on the road ahead. Even scratched and bruised and covered in mud, she looked beautiful. All he wanted to do was take her in his arms. He shook his head, forcing the thought from his mind.

Hurt by Tom's surly reply, Emily swallowed painfully. She took a sip of water from his canteen, her own having been swept away along with the rest of her belongings. An awkward silence descended between them and she was grateful for the cheerful banter coming from the back seat.

At that moment, the Jeep hit a pothole, sending

them flying through the air.

'Take it easy, mate,' drawled Rich, giving Tom's shoulder a pat.

'Sorry chaps,' Tom apologized. 'I wasn't concentrating.'

'We're unlikely to encounter any enemy patrols this far west,' Maung pointed out knowledgably.

'That's true,' agreed Rich, 'but we need to keep our wits about us.'

'I shall be jolly glad to get back to civilization,' Roland said, fishing out his cigarette case. 'I take my hat off to you chaps, always in the thick of it.'

'Most of the time we're bored out of our minds,' Rich said with a grin.

'It's the waiting and wondering that's the worst,' Tom added. 'You know they're out there but you don't know when or where they're going to strike.'

★ ★ ★

There was a break in the clouds as they drove down the hill towards Chittagong. The exotic city shimmered in the late afternoon sunshine and, beyond it, the Bay of Bengal gleamed like molten gold.

Tom pulled up outside the Palm Court Hotel.

'Thanks for the ride, Tom,' said Roland, somewhat sheepishly.

Tom nodded. If it was down to him he'd have made Thurston walk back to Chittagong. He turned to Emily. During the long drive he'd been mulling over the possibility that perhaps it wasn't too late for them. Telling himself that nothing ventured was nothing gained, he said, 'I've got a twenty-four-hour furlough coming up.' He cleared his throat nervously. 'I was

310

wondering if you might like to have tea with me?'

Emily's answering smile was tempered with caution. Though she had been dreading getting out of the car and never seeing him again, the memory of Tom's desertion was still so fresh in her mind, and as she would be leaving within weeks, she was hesitant to open herself up to any more potential heartache.

'I really would like to see you again,' Tom said, his voice soft.

'Yes,' Emily heard herself say. 'I'd like that.'

Tom grinned in obvious relief. 'Great. I'll let you know as soon as I'm in town.'

As Emily made to get out of the Jeep, he grabbed her hand. She looked him in the eye. His expression was serious.

'Stay safe, Emily.'

'I will,' she promised.

She stood on the kerb and watched them drive away.

'Well,' said Roland with a sigh of resignation. 'That's that then. You'll be back together before the week's out.'

'I should still be grieving,' Emily said as a wave of guilt washed over her. 'Kit's barely cold in his grave.'

'Now, listen here,' Roland said sternly, 'Kit's gone. Sad as that is, you of all people should know life's too short not to grab the opportunities life offers you with both hands. Tom was like a man in torment when we thought you'd been washed away. He's still in love with you. Not many people get a second chance, Emily. You'd be a fool not to take it.'

Sensing Emily's disquiet, he changed the subject. 'Right, I'm off to send a telegram to ENSA headquarters. They're not going to be very happy when I tell them that our piano is probably halfway to the ocean by now. I'll see you later.'

With her ENSA uniform stiff with dried mud, and a very visible bump on her head, Emily drew a lot of attention on entering the lobby. A female officer hurried over to enquire if she was all right.

'I am, thank you,' Emily replied. 'But I'd love a hot bath, if possible?'

'Of course. I'll get someone onto it straight away.' The woman paused. 'Thank you for what you do for our boys, Miss Rose.' She smiled. 'You visited my Jack's camp in Bawli Bazar last month. He said it boosted their morale no end.'

'It's good to know we're making a difference,' croaked Emily.

In her room she stripped off her filthy clothes and climbed into the tin bath where she lay for half an hour, luxuriating in the warm water. Of course, her thoughts were of Tom. He had changed over the years, as, undoubtedly, had she. Yet he was still her Tom. She had seen it in his eyes on the riverbank. Time hadn't dimmed his love for her. She felt a twinge deep inside for Kit but as Roland had said, he was gone. If she had a chance of happiness with Tom, she had to take it.

The water was growing cool and she stepped out of the bath, wrapping herself in a towel. The shutters were open, allowing the most air possible into the room, and the sound of the gently falling rain was incredibly soothing.

It had been a frightening day, but there had been many such days since leaving England so many weeks before and she was determined not to dwell on the darker side of her mission. She was in the middle of a war zone, after all, and her heart went out to the thousands of men and women who would never get the chance to return home. She could only pray that Tom wouldn't be one of them. She couldn't bear it if she'd found him only to lose him again.

★ ★ ★

'I think I'm ready to start performing again,' Emily said to Roland three days later. They were sitting in the hotel's shady courtyard. Palm fronds waved in the gentle breeze and the sky was clear blue, though the puddles bore witness to the torrential downpour earlier that morning. 'My throat feels much better,' she continued, taking a sip of her iced tea.

'Are you sure?' Roland asked, lowering his newspaper. 'You could damage your voice irreparably if you rush it.'

'I'm fine,' Emily reiterated. 'I saw the army doctor this morning and he's happy for me to resume touring.'

'Oh, right. Well, if the doctor said it's okay then I'm happy with that,' Roland said, turning his attention back to the morning's news. 'It says here that our troops have taken an important airfield at Myitkyina,' he read, one hand snaking out from behind the newspaper to reach for his glass.

Emily was about to comment when her attention was drawn to the figure reflected in the open patio doors. 'Oh,' she said, momentarily flustered. 'It's Tom.'

Roland lowered his newspaper and gave Emily a knowing smile. Ignoring him, she got anxiously to her feet, feeling as gauche as a lovesick schoolgirl. Catching sight of her, Tom paused in the open doorway. He cut a very dapper figure in his Royal Canadian Air Force uniform, though to Emily he seemed a little unsure of himself. He met her eyes, his fingers fiddling nervously with his cap, which he held in his hands.

'Tom,' Emily said as she approached him, her heart thumping. 'I wasn't expecting you so soon . . .'

'No,' said Tom, dropping his gaze. His highly polished shoes had picked up a coating of dust on their journey from his billet down the street to the Palm Court Hotel. 'I only arrived in town fifteen minutes ago.'

'Oh,' Emily said, her pulse quickening as the realization dawned that Tom had been so eager to see her that he had come straight round to the hotel.

'I'm sorry,' he apologized, looking slightly deflated. 'I should have sent a message first. That had been my intention but I was impatient to see you.' He smiled apprehensively.

'Well, I'm very happy to see you,' Emily said shyly. 'We've just ordered iced tea. Would you like a glass?'

'That would be nice, thank you.' Tom followed her to their table, which was situated near a marble cherub water fountain gushing brackish water into an algae-laced pool.

'Tom, good to see you again,' said Roland, setting his folded newspaper aside.

'Roland.' Tom looked at him coldly. Ignoring the outstretched hand, he sat down. As if out of nowhere, a waiter appeared, setting a clean teacup and napkin in front of Tom.

'Thank you,' he said as Emily poured the iced tea.

'You're looking a lot better than when I last saw you,' he said. 'That bump on your head's barely noticeable.

314

And your voice sounds a lot stronger.'

'It was all superficial,' Emily assured him. 'And the doctor assures me that I'm well enough to start singing again.'

'That's great,' Tom said, fishing a sprig of mint out of his glass.

'I think I'll take myself off for a stroll,' Roland said, draining his tea and scraping back his chair.

'Please don't leave on my account,' said Tom, his tone implying otherwise.

'No, no,' Roland insisted. 'I could do with stretching my legs.' He bent down to give Emily a peck on the cheek.

'Good riddance,' Tom observed drily, once Roland had disappeared into the hotel.

'I know you're angry, and you've every right to be,' Emily said, picking up her glass. 'But he's really sorry for what he did. He feels very ashamed.'

'So he should be,' Tom said bitterly. 'I can't understand why you're so fond of him. Along with Lucy, he ruined our lives. If it hadn't been for the pair of them, we'd be mar—' He broke off and looked away.

'Married?' queried Emily more sharply than she'd intended. 'Yes, we probably would be. What Lucy did was appalling, and I'm sure Roland was very persuasive. But, Tom, you made the decision to leave.' She smiled sadly. 'No one forced you. You could have stayed and fought the allegations. The truth would have come out eventually.'

Tom had the grace to look shamefaced. 'Hindsight's a wonderful thing,' he said with a regretful sigh. 'You're right. I should never have left. I was a coward. But in my defence, I wasn't thinking straight. I was petrified. Roland did a pretty good job of persuading me that everyone would believe Lucy and Rosie's version of events.'

'They both got the sack, in the end,' Emily told him. 'And I know Roland deeply regrets what he did, particularly destroying your letter. I was so angry with him when I found out. We didn't speak for a long time.' She sipped her tea. 'I only forgave him after he suffered his horrific accident.'

'I know the newspapers make much of your relationship with Roland,' Tom said, swirling the ice in his glass. 'Has there ever been any romance between you?' He tried to keep his tone as casual as he could.

'None whatsoever,' Emily assured him with a smile.

'You're aware he's in love with you, surely?' Tom said, raising one brow.

'Roland and I are good friends, that's all,' Emily said quietly.

She studied Tom's face: the set jaw, the determined mouth, the furrowed brow.

'Penny for them?' she said, with a playful smile. She was starting to feel more at ease with him now, yet she still felt reticent. Before he died, Kit had begun to chip away at the protective wall she'd erected around her heart since losing Tom, and if she wasn't careful, it was in very real danger of crumbling altogether.

'So much time wasted,' Tom said, his voice thick with regret. 'I'm sorry I didn't write again, Emily. I almost did, so many times. I've made such a mess of things.' He ran his hand across his face. 'I've written to my father, by the way.'

'Oh, Tom,' Emily sighed in relief. 'I'm glad. He'll be so pleased. Poor Ernest. He was devastated when you left. He wrote to your uncle, you know. We hoped that might be where you were headed but, sadly, he

316

received word that your uncle had passed away, so that was that hope dashed. Ernest was heartbroken.'

'I found the place deserted,' Tom said, remembering. 'My uncle's solicitor turned up while I was there to collect the mail, I . . . ' He let his words trail away. He could see his own despair mirrored in Emily's eyes as the realization dawned upon them both. Ernest's letter would likely have been amongst the pile Samuel Jones had picked up that day.

'Do you ever get the feeling the fates have been transpiring against us?' he said wryly.

Emily smiled grimly. 'It's scary how the actions of one spiteful person can have such long-reaching repercussions.'

Tom looked at Emily with a haunted expression. Perspiration had soaked through the fabric of his royal-blue shirt, forming dark circles underneath his arms and across his chest.

'I just hope my father can forgive me.'

He buried his face in his hands. To Emily's amazement she realized that he was sobbing.

'Oh, Tom.' She pushed back her chair and hurried to his side, laying a tentative arm across his shaking shoulders. He grabbed her hand in his and buried his face against her. 'It's all right,' she said softly, gently stroking his hair. 'It's going to be all right.'

41

'You must think I'm a right cissy,' Tom said sometime later as they strolled along the promenade. Storm clouds were gathering on the horizon, but for now the sky overhead was clear. Sun danced on the smooth surface of the water and a long-legged heron waded in the shallows near to a group of children playing on the mud flats.

'I think nothing of the sort,' Emily said firmly. 'We're both a bit overwhelmed. And you don't need to worry about Ernest. He'll be over the moon when he gets your letter.'

'It was just something he said that night.' Tom frowned. 'Something he implied. Maybe he didn't mean it the way it came out, but you know what our relationship was like.' He sighed. 'I just hope I get the chance to apologize to him in person.'

'You will,' Emily assured him. 'Perhaps what Roland said about everyone believing Lucy had been playing on your mind, too, so that by the time you made it home, you expected your dad to feel the same. And you were tired, Tom. Like you said, you weren't thinking straight.'

'I wasn't thinking at all,' he said ruefully. 'I just hope I get a chance to make it up to him properly.'

They fell silent, both of them aware of the precarious times they were living in. Tomorrow wasn't a certainty, for either of them.

Emily's gaze drifted towards the distant hills where plumes of smoke had been rising above the trees all day. Music drifted from an open window across the street and the promenade teemed with servicemen and women, and army nurses, making the most of the brief bout of fair weather before the next band of rain moved in. A few servicemen walked arm in arm with local girls. The food stalls lining the pavements thronged with customers, the appetizing aroma of frying food hanging on the sultry air, mingling with the tang of diesel oil and animal dung. The road between was clogged with traffic as donkey carts, military vehicles and even, to Emily's excited amazement, an elephant made their way along the main thoroughfare.

Mouths watering, they wandered amongst the stalls, close together, but not quite touching, looking with interest at the varied exotic foodstuffs on sale, the vendors beckoning them over as they vied for their business.

Settling on a samosa salad — a dish consisting of fried samosas cut into strips and mixed with fried chickpeas, cabbage and potato, swimming in a delicious broth — for which Tom insisted on paying, they took their food over to one of the rustic tables beneath a bowed tarpaulin canopy and sat down.

'This is delicious,' Emily said, tucking in with enthusiasm. She took a sip of the local beer and spluttered. 'I'm not too keen on this, though.' She pulled a face.

'It is a bit on the rough side,' Tom agreed. 'They sell better stuff in the Officer's Club.' He paused, feeling suddenly awkward. He and Emily had been getting on so well, he was reluctant to spoil things by moving too fast. But with less than twelve hours of furlough left, time was not on his side. Taking a deep breath, he took the plunge. 'There's a dinner dance at the

Officer's Club tonight and I'd be honoured if you'd accompany me.'

'A dance?' Emily wiped her lips, playing for time. Dare she risk her heart again? She was acutely aware that tomorrow morning Tom would be heading back to base. With no guarantee as to when, if ever, she would see him again, her mind was made up. Even if she never saw him again, any heartache was worth it, to spend as many precious hours in Tom's company as possible. Keeping her tone light, she said, 'It's been a while since I've been out dancing. I'd love to go, thank you.'

Tom grinned. 'I'll pick you up about seven?'

'That sounds perfect,' Emily said with a smile.

'Has there been . . . I mean . . . ' Tom cleared his throat. 'Has there been anyone else in your life?'

The loud traffic noise seemed to fade into the background as Emily took a deep breath and said, 'Yes. His name was Kit.' She gave a sad smile. 'I met him while I was performing near Dover. He was killed earlier this year.'

'I'm sorry,' Tom said, empathy reflected in his dark eyes.

'What about you?'

'There was someone. Cathy. She was killed too.'

They fell silent amidst the blaring of car horns and the braying of donkeys, remembering those they had loved and lost. Thankfully, Miss Anne's most recent letter, posted six weeks earlier, had brought the news that her friends from College Street were all safe and well. Lulu, now happily married to her GI and expecting a baby, was back living with Miss Anne while her husband was posted overseas. Leah and Barbara were still touring the length and breadth of

Britain, entertaining the troops.

'Tell me about Canada,' Emily asked, in an attempt to relieve the melancholy that had settled over them.

'It's a very vast and beautiful country,' Tom replied. 'Snow-capped mountains and huge lakes. I travelled around a lot, working where I could, on farms mostly. It's bitterly cold in winter and hot in summer.'

'I'd love to go there one day,' Emily said wistfully. 'When all this is over.'

'I'd like to take you there,' Tom said, smiling at her over his pint.

They talked for the rest of the afternoon, reluctant for their time together to end, but as the sun sank lower in the sky, Emily got to her feet.

'If I don't go now, I won't be ready for you by seven,' she told Tom.

'It's been almost like old times,' Tom said, as he walked her back to the hotel. 'I've really enjoyed myself.'

'Me too,' said Emily. They paused on the front steps. 'I'll see you tonight.'

'I'll look forward to it,' Tom said, heading off down the street with a wave.

★　★　★

Tom arrived early. Scanning the hotel lobby, he spotted Roland sitting at the bar and strolled over to him.

'Evening, Tom,' Roland nodded. His ENSA uniform had been freshly pressed by a willing member of staff, whom he suspected had a bit of a crush on him, and he'd engaged the services of a shoe-shine boy to get his mud-caked boots up to scratch. 'Pint?'

'No, thank you,' Tom declined somewhat tersely.

321

Emily might have forgiven Roland, but he certainly wasn't prepared to. 'I'm here to pick up Emily.'

'So I believe. Well, have a good time.'

'You're in love with her, aren't you?' Tom blurted out. Roland pulled a face.

'Is it that obvious?'

'Yes.'

Roland sighed. 'Look, Tom, I know sorry can never make up for what I did,' he said ruefully. 'But I am, truly. I should never have interfered that night and destroying your letter . . . ' He shook his head. 'That was despicable and totally unforgivable. I can only say that I saw Emily as a lucrative meal ticket. Like I told her, at the time I was thinking only of the career she could have, the money she could make and, yes, I think I was already a little bit in love with her, even then. I thought nothing of her personal happiness. I was offering her fame and fortune.' He shrugged. 'Who wouldn't be happy with that?'

'If you really knew Emily,' Tom said, disparagingly, 'you'd know that sort of thing would never be important to her.'

'I realized it pretty early on in our relationship,' Roland sighed. 'But by then it was too late to confess. I'd dug a pretty deep hole for myself.'

'Why did you? Confess, I mean?' Tom asked, genuinely curious.

Roland laughed. He slid his empty glass towards the hovering barman and looked at Tom questioningly. 'Sure you won't join me?'

Tom shook his head. 'Thank you, no.'

'I was going to propose,' Roland continued with a harsh laugh. 'More fool me, I thought Emily had finally exorcized your ghost and was ready to move on. Only she hadn't. I'd had too much to drink and, well, I suppose I was fed up of carrying the guilt. Anyway.' The barman handed him his fresh pint, and he sipped it, licking foam from his upper lip. 'Quite rightly, Emily was furious. She didn't speak to me for weeks.'

In spite of everything, Tom couldn't help feeling some pity for the man.

'Look,' Roland said. 'We both care very deeply for Emily. Can we let bygones be bygones, for her sake?' He stuck out his hand, his expression pleading.

Tom hesitated. 'For Emily's sake,' he said, eventually, giving Roland's hand a firm but brief shake.

'I hope you two make a go of it,' Roland said, meaning it. 'You deserve all the happiness in the world.'

'I hope so, too.'

'And here she is,' Roland said, nodding over Tom's shoulder. Tom turned to see Emily walking towards the bar. She was wearing her uniform, which had been freshly ironed. The buttons and buckles gleamed. Her hair was tied in a neat ponytail under her cap.

'You look lovely,' he said, with an appreciative smile.

'Thank you.' She turned to Roland. 'Are you sure you won't come?'

'Thank you, but I have plans of my own,' Roland said.

'What plans?' demanded Emily suspiciously.

'I have a date.'

'A date? Really?' Emily exclaimed, her brows rising almost to her hairline in surprise.

'There's no need to sound so shocked,' Roland said with an indignant snort.

'I'm just surprised, that's all.' Emily smiled. 'Who is she?'

'Her name is Hayma and she is Maung's cousin. She works in the noodle bar on the corner.'

'Well, that's great. How did you meet her?' Emily asked with interest. Roland had seldom shown interest in any other girls.

'I popped in there with some of the chaps the other evening, after our little adventure. You were resting. We got talking and, well . . . ' He shrugged. 'We seemed to get along so I asked her out.'

Emily kissed his cheek. 'I hope you have a lovely time.'

'Thanks, you too. Go on,' he said with a wave of his hand. 'Enjoy yourself.'

Roland had arranged to call for Hayma at half past seven. He checked his wristwatch. It was gone quarter past now. He paid for his drinks and, giving his appearance the once- over in the ornate mirror above the bar, snatched up his cap and strode out of the bar feeling, for the first time in a very long while, a sense of excitement. He set his cap on his head as he bounded down the front steps, whistling a jaunty tune. He had a feeling it was going to be a good evening.

★ ★ ★

The Officer's Club was an old colonial building on the quayside with high baroque ceilings and decorative chandeliers. The marble foyer was dominated by a large oil painting of Queen Victoria.

'I'm glad you came,' Tom said, taking Emily's arm as he escorted her up a grand spiral staircase.

'I'm glad you asked me,' she replied. They walked down the carpeted gallery, the walls hung with photographs of King George VI and Winston Churchill, towards the double doors of the ballroom, from whence came the sound of laughter and music.

Men and women from the Allied forces were seated at tables covered in white cloths and laid with cut glass, gilt-edged china and vibrant floral centrepieces, which gave off a heady perfume. The band struck up the opening bars of 'As Time Goes By' as Emily and Tom entered. A group of Australian nurses came in behind them, giggling over something one of them had said.

'Ah, there's Rich,' Tom said. 'He's keeping our seats.' They threaded their way between the tables to where Tom's friend was sitting with a pretty blonde girl he introduced to Emily as Abby Philips. She was a nurse with the American Army Nursing Corps.

'Whereabouts are you from?' Emily asked, taking her seat beside her.

'Oklahoma City, Oklahoma,' Abby answered. 'And you're the famous Bristol Songbird. My momma loves your songs.'

'Thank you,' Emily said, modestly.

'So, Rich tells me you and Tom knew each other way back?'

'Yes. We worked at the same hotel.'

'And now you've met up again all this time later,' Abby smiled. 'How romantic.'

Emily met Tom's eyes and she blushed.

The band finished playing to a smattering of applause as couples returned to their seats.

'We're taking a break now, folks,' the band leader said. 'We'll be back after dinner. Enjoy your meal.'

The food was delicious, and wine and beer flowed freely. For those on furlough, it was a time to let their hair down, a time to forget about the war for a while, a time to pretend that life was normal, and they were determined to make the most of it.

Tom and Rich complemented each other well. They were both easy-going and kept the two girls in fits of laughter with their jokes and amusing anecdotes about life on the airbase. Emily laughed until her sides ached, though she couldn't help thinking that, while funny now, some of the situations the men were describing must have been pretty hairy at the time.

Once the dishes had been cleared away, the band started up again, playing a Cole Porter number: 'Don't Fence Me in'.

Tom turned to Emily. 'Would you like to dance?'

With his hand resting gently on the small of her back, he escorted her onto the dance floor. Amidst the swinging, gyrating crowd, he took her by the hand and they jitterbugged around the room. Neither of them were brilliant dancers, but what they lacked in style and finesse they made up for with enthusiasm. Emily had never enjoyed herself so much and they worked their way through a variety of dance steps along with dozens of other couples.

'I really enjoyed that,' she panted as they made their way back to their seats while the band took another well-earned break.

'I'm so hot,' Abby said, fanning her flushed cheeks with her napkin. 'Get me a shandy, please, darling,' she said to Rich.

'Coming right up,' he said with a grin. His face glistened with sweat and he ran his fingers through his sandy hair, making it stand up on end.

'Dancing's not really my thing,' Tom said, downing half his pint. 'But that was a lot of fun.'

'I don't think I've enjoyed myself so much in a long time,' Emily admitted, pulling her shirt away from her damp skin. It was very warm in the ballroom. The windows were open but the sea breeze brought little relief, nor did the fans labouring overhead.

Rich returned from the bar with a shandy for Abby and a tall jug of iced tea. They chatted amiably for a while about their respective homes, people they knew, places they'd been.

'I wonder how Roland's date is going?' Emily mused to Tom during a lull in the conversation. 'Roland's my agent, and chaperone,' she explained to Abby.

'Oh, yes, I met him when you toured the field hospital where I was stationed,' Abby said. 'He seems a nice man. I hope it works out for him. Though in these uncertain times it's best not to think too far ahead.'

'We'll take each day as it comes,' Rich said cheerfully. 'And be glad for the time we have.' He gave Abby's shoulders a squeeze. 'It's stifling in here. Shall we take a walk on the terrace?'

'I could do with some fresh air too,' Tom said to Emily.

They followed Rich and Abby downstairs and onto the covered terrace. Other couples had had the same idea and most of the rattan chairs were occupied. A few soldiers stood on the edge of the terrace, just out of reach of the water dripping from the overflowing gutter, smoking and telling bawdy jokes. The nocturnal chorus was in full voice. Out of the darkness came the deep-throated croak of a male bullfrog, followed by a distinct plop.

'It's much more refreshing out here,' said Tom as he and Emily strolled across the wide terrace. Standing looking out through a curtain of warm rain over the darkened grounds, it seemed the most natural thing in the world that Tom should take hold of her hand. Entwining her fingers in his, Emily breathed in the scent of his aftershave mingling with the sweet smell of damp earth. In that moment she didn't want to be anywhere else on Earth.

'The past eight years have been torture,' Tom said suddenly, his courage buoyed by the romance of the evening. 'I really missed you, Emily.' He kept his voice low enough so only she could hear.

'I've missed you too,' Emily whispered, leaning into him.

Flashes of orange lit up the far-off hills as the sound of distant gunfire shattered the night, a stark reminder that beyond the border the war still raged. Suddenly, Emily was filled with the overwhelming urge to tell Tom how she felt. If she made a fool of herself, so be it, but she knew, deep down, that he loved her as much as she did him.

'Tom,' she said, turning to face him. She took a deep breath. 'There's something I need to say.'

'What?' His tone was a mixture of apprehension and expectation. Emily hesitated. Ice clinked against glass and all around them people were talking and laughing. If it wasn't for the rain, which was coming down in stair rods now, she would have suggested they find somewhere a little more private.

She realized Tom was patiently waiting to hear what she had to say and she gave herself a mental shake. *Have some gumption, girl*, she told herself sternly.

'I'm still in love with you,' she blurted out. 'Despite my feelings for Kit, I never stopped loving you.' Breathless, she studied his face, anxiously awaiting his reaction. His response was to let out a loud whoop and swing her off her feet.

'You have no idea how long I've dreamed of hearing you say that, Emily Baker. I love you too,' he proclaimed loudly. 'More than you'll ever know.' He kissed her, eliciting cheers and whistles from those standing nearby.

'About time,' called Rich, grinning at them from across the terrace, his arm draped around Abby's shoulders. 'He's been like a bear with a sore head ever since you showed up at our camp.'

Tom raised his hand in acknowledgement and gently steered Emily towards a pair of rattan chairs that had just become vacant. Sitting beside him, their hands entwined, Emily felt that she had never been happier. She refused to think about tomorrow when Tom would return to base. She had the here and now, and with that she had to be content.

★   ★   ★

The rain cleared just before eleven and the clouds parted to reveal a star-studded sky. The water shimmered pearl-white in the moonlight as Emily and Tom walked hand in hand along the promenade. The market stalls had long since packed up and the street was deserted but for the odd sentry on foot patrol and groups of military personnel on their way home from a night out.

'I don't want to lose you again,' Tom said as they paused to gaze out across the water. The engine of some sort of vessel throbbed far from shore and Emily felt a faint prickle of unease, but from further upriver came the sound of a shot being fired and the noise of the engine faded as it retreated.

329

'I don't want to talk about tomorrow,' Emily said. 'Let's just enjoy the time we have now.'

'We need to talk about our future,' Tom said earnestly. He gripped Emily's hands in his and, to her total surprise, he dropped down onto one knee. 'Emily, will you marry me?'

'Tom!' Emily gasped. She rocked back on her heels, giddy with shock and exhilaration. 'Are you sure?'

'I've never been surer of anything in my life,' replied Tom.

'Then, yes!' Emily shrieked. 'Yes, yes, yes!'

Pushing himself up off the damp ground, Tom grabbed Emily in his arms and hugged her tight. 'God, Emily, you've just made me the happiest man alive,' he cried, kissing her hard on the mouth. 'I feel like shouting it from the rooftops.' He grinned. Cupping his hands around his mouth he yelled out over the water, 'I'm going to marry Emily Baker!'

'Hush!' Emily laughed, grabbing his arm as barking drifted up the street. 'Look, you've set the dogs off now.'

'I don't care,' declared Tom, cupping her face in his warm hands and kissing her again. 'I want everyone to know that you're going to be my wife. I know a few of the guys in my squadron who'll be green with envy when I tell them,' he added with a chuckle.

'Will people say we're mad, do you think?' Emily asked sometime later. They were sitting on a rock overlooking the river. The eastern horizon was tinged with gold as the sun began to make its appearance. They had sat up talking all night, desperate in the knowledge that their time together was short. 'They'll think we're rushing things.'

'Emily, we've waited eight years for this. If I hadn't

been such a stupid idiot, we'd have been married years ago.' His smile faded somewhat. 'I've got a few days' leave due in early June. What date do you leave?'

'We leave for Calcutta on the ninth,' Emily said soberly. She was already dreading going home and leaving Tom behind.

'All right,' Tom said. 'I'll speak to my brigadier general and the chaplain. I'll send word as soon as I've got a date.' He grinned at her in the waning moonlight. 'Just think, in about three weeks' time, you'll be Mrs Thomas Harding.'

Emily smiled. 'We must let Ernest know the good news. He'll be so pleased to hear we're getting married at last.'

They stayed where they were, watching the sun rise above the jungle, a blazing orange fireball streaking the sky with crimson, pink and gold and bathing the landscape in its hazy glow. The colours were reflected in the flowing river, a soft mist rising gently from its surface. Finally, the early-morning tranquillity was broken by the arrival of the market traders and the traffic building up on the thoroughfare.

'I suppose I should get you back to your hotel before your reputation is compromised,' Tom teased, stifling a yawn as he stretched his arms above his head to relieve the crick in his spine.

Emily's answering smile was tinged with sadness. 'What time do you have to be back at base?' she asked. 'Do you have time to join me for breakfast?'

'We've got to leave within the next half-hour,' Tom replied with a rueful shake of his head.

★ ★ ★

331

'I'll miss you,' Emily said at the bottom of the hotel steps.

'I'll miss you too,' Tom said, giving her fingers a squeeze. 'I'll write and let you know once I've set a date.' He smiled. 'See you in three weeks.'

'I'll be counting the hours,' Emily said, smiling bravely as she watched him walk away.

42

She found Roland in the dining room.

'Well, well, if it isn't little Miss Stop-out,' he said, grinning at her over his copy of the *Daily Express*. 'All right,' he said, eyeing her suspiciously as he folded his newspaper and laid it beside his empty plate. 'You look like the cat that got the cream. Out with it.'

'Tom and I are engaged,' Emily whispered gleefully, glancing around at the tables of servicemen and women to make sure no one was paying them any attention. But having greeted her with cheerful cries of 'Good morning, Miss Rose,' when she'd entered the dining room, they had now turned their attention back to their own conversations.

Smiling at Roland's obvious astonishment, Emily pulled out a chair and sat down. A waiter hurried over with a glass of freshly squeezed orange juice, and she thanked him. It was hot in the dining room and she could feel herself perspiring already.

'Engaged?' Roland said with a frown as she gulped her drink thirstily. 'Isn't that a bit quick?'

Emily scowled at him. 'You're the one who told me to grab any chance of happiness with both hands.'

'I just thought you might have taken things a little slower.' Roland said, taking a sip of his coffee. 'Got to know one another again, that sort of thing. People can change a lot in eight years, you know?'

'Not Tom,' Emily said firmly, her gaze drifting to the baskets of exotic fruits adorning the buffet table. To one side, a middle-aged chef fried bacon and flipped eggs for the three army officers waiting in line. 'Have you eaten?' she asked, eyeing Roland's pristine plate. He shook his head.

'I was waiting for you. When you didn't surface, I went up to your room and imagine my horror when I realized that you'd been out all night.'

Emily couldn't help laughing at his mock-scandalized expression.

'I assure you, Tom was the perfect gentleman,' she said primly. 'I'm starving. Shall we?' She got up, pushing back her chair, and went over to the buffet. Intricate floral arrangements were interspersed among the fruit baskets, their delicate perfume filling the room. The patio doors were open and the surrounding foliage reverberated with birdsong and the increasingly tiresome whine of cicadas.

'So, have you set a date?' asked Roland, helping himself to a portion of freshly chopped coconut.

'Early June,' Emily said, loading her plate with slices of papaya, banana, strawberries and rambutan, a small translucent white fruit that she had grown particularly fond of during her time in Southeast Asia.

Roland's brows shot up. 'June?'

'Yes, hopefully,' replied Emily, licking papaya juice from her fingers. 'Tom will let me know once he's sorted a date.'

'But,' Roland began, perplexed, 'we leave on the ninth.'

'I'm aware of that, Roland. Tom and I won't be the first couple to marry in wartime and have only a few days together. In fact, a girl I know back home only had a couple of hours with her husband before he had to return to his unit. If Tom and I manage a couple of days, I shall count myself very fortunate.'

As she returned to the table, she suddenly remembered Roland's date. 'How rude of me,' she said, sitting down and picking up her napkin. 'I haven't asked about your evening!'

'It was pretty good, actually,' replied Roland, dousing his eggs and bacon in HP Sauce. 'Hayma and I have arranged to see each other again this evening. Perhaps you'd like to meet her?'

'I would love to,' Emily agreed eagerly, peeling her banana. Before she arrived in the Far East, it had been years since she'd eaten one, and she endeavoured to have at least one a day, knowing how much she would miss them once she got back to England. 'We need to get hold of Maung,' she told Roland, swallowing the last bite of her banana and dabbing her lips. She glanced over at the huge bunches piled on the buffet table but resisted going back for another one. 'We need to start touring again. We've been idle far too long.'

Despite having had no sleep, she didn't feel in the least bit tired. She knew she was running on adrenalin and that, come mid-afternoon, she'd be exhausted, but she'd been out of action long enough and keeping busy would stop her worrying about Tom.

'Have you managed to find a replacement piano yet?'

'As a matter of fact, I have,' replied Roland with a triumphant grin. 'A nearby mission station was destroyed by the Japanese a few months ago. Lots of people killed,' he said with a grimace. 'Horrible business. But they had a small piano, which, amazingly, survived unscathed. The parents of one of the nuns have got it in their back room and Maung says we're welcome to use it for as long as we like.'

'That's kind of them. Can we arrange for Maung to pick it up within the next hour?'

'All right. I'll get one of the errand boys to get a message to him. You should have had some of this bacon,' he said, smacking his lips as he mopped up egg yolk with a slice of bread. 'It's delicious.'

★ ★ ★

Emily worried about Tom constantly. Each time she heard planes overhead, she would run to watch them, shielding her eyes from the glare of the sun. Of course, she had no way of knowing if Tom was in any of them, but she knew he flew planes that dropped life-saving supplies to remote villages that were cut off by the Japanese.

There had been some heavy fighting in recent days and casualties were high. Visiting one field hospital near Pyin Oo Lwin, Emily's heart had almost broken at the sight of the badly wounded soldiers filling the makeshift wards. The hospital tents were hot and humid, reeking of blood. The nurses battled tirelessly against the heat and insects and the endless monsoon rains and floodwater that seeped into the wards, bringing with it disease and infection. That day, Emily sang only a handful of songs, preferring instead to sit at the men's bedsides. To the soothing tinkle of Roland's piano, she had held the hands of the dying and spoken words of what she hoped was comfort to those whose lives would be forever changed because of the injuries they had sustained.

She'd had to swallow her tears while sitting with one young man, a nineteen-year-old boy from Nottingham called Ian, whose lower jaw had been blown away. With the use of pencil and paper, he communicated to Emily that he had a fiancée back home and he was terrified she would leave him once she knew the extent of his injuries. Emily had been at a loss as to what to say, so she'd just sat and held his hand while he wept softly into his bandages.

★ ★ ★

The following Sunday, there was a message from Tom waiting for Emily at the reception desk. He had spoken to both the brigadier general and the chaplain and the wedding date was set for June 6th at ten o'clock in the military chapel. Rich would be Tom's best man, naturally, which left Emily with the dilemma of who to have as her maid of honour. Had she been getting married in England, Betty would have been her obvious choice. She pursed her lips. She'd only met Abby, Rich's girlfriend, once and while she was on good terms with the few female military personnel at the hotel, there wasn't anyone she would class as a friend. Roland would give her away, of course; he had agreed readily when she'd asked him. And now she wondered whether Hayma would consent to be her maid of honour.

They had met for the first time at Hayma's noodle bar the previous week and the two women had formed an instant bond. At twenty-five, Hayma was thirteen years younger than Roland. She was a shy and unassuming woman with flawless skin and raven-black hair, which she wore in a neat ponytail that reached her tiny waist. She favoured traditional dresses, which she wore in a variety of vibrant colours. In her drab olive-green ENSA uniform, Emily had felt like a dull sparrow by comparison.

She had arranged to meet Roland and Hayma at the Officer's Club that afternoon and she resolved to ask her then. To her delight, Hayma accepted with obvious pleasure. They were sitting on the shaded terrace overlooking the pond. Iridescent dragonflies skimmed the water's rippled surface and a solemn-faced stork waded between the lily pads. In the distance, the jungle steamed beneath a bank of thick cloud but the sky over the city remained clear.

'Thank you, Hayma. I really appreciate it. It's going to be a very small wedding,' Emily explained over a jug of iced tea and slices of delicious semolina cake. 'Only about eight people in all, I think. I thought we could come back here for a meal afterwards. What do you think?'

'Excellent idea,' Roland agreed. 'They put on a good spread here.'

'Good. I'll speak to the manager on my way out.'

★ ★ ★

With only just over a week to go until her wedding day, Emily could hardly contain her excitement, but she was kept busy every day performing or visiting recuperating soldiers. She'd heard from one of the nurses that Ian, the young soldier with the badly damaged jaw, had been evacuated home to England. She hoped fervently that his fiancée would stick by him. The poor boy had a long and difficult road ahead. Hopefully he wouldn't have to travel it alone.

Tom was constantly in her thoughts. She couldn't help but think that she and Tom were somehow jinxed, and that something would happen to stop the

338

wedding, but Tuesday the 6th of June dawned bright, sunny and hot. Though a thick bank of rain clouds hovered on the horizon, they seemed in no hurry to move closer, and so it was in glorious sunshine that Emily, Roland and Hayma walked the two blocks to the military chapel. Hayma looked resplendent in a pale pink traditional dress with a matching parasol, and Emily and Roland wore their ENSA uniforms. Three RCAF vehicles were parked alongside the kerb outside the chapel. The flags of the Allies drooped in the still, hot air, flagpoles gleaming in the sunlight.

The chaplain met them on the steps of the old stone church. He was a good-looking man of about forty, deeply tanned, his dark hair streaked with silver. He saluted Roland and Emily, and smiled.

'It's a lovely day for a wedding,' he said. 'If a little warm.'

Emily, already perspiring under her uniform, could only agree. She doubted she'd ever get used to the humidity.

'Shall we?' At Emily's nervous nod, the chaplain turned on his heels and led the way into the church. The chapel's interior was built of thick stone and was refreshingly cool and dim after the white heat of the morning sun. Tom and Rich stood at the altar, side by side. As Emily and Roland followed the chaplain through the carved wooden archway, Tom turned and smiled. He was wearing his dress uniform and holding his cap in his hand. Emily could see her own thoughts and emotions reflected in the expression on his face, and she felt herself beginning to well up.

'Don't you dare cry,' Roland hissed in her ear. 'You'll make your mascara run.'

Emily choked on a laugh and then all at once she

was at the altar and Roland was kissing her cheek and the chaplain was placing her trembling hand in Tom's.

'Dearly beloved,' the chaplain began, peering over his spectacles at the congregation, which was made up in its entirety of Brigadier General Lewis, Rich and his girlfriend Abby, Maung, Hayma and Roland. 'We are gathered here today to join this man and this woman in holy matrimony.'

Some twenty minutes later, Captain and Mrs Thomas Harding emerged into dazzling sunlight.

'Congratulations, my dear,' Brigadier General Lewis said, kissing Emily on the cheek. He shook Tom's hand. 'Well done, Captain.'

'Thank you, sir.' Tom beamed.

They posed for photographs outside the church before piling into the waiting Jeeps for the short drive to the Officer's Club where the staff had prepared a delicious three-course meal of smoked salmon and cold chicken salad followed by sticky rice cake, a popular local dessert, flavoured with peanuts and coconut.

The brigadier general raised a toast in their honour before, hand in hand, and amidst a shower of dried rose petals, Emily and Tom hurried down the steps to where a bright green tuk-tuk decorated in colourful flowers waited to whisk them away on their honeymoon.

It was a short ride to the small wooden shack nestled in the hills above the city. Owned by another of Maung's many cousins, it afforded a breathtaking view of the city in a peaceful, tranquil setting.

While Tom paid the tuk-tuk driver, including a hefty tip that had the man grinning from ear to ear, Emily wandered over to the little shack and peered in the window. The interiors looked rustic and very basic but spotlessly clean. The perfect place to spend their short honeymoon.

'Have I mentioned how much I love you, Mrs Harding,' Tom said, coming up behind her to nuzzle her neck as he pushed the door open with his foot.

'You may have done,' Emily said, her smile turning to a shriek of laughter as Tom picked her up and carried her inside, dropping her rather unceremoniously on the double bed where he kissed her long and hard on the mouth.

There, in the middle of the hot, sultry afternoon, they made love for the first time. By the time their desire for each other was slaked, darkness was falling. Easing himself out of the bed, Tom padded naked to the open doorway to retrieve the bags and the provisions they'd brought for the next two days. Refusing to dwell on the fact that they only had two more days together, Emily flung on her thin cotton gown and set about preparing a simple meal on the temperamental kerosene stove. They ate sitting on the doorstep, looking out over the dark city.

Emily set her plate aside. Leaning against the doorframe, she sighed.

'What is it?' Tom asked, reaching for his bottle of beer.

'If only we had more time together,' she said, a catch in her voice.

'Once this war is over, we'll have all the time in the world,' Tom said, getting to his feet and extending his hand to Emily. 'But in the meantime, let's not waste a single minute of the time we have got.'

Taking his hand, Emily got up and followed him inside.

43

Emily and Tom returned from their three-day idyll to find the hotel buzzing with news of the D-Day landings. The daily newspapers were full of reports of the great Allied invasion and the general mood amongst the military staff, pausing in their duties to congratulate Tom and Emily on their marriage, was one of cheerful optimism.

However, the success of events halfway across the world did little to ease Emily's heartache as she and Tom stood beside the covered Jeep idling at the kerbside, windscreen wipers swishing back and forth in a valiant effort against the torrential downpour. The sky above was dark and sombre, perfectly reflecting Emily's mood.

'Promise me you'll stay safe,' she whispered, her tears mingling with the rain streaming down her face.

'I'll do my best,' Tom said with a wry smile, his thumb caressing her cheek. 'I've got everything to live for, Emily,' he said, turning serious. 'I won't take any unnecessary risks.' He kissed her. 'You take care, and never forget how much I love you.'

'I love you too,' Emily sobbed as, with one last squeeze of her hand, Tom got into the Jeep and the driver pulled away from the kerb, joining the slow-moving stream of traffic moving along the waterfront.

'Come on, Emily,' said Roland, coming up behind her with an umbrella. 'Let's get you inside.' Putting his arm around her shoulders, he steered her up the steps and into the hotel lobby. Emily took a deep breath in an effort to compose herself. She wasn't the only woman separated from her husband by the war. It was time to pull herself together and get on with her life until this wretched war was over and she and Tom could be together again.

They left Chittagong at eight the following morning in Maung's trusty Jeep. They had a six-hour drive ahead of them, a hazardous journey that was made even more treacherous by the torrential rain. Huddled beneath the leaking tarpaulin cover, they spoke little. Emily kept reliving the memories of her honeymoon. She was missing Tom so much it was a physical ache inside her. She was so wrapped up in her own misery that she failed to notice Roland's torment. It was only during a brief break in the weather when they stopped to buy some fruit from a roadside stall that she witnessed the extent of his anguish. Having chosen a basketful of fruit, Emily called over to Roland to see if he wanted anything. To her dismay, he was slumped in the front passenger seat, his expression bleak. Leaving Maung to haggle with the stallholder over the price of her bananas, she hurried back to the Jeep.

'Oh, Roland,' she said, leaning her arms on the door. 'How selfish of me. I didn't even stop to consider that you're hurting too. But you'll write to Hayma, won't you?'

'No,' Roland said shortly. 'There's no point.'

'Why not?' Emily exclaimed in surprise. 'It was obvious she was fond of you too. Who knows what might develop in time?'

'Nothing is going to develop, because I'm not going to pursue this.'

'But—'

'I'm too old for her, Emily,' Roland interrupted roughly. 'She's young and beautiful with her whole life ahead of her. Not to mention that our homes are continents apart.'

'The war will be over one day, Roland,' Emily said, with a brightness that belied her own anxieties. Right now, each day she was parted from Tom felt like a lifetime. 'You and Hayma will be able to be together again.'

'By then she will have met someone else.' Emily was about to reply but Roland silenced her with a wave of his hand. 'The subject is closed,' he said, slouching low in his seat and pulling his cap down over his eyes. 'I don't want to hear another word.'

★ ★ ★

They reached Dakha at two in the afternoon. Maung dropped them off at the Officer's Club and, after bidding him a heartfelt farewell, Emily walked down the street to the telegraph office where she sent a telegram to Tom's father informing him that she and Tom were married. As she paid the fee, she couldn't help smiling to herself as she imagined Ernest's delight at the news.

The following morning, they put on a performance for the officers and troops before catching a late-afternoon flight to Calcutta. The flight was plagued by turbulence, which had Roland reaching for the sick bag more than once, and they were both relieved when they finally touched down that evening.

They spent another two days in Calcutta, visiting the troops and hospitals, before flying on to the garrison in Rawalpindi where Emily and Roland put on a show for the officers and their wives.

Their homeward journey was long and tiring, and by the time they touched down at a small airfield near Bristol in the last week of June, Emily felt, and looked, exhausted.

★ ★ ★

'Emily!' Miss Anne had the door open before Emily was even out of the car.

'Hello, Miss Anne.' Emily smiled, turning to Roland. 'Will you come in for a cup of tea?'

'I won't, thank you,' Roland declined. 'Good afternoon, Miss Anne,' he called, leaning across Emily and waving.

'I'll see you, then?'

'Yes. We both deserve a few days off. I'll be in touch next week.'

Shouldering her bags, Emily watched Roland drive off before dragging herself wearily up the steps.

'Congratulations, Mrs Harding,' Miss Anne cried, meeting Emily on the doorstep and flinging her arms around her. 'I was so pleased to get your wonderful news. It bucked me up no end, I can tell you.' She bustled Emily into the hall. 'The kettle's on and there's plenty of hot water if you want a bath.'

'I'd love one,' Emily said, stifling a yawn. Her eyes darted through the open parlour door to the letters propped up on the mantelpiece. Following her gaze, Miss Anne beamed.

'They're all for you. Two are from your husband,' she said cheerfully. 'They're postmarked a week apart but they both arrived yesterday morning. Go on, love. You read your letters and have your bath. I'll bring your tea up.'

'Thanks, Miss Anne.' Emily gave her landlady a hug. With Nellie gone and Lulu back living with her parents while she awaited the birth of her baby, and the rest of the girls away touring much of the time, Emily often worried that Miss Anne might suffer from loneliness. But whenever she broached the subject in her frequent letters home, her landlady was always quick to insist that she was kept so busy with her volunteering roles and a variety of activities that she seldom had time to catch her breath, never mind feel lonely.

Stretched out in the tub, Emily unfolded the first of Tom's letters. He'd written the moment he arrived back at base. It was full of memories of their lovemaking and the joy he felt at being her husband. Just reading it took Emily right back to the little rustic shack nestled in the Chittagong hills.

The second letter was more about daily life at the base. At every stop on their homeward journey, Emily had posted a letter to Tom and, by the time he had written his second letter, he had received two of them. Delivering mail to remote jungle camps was a dangerous mission for the supply planes and Emily knew from experience that it was usual to receive five or six letters in one drop.

There was also a letter from Betty, which included a pretty studio portrait of the three children, and her hearty congratulations on her marriage.

I'm ecstatic for you, Emily, Betty wrote with unbridled enthusiasm. *I always knew you and Tom were destined to be together.*

The rest were fan letters that ENSA had forwarded on to her. She read them fondly. Most were from troops thanking her for taking the time to visit their base. It

346

was heart-warming to read how she had cheered so many young men, giving them hope to fight another day.

A few were from grateful mothers, wives or sweethearts, thanking her for offering comfort to an injured serviceman far from home. Their gratitude brought tears to Emily's eyes. But the letter that brought her the most joy was from a Miss Cynthia Woodward, postmarked Nottingham.

Cynthia was the fiancée of Ian, the young nineteen-year-old soldier Emily had met in the field hospital near Pyin Oo Lwin who had lost most of his jaw.

★   ★   ★

Dear Miss Rose, Cynthia wrote in her neat, looping script.

I am writing to thank you for the kindness you showed to my Ian when he was in hospital in Burma. He is now in hospital here in Nottingham where he is awaiting surgery to mend his shattered jaw. The doctors are confident that, in time, he should be able to eat and drink, after a fashion, but he will most probably be required to wear some sort of face covering when out in public.

I am so grateful to you for taking the time to sit and talk with him when he was going through what was a very dark time for him. Ian said you were like an angel, miss, and that you gave him the strength to keep going when there didn't seem to be much point. We shall be married as soon as Ian is strong enough. With fondest wishes,
Affectionately yours,
Cynthia Woodward (Miss)

Emily made a mental note to jot down Cynthia's address in order to send her congratulations on the upcoming marriage. Ian's war was over. For Cynthia, at least, the sleepless nights and endless worry were a thing of the past.

Realizing that her bathwater had cooled to an uncomfortable temperature, Emily gulped down the rest of her tea and got out. In her dressing gown and slippers, she went downstairs, finding Miss Anne in the kitchen shelling peas, the back door open to the summer breeze.

'Feeling better?' the older woman asked, looking up at Emily loitering in the kitchen doorway.

'Much,' Emily said, coming into the kitchen and pulling out a chair.

'You've caught yourself quite a tan,' Miss Anne pointed out. She frowned. 'You're looking a bit peaky underneath it though,' she said with concern. 'Are you unwell?'

'No,' Emily replied slowly. 'In fact, my monthlies are a week overdue.'

Miss Anne's brows rose and she dropped her pea-pod in the bowl. 'Oh, Emily,' she breathed joyfully. 'Do you think you're expecting?'

Blushing, Emily nodded and smiled. 'Obviously it's very early days and there could be a hundred and one reasons why I'm late but, well, I just feel . . . different.'

Miss Anne clapped her hands. 'Oh, I'm so pleased. This calls for a celebration,' she said, pushing back her chair. 'A double celebration.'

'Double?'

'We must toast your wedding, too,' Miss Anne said. 'I've got one bottle of my elderflower cordial left in the pantry. I'll fetch it while you get the glasses.'

They carried their glasses outside into the yard. Slanting rays of sunlight beamed through the latticed fence. Sitting on the warm bench, bees humming amongst the pea vines and potato plants, Emily set her glass on the flagstone and leaned back on her hands, turning her face to the sun's warmth. It was the perfect summer evening. A blackbird sang above her head, perched in the lofty heights of next door's pear tree. A large tabby cat sat on the coal bunker, eyeing it with arrogant disinterest.

'Now tell me all about your wedding,' Miss Anne said. 'What did you wear?'

'My uniform,' Emily said, with a wry lift of her eyebrow. 'It was a nice service, though, and Tom's unit commander arranged a lovely meal at the Officer's Club for us afterwards. We only had three days together,' she said, shaking her head sorrowfully.

'Now, now,' Miss Anne chided her, patting her arm. 'Now's not the time for melancholy. This is a celebration. Cheers. Here's to you and your Tom, and to that precious new life inside you.'

'Thank you,' Emily said, raising her glass to her lips.

'And may this blasted war soon be over,' Miss Anne said vehemently.

'I'll certainly drink to that,' said Emily with a laugh.

44

The view from the bus wending its way down from Shaftesbury to Motcombe was of a winter wonderland. The hedgerows and fields sparkled with frost. Bare trees stood sentinel along the roadside, stark against the whiteness, and a flock of geese flew in a V formation across a colourless sky.

Emily tucked a strand of hair behind her ear and cautiously adjusted her position, resting her gloved hands on her rounded stomach. It was early December and she was six months gone. Her stomach already strained against the confines of her coat buttons and the midwife she'd seen back in Bristol had warned her, quite gaily, that Emily was on track to give birth to a 'whopper'. And while she wasn't looking forward to the prospect of giving birth to a 'whopper', she was pleased her baby appeared to be strong and healthy. Especially as Lulu had recently given birth to a little girl, weighing just five pounds, two ounces. For a few weeks, it had been touch and go for the poor mite but, thankfully, baby Jemima had proved herself quite the little fighter and, according to Lulu's last letter, was thriving.

The bus rounded the corner, jolting Emily back to the present. She gazed out of the steamed-up window, as the bus pulled up outside the Methodist church opposite Ernest's cottage. Getting awkwardly to her feet, she picked up her suitcase and followed the handful of other passengers off the bus.

The cold air took her breath away, and she took a

moment to gather her thoughts before crossing the street to her father-in-law's home.

She had carried on performing for as long as she could, having the waistband of her uniform taken out twice before the letter from the ENSA headquarters had arrived relieving her of her duties.

In his letters, Tom was excited about the prospect of becoming a father but worried about Emily staying in Bristol, which was still experiencing the occasional bombing raid. Miss Anne seconded his concerns, and so, after several letters flying back and forth between Dorset and Somerset, it was decided that Emily would stay with Ernest. That morning she'd said a tearful goodbye to Miss Anne, and Roland had driven her to the station.

'You will visit, won't you?' she'd asked Roland as they stood on the crowded platform.

'Of course I will,' he said, with a grin. 'I'll bring Miss Anne down for a run in the country. She'll enjoy that.'

She hoped Roland would be true to his word, not just because she would miss him, but because she worried about him. In the months since returning to England, he had failed to regain his joie de vivre. She knew he was pining for Hayma and deeply regretted his decision not to pursue the relationship further, but she was powerless to help him. She had thought of asking Tom if he might be able to contact Hayma on his next visit to Chittagong but his unit had been moved further east and anyway, he wrote that with things heating up in Burma, he wasn't expecting to get leave any time soon.

* * *

'Emily, welcome home.' Ernest came hurrying down his front path to give Emily a clumsy embrace and take her bags. 'Come on in. The kettle's on and I've added another shovelful of coal to the fire.'

Once inside, Emily took off her coat and hung it up. She went into the cosy parlour while Ernest took her bags upstairs.

'Take the weight off your feet, love,' her father-in-law said, appearing in the doorway and indicating the chair closest to the blazing fire. 'I'll make us a pot of tea.'

'You don't have to wait on me, Ernest,' Emily called into the kitchen after him. 'I'm expecting a baby. I'm not ill.' Nevertheless, it was a relief to sink into the comfortable armchair and rest her aching back.

'You're the expectant mother of my first grand-child,' Ernest said from the doorway. 'If I want to wait on you, I jolly well shall.'

Once Emily had quenched her thirst with a cup of Ernest's strong tea, he took her upstairs to show her where she would be sleeping.

'I thought you'd need the bigger of the two rooms,' he said, when Emily expressed surprise at being offered the master bedroom. 'I'm perfectly all right in the back bedroom.' He waved away her protests and flung open the doors of the double wardrobe. 'You've got plenty of hanging space for your clothes, and I thought the chest of drawers will do for the baby's bits and pieces.'

'But this is your bed, Ernest,' Emily tried again. 'I feel terrible depriving you of your bed.'

'I insist,' Ernest said, sternly. 'And once Tom comes home, you'll need the extra space until you find somewhere of your own. Now, I don't have indoor plumbing. The tin bath is hanging in the privy out back. I usually have my bath on a Friday, but if you'd like one now I'm quite happy to get it ready for you?'

'That's not necessary, Ernest, thank you,' Emily told him, touched. She walked over to the window and looked down at the frosty street, trying to picture a day when Tom would be sharing this room with her. The thought brought a lump to her throat.

'I'll leave you to unpack,' Ernest said. 'Take your time. Supper will be ready when you are.'

In reply, Emily walked over to her father-in-law and hugged him. 'Thank you,' she said. 'For everything.'

'Oh, now, let's have none of that,' he said gruffly, his eyes suddenly suspiciously bright. 'I'm just over the moon that you and Tom are married at last, and that he and I are reconciled. I've written to him, telling him I accept his apology. To think he could believe I was ashamed of him. Disgusted, even? I can't even remember what I said but . . . ' Ernest shook his head, perplexed. 'I know I wasn't there for him when his mum died. That's why I insisted he stay with me when my sister immigrated. I wanted to make it up to him. I love him, you see? I could never be ashamed of him. I knew he hadn't done what he was being accused of.' He sighed. 'We've so much time to make up for,' he said regretfully.

'You'll have plenty of time for that when he comes home,' Emily said stoutly, wincing as the baby kicked at her ribs.

'Going to be a footballer, is he?' Ernest said, smiling at her bump.

'Betty reckons I'm having a boy, too,' Emily said, massaging the base of her spine with a rueful smile. 'I had a craving for salty crackers.' She raised a sceptical eyebrow. 'Apparently that's a dead giveaway.'

Ernest chuckled. 'Well, we've got a fifty-fifty chance of being right.'

Left alone, Emily sat down on the double bed. It was comfortable, covered with a colourful patchwork bedspread and plump, goose-down pillows in pale blue slips. The curtains were blue, as was the hand-woven rug covering the stained floorboards. With the sound of her father-in-law's whistling drifting up the stairs, Emily opened her suitcase. Laid across the top, wrapped in tissue paper was the red dress Tom had bought her all those years ago. She unwrapped it, running her fingers over the soft velvet and hung it in the wardrobe.

★　★　★

Christmas came, bringing deep snowdrifts and disruption to the trains. Roland and Miss Anne, driving down from Bristol on Christmas Eve, arrived three hours later than expected.

'I had to dig the car out of snowdrifts three times,' Roland grumbled, stamping snow from his shoes as he unwound his scarf.

'It was an eventful journey,' Miss Anne agreed, her cold cheeks turning crimson in the sudden warmth as she took off her gloves and coat. 'But thank goodness we had planned to drive, what with the trains being cancelled.'

'How did you justify using the petrol?' Ernest asked Roland coolly. Emily had filled him in on Roland's involvement in Tom's disappearance, and it was only on Emily's account that Ernest allowed him to set foot in his house.

'I'm performing for the American airmen at Coombe House tomorrow afternoon,' replied Roland equally coolly. 'Which makes this trip a legitimate expense.'

'Right, Emily,' Miss Anne said, squeezing between the two men. 'Is there anything I can do in the kitchen?'

'You sit down and relax, Miss Anne,' Emily said. 'I've got everything under control. Roland, a drink?'

'Whisky, if you've got it, please?'

Ernest gave him a look, but went and fetched the bottle from the kitchen and, grabbing two glass tumblers, poured a drink for himself and Roland.

'Thank you, sir. Merry Christmas.' Roland raised his glass in salute.

Leaving the two men regarding each other awkwardly in the parlour, Miss Anne joined Emily in the kitchen.

'He was really nervous about coming here, you know,' she told Emily, lowering her voice. Emily glanced at the doorway. She could hear the gentle tick of the mantlepiece clock and crackle of the flames but, otherwise, the parlour was silent. Her shoulders slumped.

'I know Ernest wasn't keen on having Roland here. I have tried to explain things to him but I know he's trying to find it in his heart to forgive Roland for what he did to Tom.' She sighed, lifting the lid off the pot of rabbit stew.

'My, that smells good,' Miss Anne said. Emily was about to reply when they were startled by a shout of laughter from the parlour. Exchanging perplexed glances, Emily and Miss Anne hurried to the parlour door.

Roland and Ernest were huddled around the small

card table, playing dominoes and laughing. Emily and Miss Anne exchanged another bemused glance.

'Roland has apologized for his shameful behaviour and I've accepted,' Ernest said, not looking up from his game. 'So we'll say no more about it.' Emily glanced at Roland, who shrugged and gave her a sheepish grin.

'Right,' she said. 'Good. When you've finished your game, supper's ready.'

★ ★ ★

'So, what exactly did you say to Ernest yesterday?' Emily asked Roland. She glanced over her shoulder but Ernest and Miss Anne were some way behind. It was Christmas Day and they were walking back from church, snow crunching beneath their feet. The landscape was dazzling in its brightness, making Emily's eyes water.

'More or less what I told you, and Tom,' Roland replied. 'That I was a selfish idiot, with scant regard for Tom's and your feelings and that I regretted my actions almost from the moment you and I got to Bristol.'

'And he accepted your apology just like that?'

'He muttered something about the season of goodwill and letting bygones be bygones,' Roland said, shoving his hand in his coat pocket. 'He's a good man, Emily, and Tom is just like him. You're a fortunate woman.'

Emily grinned. 'I am, aren't I?'

'How is your friend, Betty?' Roland asked. 'And the children?'

'They are all well, thank you. They're spending a

couple of weeks with Edward's parents in Ferndown.' She glanced over her shoulder as they emerged from Church Walk onto the main road. 'Miss Anne and Ernest seem to be getting on well.'

'They do,' Roland agreed, stepping aside to avoid a group of children running up the street. One pulled a smaller child on a wooden sledge, an exuberant Labrador gambolling alongside them. 'I think they're both a bit lonely.'

'And what about you?' Emily asked softly, turning to look at him. 'You still miss Hayma, don't you?'

'Emily,' Roland said, a warning note in his tone. 'Like I said back in India, the subject is closed.'

'Perhaps if you wrote to Palm Court Hotel,' Emily persisted. 'Someone could get a message to her.'

'Leave it, Emily,' Roland snapped. They walked on in silence for a few steps, then Roland said, in a lighter tone, 'Your latest record has done very well.'

'I'm very pleased,' Emily said, accepting the olive branch with equanimity. 'I had a nice review in the local newspaper.'

'You deserve it,' Roland said, opening the gate and standing aside for Emily to walk up the neatly swept path. 'I never got the chance to say anything yesterday,' he continued, following Emily into the cottage, 'but I've received several offers from film productions companies offering you a part in one of their films.'

'But I can't act,' Emily said in surprise, hanging up her coat and going through to the kitchen to check on the turkey roasting in the oven.

'I think it's your voice they're interested in rather than your acting skills,' Roland said, leaning against the dresser, arms folded across his chest.

Emily shut the oven door and straightened up. 'I

don't think so. I've had a wonderful career and I'm really glad I could do my bit for the troops — I'm still getting letters thanking us for everything we've done — but, and I've thought long and hard about this, I think it's time I called it a day.'

Roland stared at her. 'You're quitting?'

'I'm having a baby, Roland, and, God willing, this war will be over before very long and Tom will come home. I just want to enjoy being a wife and mother for a while.'

'But ... when the war is over, that's when your career will really take off.'

Emily smiled at Roland fondly. 'You're a dear friend and a great agent. You'll go on to represent some huge stars, I'm sure of it. They just won't be me.'

'You've made up your mind, then? It's all decided?' he said, somewhat petulantly.

'Yes,' Emily said as the front door opened and Ernest and Miss Anne came in, laughing and stamping their feet. 'I have.'

45

January 1945

As well as bringing encouraging news of Allied conquests and the retreat of German forces in Belgium, January also brought reports of fierce battles raging across central Burma as the Allies launched a bitter offensive against the Japanese in their attempts to capture Meiktila and Mandalay. Emily and Ernest listened to the news on the wireless every night and lived in constant fear of the dreaded telegram.

Early February, the newspapers were filled with horrific images of ill and dying prisoners in the recently liberated Auschwitz and Birkenau concentration camps in Poland, and a nation listened with growing disbelief to news broadcasts that revealed the full horror of the atrocities carried out there.

Closer to home, German rockets continued to rain down on London in the first few weeks of the year, killing thousands of civilians and destroying hundreds of lives.

For Emily, despite her worry over Tom, life carried on at a more sedate pace. She met up with Betty and Molly regularly in one or the other of Shaftesbury's many tea shops and she had confided her fears of the upcoming birth to them several times. While they had both been quick to reassure her, it was in the early hours when sleep eluded her that she couldn't keep the memories of her mother's untimely death in childbirth at bay. During the day she was too busy to fret, replying to the many fan letters that continued to arrive for her. She wrote to Tom twice a week, too, and to Miss Anne and Roland once a fortnight.

One morning in early March, she went out to hang the washing. She set the laundry basket on the dew-soaked grass and arched her back, gently massaging the base of her spine and breathing in the fresh spring air.

It was a beautiful morning. Fluffy white clouds scudded across a pale blue sky and the surrounding hills shimmered in the hazy sunshine. The base of the crumbling stone wall was a riot of yolk-yellow daffodils and purple and gold crocuses. Newly born lambs bleated for their mothers in a nearby field and she could hear a cuckoo calling in the little copse behind the house.

Bending over to pick up a sheet, she gasped and clutched at her stomach as a powerful contraction rippled through her abdomen. It passed as swiftly as it had come, leaving her slightly breathless. She waited a moment but no further cramps were forthcoming. She finished pegging out the washing and returned to the cottage, where Ernest was sitting beside the stove reading the newspaper.

'Are you all right, love?' he asked, lowering his paper and regarding her with some concern. 'You look a little pale.'

'I'm fine, I think,' Emily said hesitantly. 'Oh!' She grabbed the edge of the dresser, bent almost double by the strength of her second contraction. She raised her eyes, meeting Ernest's anxious gaze. 'I think the baby's coming.'

Hastily folding his newspaper, Ernest leapt to his feet. 'I'll get Mrs Mullet.' Without taking the time to change out of his slippers, he dashed from the kitchen. Seconds later, the slam of the front door reverberated through the tiny cottage.

The pain receded, and Emily exhaled in relief. Despite her initial anxiety, now the ordeal was upon her, she felt strangely calm and exhilarated at the thought that, hopefully very soon, she would be holding Tom's child in her arms.

She heard the front door open. 'It's only me, Emily,' called Mrs Mullet as the door closed with a gentle click. 'I've sent Ernest to telephone for the midwife,' she said, seeing Emily in the doorway. 'And I've told him to stay at mine. He'll just be in the way here. Right.' She pursed her lips, looking Emily up and down. 'How close are your contractions?'

'I'm not sure,' admitted Emily. 'Quite close.'

'Let's get you up to bed and then I'll put the kettle on.'

By the time the midwife arrived twenty minutes later, Emily's contractions were coming thick and fast.

'You're doing very well,' Nurse Dot Hodder said, with a smile of encouragement. She looked to be about fifty with short, wavy, greying blonde hair. 'Mrs Mullet, a cup of tea would be splendid, if you please.'

'Yes, of course,' Mrs Mullet said, hurrying from the room.

'Is Dad away fighting?' Nurse Hodder asked, timing Emily's contractions on her watch.

'Burma,' Emily hissed through gritted teeth. Nurse Hodder pulled a face.

'My son's over there too,' she said, placing a cool hand on Emily's stomach. 'You visited his base last year. He wrote and told me how much your visit lifted their spirits.' Her smile slipping momentarily, she said,

'I really admire you for what you did for those lads. It let them know they weren't forgotten. And it sounds pretty grim out there at the moment.' She smiled brightly, taking her tea from Mrs Mullet. 'Well, this one isn't hanging about. I think we're almost there.'

'I can see baby's head,' she said, ten minutes later. 'Now, Emily,' Nurse Hodder went on calmly, 'Baby is quite big, so I'm just going to help manoeuvre the shoulders out.'

Gripping Mrs Mullet's hand, Emily gave a long, low moan as another contraction tore at her stomach.

'Squeeze as hard as you like, Emily,' Vera said, using her other hand to run a cool flannel over Emily's brow.

Emily felt Nurse Hodder's hands between her legs and then a wet, gushing sensation as her baby slithered out into the midwife's waiting arms. The room was filled with the high-pitched wail of a newborn baby.

'It's a boy, Emily,' cried Nurse Hodder triumphantly. 'A perfectly lovely baby boy.'

'He's beautiful,' Emily breathed, taking the swaddled bundle in her arms and gazing in awe at the red, screwed-up face and gently stroking the whorls of dark hair.

'He is very bonny,' agreed Nurse Hodder.

'He's gorgeous,' Vera said, misty-eyed. She went downstairs to make them all a well-earned cup of tea and to let Ernest know he had become a grandpa, while Nurse Hodder cleaned up the baby and made Emily more comfortable.

'Have you thought of a name?' the midwife asked, lifting the baby onto the scales.

'Jonathan,' said Emily, leaning back against her pillows. 'Jonathan Thomas Harding — Johnny for short.'

'Well, little Johnny weighs a whopping nine pounds, five ounces.' Nurse Hodder beamed and placed the sleeping baby in Emily's arms.

'Hello,' came Ernest's voice from the bottom of the stairs. 'Is it all right for me to come up?'

Nurse Hodder looked at Emily, who nodded and smiled. The nurse went to the door and called out, 'Come on, Grandpa. Come and meet your new grandson.'

The sound of hurried footsteps pounding the stairs heralded Ernest's arrival. He stood motionless in the doorway, drinking in the tableau of his daughter-in-law sitting up in bed, her chestnut-brown hair tumbling over her shoulders as she cradled her newborn son in her arms.

'Come in, Ernest,' Emily said with a smile. Ernest crossed the room, approaching the bed with an expression of awestruck wonder. He was followed by Mrs Mullet carrying a tea tray.

'Isn't he gorgeous?' she said, setting the tray on the chest of drawers. 'You're a fortunate man, Ernest Harding. You should be very proud of Emily.'

'I am,' Ernest said, peering down at his grandson. Emily adjusted her position, gently moving the swaddling blanket aside so he could see Johnny's face clearly. He smiled broadly. 'Ah, he's a bonny lad,' he said, his voice hoarse with emotion. 'He looks just like my Tom did when he was born.'

They stood around the bed, drinking tea and chatting until Johnny woke up, bawling lustily, his face turning red and his little arms flailing wildly.

'I think the little mite's hungry,' observed Nurse Hodder, finishing her tea. 'Come on, we'll leave you to it, Emily. I'll call again in the morning to see how you're getting on.'

'Thank you.' Emily smiled up at her, gratefully.

'I'll get over to the post office and send a telegram to our Tom,' Ernest said, kissing the top of her head.

'Would you send one to Roland and Miss Anne as well, please?' Emily called after him.

'Of course,' he replied. 'What about your other friends?'

'I'll call in on Betty when I go up to town later,' Mrs Mullet told him. 'She'll let Molly know.'

They quietly left the room, leaving Emily alone with her baby.

With Johnny nuzzling gently at her breast, her thoughts turned to Tom. His unit was in the thick of the fighting and she worried about him constantly. In his letters, he was always so upbeat and optimistic, insisting that it wouldn't be too long before they were together again and expressing how much he was looking forward to the birth of their child. He'd always said he didn't mind whether it was a boy or girl, but Emily knew he'd be over the moon that he had a son.

★ ★ ★

Roland and Miss Anne arrived the following day.

'Roland, where on earth did you get that teddy bear?' Emily laughed when he followed Miss Anne into the room carrying the most enormous knitted toy bear Emily had ever seen.

'My sister knitted it,' Roland said, with a soppy grin as he plonked the floppy bear in the rocking chair.

'We were a sight waiting on the platform with that thing, I can tell you,' Miss Anne said, coming over to give Emily a hug. 'You look ever so well, dear. Doesn't she look well, Roland?'

'Radiant,' Roland said with a grin.

Having had a bath and washed her hair, Emily had changed into a fresh nightdress in readiness for her guests. Johnny lay in her arms, swaddled in a soft white shawl she had crocheted herself.

'He's a handsome little boy,' Miss Anne said admiringly. 'And a good size, too.'

'He is quite remarkable,' Roland said, peering down on the sleeping infant. 'I can see a lot of Tom in him.'

'Ernest said he's the image of Tom when he was a baby.'

'He is that,' said Ernest from the doorway. 'And Tom was a nine-pounder too.'

'Well, like I said in my telegram,' Miss Anne said, suddenly all business-like, 'I'm going to be staying for a while, at least until your ten days' lying-in is up. Is that all right with you?' she asked Ernest.

'By all means,' he said quickly. 'I've changed the sheets on my bed for you. I'm happy to bunk down in the kitchen for a couple of weeks.'

'That's very kind of you,' Miss Anne said, flushing slightly under her face powder.

'Roland, you can bunk down with me for the night. I take it you're still planning on heading back tomorrow?'

'I am,' Roland replied. 'My train leaves at four-fifteen in the afternoon.'

'Oh, good,' said Emily. 'At least we'll have the day together.'

'You need your rest, missus,' Miss Anne said in a mock-scolding tone.

'Oh, I feel absolutely fine,' Emily protested. 'Johnny

slept most of the night.'

'Hmph,' Miss Anne snorted. 'That won't last. Roland, pass me my bag, will you? Let me show you what I've brought for Master Johnny.' Roland handed over the red and brown carpet bag. 'I've been busy knitting.'

'What do you say to a quick pint in the Royal Oak?' Ernest said to Roland. 'We can wet the baby's head.'

'Sounds a grand idea,' replied Roland. 'I'll see you later, Emily, Miss Anne. See you later, little chap.' He gazed down at the baby sleeping peacefully in his mother's arms, his expression wistful. 'He's absolutely adorable, Emily. You and Tom are really blessed.'

The men had barely left when Mrs Mullet let herself in the front door.

'I've just seen the boys leave,' she said, coming into the bedroom, her face lighting up at the sight of the baby. 'Off down the pub, are they? Good, they'll be gone for a while then. Gives us plenty of time for a nice chat over a cup of tea.'

'Miss Anne was just showing me the lovely cardigans and bonnets she's knitted for Johnny,' Emily said. 'They're exquisite, Miss Anne. Thank you so much.' Then, unexpectedly, Emily burst into tears. 'Oh, Miss Anne,' she sobbed. 'I wish my mum and dad could have met Johnny. They'd have loved him so much.'

'Oh, Emily love, you're bound to feel their loss more keenly now you're a mum yourself. Every girl needs her mum at a time like this.' She gave Emily's shoulder a squeeze. 'But you can be sure they'll be watching over you.'

Emily wiped her eyes. 'Do you really believe that?' she hiccupped.

'I do,' replied Miss Anne firmly.

'I'm sorry I'm so down when I should be so happy.'

'You've nothing to be sorry for,' Miss Anne comforted her.

'You've a touch of the baby blues, Emily love,' added Mrs Mullet knowingly. 'You'll feel brighter in a day or two.'

* * *

Roland left the following afternoon, promising to return for a visit as soon as possible. Miss Anne stayed the full ten days. Confined to her bedroom, Emily could hear only snippets of the conversations between Miss Anne and Ernest but it appeared the two had grown quite fond of each other.

On the day of Miss Anne's return to Bristol, Emily stood by her open bedroom window, winding Johnny after his feed. She looked down on the garden where Ernest was sitting on a deck chair taking a break from tending his vegetables. His half-dozen chickens clucked and scratched in the dirt around his feet. As Emily watched, Miss Anne came and sat beside him. She had brought her knitting and, for a while, they seemed content to sit in companionable silence.

'Well,' she said at length, her words drifting up to Emily in the bedroom above, 'I'd better make a start on the dinner if I'm to eat before I leave to catch my train.' She wound up her ball of pastel blue wool, which she was knitting into a bonnet for Johnny, and smiled at Ernest, stretched out in his deckchair. His one concession to the unseasonably warm March weather had been to remove his tie and undo the top button of his fawn and cream striped shirt. 'You'll be glad to have your bed back, no doubt,' she said.

367

Ernest grunted. 'I've been comfortable enough.'

'I don't believe that for a minute,' Miss Anne said with a laugh. 'You're a generous man, Ernest Harding, and the way you dote on that little mite is heart-warming to see. It makes my leaving so much easier to bear, knowing Emily and Johnny have you looking out for them.'

Her words made Emily smile, but it was a smile tempered by sadness. She had grown used to Miss Anne's solid presence around the cottage. Having to say goodbye would be a wrench.

'Well now,' she heard Ernest say, as she was turning away to lay Johnny in his cot. 'Once our Tom comes home from the war, he and Emily will want a place of their own and, the way I understand it, you're rattling around your big old house in Bristol by yourself and I'm going to be here on my own. Why don't you consider coming to live with me? We're comfortable with each other.'

'Like a pair of old slippers,' Miss Anne quipped.

Ernest gave her a look. 'You'd be welcome to Emily's room,' he continued. 'You said yourself how much you've fallen in love with our little village.'

'It's a very tempting invitation, Ernest,' Miss Anne said slowly. 'Home isn't the same now, what with Emily and Lulu married with families of their own and our darling Nellie gone . . .' She sighed. 'And I doubt very much that Barbara and Leah will be back to stay once the war's over.'

From her vantage point, Emily saw Ernest give a little shrug. 'There's no hurry to decide,' he said. 'The offer's there, if you want it.'

'I'll think about it,' Miss Anne promised. 'And now, I really must get on with the dinner. I don't want to miss my train.'

46

May brought the news that Adolf Hitler and his wife Eva had committed suicide and of Germany's subsequent surrender.

Celebrations erupted all across the country with crowds massing in Trafalgar Square and up the Mall to Buckingham Palace where King George VI and Queen Elizabeth, accompanied by the princesses and the prime minister, appeared on the palace balcony to wave to the cheering crowd.

Emily and Ernest huddled around the wireless. Johnny lay in his pram gurgling contentedly to himself. He was two months old and had just started to smile.

'That's it then,' Ernest said, leaning back in his chair. 'It's over.'

'In Europe at least,' Emily said solemnly. She hadn't heard from Tom in over two months. He had never acknowledged her telegram informing him of Johnny's birth and her subsequent letters had remained unanswered. Her sense of dread had been growing daily.

'We may allow ourselves a brief period of rejoicing,' the prime minister, Winston Churchill, continued, his familiar voice filling the small parlour. 'But let us not forget for a moment the toil and efforts that lie ahead. Japan, with all her treachery and greed, remains unsubdued.'

Emily dabbed at her wet eyes with the corner of her handkerchief. Ernest reached over and turned the wireless off and they looked at each other in silence. Outside, the street was filling up as neighbours spilled from their homes, laughing and singing, and suddenly the pealing of church bells rent the air.

She got up and crossed to the window. The street was bustling, mainly with women and old men and children. Someone was wheeling a piano along the road.

'I'm not sure I feel like celebrating all that much,' said Ernest.

'No,' Emily agreed. 'I'm relieved that it's over, obviously, but so many lives have been lost, and while we don't know whether Tom's . . . ' She broke off, unable to voice her fears. She looked up to see Mrs Mullet coming up the garden path. A moment later, she was rapping on the door.

'Aren't you coming out to celebrate?' she said when Emily opened it. 'Come on, the whole street's out here. Margaret's dragged her piano out. We're going to have a singsong and everyone's rummaging about in larders to see what they can find. I found a tin of pears.'

'Mrs Mullet, I don't think we're up for celebrating—' Emily began but Vera interrupted her.

'Look, Emily, I know you and Ernest are worried sick about your Tom, and rightly so. I'd be the same if it was one of my boys. But for the first time in years, we've got a future to look forward to. Come on,' she cajoled gently. 'Just for half an hour or so?'

Emily looked back at Ernest who shrugged. 'I'll get my jacket,' he said.

'All right. We'll come for a bit,' Emily said. 'I think I might have a tin of peaches at the back of the pantry. I'll bring it over, and whatever else I can find.'

The street had the air of a party about it when Emily wheeled Johnny's pram down the front path. She had taken some time to change her dress and reapply her lipstick, and Ernest was wearing his Sunday-best shirt.

Margaret was banging away at the piano and people were singing all the old wartime favourites.

'Come on, Mrs Harding,' one woman called to Emily. 'Give us a song.'

The plea was taken up by several other women in the street. Emily hesitated.

'Oh, I don't know,' she said, looking around. Tables had been laid along the pavement and whatever could be spared had been brought out to share. Emily placed her tinned peaches on the table along with a box of broken biscuits she'd found at the back of the pantry shelf.

'Please, Mrs Harding,' another woman pleaded.

'Oh, yes, all right then.' Emily smiled. Margaret beamed and struck up the tune to 'The White Cliffs of Dover'.

Standing in the middle of the street in the warm May sunshine, Emily began to sing. Many of her neighbours joined in and those that didn't sing swayed quietly from side to side, rocking babies or holding on to toddlers, while slightly older children ran about, laughing and shouting, relieved that the grown-ups appeared to be happy once more.

As the afternoon wore on, and the men came home from work, the pub landlord brought out kegs of beer. The piano was abandoned in favour of a gramophone and Emily stood by her gate, gently rocking Johnny in her arms and smiling as she watched a group of teenagers jitterbug in the street to Benny Goodman.

'It's strange to think we'll never have to worry about bombs and such again, isn't it?' Mrs Mullet said, coming to stand beside her. 'I just thank God it's over before my boys were old enough to enlist.'

'It's been a difficult six years,' Emily said, thinking of Nellie and Kit. So many lives sacrificed because of some egotistical megalomaniac.

She was about to voice her thoughts out loud when she realized the street had fallen silent. She followed the direction of everyone's gaze, her heart plummeting at the sight of the telegram delivery boy pedalling down the street.

The street seemed to collectively hold its breath. Even the children had gone quiet, the littler ones burying their faces in their mothers' skirts. Emily buried her face in Johnny's hair, savouring his sweet, baby smell, wondering which of them was about to have their world shattered.

She heard the squeal of bicycle brakes and looked up. Icy fingers of dread ran down her spine as the delivery boy stopped right beside her.

'Greenstone Cottage?' he asked Emily, his big dark eyes solemn. Behind her, Ernest groaned. Her throat too dry to speak, Emily could only nod in reply as the colour drained from her face. The boy took the telegram from his basket and held it out to her. He had a very sad face for one so young, she found herself thinking. She wondered if that was the reason he'd been given the job, or had years of delivering bad news simply sapped him of all his joy?

Barely noticing that Mrs Mullet had removed Johnny from her arms, Emily took the telegram with trembling fingers.

'Come on, lass. Let's go indoors.' Ernest was at her side. With his hand resting lightly on her arm, he gently steered her through the gate and up the path. Mrs Mullet followed with the baby.

Emily caught sight of herself in the parlour mirror. She looked pale and wan, and utterly terrified.

'Do you want me to open it?' Ernest asked gruffly. Emily shook her head. She was shaking like a leaf.

Taking a deep breath, she slit the envelope open and pulled out the telegram. Letting out a sharp cry of dismay, she groped for a chair, falling into it heavily as her knees buckled and her legs gave way.

'He's a prisoner of war,' she keened, barely able to meet Ernest's stricken gaze.

'Well, that's a good thing, isn't it?' Mrs Mullet said, her eyes darting between Ernest and Emily. 'Or, at least, it's better news than it could have been,' she amended.

Emily didn't reply. During her time in Burma, she had heard rumours about the barbaric way in which the Japanese treated their POWs. To the Japanese, surrender was seen as a sign of cowardice and to allow oneself to be captured by the enemy was viewed as an unthinkable betrayal of one's honour.

She could only pray that Tom was strong enough to withstand whatever torments his captors inflicted upon him.

47

Nong Pladuk POW Camp, Thailand

Tom groaned and opened his eyes, squinting in the dazzling sunlight that filtered through the attap ceiling. His whole body ached as though he'd suffered a severe beating and he was bathed in sweat. He lay motionless, listening to the laboured breathing and grunting of his fellow POWs. There were three hundred of them crammed into six hundred square feet.

His fevered mind attempted to work out the date. He'd been captured in late February when he and his crew had been forced to bail out of their plane. For three days, they had managed to evade the Japanese as they attempted to make their way back to camp, until their luck had run out. At first, Tom had expected to be shot immediately. Sometimes, when the Korean guards were particularly brutal in their treatment, he wondered if it wouldn't have been a mercy. Then his thoughts would turn to Emily and his baby. It would be four months old now and he didn't even know if he had a son or a daughter.

He moaned softly, imagining the torments Emily must be suffering, not knowing what had become of him. With trembling fingers, he traced the marks he'd painstakingly gouged into the wooden floor with a piece of sharpened stone, which he kept concealed amongst the woven bamboo fronds that made up the walls of the hut. It was the middle of July and he had been a prisoner of war for four and a half months.

After his capture, he and his fellow crew members had been marched through the jungle for several days until they reached Rangoon where they joined a group of thirty captured Allied servicemen. Loaded onto a cattle truck, they were driven over five hundred miles to the prison camp situated forty miles west of Bangkok.

The journey had taken fourteen hours over rough terrain with the men enduring uncomfortable, cramped conditions with no food and very little water to sustain them in the sweltering heat.

They had arrived at Nong Pladuk prison camp early in the morning. There was a lot of shouting as the back doors had clanged open. The brightness was dazzling after the dimness, making Tom's eyes water as he'd squinted at the guards swarming around the truck. They brandished rifles and bamboo canes, shouting in halting English for the men to come out.

Dazed and confused by lack of food and water, and from sheer exhaustion, the men had half-staggered and half-fallen out of the truck. They'd huddled in a bewildered group massaging cramped muscles and aching joints.

Tom and Rich stayed close together, surveying their surroundings in mounting horror as prisoners began emerging from the bamboo huts. Terribly emaciated, they looked like living skeletons. Many bore the scars of severe beatings and others were covered in weeping lesions and insect bites that had become hideously infected.

A Korean guard prodded Tom roughly with the butt of his rifle, shouting at him to turn around. The

375

guards made them stand in line and they walked up and down, shouting in their faces. They had been made to stand like that for several hours as the sun rose high in the sky, its white heat burning down on their bare heads. Tom had begun to feel light-headed, but he'd forced himself to focus his thoughts on Emily and his baby.

Two of the men had fainted, and were dragged away by the guards. Tom never saw either of them again.

Finally, they were allowed to make their way to one of the huts. There were six huts in all, each built to house between two to three hundred men. A simple wooden frame covered in bamboo matting, the huts stood on stilts, two feet off the ground. Railway sleepers had been piled in front of the entrances to form steps.

The new arrivals were allocated a sleeping space and then they were led back outside and put to work. With his horticultural experience, Tom had been set to work in the prison vegetable garden. The earth was often as hard and unyielding as concrete, which made for back-breaking work under a blazing sun, yet it offered him the opportunity to divert a few potatoes and other vegetables from their journey to the camp commander's table to supplement the POWs' meagre rations of rice and green leaves.

With the gruelling work and poor diet, the weight fell off him. Many of his fellow POWs suffered from dysentery and skin disease. Punishments meted out by the sadistic guards were swift and brutal, and there were several deaths in just Tom's first week.

Like the other inmates, Tom and Rich quickly learned to keep their heads down. They accepted the daily humiliations carried out by the guards without flinching, worked hard and tried to keep their spirits up. The worst and most trying day for Tom had been when he returned to his hut one evening to find one of the guards looking at his photograph of Emily. Forcing himself not to react, he'd politely asked for the photograph back. The guard, a young Korean man with bad acne and rotting teeth, had simply laughed in Tom's face. Tucking Emily's picture in his breast pocket, he'd turned his back on Tom. With no consideration for the consequences, Tom had grabbed the man by the shoulder. Ignoring Rich's whispered warning, he'd spun the man around.

'Give it back,' he'd hissed angrily, but the guard had only grinned. Slowly, he'd taken the photograph out of his pocket and, in front of Tom, torn it into tiny pieces.

'Bastard!' Tom shouted, lunging forward to grab the guard by his collar. The guard shouted, lashing out at Tom with his rifle as Rich and several of the other prisoners attempted to drag Tom off him. Within seconds, reinforcements had come racing into the hut, shouting and lashing out indiscriminately with rifles and bamboo sticks.

The incident had ended with Tom being hauled off to the punishment tank, a small wooden cell in which he spent three days without food or water, except what his fellow POWs could smuggle to him through the tiny slit. It was unbearably hot during the day, but at night he shivered with cold. On his release, he'd been delirious from dehydration and lack of food.

Despite his ordeal, his greatest dismay was the loss of Emily's photograph. At night he lay in his bed, reliving their wedding night and wondering if he would ever get to see her again.

Now, he sat up and stretched his aching body. Beside him, Rich stirred and moaned in his sleep. Tom regarded his friend sadly. Rich was a shadow of his former self. Once a big, sturdy man, he was now little more than skin and bone. Even so, he had never lost his sense of cheerful optimism and had been a tower of strength to Tom on more than one occasion.

Tom winced as his stomach growled ominously. He'd been suffering from a bad stomach lately and was worried he'd picked up dysentery. He didn't relish a visit to the sanatorium. Too many men had gone in and never returned.

The men were waking up now, coughing and spluttering as they dragged themselves to their feet, preparing to face another day in hell. Tom shook Rich gently by the shoulder. His friend mumbled something and rolled over.

Tom looked at him in alarm. 'Come on, mate,' he urged him. 'Don't give the bastards an excuse.'

Rich's eyes stayed closed. Tom shook him again. Rich's skin was dry and hot to the touch and now Tom noticed his shallow breathing.

'Rich. Come on, mate, wake up.' There was no way he was going to let Rich die. After all, he owed him his life. Rich merely groaned again. The man who occupied the space beside Tom, an Englishman from Manchester called Sam, came to crouch down at Rich's side, a worried frown on his thin, weathered face.

'He looks in a bad way,' he remarked. 'There's a chap in the hut next door by the name of Roger. He's a medic and works in the San. If you can get your

378

friend through roll call, I'll get Roger to have a look at him. He's got access to medical supplies and he's got a contact on the outside.' Sam looked grave. 'Do you think you can get him up? If the guards see him like this, I don't fancy his chances.'

'I'll get him up,' Tom said with grim determination. It took two of them, but they finally managed to get Rich up and out of the hut. With approximately eighteen hundred men at roll call, it was easy to hide Rich in the midst of the crowd. He was conscious enough to remain upright with Tom and another older POW supporting him on either side. Thankfully, the guards were in a particularly benevolent mood and didn't keep the prisoners standing out in the hot sun longer than it took to satisfy themselves that everyone was accounted for.

The moment they were dismissed to go to their various jobs, Tom and Sam smuggled Rich back into the hut. Tom remained with him while Sam went off to find Roger. It was twenty long, nerve-wracking minutes before Sam returned with the medic.

Roger was a tall, naturally thin man whose role as unofficial camp doctor had afforded him extra rations, much of which he shared with his fellow POWs, but even so, he was as thin as a rake. His skin was tanned a deep mahogany and looked leathery. He walked with a stoop like a man much older than his thirty-five years.

'Malaria,' he diagnosed after a brief examination. 'I'll get you some quinine from the medical stores.'

Leaving Rich to sleep, Tom shook Roger and Sam by the hands and headed for the camp gardens. He was fairly confident that his absence wouldn't have been discovered. The guards seldom troubled themselves to venture that far across the camp and, if they had, he trusted the other prisoners to cover for him.

He spent the next few hours toiling in the heat. Just as the sun reached its zenith, a triumphant shout went up across the camp. Leaning on his hoe, Tom looked up.

'Mail,' one of the other POWs told him jubilantly, throwing his shovel to the ground and setting off across the yard. 'Coming?' he asked Tom over his shoulder.

Laying aside his hoe, Tom followed at as quick a pace as his aching muscles and joints would allow.

POWs poured from all over the camp. A middle-aged man with grey hair who was simply known as the Colonel stood on an upturned orange crate, calling out names. The guards loitered nearby, or reclined on the shady veranda of the wooden guard hut, but showed little interest in the proceedings.

As the Colonel called out names and the lucky recipients came forward to a smattering of applause, Tom hardly dared hope there might be a letter for him, and so it was with disbelief that he heard his name called across the dusty yard.

Hobbling as fast as he could, the hardened soles of his feet impervious now to the rough ground, he joined the queue of POWs anxiously waiting for their letters. He could barely contain his impatience and practically snatched the small bundle of letters from the Colonel's assistant.

Hurrying to find a shady spot, Tom crouched down in the dust, tears blurring his vision. There was a note attached to his bundle of mail that had been sent on by his unit commander, Brigadier General Lewis. With shaking fingers, he ripped open the telegram, his breathing ragged as he absorbed the news that he had a son. He let out a sob and closed his eyes. He had a son. Feeling as though his heart might explode, he opened the other letters, weeping softly as he read Emily's words. Jonathan, his son was called Jonathan. He tested the name on his dry, cracked lips. 'Jonathan, my son,' he whispered.

It was clear from Emily's letters, dated March and April, that she hadn't heard any news of him for some time and was growing anxious. A whistle blew, signalling that the guards had run out of patience, and the men shuffled back to work.

Tom folded his letters and tucked them into the waistband of his shorts. He had a son. He couldn't keep the smile off his face, though he was careful not to let the guards see. Just looking happy could earn him a beating.

★ ★ ★

That evening, he shared his good news with Rich, who appeared a little better after his first dose of quinine, and his fellow POWs. Those who had no news to share were good-natured in their responses to those who had, and conversation in the hut that evening was livelier than it had been for a while.

The guards cared little how their charges occupied themselves during the evenings, and the men often put on plays or musical entertainment, sometimes even performing for the camp guards. To Tom's amusement, his status had been elevated somewhat when his fellows learned that his wife was none other than the Bristol Songbird, Emily Rose.

Their easy banter was interrupted by the appearance of one of the guards blocking the doorway. It was raining, moisture seeping in through the bamboo matting and soaking into the attap roof.

The men were immediately on their guard, straightening up. The tension in the air was palpable as they bowed to the young Korean guard, who stared back at them with a slightly apprehensive smile. Tom hadn't seen him before and reasoned that the boy must be new. The guard said something they couldn't understand and held out his hand, motioning for them to take whatever it was he held.

Sam, the hut's elected leader, approached the guard. 'Write,' the man said, thrusting out his hand.

'Ah,' said Sam, taking the items from the guard. 'Thank you.' He bowed as he backed away. 'It would seem, chaps,' he said, handing out the small, brown cards, 'that we're to fill out these postcards to send back home.'

Tom looked at the thin piece of card. At the top in bold black letters, it said:

IMPERIAL JAPANESE ARMY

Below was a space to fill in the name of the POW camp, the state of his health, and his occupation in the camp. Pens and pencils were a scarce commodity in the camp, and it was late in the night before Tom managed to scratch a few words on his card. In the tiny space provided to write a personal message, he wrote quickly, *Look after yourself and our precious son. With love to you all, Tom.*

The same guard came back in the morning to collect them and Tom could only hope and pray that Emily would receive it and know that, for the moment at least, he was all right and thinking of her.

48

Emily glanced through the kitchen window to where Johnny slumbered in his pram in the shaded garden. It was the middle of September and Johnny was six and a half months old. He was a sturdy, cheerful little boy who had a wide gummy smile for friends and strangers alike. When she took him out for a walk in his pram, she seldom got to the end of the street without some neighbour or other hurrying out of their cottage to fuss over him.

She dumped the potatoes she had been peeling into a pan of salted water and set them on the stove to boil. Wiping her hands on a tea towel, she went to stand in the doorway, leaning against the doorframe, savouring the last of the summer's warmth on her face.

Although the days remained mild and dry, the nights were turning chilly, and when Emily had opened the door first thing that morning, the garden had been shrouded in spiderwebs, each intricate strand glistening with dew. Swallows were gathering on the telegraph wires and the leaves were beginning to turn. The breeze carried the distinct smell of autumn.

It had been just over a month since the Japanese had surrendered. Like everyone else, Emily had seen the heartbreaking images of POWs in the Far East. On a recent trip to the cinema with Betty, she had had to leave before the film started when Pathé News showed footage of POWs being liberated from a camp somewhere in Thailand, unable to witness the sight of the emaciated, gaunt figures being helped into waiting trucks, knowing that Tom could possibly be among them.

She had heard nothing from him since the surrender, nor from the war office. Her only correspondence had been a simple postcard telling her little more than the fact that he was alive and incarcerated in Nong Pladuk. He had mentioned Johnny so she knew he had received at least some of her letters.

Every day she lived in fear, awaiting the knock on the door and the dreaded telegram. She was grateful for her friends, who had rallied around her. Betty, Molly and Emily met up at least twice a week. Three-year-old Olivia adored Johnny and was quite happy keeping him entertained while the women chatted over a cup of tea. Edward was home now, having been discharged from the army at the end of May, and working in town.

Roland came down as often as his work commitments allowed. Despite Ernest's initial reservations, the two of them got along well, often ambling over to the Royal Oak pub on a Saturday evening together for a pint and game of dominoes.

Emily wrote regularly to Leah, Barbara and Lulu, and heard back from them often in return. Leah had been taken on permanently by the White Star Line and was currently performing aboard one of their cruise liners sailing between Southampton and Cape Town. Every other week or so, Emily would receive a postcard from her picturing yet another exotic location. Barbara was recently married and living in Portsmouth with her naval officer husband, whom she had met whilst touring the south coast, and Lulu, finally reunited with her American GI husband, was living in Milwaukee. She wrote that Bobby had a huge family,

384

all of whom doted on his 'quaint English wife' and absolutely adored little Jemima.

With all 'her girls' having now flown the nest, Miss Anne had put her house on the market. The estate agent was confident it would sell quickly and, in the meantime, she was renting the small cottage a few doors down from Ernest and Emily. Miss Anne and Ernest had become a familiar sight around the village and were regarded by most to be a couple, although they both took great pains to insist that they were nothing more than good companions.

Emily walked across the lawn to check on Johnny slumbering in his pram under the apple tree. She watched him for a long moment, marvelling at his perfect features, her heart aching with maternal love and pride. He seemed to grow more like Tom every day.

She heard the click of the latch on the front gate and, on cue, Mrs Mullet's dog started to bark. A recent acquisition to the Mullet family, Shelby the fox terrier had belonged to an evacuee boy who hadn't been able to take him home to London. Shelby hated the postman. Emily hurried indoors to find the letter face up on the doormat. It looked official and had a foreign postmark. She picked it up, her heart racing, and ripped it open. Unfolding the single sheet of official military-headed writing paper, she scanned the typed script.

Dear Mrs Harding,

I regret to inform you that your husband, Captain Thomas Harding, is being treated at St Hilda's Military Hospital in Chittagong for dysentery and malaria. I'm afraid that due to the severe malnutrition and dehydration he suffered during his incarceration at Nong Pladuk POW camp, his condition is being classed as critical.

Though it is my regret to inform you that Captain Harding is so dangerously ill, I must hasten to add that our wonderful medical team here at St Hilda's are doing everything in their power to bring about a full recovery.

I trust this letter finds you and your son in good health.
Yours sincerely,
Brigadier General Lewis.

Emily sat at the bottom of the stairs. She read the letter again, searching for a glimmer of hope in the brigadier's words, taking consolation from the fact that he had insisted the medical staff were doing all they could to save Tom's life. Dysentery and malaria; both illnesses could prove fatal if not treated in time. She just prayed that it wasn't too late for Tom.

She was still sitting there twenty minutes later when Ernest and Miss Anne returned from their trip to Shaftesbury.

'Emily! What's happened?' Miss Anne said, instantly concerned.

'Is it the baby?' Ernest asked, standing in the doorway, his entrance barred by Miss Anne, who had dumped her string shopping bags on the floor. 'Tom?' His face paled.

'He's sick,' Emily said, passing the letter to Ernest as Miss Anne squeezed herself onto the step next to Emily and gave her a hug. Ernest read the letter in grim silence.

'Well, he's alive,' he said, handing the letter to Miss

Anne. 'We can be thankful for that, at least.' He picked up the shopping bags, gathering up two tins of evaporated milk that had rolled across the carpet, and took them into the kitchen.

'He's in the best place, love,' Miss Anne said, folding the letter and handing it back to Emily. 'All we can do is pray that he recovers. At least you can write to him care of the hospital.'

'Tom will be all right,' Emily said firmly. 'I have to believe that.'

'Of course he will,' Miss Anne assured her with slightly more optimism than she felt. 'He's a fighter. He won't give up. Not when he knows he's got to get well for you and the little one.'

Emily gave Miss Anne a wan smile, her shoulders drooping wearily as she followed Ernest through to the kitchen to finish preparing the midday meal.

★　★　★

The following Thursday Emily was returning from the post office. The air was decidedly cooler and she shivered in her thin summer coat. The sky was clear but the sun had already lost much of its summer warmth. Something rustled the leaves above her head and a squirrel scampered along the iron railings. Johnny, propped up in his pram, snug as a bug in his blue knitted hat and coat, shouted in delight. He gave Emily a beaming toothless smile to which she couldn't help but respond. He really was the most adorable child.

Coming along the street, she was surprised to see a car parked outside Greenstone Cottage. Crossing the road, she bumped the pram up the kerb and pushed open the front gate. She had barely got halfway up the path when the front door opened and Roland stepped out onto the doorstep grinning like a Cheshire cat.

'This is a surprise,' Emily said, engaging the pram's brake and going to give him a hug. 'You didn't say you were coming down?'

'It was a bit of a spur-of-the-moment thing,' he said, kissing her cheek.

'Thank you for the sailor suit,' she said, unbuckling Johnny from the pram. 'It was very thoughtful of you. Say hello to your Uncle Roland, Johnny,' she said, passing the baby to him.

'My pleasure,' Roland replied, grinning at the chubby baby in his arms.

'You look very pleased with yourself, I must say,' Emily said, going ahead of him into the cottage. She stopped in surprise, scarcely able to believe her eyes. On the parlour sofa, next to Miss Anne, a cup and saucer balancing on her lap, sat Hayma.

'Hello, Miss Rose,' Hayma said with a small bow.

'Hayma, hello. Gosh! What a surprise.' She turned to Roland with raised eyebrows.

'The look on your face.' He grinned. 'Priceless.' Still holding Johnny, he went to sit beside Hayma. She smiled at the baby and tickled his chin. Johnny opened his mouth and gave her one of his gummy smiles.

'Your baby is very sweet, Miss Rose,' Hayma said.

'Thank you,' Emily replied, perching on the edge of the armchair closest to the fireplace, where Ernest's slippers were warming in front of the glowing coals. 'And call me Emily, please. So, when did you come to England?'

'Last week, Miss ... Emily,' Hayma said with a

toss of her long, raven-black hair. She was wearing a calf-length, turquoise silk dress and silver bangles on her slender wrists.

'Last week. You kept this very quiet, Roland,' Emily said, giving him a look.

'I didn't know she was coming,' Roland protested. 'I got the shock of my life when I saw her standing on my doorstep.' He squeezed her hand. 'But it was the best kind of shock,' he said, smiling at her fondly.

'It's a rather sweet story,' Miss Anne said, getting up to replenish the tea.

'I find address of ENSA,' Hayma said with a smile. 'And after war is over, I sell my noodle bar and travel with English family on ship. I am their ayah. When we dock in Southampton, I go to London, to ENSA office and a nice lady, she give me Roland's address in Bristol.'

'How adventurous of you, coming all this way by yourself,' Emily said, admiringly.

'It was easy,' Hayma said with a shrug of her slender shoulders. 'I stay in hotel in London, then get train to Bristol.'

'This is the part I love,' said Miss Anne, returning with the tea and a clean cup for Emily. 'While you finish your story, Roland, I'll take Johnny upstairs. He's due a nap and he probably needs his nappy changing too.' With some reluctance, Roland relinquished his hold on the child and Miss Anne took him off upstairs.

'I was in my lodgings,' Roland said, taking up the story. 'It was last Wednesday?' He turned to Hayma who was shaking her head.

'Tuesday,' she corrected him.

'Yes, that's right. It was Tuesday. I'd just signed a

new contract with a young Welsh lad. Voice like an angel, but that's beside the point. I was in my room when one of the other lodgers knocked on my door to tell me I'd had a delivery. I was in the middle of something so I didn't go down right away.' He grinned. 'I'm lucky you didn't get fed up and leave,' he said to Hayma. 'Anyway, I did go down eventually. There wasn't anything in the hall so I was about to go back upstairs again, thinking the bloke had made a mistake, when he reappeared and told me my delivery was in the front room. I went into the parlour and, well, I thought I was hallucinating at first. I couldn't believe my beautiful Hayma was standing in front of me.'

'He said, "Pinch me, I must be dreaming," so I did,' Hayma laughed.

'And she can pinch, believe me,' Roland said. 'I've still got the bruise to prove it.'

'That's so romantic,' Emily said. 'I'm so happy for you both. Roland's been pining for you ever since we left Chittagong,' she told Hayma.

'I have indeed,' Roland admitted sheepishly. 'Thank goodness Hayma had the sense to take matters into her own hands. We can't stay long, I'm afraid,' he said, spooning sugar into his tea. 'We're on our way down to Weymouth. One of my acts is performing at the Pavilion this evening. I thought we'd book into a B & B and have a few days by the sea.'

'That will be lovely for you both,' Emily said, slightly envious. Her expression grew troubled, and Roland, always astute when it came to Emily's emotions, reached over to pat her arm.

'I know it's hard but try not to worry.'

Emily smiled sadly. 'Easier said than done. It's the

not knowing. That's the worst. I can't sleep at night, I'm so sick with worry. And Ernest is too, though he tries to hide it, for my sake.'

'The doctors will be doing everything they can, Emily.'

'I know,' she sighed.

'Where is Ernest anyway? I'd have liked him to meet Hayma.'

'He's working. He was on the late shift today, so he only went in at eleven. He'll be sorry he missed you, Hayma.'

Miss Anne came down the stairs just as Roland and Hayma were getting up to leave.

'We'll call in again in a few days' time,' Roland promised as Emily walked them to the car.

'Yes, do,' she insisted. 'Hopefully you'll get to see Ernest then too.' She leaned on the gate. 'I'll come up to Bristol once you're settled, Hayma. We can take Johnny to the zoo or something.'

'That would be nice,' Hayma said. 'I will look forward to it. Goodbye, Emily. It is nice seeing you again.'

'And you,' Emily replied. Roland helped Hayma into the passenger seat and shut the door. He paused beside her. 'Keep your chin up.'

Emily nodded. 'I will. You take care now.'

Roland gave her a kiss and got into the car. Standing by the gate, she watched them drive away. She waved until they turned the corner, then went inside and shut the door.

Epilogue
1946

Emily spread the picnic blanket on the warm, damp grass. The meadow was awash with daisies and golden buttercups, and the clear morning air resonated with birdsong and the bleating of newborn lambs.

She lifted Johnny out of his pram and sat him on the blanket. It was mid-March. Johnny had taken his first steps on his birthday, two weeks earlier. He gave her a big, toothy grin and, hauling himself upright, lurched forward on unsteady legs towards the wicker picnic basket.

Emily grabbed him and swung him up into the air, making him giggle in delight. He was a delightful little boy, loved by all who knew him, especially his Grandpa Ernest and Grandma Anne. Miss Anne and Ernest had married on Christmas Eve. Emily had been their maid of honour. They had all hoped that Tom might make it home in time to act as best man, but he was still in Canada awaiting his demobilization papers.

Late last autumn they had received the welcome news that Tom's condition was no longer considered to be life-threatening and he was being evacuated home to Canada.

Ernest and Miss Anne had toyed with the idea of postponing their wedding until Tom could get back, but, in the end, they'd decided against it. There was no guarantee of when he would be able to get back to

England and neither of them were getting any younger. In the end, Mr Mullet had acted as best man.

Barely five days later, they had gathered for Roland and Hayma's wedding in Bristol. The ceremony at St Mary Redcliffe church was on an altogether grander scale than Miss Anne and Ernest's, and afterwards, they'd held a lavish reception at the Bristol Harbour, attended by many well-known names in the music and entertainment industry. Roland and Hayma had left the following morning for a fortnight's honeymoon in Paris.

Emily set Johnny down and rummaged in her bag for the toys she had brought to keep him occupied. She sat down beside him, her legs curled underneath her, and helped him set out his toy animals. Every so often, she gazed back towards the cottage. Smoke curled from the chimney pot. A row of nappies flapped on the clothesline.

She'd had to get out of the house. The waiting was driving her crazy. Ever since she'd received Tom's letter telling her he was on his way home, she had been like a cat on hot bricks, unable to be still for a moment. She didn't know how she would get through another week.

Johnny clambered onto her lap and she rocked him gently, stroking his soft curls as she began to sing the lullaby her own mother had sung to her so long ago,
'Lay down your head, sweet little child,
Mama and Papa are here by your side ...'
She heard the faraway whistle of a train and the slow chug of a tractor in the adjacent field. A tightening in her chest prompted her to turn around. The song died on her lips. Shielding her eyes from the sun's glare, she watched the figure of a man walking

towards her. She got slowly to her feet, lifting Johnny onto her hip. Blood pounded in her ears and her heart started to race.

'Tom?' she breathed as the figure waved and broke into a run.

'Emily!'

'Tom!' she screamed. Startled, Johnny burst into tears. Hushing him, she started to run towards Tom. They met in the middle of the empty meadow, laughing and crying as they hugged each other. Johnny buried his face in Emily's neck, his cries escalating.

'I went to the cottage,' Tom said, drinking her in with his eyes. 'Dad said you were out here.'

'I wasn't expecting you until next week,' Emily said between sobs, clinging to him with all her might. Tom pressed her against him, kissing her fiercely on the mouth. 'You said four weeks.'

'Four weeks from when I sailed, yes,' Tom said. 'It would have taken my letter at least a week to arrive.'

'Oh.' Emily blinked back tears. 'I think I miscalculated.'

'Emily,' Tom said. 'Does it matter?'

Emily laughed through her tears. 'No, it doesn't,' she said, jiggling Johnny up and down on her hip. He stopped crying, staring at Tom with avid interest. 'Say hello to your son,' Emily said, with a shaky smile.

Gently Tom took the boy into his arms. 'Hello, little chap,' he said softly. 'I'm your daddy.'

'Dada, Dada,' Johnny shouted, looking inordinately pleased with himself.

'He just called me Dad,' Tom exclaimed. He was beaming with such pride, Emily didn't have the heart to explain that Johnny called everyone Dada, whether it was his Grandpa Ernest, the postman or the Mullets' fox terrier.

'I thought about you every minute of every day,' Tom said earnestly.

'I can't believe you're really here at last,' Emily said tearfully as Tom's arm tightened around her.

'Believe it,' Tom said softly, his free hand cupping the back of her head as he gently brought her face to his. 'I'm here, and I'm never going away again, ever,' he promised. Then he kissed her.

★　★　★

An hour later Ernest and Miss Anne emerged from the cottage. They leaned against the three-bar gate and watched the little family seated on the rug in the middle of the meadow. The mother was setting out the picnic things while the father played amongst the wild flowers with the little boy. He caught him up in his arms and swung him over his shoulder, the toddler's shrieks of uninhibited laughter resonating across the meadow.

Ernest and Miss Anne looked at each other and smiled. Hand in hand, they opened the gate and went to join their family.

Acknowledgements

Grateful thanks, once again, to my agent, Judith Murdoch, for her patience and encouragement. To my editor, Alice Rodgers of Simon & Schuster UK Ltd, thank you for your continued support and guidance. I love your enthusiasm for my writing.

To my copy editor, Paul Simpson, thank you for your meticulous attention to detail and for making sure my novel is historically accurate. If any mistakes remain, they are mine and not yours. And to all the staff at Simon & Schuster UK Ltd, a huge and grateful thank you.

Thank you to my husband, John, my children, grandchildren, and all my family and friends who have encouraged and supported me every step of this amazing journey.

And finally, thank you to you, the reader. I hope I never disappoint.

Other titles published by Ulverscroft:

THE SHOP GIRL'S SOLDIER

Karen Dickson

Southampton, 1905: Ellie-May and Jack have been inseparable since birth. They are best friends, having grown up together on the same street. But when Jack and his mother fall on hard times they are thrown into the workhouse, and he and Ellie-May are forced into a goodbye. Four years later, now aged sixteen, Jack returns to Southampton and is reunited with Ellie-May. Quickly they both realise that their feelings for each other go beyond friendship, and with Jack home for good the pair are finally free to be together. But when WWII approaches, Jack's duty to his country is hard to ignore and when he enlists to fight, they are once again torn apart. Will Ellie-May and Jack find their way back to each other before it's too late?